UNDERCOVER LION

Part 2 of The Pride of Lions

ANTOINETTE GEORGE

This series of books is dedicated to my late father.

History always fascinated him and I believe that's where my love of the subject comes from. He always encouraged me to read anything and everything, just as he did, and he was a fount of knowledge on all sorts of random subjects.

I'm not sure what he would have made of all my books, but he was always supportive of everything I tried to do and I like to think they would have amused him no end.

It's many years since he passed, but I still love and miss him a lot.

The Granville Legacy: Set Two
THE PRIDE OF LIONS

Nicholas de Bresancourt was an aristocratic but penniless refugee of the bloody French Revolution from which he'd escaped as a four-year-old orphan, thanks to Francis Granville and his friends. Nicky had lost everything: family, estate and fortune, and grew up hating those responsible in France for ending countless innocent lives on the guillotine and then Bonaparte, whose megalomania had put his country through so much further upheaval and war. With no other means to support himself or earn a living, and his pride refusing to allow him to accept the charity of his wealthy adoptive family, Nicky has joined the British army, keen to serve and help end the interminable war in Europe.

With Francis as a mentor, Nicky has matured into a charismatic, capable man and a clever fighter, as well as a lover of many women. He is also trilingual, thanks to growing up and being educated at an English school with a Spanish step-mother and French step-father. He is therefore ideal material to work undercover and put his talents to use on behalf of his adopted country. First, as an agent liaising with the Spanish rebels and guerrillas as the British endeavoured to drive the French out of Spain during the Peninsular War, and then as a full-blown spy for an anonymous Whitehall Department and Wellington, on the trail of a dangerous and ruthless French agent operating in both Spain and France: a man with a long-standing, personal vendetta against The Shadow, the man he suspected had caused the death of his father.

Part 2: Undercover Lion

Spain 1813

Obsessed with the mysterious woman he's had to leave behind in London, Nicky must nevertheless turn his mind to his mission. He has to run to earth and stop Frederick Bernheim, the agent now plotting to de-stabilise Wellington's increasingly successful military efforts in Spain.

Frederick Bernheim, son of the man responsible for the demise of Nicky's parents, his own nightmare incarceration in a grim fortress prison at the age of only four, and guilty shortly after of the nearly causing the death of several of his adoptive relations who had saved his life and helped him escape from France. The coincidence is both surreal and frightening, and memories of what happened to him have plagued Nicky ever since and coloured his whole life.

Despairing of finding any clue to trace his target and now operating deep under cover, disguised as an itinerant singer working in common bars and hostelries, Nicky finally gets a lead through a chance meeting with a young prostitute. However, he's in Madrid and cut off from Wellington's forces.

With no other help to hand, he runs to earth an old gypsy associate of Francis Granville from his Shadow days, and it's down to just the two of them to thwart Bernheim's nefarious plans and dispense with the man himself. However, as Nicky discovers, he's even cleverer and more dangerous than his late father...

Historical Landscape

Dear Readers,

If you're following the continuing saga of the life and times of Francis Granville, I hope you're going to enjoy this sequel story about Nicholas de Bresancourt, Duke of Valenciennes, adopted son of Edouard and Carlotta de Mornay. The twisting and turning plot is full of even more adventure and drama, love, passion, steam, fascinating characters (some new and some familiar) and of course, a really evil villain! And lions…. Rawwwwr!

But it's also based on what I think is a fascinating period of history, both English and European. If you aren't very familiar with this era, its revolutions and wars, or it's been too long since you were at school (!), I thought I'd give you a brief overview which will help put the events in the story into perspective. There are a couple of maps here as well (in case your geography is also a bit hazy) to help you understand what was going on in Spain while the British army was there, and then back to southern England and northern France where of course the main characters have their roots.

Historical enemies down the centuries, probably since William the Conqueror invaded England back in 1066, and the English controlled part of France during the Hundred Years War in the Middle Ages... during the 1700s, Britain and France were yet again involved in significant wars both in Europe and far from their shores. From the beginning of the century in 1704 when John Churchill, Duke of Marlborough, (the ancestor of Winston Churchill), resoundingly defeated the forces of French King Louis XIV and his allies at Blenheim, the old rivalry continued unabated. Both nations vied with each other for supremacy as they sought to either influence who ruled the various countries of Europe, or colonise new territories around the globe, in North America, Africa and the Far East, seeking both power and influence as well as new trading opportunities.

By this time, Great Britain, or more specifically the all-powerful British East India Company, controlled large areas of the Indian sub-continent as it expanded its commercial interests across south-east Asia. Army units fought various wars in alliance with local rulers until eventually, the decisive battle between the British and the French at Wandiwash in 1760 cleared the way for Britain to become the main European power in India and it became a springboard for further expansion of trade and influence throughout that part of the world, all the way down to Australia where the first convicts landed from a small fleet of British ships in Botany Bay in 1788. A penal colony was subsequently set up near there and thus began the colonisation of Australia by the British (who incidentally just beat the French to it; they landed in Botany Bay 6 days before the French expedition arrived.)

Although a British commanded army continued to have a significant presence in India after 1760 and be involved in local battles well into the 19th century, the focus of the British and French animosity turned west and both countries became embroiled in the American Revolutionary War from 1775-83.

France's help was a major contribution towards the United States' eventual victory and resulting independence. However, as a cost of participation in the war, France accumulated over 1 billion *livres* in debt, which significantly strained the nation's finances. The French government's failure to control spending compounded many other growing social problems and led to serious unrest in the nation which eventually culminated in the Revolution in 1789.

Thereafter, while Britain came to terms with the loss of its American colonies, France was in turmoil and descending into anarchy.

At the start of 1791, the other monarchies in Europe became concerned at the serious Revolution happening on their doorsteps and they considered whether they should intervene: either in support of King Louis XVI, to prevent the spread of revolutionary fervour across the continent to their own countries, or to take advantage of the chaos in France to expand their own borders. By 1792, France found itself at war with its neighbours and after a series of small victories, a series of defeats followed and this downturn allowed the radical Jacobins to rise to power and impose the Reign of Terror. This inevitably led to Louis XVI and Marie Antoinette, along with large swathes of the French aristocracy and upper classes, meeting a grisly end on the guillotine. Tens of thousands were either executed or murdered across France in under a year during this most bloody period of French history.

From 1794, the war situation turned again and improved dramatically for the French. A hitherto unknown officer from Corsica, one Napoleon Bonaparte, had been rapidly rising through the ranks. Appointed Brigadier General in 1793 at the age of only 24, he began his first full campaign in Italy in April 1796. Within a year, French armies under Bonaparte were overwhelming their enemies and one by one the European states sued for peace.

By the start of 1800, Britain was becoming ever more alone in its successful resistance to Bonaparte. Its maritime supremacy was of growing importance as a series of naval victories secured control of the Mediterranean while it endeavoured to blockade France by sea. There was a brief peace and break in hostilities in 1802, but inevitably it didn't last.

Bonaparte's star continued to rise, he was an extremely capable military general and his victories made him increasingly popular in France where he continued to consolidate his own political power. In 1804, he was crowned Emperor Napoleon I as his armies continued their conquest of Europe. However, at sea, Britain reigned supreme and Nelson's famous victory at Trafalgar in 1805 decimated the French and allied Spanish navies and prevented a potential invasion of England itself.

Fuming and frustrated by the old enemy across the Channel and hoping to isolate and weaken Britain economically, as she was trying to do to France through her naval blockade, in 1806 in retaliation, Bonaparte introduced and tried to enforce his 'Continental System'. This was a large-scale embargo on British trade, and even the post, which forbade the import of British goods into any European countries allied with or dependent upon France. But it was ineffectual as smuggling became rife and trade simply continued through Portugal, Spain and Russia, much to his irritation. As a result, Bonaparte launched an invasion of Portugal, the only remaining British ally in continental Europe. After occupying Lisbon in November 1807, he seized the opportunity to turn against his former ally, deposed the reigning Spanish royal family and declared his brother King of Spain in 1808. The Spanish and Portuguese revolted, and Britain supported them, and so began the Peninsular War.

Bonaparte did well when he was in direct charge, but problems and losses followed his departure from Spain to re-focus his attention on subjugating and controlling central and eastern Europe, leaving his Marshals to run the campaign. He severely underestimated how much manpower would be needed, and the effort in Spain was a drain on that as well as money and prestige, and ultimately failed. Especially once an able British commander, Sir Arthur Wellesley, was put in total charge of the British army, supported by the Portuguese and Spanish rebels and ruthless guerrillas. Wellesley had recently arrived after a victorious tour of duty in India. His success in the Peninsular War saw him elevated to become Duke of Wellington and eventually the two opposing military leaders faced each other at the epic Battle of Waterloo in 1815. After that, Europe enjoyed nearly a century of relative peace and prosperity.

Against this background, England in 1812 was itself experiencing a difficult year.

The war against Bonaparte and the French seemed never-ending and was a constant drain on the country's finances. In particular, action in the Peninsula was at a critical point as Wellington's fortunes continued to ebb and flow in his efforts to push the French out of Spain and back into France. In Europe, meanwhile, Napoleon's ego had made him cast his eyes east and the French were now marching on Russia. There seemed to be no stopping his megalomania. On the domestic front, the Government continuously watched public feeling, wary of radicals who sought social change and in May, to the shock of the country, the Prime Minister, Spencer Perceval, was assassinated in Parliament, in the lobby of the House of Commons. And if all that wasn't enough, tensions with the new United States caused an outbreak of hostilities between the two nations in June, known as the War of 1812 (which actually lasted until early 1815) with Britain subsequently having to defend its colonies in Canada from American incursion.

And the middle of 1812 is where Pride of Lions starts. So read on and find out what Nicky, Francis and their eccentric family and friends get up to as their tale continues some 20 years on from where Behind the Shadow finished in 1792…

Apologies for the boring history lesson, I trust it hasn't sent you to sleep! But I hope you move on and enjoy the fiction story now as much as I enjoyed writing it. And if by chance you are interested in little historical anecdotes related to events in my books, keep an eye on the blog on my website where I occasionally write further musings: https://antoinettegeorge.com/blog/

Antoinette…

Channel Coasts of England & France,
1790-1816

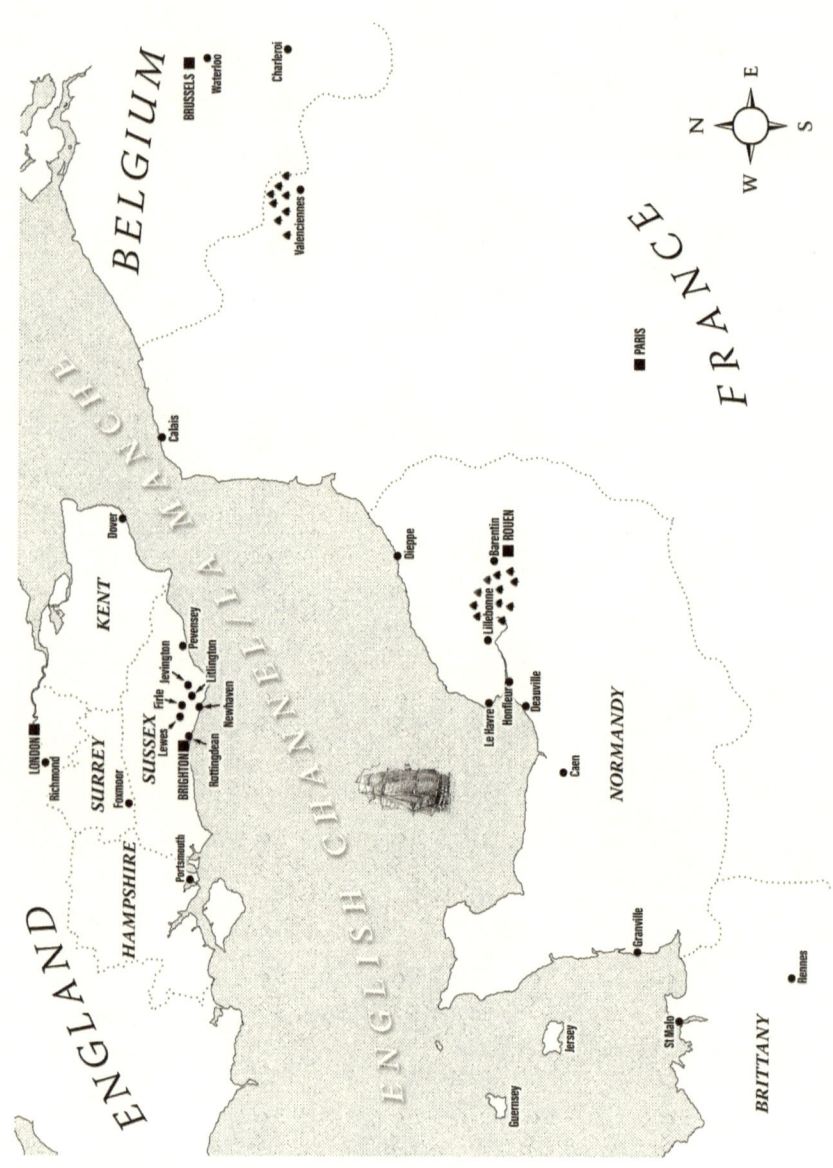

ENGLAND

BELGIUM

FRANCE

BRUSSELS
Waterloo
Charleroi

Valenciennes

PARIS

Calais

LA MANCHE

Dover

KENT

SURREY

Richmond
LONDON

Foxmoor

SUSSEX
Lewes
Pevensey
Jevington
Fifle
Littlington
Newhaven
BRIGHTON
Rottingdean

HAMPSHIRE

Portsmouth

ENGLISH CHANNEL

Dieppe

Lillebonne
Barentin
ROUEN

Le Havre
Honfleur
Deauville

Caen

NORMANDY

Granville

Jersey

Guernsey

St Malo

Rennes

BRITTANY

N
E
S
W

Southern France, Spain & Portugal with the Main Battle Sites of the Peninsular War

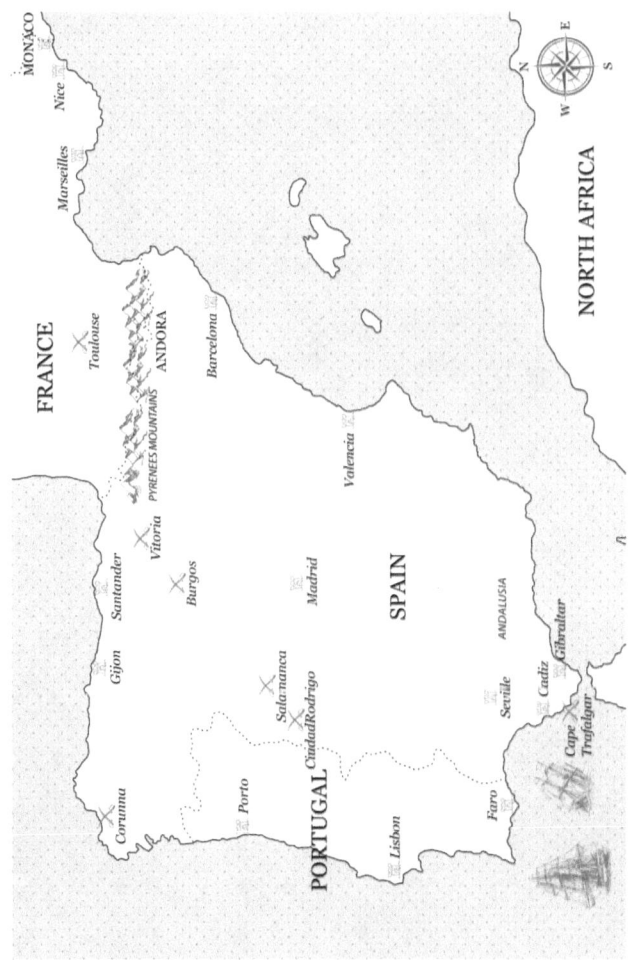

Chapter One

Nicky was sitting at the bar in a scruffy *taberna* in a dirty back street of Madrid, desultorily sipping his glass of wine and smoking a cheroot while he contemplated his next move. December was approaching and Wellington's prediction about the French had been proved right. They had regrouped and fought back. Confronted with forces attacking him from two sides, Wellington had been forced to abandon his siege at Burgos and retreat westwards yet again, nearer to the border with Portugal. The allied British and Portuguese army was in disarray, on the back foot and outnumbered, and it was their good fortune that Marshal Soult, who was chasing them, rather strangely declined to attack on the old Salamanca battlefield. Such are the fortunes of war and it was undoubtedly Wellington's lucky day.

Madrid was now re-occupied by the French though they had not left a garrison there, instead choosing to chase the Allied forces with all men available. The city was therefore in turmoil and things were not looking good for the British. However, Nicky had faith in their commander and was certain Wellington would sort himself out, regroup his forces and fight his way forward again after the winter.

However, in the interim, he himself was isolated, with still no sign of Bernheim or any of his associates.

As he leaned on the deserted bar, waiting for the evening's clientele to drift in, a young girl entered and perched on the stool next to him, eyeing him to assess his worth as a potential customer. He turned and smiled down at her, his lips curling in a charming smile. She couldn't have been more than fifteen, sixteen at most, he decided, her dark hair waving down her back and black eyes flashing. The epitome of the type of women he'd teased Wellington about, if a tad younger, making him grin to himself. However, despite what she obviously was, this girl looked young and still unspoiled and in a flash of memory, reminded him in a vague way of Sooty as she'd been at the same age - all bravado and innocence, very slender and still developing her figure, on the cusp of womanhood. Except, this girl knew exactly what she was doing. He sighed; she was too young to be selling herself to any man who would pay a few coins.

The young girl grumbled at him, "You're only the singer, aren't you?" realising who he was when she spotted a guitar on the floor leaning against his stool. Like her, he was there to earn a few *escudos* if he was lucky, she concluded, so was unlikely to spend even a few *reales* on her, when he no doubt needed to buy himself some dinner.

"Afraid so, *Señorita*, just a poor singer," but Nicky's eyes sparkled as he grinned at her, the smile lighting up his handsome features. "And you are...?"

"I'm Rosita," she announced grandly, tossing her head and thrusting out her chest in an effort to make her small, pert breasts seem more prominent.

"Are you indeed," his soft voice whispered, amusement obvious in his tone.

She grinned saucily back at him and winked. "I certainly am." Tilting her head to one side, she then asked thoughtfully, "I ain't seen you 'ere afore. Is this the first time you've sung in *Las Miraflores*?"

"Nah, I've been 'ere a coupla times, but I've been workin' around the city centre recently; more punters," he shrugged. "I've played an' sung at most of the *tabernas* and cafés there now, so I thought I'd come back 'ere an' see what was on offer. Are you expectin' it to get busy later?" Nicky's accent was choice and common. His beloved late step-mother would have cringed to hear it.

"Dunno, mebbe," she shrugged also. "With all the comin's an' goin's, first *los soldados Franceses*, then *los soldados Ingleses*, no one knows from one night to the next 'ow busy it's gonna be. Not good news for a poor workin' girl like me," she grumbled again and sighed.

"Mmmmm," Nicky nodded vaguely, wondering to himself if he should wander off and find a busier hostelry. But as he looked down at the young girl again, she smiled at him and he decided he might just as well stay there. At least she was pretty and amusing, certainly better fare than some of the other women he'd been forced to spend nights with recently in his search for information.

As he drank some more of his cheap wine, Rosita eyed him more closely. "Did you ever work at *El Toro Negro*?" she asked curiously.

"Yeeeees, for a few nights," he answered slowly. "Why?"

Her eyes lit up. "I bet it was you!" she exclaimed, narrowing her eyes as she looked him up and down in an assessing, womanly way, a professional way, especially at the front of his disreputable breeches, smiling wickedly.

"Me? What am I supposed to 'ave done?" he laughed. "Not guilty, whatever it was," as he held up his hands.

"Do you 'member a girl there called Madalena?" Rosita asked. "She worked the bar most nights."

Nicky thought back. Endless *tabernas*, names and faces drifted across his memory; how many bar workers and serving girls called Madalena had he met? He hadn't a clue. "Hmmm, I'm not sure, why?"

Rosita giggled naughtily. "I share a room with 'er sometimes, an' you fit the description she gave me of a man she met." She looked him up and down again, taking in the tousled, long tawny hair, wide shoulders and muscled chest, flat stomach and firm thighs in the tight, almost indecent breeches. "She said there was an itinerant singer there for a few days, a coupla months back, who gave 'er the best night of 'er life. She can't stop talkin' 'bout it."

Nicky burst out laughing. "It's probably someone else," he demurred. "Spain is full of itinerant musicians an' dancers tryin' to earn a livin' while this fuckin' war drags on."

3

"Oh, I don't think so," Rosita said slowly, leaning forward to run her fingers through his still bleached hair, down his neck and into the opening of his scruffy shirt. "What's your name?" she asked softly.

He looked back at her. "Most people call me León," his lips curled in a lecherous smile and he leaned towards her to bend down and growl in her ear. "Rawrrrrrr... do you want me to scratch your itch too, then?" and he ran his fingernails, grown longer to play the guitar he carried, round her neck and down her back.

Rosita felt a shiver run right down her spine and her belly spasmed with a coil of lust as she stared into his golden irises."Diiii-osss!" she muttered, rolling her eyes and fanning herself with a hand, "NOW I understand Madalena," as Nicky merely sat back and grinned wickedly at her, his perfect white teeth standing out against his still swarthy features.

"Tal vez, más tarde, Querida?" "Perhaps later, Sweetheart?" he whispered and Rosita's heart thumped in her chest.

The bar gradually filled up. Rosita waited at the tables, actually turning down a couple of offers for her favours from paying customers in hopeful expectation of a night with the attractive man who was now sitting strumming his guitar, occasionally singing a traditional melody to entertain the punters.

Nicky had originally only learned to play the guitar as a small boy to please his Madre, as he called his late Spanish step-mother, to keep her entertained with a small reminder of her homeland. As he sat and played that evening, memories of her dancing around the drawing room in their house in Chelsea or their country home at Arlington, as he'd sat and practised a flamenco tune, made him smile sadly. It was she who had taught him some of the traditional Spanish songs he was singing now. As he played, Nicky's eyes lifted towards the ceiling, wondering if she was truly looking down on him. He rather hoped she was.

In the early hours, once the last of the customers drifted off and after Rosita had helped the landlord clear the tables and tidy the bar, Nicky begged the use of one of the two unused rooms upstairs in lieu of payment for his services and held out his hand to the young girl in invitation to join him.

He peeled off her cheap peasant clothes gradually as they lay on the thin mattress in the small attic room, making her cry with pleasure, literally shedding a few emotional tears, as he slowly kissed and caressed down the length of her body. Totally unused to such gentle and loving consideration from any man, Rosita writhed and gave herself up to the passion that was overwhelming her senses, experiencing a depth of feeling deep inside that she'd never known before. As he turned her over and started to kiss down her spine towards her soft, rounded buttocks, Nicky couldn't help but notice the remains of several deep weals across her back. Rising to look more closely at the barely healed scars in the dim moonlight coming in the window, he whispered in shock, "Who's done this to you, *Querida?*"

Rosita rolled over onto her back again, looking up at him in embarrassment. "Oh, 'tis nothin'. I'm sorry... please..." she hesitated, "please don't stop, just ignore them."

Nicky looked back at her seriously. "Nothin'? How can you call that nothin'?" he asked angrily and pushed her over to inspect the nasty weals again. "You've not been beaten, you've been whipped, hard," he bit out. "D'you 'ave a pimp who did this, or was it a customer?" His eyes flashed. "Tell me, *Querida*. I swear if it was your pimp I'll go an' do the same to 'im! *Christos*, you're just a young girl!" He looked at her assessingly, "'Ow old are you anyway, Rosita? Don't you 'ave any family? If you don't mind me sayin', you speak much better than most of the other girls, 'ow the 'ell did you get into this life?" Nicky always tried to match his common accent to the other person, mainly to make them feel more at ease, so had been relieved to speak much more normally with Rosita, merely dropping a few consonants here and there. Ashcroft would undoubtedly have been fascinated and impressed by his communication strategy!

"I'm fifteen," she whispered, frightened she'd angered or put him off and he would throw her out. "My parents were killed a few years back; the war..." she shrugged sadly. "They 'ad a small bookshop 'ere in Madrid, but I've no relations an' I was left to fend for meself after they died or I'd 'ave starved. I... I've been by meself since I was eleven, nearly twelve." Nicky's shocked expression made her even more apologetic. "I'm sorry, I'm sorry, it wasn't a pimp. I don't 'ave one... it was... it was just a customer. Please don't make me go; please, León, I'll do anything, whatever you want... I'm sorry," and she leaned up to grasp his hand and kiss it pleadingly.

Nicky pulled the trembling young girl into his arms and gently soothed her, softly rubbing his hands up and down her back and bending to kiss her face, down her neck and shoulders to her small, rounded breasts. "'Ush now, *Querida*, stop apologisin'. You don't 'ave to go anywhere. I just can't stand the thought of anyone abusin' you like this, the man must be an animal. Did you know he was like that when you went with 'im? Whatever 'e paid you, it wasn't worth it."

Rosita sighed and relaxed back into Nicky's arms, waves of pleasure once again roiling through her body as he caressed away her fears and distress. "Yes... no," she stuttered and Nicky looked at her, confused. "I only went with 'im as a favour to Carmelita. Madelena an' I rent a small room in a tenement where she also stays, 'cept 'er rooms are nicer than what we can afford. This bloke is one of 'er reg'lars. I'd never seen 'im before that night though. She goes out to 'is villa, 'e lives just outside Madrid." The young girl shuddered at the memory. "Carmelita enjoys that sort of man, an' that's what she specialises in," she whispered. "Perversion, pain... d'you understand?" Nicky nodded distastefully. "One day last month when 'e sent for 'er, she was, um, indisposed at the time." Rosita shrugged and hurried on, women's monthly problems that broke into their income generation something they simply put up with. "So she asked me to go in 'er place. She didn't wanna lose 'is custom, y'see," she shuddered again and Nicky hugged her closer. "She... she said 'e was a bit perverted, but I never expected nothin' like the things 'e did to me. I thought I'd done most stuff but..." reliving the memory brought tears to her eyes. "That whip, *Dios*, the pain, but the more 'e thrashed me with it an' 'is ridin' crop, the more aroused 'e got, an' when 'e took me, I thought 'e would strangle me. It was terrible it was. I don't know 'ow Carmelita puts up with it!" She buried her face in Nicky's warm chest and he hugged her close.

"Who is 'e, Rosita? Tell me an' I'll pay 'im a visit," Nicky bit out. "I'll give 'im a taste of 'is own fuckin' medicine an' see 'ow 'e likes it." He would have no truck with a man like that. Nicky hated perverts and bullies who abused or hit women and children; he'd come across enough evidence of it, even in the upper echelons of the Ton. Affairs with wives who'd revelled in the pleasure of a caring man for a night or a stolen afternoon here or there, one who could make them forget their nightmare existence with a man in an arranged or loveless marriage, especially one who enjoyed beating or forcing them. He'd discovered many gently raised Ladies who'd been extremely ignorant of the wide variety of sexual pleasures or diversions that existed, even if many of their husbands weren't. Often, the marriage bed had come as a distasteful shock to them if their husbands weren't patient, caring or inclined to explain matters to them and introduce their 'idiosyncrasies' gradually.

"I dunno 'is name," Rosita replied. "'E just sent a small carriage for Carmelita with blacked out windows so I've no idea where 'e lives, an' the carriage took me 'ome after... afterwards. Creepy it was. All I know is that 'e's French an' 'e's quite aristocratic like, an' 'e did pay me well. But I swear I'll never go back there again even if 'e offered me double, or triple. 'E's...'e's crazy. Black cold eyes, like 'is 'air; gave me the shivers... like the Devil."

The hairs stood up on the back of Nicky's neck. But he carried on caressing Rosita, once more pushing her down into the mattress and running his fingers up and down her thighs and around to her bottom; teasing, tantalising and driving her wild. As she moaned beneath him, he whispered, "Bastard French. Are you sure you didn't get 'is name or 'ave any idea where 'e lives, *Querida*? I'd be 'appy to go an' beat the 'ell out of 'im for you. Now that would give ME pleasure..."

Rosita laughed as she rolled over and pushed him back down, determined to please this handsome and considerate man as much as he was pleasing her. "Aaah, my 'ero," she purred, "but I just wanna forget about 'IM. I don't know 'is name or where 'e lives, south of Madrid I think we went, I just dozed off while we drove, but 'e 'ad the letter B embroidered on 'is shirt an' kerchief. B for *bastardo* no doubt," and as she laughed again she bent to run her tongue around his navel and then start to kiss her way lower. "Enough of the bloody *Francés*. You want pleasure then, my vengeful lion? Why not let Rosita do that for you? My customers tell me I'm very good..." and her mouth opened over him.

Nicky felt as if his brain and body were split in two. Half was revelling in the pleasure Rosita was giving him while the other half was seized with the information she'd just innocently imparted. An aristocratic Frenchman, with a perverted, cruel and vicious nature, dark hair and dark eyes, living in a secluded villa south of Madrid who obviously wanted to keep his name, location and whereabouts a secret... and his initial was B. It was too much of a coincidence. Finally, finally, after all these months he had a lead.

But there was nothing he could do until the morning, so being Nicky, he simply gave himself over to the delights of the night and the seductive young girl who was sharing them with him.

Rosita wailed loudly with intense pleasure as Nicky brought her to a shuddering climax and as she lay back against the dingy pillow, panting, she looked up at him in stunned wonder. "That was quite somethin'" she whispered breathlessly. "You're quite somethin'," and he smiled at her, his eyes twinkling. "Now I really understand why Madalena raved." She put her hand up and caressed his lightly bearded cheek, "Thank you, León. I've... I've never experienced anythin' quite like that afore. Most men, right from my first, all the men I go with, all they want is their pleasure. I just lay there an' pretend an' make the right noises while they rut away, but you... you... I 'ad no idea it could be so good."

"You mean you didn't pretend to enjoy that?" Nicky laughed and leaned down to kiss the tip of her nose, "*Querida* let me show you just 'ow good it can really be..."

Twice more he brought her to a shimmering, intense climax, laughing at her uninhibited, unbounded enthusiasm, the last remnants of her innocent youth still obvious as she actually blushed at some of the teasing things he did to enhance her pleasure. As Rosita lay back in his arms, sated and sleepily exhausted, she turned to look at him, running her fingers through his tousled mane of thick hair. "You're a very special man, León," she whispered.

"Not really, *Querida*. You just keep meetin' the wrong type of men. I'm nothin' special," he demurred.

"Oh yes, you are, believe me." She looked into his eyes, suddenly older beyond her years and sighed. "Isn't there a woman in your life? I'm amazed there isn't a queue out there fightin' over you."

He grinned at her. "Aaah, *Querida*," he sighed as he thought of Bella and of *Lionesse*, "women just cause me endless problems. Besides, I'm penniless, 'omeless, I've nothin' to offer, other than me an' my guitar."

She laughed back at him. "You fool," she whispered. "You big, soft-'earted fool. As if anyone would care about that if they could 'ave you, all to themself."

The following morning, Nicky made love to her again, one final time before they got up to go their separate ways, something about Rosita bringing out the long buried, caring, protective side of him he used to feel for Bella, his little Sooty. He hadn't just fucked her as he did many of the women he'd engaged with, he'd taken care with her, wanting to simply bring some pleasure into her hard and meaningless existence. As she reached up to kiss him goodbye, he pressed a clutch of gold coins in her hand. "Get away from 'ere, *Querida*," he said softly. "You're too good for this life. Go south or east, to the coast; find someone more deserving of you," adding warningly, "an' whatever you do, don't go near that pervert again, no matter what 'e pays you."

Rosita gasped as she saw the money in her hand and tears filled her eyes as she looked up at him. "Whatever are you doin'? You can't afford to give me this..." and she tried to give the coins back to him.

Nicky merely smiled at her and chucked her under the chin, giving her a quick kiss. "Easy come, easy go, *Querida*," he shrugged. "I'll just 'ave to sing a bit louder or for a bit longer, or find a rich widow," and he grinned as he spun her around, swatted her on the bottom and sent her on her way. He'd have given her far more had she but known it, but it would have raised too many suspicious questions. He hoped to God she took his advice.

As Rosita wandered off down the deserted street, Nicky appeared to go back inside the tavern, but as she rounded the next corner, he turned and slowly made his way after her, keeping at a distance and staying in the shelter of shop doorways. He smiled as he watched her stroll along in the morning sunshine, her hips swinging, singing happily to herself. Again he thought of Bella, his Sooty. It had to be the hair, or maybe her general enthusiasm and energy for life, like an exuberant young dog, but there was something about her that reminded him of the young woman back in England who'd been a part of his life for as long as he could remember and who he had no idea what to do with. Maybe that was why he'd been so taken with Rosita, he was nostalgic for home and his family. He shook his head and returned his attention to where she was leading him.

Making her way down a maze of dank alleyways, she eventually arrived at a dingy tenement building and disappeared inside. Finding a deep doorway further back up the alley, he loitered in the entryway to another tenement and leaned back against the wall, watching the entrance to her building and who was coming in and out.

There was little movement over the next hour or so and, finally realising that the women who lived there would probably be sleeping off the excesses of the previous night before venturing out again in the late afternoon or early evening, he returned to the *taberna* to pick up his things and find a room in another inconspicuous inn, from where he could move around without anyone noticing.

For the next few days, Nicky watched Rosita's tenement. He saw her come and go and also spotted Madalena, finally remembering her from his brief time at *El Toro Negro*.

While Rosita and Madalena were out, he approached and casually asked one or two of the other residents if Carmelita was around. One young girl shook her head and told him she was often away for days, sometimes weeks at a time if she'd found a wealthy customer. Having no idea what the woman looked like, he also enquired about that and was told Carmelita could always be recognised by the small scar she carried above one of her dark eyebrows. He also confirmed what Rosita had told him, that she catered for a certain type of client. His senses recoiled at the prospect of involving himself with a woman who enjoyed Bernheim's particular form of entertainment.

Working at *Las Miraflores* several evenings a week, Rosita had hoped Nicky would return there. She even called into all of the other cafés and *tabernas* in the area to see if he was singing there, but there was no sign of him and none of the other working girls in the area had seen a man of his description. She sighed sadly, he seemed to have disappeared into thin air as mysteriously as he'd appeared.

Alone in the damp and dingy room she shared with Madalena, she pulled out the small soft bag she kept stuffed deep inside her thin mattress and counted out the coins saved there. With the gold Nicky had given her, she reckoned she almost had enough to leave Madrid and make a new life for herself somewhere far from there. She thought she would follow his advice and head for the coast, see if she could find herself a place as a house or kitchen maid in some respectable villa or lodging house and escape the sordid life she was currently leading. It was nearly Christmas, so with the extra money she could make from helping in the local bars as well as from drunken punters, she thought she would leave in the new year; a new year and a new start, but she just needed a little bit more money. She needed the cost of transport to the coast, money for a room to live in temporarily and to feed herself, and some sensible, demure clothes... until she found herself some proper employment.

Rosita looked at the coins again and tried to estimate how much more she would need. Not a lot, but still a fair bit. Once she'd left Madrid and finished with selling herself, she vowed she would never return to that way of life again, so she had to make enough to ensure it didn't happen. That meant just a few more punters, and the ones who wanted more than a quick fuck would pay more. Christmas was good as the men tended to get drunk and treat themselves, and spend a bit more indulging their little fantasies and foibles, or idiosyncrasies, or perversions. That was how to get more money. She grimaced in distaste, but it was now a means to an end, and not for much longer. Just a few more punters...

Chapter Two

Christmas was only a few days away and Nicky was still waiting for Carmelita to appear. He was watching the tenement but hadn't seen Rosita for nearly a week. Early one afternoon, there was a bit of a commotion and he watched as Madalena rushed out through the entry door looking distraught. Wondering at the cause of her upset, he followed curiously as she hurried towards the banks of the Manzanares river. She made her way to the Toledo Bridge and as Nicky watched, rushed over to where a small group of people were standing on the riverbank, under the first of the stone arches. As the group of mainly women, mostly local prostitutes by their appearance, parted to let Madalena through, Nicky saw a bedraggled body lying on the ground at their feet. A creeping feeling of *déjà vu* ran up his spine as he, too, moved nearer. He heard Madalena wail as she bent over the still form and the group started to break up and slope off as a couple of militia approached. He caught one of the weeping women, asking the question to which he feared he already knew the answer. "Who is it, the girl there?" he asked, passing a coin into her hand.

"'Tis Rosita," she sobbed, pocketing the coin out of habit, obviously too distracted to care what it was. "Some bastard's broken 'er neck.

Thrashed 'er first an' all, good an' proper, looks like th' bastard took a whip or crop to 'er," the woman wiped her eyes as Nicky blanched. "She was only a babe, so sweet she was," she muttered. "Shud be strung up by 'is bollocks fer doin' that, an' that'd be too good fer 'im," and she spat venomously. "That's th' third girl's bin found 'ere in th' past six months, all strangled or wiv their necks broke; 'bout time th' 'thorities did sumthin' 'bout it. But they won't do nuffin', as usual. Fuckin' men!" and she spat uncouthly again.

"Three?" Nicky whispered, grimacing.

"Yers," nodded the raddled prostitute. "Shockin' ain't it? Bet it's th' same bastard did fer 'em all, an' jes' leaves 'em 'ere fer th' crows."

"Were they all whipped or thrashed too?" Nicky really didn't want to know, but knew he had to ask.

"Nah, but those wot weren't 'ad bin beaten real good, covered in bruises they was; fuckin' pervert!" she swore. "I'd like ter take a knife to 'im I wud, castrate th' bastard," and with that, she wandered off, swearing and shaking her head as she went.

Nicky stood still for a few minutes, absorbing the horror of what he'd just learned. Had Bernheim been responsible for this as well as the other girls? Surely not, he thought, the man had bigger things on his mind than the murder of some common prostitutes. But the evidence, such as it was, pointed that way. On the other hand, the world was full of perverts, weirdos and brutal men – and the evidence was circumstantial. But Nicky's gut instinct told him his first assumptions were right, it was too much of a coincidence. He shuddered. The man obviously had a vicious nature and bestial appetite. For the first time, a glimmer of fear ran down his spine as he remembered how Ashcroft had described the bloodied remains of his former agents.

Madalena was kneeling over the body as he approached. She looked up as his shadow fell over her, tears still rolling down her face. "León!" she gasped. "What're you doin' 'ere?" Nicky kneeled down next to her, his eyes staring at the cold white face and long, wet black hair which half covered it. Rosita's head was lolling at an odd angle and he could see the tell-tale bruising round her neck. "Rosita said you'd gorn," Madalena choked out, "she went lookin' fer yer, she woz worrit you'd given 'er all yer money an' you'd got inter trubble." She shook her head sadly as she looked up at Nicky and reflected, soft tears still falling. "So soft 'earted she woz. She'd bin a nice girl once, then 'er parents got killt by th' fuckin' *Francés*. Shot where they stood in their bloody bookshop they woz, jes' cos they didn't fink Bonaparte's bruvver shud be king as 'e ain't Spanish, an' Rosita woz 'idin' under th' counter, that's 'ow she 'scaped. They set fire ter th' place an' all. Nothin' left after that, she 'ad nowhere ter go, only th' streets."

Nicky's stomach roiled with anger and pity as Madalena put her hand on his arm. "She told me 'ow good yer'd bin to 'er, she woz goin' ter go away, said yer'd told 'er to. Asked me ter go wiv 'er, she did. Safer that way, two of us tergether, lookin' out fer each uvver. We woz goin' after Christmas, we jes' needed ter save a bit more money," and another bout of sobs overtook her. "I told 'er an' told 'er not ter go wiv that bastard agin, not after what 'e did afore, but Carmelita sent a message sayin' 'e'd asked fer 'er, partic'lar like, said 'e pay 'er well fer 'er trouble. So off she went, said she cud put up wiv it jes once more, said it wud be th' last time an' th' money wud be 'nough ter make it worfwhile." She wailed, "Fat lot of use to 'er now," and she howled with grief.

Nicky put his arm around the distraught and sobbing girl. "Yer mus' tell the Authorities, yer know 'e did it, why don't yer report 'im? Was it 'im who did fer the others? Do yer know?" he asked curiously.

"I dunno," Madalena husked quietly as she tried to pull herself together, "but I wudn't be s'rprised, an' I can't tell nobody. That Carmelita, she's a nasty piece o' work; she frightens me, she duz, an' she'll 'ave me if I say anythin' or squeal ter th' 'thorities'. Cut me wiv a knife most like. I shudn't even talk ter yer, but yer knows 'bout it already, an' yer knew Rosita." She looked up at Nicky again, "I just wanna git out of 'ere, away from all this shit. I've 'ad 'nough too. I wanna be an 'ousemaid or kitchin maid. Rosita said we could if'n we tried. I don't care if I scrubs floors or clean chamber pots; anythin's better than sellin' meself ter arseholes like 'im."

A thought struck her as she wiped her eyes with her grubby skirt, "What're you doin' 'ere anyways?"

"Me? Oh, I've bin buskin' over t'other side of th' city an' picked up a bit o' casual work in a stables; that's why I 'aven't bin around fer a while. Gotta earn th' cash where I can gets it. I was on me way ter find Rosita ter see what she was doin' fer Christmas, an' then when I got ter yer lodgins someone told me what 'ad 'appened, so I came down 'ere an' then I saw you."

"Oh, I'm so sorry," Madalena sighed. Thinking him the kind-hearted but penniless bar singer they'd both known, she added, "I s'pose yer cud do wiv yer money back now?" she sighed sadly. "I'll geddit fer yer when I go back ter our room; I knows where Rosita 'id 'er stuff," she offered, somewhat to Nicky's surprise; he didn't expect such honesty, or generosity, from a poor prostitute.

"*Dios...* no," Nicky muttered. "You keep it fer yerself. Rosita would 'ave wanted that. Just get away from 'ere as quickly as possible. Er, d'you know where Carmelita is, by the way?" he asked idly.

"Nah, bin away fer weeks wiv some man she 'as, but she'll be back soon, in a coupla days prob'ly. It's Christmas, remember? Lot o' work fer us girls round 'ere at Christmas," she sighed, "but I'd rather not face 'er, not after this."

"Go now," Nicky said as he drew her to her feet and hugged her. "Do what I told yer. Take Rosita's money an' go as quick as yer can." He looked down at the dead girl in front of them, sorrow etching his features. "She was so young, so sweet, so full of life," he whispered sadly.

"She woz very taken wiv yer, León, y'know, an' yer seem so sad. Did yer like 'er too?"

Nicky sighed. "She reminded me of someone, someone I grew up with," he murmured almost to himself. Then, "I'll make that bastard suffer if I ever get me 'ands on 'im." He whispered his words with such intense venom, Madalena gasped.

"León, NO! Yer musn't git involved; 'e's bad news, let 'im be an' foller yer own advice. Git away from this shitty life 'ere." She looked at him hopefully, "I don't s'pose yous fancy comin' wiv me? If yer knows 'orses, yer can find work easy 'nuf anywhere we goes..."

Nicky laughed sadly. "No, *Querida*, I'm not th' man fer you, sweet as you are too. I need ter stay 'ere in th' city an' make meself some more money. As yer say, it'll soon be Christmas," and he put his hands in his pocket and pulled out some coins which he pressed into Madalena's hand. "'Ere, take this, make sure she gits a proper funeral, hmmm?" He looked deep in the girl's eyes, "An' then you go, go as quick as yer can, an' forget all this. Th' sooner th' better, an' keep well away from Carmelita."

Madalena looked up at him, "God bless yer, León. Rosita woz right, yous are a special man," and she actually crossed herself.

Nicky merely smiled sadly at her, shaking his head, before he turned and walked slowly away.

He went back to his solitary vigil, a cold hardness now settled over his heart. His gut instinct was rarely wrong and it told him Frederick Bernheim was responsible for the dead women. Like father, like son; he wondered how alike they looked. He'd never forget the father, Edgar Bernheim; the man's face was scorched into his memory and he'd never forget what had been done to him and his parents in the terrible dungeons of Rouen Fortress on his orders, some of it by his own hand. Nor the bloody massacre of the servants and retainers the day he and his so-called militia had pitched up at the family chateau. That evil man, now his son too, had destroyed so many lives between them, including his, also nearly Francis's. He was now even more determined to put a stop to Frederick Bernheim before he destroyed anyone else.

Chapter Three

Carmelita returned three days later and Nicky recognised her instantly by the scar on her forehead. It was Christmas Eve. Earlier that morning he'd watched from a distance as Madalena and a few of the other girls had attended the quiet little funeral in a small churchyard near the outskirts of the city. After they left, he went over to the newly dug grave and laid a solitary flower, a rose like her name, on top of the mound of earth, before he, too, returned to the alley, to wait for the woman he was sure could lead him to Rosita's murderer and Ashcroft's quarry.

He watched as Carmelita disappeared inside the tenement, carrying just a small bag. She came out a few hours later, dressed for the evening. Not as scruffy as most of the other working girls, she wore black, her clothes better fitting and slightly finer quality. She had a sultry look about her but to Nicky, she nonetheless appeared exactly what she was. He followed her as she made her way to a small *taberna*, a slightly more refined type of clientele here. By the end of the evening, she'd found herself a customer and left with him.

Nicky had already thoroughly searched her rooms in the tenement and found nothing. He had no idea how involved she was with Bernheim but she was his only lead. He simply had to wait until she was summoned by him again, but he needed to know if she was more to the man than just his favourite whore, or if she knew more about him, his real identity and unscrupulous personal plans. He also wondered if she knew any of his accomplices.

The next day was Christmas Day. Nicky wandered round the quiet city centre and on impulse went into the Basilica de San Francisco to light a candle for his step-mother, wondering if she'd ever been there herself. He wondered, too, whether the Dowager was still alive and knelt quietly to say a short prayer for her. He then sat in the peaceful and quiet interior, gazing up at the stunning, frescoed cupola, his mind drifting back to England; he wondered what his family were doing.

In England, the family were gathered at Firle Manor. Francis had retreated to his study as the only sane place in the whole house, even if he couldn't keep out the noise. His raucous sons were all at home and had brought some school and university friends with them. His daughter was still exercising her lungs for England and now she could crawl, nothing was sacred in whatever room she was in. He sat down to try and work but eventually gave up when a loud scratching and barking at his door disturbed his train of thought. He got up to let Bubbles in, the latest descendant of the Duchess's original mountain of a hound, Fluffy, with Duchess, his mate. The Pyrenean Mountain Dog was obviously also retreating from the mayhem outside. Following the giant, white, long-haired creature who plodded across the room, Francis went to sit down in front of the fire, nursing a glass of fine port and smoking a cigar while he idly twirled a soft furry ear.

Unlike his predecessors, Fluffy in particular, in some ways Bubbles was really more Francis's dog than his wife's. When they'd decided to keep him as a family pet from the last and unexpected litter which had sadly caused the death of Bubbles' mother, Cat had been pregnant with Elizabeth. She'd been upset enough about losing the dog and fraught about avoiding yet another miscarriage, common in the early stages of pregnancy, the protective, worried, fussing Francis had taken over exercising and trying to train the exuberant puppy into some measure of obedience. The dog had become very attached to him and the feeling was mutual, even though Francis wouldn't admit it. Bubbles now sighed with pleasure and collapsed with a sleepy woof on the hearth rug while Francis wondered what he should tell the family about the news, or rather no news, from the Peninsula. Nicky's letter was burning a hole in his jacket pocket. He'd received it a couple of weeks previously and had decided to keep it as a surprise for everyone for Christmas. He'd laughed when he'd read the hastily scribbled note, but the news he'd received from Ashcroft this past week was more depressing.

Wellington had retreated back to the Spanish border with Portugal and the French forces were now located between him and Madrid. Something had gone wrong with the logistical arrangements during the retreat and it had been a shambles. Bedraggled men were literally starving and fending off skirmishes, while stragglers were being taken prisoner in alarming numbers by the pursuing French, including Wellington's second-in-command, General Edward Paget. Nicky hadn't been seen nor heard from since he'd left the English camp besieging Burgos in mid-October, sent away with instructions from the head of the Allied forces to continue searching for Bernheim. Marauding French squads were all over the countryside, Reynard had heard nothing at all from Nicky since he'd returned to Spain and Francis hoped he was in Madrid. He'd heard the French hadn't bothered to garrison the city when they'd recaptured it, so providing he kept his head down, Nicky should be all right. But Francis nonetheless fretted at the sparsity of news or information. He just hoped that no news was good news. After much consideration, he decided to say nothing to the family, merely let them read Nicky's letter. He certainly didn't want Bella to fret unnecessarily, he knew she worried enough as it was. She'd been kept busy redecorating his late grandmother's house, but her increasing girth was starting to tire her and she still insisted on keeping a personal eye on the activities at her two gaming houses. He grinned to himself that at least she'd now given up making personal appearances there. No costume in the world could hide her obvious condition and it would have been impossible to keep her identity a secret, no matter what mask she was wearing.

Shouts and shrieks percolated through his door and noises of what sounded like a fight or serious fracas further down the corridor. With a smiling sigh he rose to his feet to go and sort it all out. A house full of boys and young men, the sons and daughters of some of their neighbours, plus the children of his wife's sisters, was no place for anyone wanting peace and quiet, especially on Christmas Day.

Later that evening, Bella sat alone in her bedroom, Nicky's note clutched in her hand. The Duke had produced it for everyone to read over their Christmas dinner and it had been received with smiles of relief and poignant humour as it had been passed around the table. The update on Wellington's recent military setbacks had finally reached the newssheets so they all understood the situation in the Peninsula was difficult. She'd quietly cornered her uncle after the meal and asked if he'd had any further private information, but he'd shaken his head, reassuring her yet again it was not surprising given the position of the French forces. Francis tried to reassure her saying no news was good news and it had only been a few months since he himself had received any reports from Spain, but it didn't do much to calm her constant concern for Nicky's safety.

As she re-read his scribble for the umpteenth time, her hand crept over her rounded belly. She could feel the child moving inside her as she lay back on her bed and tried to picture him sitting in some army tent, jotting down the careless note for them all. Large tears ran down her soft cheeks and she sent up a fervent prayer to God to keep her beloved safe, wondering what he was doing on Christmas Day in Spain.

Chapter Four

Nicky came out of the Basilica feeling a bit more at peace with himself, turning up the collar of his jacket against the damp chill. He continued his meanderings around the quiet streets, trying to decide about the best way to approach Carmelita. Somehow, he didn't think a romantic tavern singer would hold out much appeal to her, unlike the other working girls such as Madalena and Rosita, whom he'd picked up to question over the previous weeks and months, so he would have to change his character into someone who would interest a woman like her. His mouth grimaced in distaste, but he would do whatever was necessary to prise what information he could from the fearsome prostitute.

He went back to his lodgings and ordered something to eat. He lay back on his bed after considering how to deal with Carmelita and then slept for a few hours before getting up to wash and change into a cleaner set of clothes and smarten himself up from his usual slightly scruffy appearance. Before he left, he took an item out of his saddle-bags and stuffed it down the inside of one of his boots.

He went back to the bar where he'd seen Carmelita the previous evening and parked himself at a table, waiting to see if she'd appear.

He was sitting in a quiet corner, nursing a glass of wine and smoking a cheroot, when she sauntered in. The place was now full of Christmas revellers and he'd already turned down approaches from a couple of other girls making their way around the tables, looking out for a punter for the night, hopefully full of Christmas cheer and feeling more generous than usual.

Nicky watched through narrowed eyes as she positioned herself by the bar and quietly surveyed the room, eyeing up the men sitting around the tables and their potential for her. Not a girl like Madalena or Rosita, she was older, a striking-looking woman in her late twenties or early thirties, he surmised. Tall and black haired with full red lips and a luscious, voluptuous figure, she was once more dressed in black with the odd red trimming to lessen the severity of her outfit and make it less funereal, not that the low-cut gown would be suitable to go anywhere near a solemn burial service. Her dark eyes were cold and hard and the small scar over her eyebrow lent a somewhat forbidding mien to her face. He could well understand why the other girls were slightly frightened of her and wondered what type of man would find her appearance appealing, although he had to admit to himself her sultry, sensual looks would be to some men's taste, even if not his own.

As her eyes continuously scanned the bar, assessing the customers as they came and went, they momentarily locked with Nicky's as he raised his to look at her, but apart from a mere pause, she made no move or acknowledgement of him and continued with her roaming gaze. He returned to his drink, lit another cheroot and waited, ostensibly ignoring her.

She spent the next half hour sauntering around the tables, flirting with the groups of men and then finally she insinuated herself over to the corner where Nicky was sitting in solitude. "Holá, Guapo," "Hello, Handsome, all by yourself for Christmas?" she purred.

"I was rather hoping you'd come and join me," Nicky answered, his smile curling as he looked directly into her eyes and he held out his hand, indicating her to take a seat at his table. As she sat down, he caught the eye of one of the serving girls and she brought over another bottle of wine and a glass. He poured a drink for Carmelita and silently toasted her as their glasses clinked.

They talked desultorily for a while, skirting around anything personal. Nicky got the impression that behind the hard, seductive exterior, there lurked quite a clever mind. "I'm Carmelita, by the way," she offered as he refilled her glass, "...and you are?"

"I'm Nico," he responded. "Nicolás León, at your service," inclining his head briefly.

"So, Nico, what do you do?" She was obviously assessing how much he could afford to pay for her services.

"Oh, this and that," he replied vaguely. "Sometimes I'm a musician, but I mainly deal with horses now. Trading, training, occasionally dealing with difficult horses for their rich owners."

"Really," she muttered, obviously not particularly impressed, deciding that sort of occupation wouldn't pay much.

"Oh, it has its moments," he raised an eyebrow and looked her up and down, "but I have a little sideline as well."

"What sort of sideline?" she queried, quirking her own scarred eyebrow.

"Wouldn't you like to know," he smirked archly. "But since we are vaguely in the same type of business I'll tell you." Nicky leaned towards her slightly to speak softly. "When the wives of the horse owners want to be ridden by a real man, I'm happy to oblige, because they'll recommend me to their friends for some afternoon siesta entertainment while their husbands are otherwise occupied with business or their mistresses." He lolled back in his chair again with a lecherous expression on his face while she looked him over with a critical eye, inspecting his chest, then down to his tight breeches – where they paused.

"Do you now. How... ah... interesting. Well, well, well." She returned her assessing eyes back up to his. "So, with all these available ladies, what are you doing here by yourself then?"

"Well, that's all about satisfying THEM and getting paid for my trouble. It's Christmas today, so I thought for once I might satisfy MYSELF with what I like," he said with an enigmatic look.

"Oh yes? And what do YOU like that satisfies you?" she purred.

"Me? Ah, well, you see, I get fed up dealing with women who just lie back and expect me to pleasure them. I want someone a bit more feisty, who likes a bit more, ah… excitement, more passion, something that caters to my particular tastes."

"And what tastes are those?" she whispered brazenly.

Nicky looked at the woman opposite him. Her eyes were suddenly more alive, more lascivious and interested. "Well," his eyes glittered coldly, "I get great satisfaction when I persuade a horse to do my bidding, perform tricks for me, do precisely what I want." He raised his eyes now to Carmelita, "I find it's the same with a woman." At that, he bent down to pull the riding crop from his boot that he'd placed there earlier, flexing it between his hands, his eyes looking deeply into hers with a questioning, raised eyebrow.

"Such tastes don't come cheap," she whispered.

"It's Christmas," he murmured back, "and I like to treat myself now and again."

Carmelita leaned over and whispered a price in his ear which almost made him raise his eyebrows, but Nicky laughed to himself. Ashcroft expected him to do whatever it took and he presumed a night with this depraved creature definitely counted as such, so he threw a handful of gold coins down on the table in front of her, watching as her greedy eyes lit up. As Carmelita scooped up the coins and they quickly disappeared into a hidden pocket of her gown, he rose and held out a hand to her. "There's more where that came from if you please me," he said meaningfully and then threw more coins down on the table to pay for the wine before leading her out of the tavern.

They strolled down the street and into a nearby hostelry where Nicky took a room for the night, merely telling Carmelita his lodgings were on the far side of town and he was in a hurry to enjoy her favours. As soon as they entered the dingy room she turned on him to cover his face in kisses and then kiss him on the mouth, carnally and vora-ciously. Nicky reared back slightly, but as he pulled her into his arms and started to return her kiss, she writhed against him and moaned in passion. From the corner of his eye, he saw her clawed fingers come up to scratch him.

"No!" he bit out as he managed to catch her hand before it made contact with his skin and he pulled her head back by her hair. As she was pulled away from him momentarily, she looked into his face, smiling maliciously before curling her other hand round his neck and pulling his head down to her mouth again. She kissed him hungrily and once more he felt her claw-like fingers creep up his shirt towards his neck. "I said NO!" he rasped more angrily. "Stop it. I don't wish to have your claw marks on me."

She leaned back again and laughed at him. "Then make me," she purred and kissed him again. Her hands roved up and down his body, curling around the front of his tight breeches, squeezing hard and caressing, then rose up towards his chest where he felt her sharp nails claw at his skin, scratching deeply inside his now open shirt front.

"I said NO!" his voice laced with anger.

"And I said MAKE me," she rasped malevolently.

Nicky realised now just what sort of a night he had in front of him. He felt as though he'd crawled under a stone and been confronted by a female scorpion. His mind reeled back to Wellington's ironic comment. He was nauseated, but knew that if he was to find out anything about Bernheim and his whereabouts and plans, this was the only woman who could lead him there. Despite his revulsion, he would need to play her distasteful games and pretend to enjoy them, and he wondered at the sort of man who would pay for this activity, definitely not him unless he had to. King and his adopted country he told himself. Ashcroft and Wellington should be proud of him. He lifted his hand and slapped her across the face.

Carmelita laughed at him, throwing her head back with pleasure and scratched his chest again. "Call that a slap. Try harder," she ordered.

She was insatiable. Nicky had made love to and fucked countless women, had played all sorts of games with them, but none had been like this, not that this could remotely be called making love or anything like it, not even a satisfying fuck; his idea of games were pastimes that titillated, teased or pleasurably tormented, all to enhance the ultimate pleasure. Not this.

With Carmelita, the whole thing was a sex act, dirty and deviated.

He felt like he was being eaten alive as she'd worked her way down his body, licking, biting and scratching him. Giving credibility to his story, he'd slapped her hard then thrashed her with his riding crop, her creamy buttocks going red from the force of his blows and she'd climaxed as he'd roughly chafed and pinched her sex as he'd hit her, screaming out with intense pleasure, begging him to hit her harder. It was no prostitute's act, he could tell; she was soaking wet and revelling in the depravity of it. Finally, he'd bent her over the bed-board, driving hard into her, bending her arms up behind her back as he did so, making her cry out with agony, then ecstasy, as she'd found another release. It seemed the more he hurt her, the more pleasure she found. But she wasn't submissive in the normal sense, she was vicious and revelled in being tamed. As they'd both finally collapsed on the bed, exhausted and panting, she was like a pleasured feral cat, curled around his body, while he lay there, sickened by the whole episode.

"Well, well, Nico," Carmelita purred over him. "You're quite the lover, aren't you? I've not had that much pleasure from many men. You certainly know what you're doing."

He forced himself to smile down at her. "I'm glad I pleased you, *Querida*, you're quite a woman yourself. You certainly pleased me, well worth the money. Do you have a particular protector at present in your life, or someone who has first call on your favours?" he asked idly.

She looked at him through narrowed eyes. "And why would you want to know that?" she asked warily.

Nicky merely shrugged, face impassive. "Only that I'd quite like to see you again, do this again," he let his hand move down her body, his long, guitar-player's nails scratching deep into the skin of her back, making her arch against him and moan. "But I wouldn't want to upset anyone if someone as fascinating as you is otherwise taken."

"I'm my own mistress. I please myself," she replied assertively. "I don't have or need a pimp. I have a few regular customers who have particular 'appetites', as you obviously do, but I belong to no one man."

"Hmmm," Nicky muttered, bending his head to bite down hard on first one then the other of her nipples making her writhe and moan more. "And just what do these other customers do for you, or you for them, these 'particular appetites' that you all particularly enjoy? Tell me about them and what they do that pleases you; it may be that it would please me too, my own personal appetite is quite wide ranging, in various directions, depending on my mood..."

As he spent the next couple of hours indulging and satisfying Carmelita's perverted whims and allowing her access to his body as she wished, thinking she was pleasing him in turn to earn her money, Nicky finally managed to learn that one regular was a degenerate old goat, an aristocrat with plenty of money to indulge his twisted fantasies, who paid her well to visit his country villa for a week or so whenever he could escape his family in Madrid. There was another who liked to be beaten and subjugated, another of her specialities, he gathered. Finally, just as he tormented her to the heights of her depraved passions, he learned of her other lover – the Frenchman.

The Frenchman. A man with very distinct desires, according to Carmelita. He summoned her from time to time and she went. But that was all Nicky could tease out of her. No details of what they did or where. When Carmelita eventually fell into a sated slumber, Nicky lay wide awake and knew he'd have to continue this sordid relationship for a while in an effort to find out more: where Bernheim was based and anything else he could persuade the prostitute to reveal.

They went their separate ways in the morning. Carmelita told Nicky that if and when he wanted to see her again, he only had to leave word at the bar where they'd met earlier and she would come there to meet him.

Nicky went back to his lodgings and ordered a bath. As he scrubbed at his skin, looking distastefully at the scratches and teeth marks, he felt as if he'd sunk to the bottom of a pit of depravity and his mind drifted to Rosita and how she must have felt each time she went with some dirty, stinking man, old enough to be her father or grandfather, only to end up with Bernheim, courtesy of Carmelita. What he still didn't know, however, was whether Carmelita knew what Bernheim had intended to do to the young girl. Whatever it took, Nicky promised himself he would find out.

As he sat and soaked in the warm water, Nicky's mind drifted back to his long-ago childhood in France, when he was nearly five years old and a prisoner, along with his parents, of Bernheim's father in the old Rouen Fortress. His parents hadn't survived, but Marie-Catherine Granville had risked her life to rescue him from the clutches of Dupont, Bernheim's sadistic lieutenant and right-hand man. His step-mother and Francis had arrived just in time to save her and then sneak him out with them when they'd made their escape. Cat had suspected he was about to be molested by Dupont when she'd found him in the man's quarters and guessed it might not have been the first time, but it was a subject no one had ever mentioned or discussed. Everyone assumed they'd got him out in time, avoiding any serious abuse and then, with love, care and the passage of time and him being so young, he'd forget about it.

What Nicky had never spoken about to anyone, even in his adopted family, was that Dupont had indeed forced him to carry out disgusting acts and not just once or twice; he'd forgotten nothing.

He'd been beaten, starved, physically and sexually abused in the worst ways, on and off for months on end. His pregnant mother had miscarried and died next to him in the cramped, windowless, dank and fetid cell he'd shared with her, deep in the dark bowels of the fortress, unable to sustain the beatings and vicious treatment meted out to her by Bernheim and his lieutenant. Unfortunately for the little boy, after her death, Bernheim had instructed Dupont to start on him, in the hope that the little Ducal heir might know some if not all the details about his inheritance which could be further and quietly investigated.

Antoine de Bresancourt, the Duke, his father, incarcerated on trumped up charges of treason, had been proud and disdainful to the end, withstanding everything Bernheim had thrown at him, the most appalling and vicious torture of which Nicky had seen the results: battered and bruised, missing teeth, finger and toenails, terrible burns and much more. Still, he'd gone to his grave either in or on his way to

Paris, a broken man but with his secrets intact, much to Bernheim's intense frustration.

Whether Bernheim knew or cared that Dupont had already earmarked the little boy for his special brand of servitude and torment, or had made a start on it even before his parents had died, Nicky didn't know, but it didn't matter. His fond childhood memories of life within the slightly eccentric Granville family with his step-mother and step-father, were now hazy, but the perversion, degradation and pain to which he'd been subjected at the hands of Dupont, had never left him. Although the nightmares had finally faded long ago, only occasionally surfacing when he was anxious or stressed, he had never, ever, forgotten and knew the memories would stay with him until he died.

He'd grown up feeling protected and safe in the care of a close, loving and happy family. Neither his gentle step-father nor loving step-mother had ever laid a hand on him when he'd been naughty, although both Cat and Francis had paddled his backside on occasions when he'd been up to serious mischief. But strangely, that hadn't disturbed him at all. He knew deep down how much they loved him and invariably, Francis had abandoned his efforts and chuckled at him afterwards, telling him he'd been just as bad at his age. Cat merely gave up and cuddled him as neither were capable of seriously disciplining anyone they cared about, especially their children, him, Bella and their pets. When he'd become a young man, sex to him had always been a pleasure. Chasing and charming, first girls, then women, for endless enjoyment – his and their own – all laughingly encouraged by Francis, his rogue of an adopted uncle. He'd racketed around London with his rakehell friends, up to all kinds of lascivious and amorous activities, but he scrupulously avoided anyone or anything remotely depraved, perverted or sordid. He knew all about it, had made it his mission to be aware of every facet of sex, just wouldn't indulge personally. As he'd even told *Lionesse* that first night, he'd play most sex games for fun, his or someone else's, but he wouldn't tolerate pain, nor serious perversion. He had his own very personal code. To him there was a great difference between erotic teasing and enjoyment against coercing someone to do something either they weren't happy with, or was against their will.

But now he'd found himself involved with just the type of woman and activity he'd avoided like the plague all his life, as well as a man with connections to a past he'd endeavoured for years to forget. That man was probably even more evil and repugnant than his father, if that were possible, the beast who had destroyed his parents and very nearly, him.

Nicky put his face in his hands and shuddered. He knew he had to continue with his mission and not let any demons come back and haunt him, to destroy the life he'd made for himself.

Chapter Five

Over the next few weeks, Nicky kept watch on Carmelita's movements. She had a regular round of *tabernas* and cafés where she worked the customers, only going off with one if they appeared to have money. She obviously wasn't interested in spreading her legs for a mere few coins, like most of the other prostitutes. She disappeared for a week but he'd followed her as she set off, knowing she'd gone to stay with her elderly aristocratic client. Nicky officially saw her twice and went through a similar routine with her as the first night, trying to close his mind to what he was doing to keep her happy and let her think he was getting his particular 'appetite' satisfied. She was very close-mouthed about her Frenchman and Nicky had to be extremely careful not to be obviously probing. All he could ascertain was that she hadn't seen him for a while.

Meanwhile, in all the hostelries and meeting places around the city, gossip was now rife that Bonaparte was retreating from Russia. Nicky had also heard that Wellington had fallen right back to the Portuguese border during a calamitous winter retreat but knowing the determination of the man, he was sure he was regrouping and would strike out again once the weather improved. He wondered how the news about Bonaparte would affect the situation in Spain, but being cut off in

Madrid there was little he could do other than listen to rumour and speculation. He had no way of contacting the British forces, nor Ashcroft at the moment, and it was too far for him to make his way west to the border. Now he finally had a lead on Bernheim after all this time, he needed to remain in Madrid and follow things through.

One evening, he followed Carmelita to a back street *taberna* where she'd never been before. There was something different about her demeanour this time, however, and her dress was far more restrained, though still black. She frequently looked around furtively as she hurried along down the alleyways and the premises she finally entered was small, dark and discreet. Nicky had concealed himself in a doorway further back and sat in the shadows, hunched over with a blanket covering his head and body, looking at first glance like many of the poor beggars who haunted the streets; he'd acquired the blanket from one of them in exchange for a few coins. It stank, but it did the job perfectly.

The alley was deserted and the *taberna* didn't appear to attract many customers, but shortly after Carmelita disappeared inside, a dark, swarthy-looking man with a scarred face hurried in after her. Then, HE appeared. He approached from the other direction, tall, slender and dark haired, with a voluminous cloak swirling around him. He hurried along in the shadows of the doorways, his booted feet almost silent on the slick, damp cobbles. He looked around briefly before entering the hostelry and that was when Nicky caught a glimpse of his face. Impassive. Sinister. Cold obsidian eyes. High cheekbones. Pale olive skin. Thin lips. Dark hair. Nicky had never seen him before, no one had a proper or exact description, but he knew it was Frederick Bernheim. He didn't look exactly like his father, but he had some of his features and their tall and slender build was similar. There was just something about him which made Nicky shiver in recognition as the dreadful memories of so long ago returned in spades and danced round his brain.

He waited several minutes before rising to his feet and crept silently along the alley towards the *taberna* entrance. There was a small murky window beside the door and he peered carefully inside. Through the gloom, he could just about make out the three figures sitting in a quiet corner, heads down, deep in discussion. As he watched, Bernheim produced some papers and the trio pored over the documents while Bernheim obviously gave them instructions.

Nicky was in a dilemma. Who of the two men should he follow? Bernheim himself, perhaps, to discover where he lived, or the mysterious other man to ascertain who his accomplices were? As he contemplated his dilemma, he watched as the meeting broke up and Carmelita leaned up to kiss Bernheim. The man merely stood there, unresponsive, as the wanton Spanish woman curled herself around him, whispering in his ear. He paused for a moment then gave her a brief nod and they disappeared into the back darkness of the murky bar while the third man made his way back towards the door. Nicky turned hurriedly to conceal himself and when the scarred man emerged, he took a quick decision and began to follow him.

The man made his way down squalid streets with Nicky doggedly on his trail. Eventually, he arrived at a tenement building similar to that occupied by Carmelita and the other prostitutes and disappeared inside. Noting the location, Nicky turned and made his way back to the *taberna*, hoping that Bernheim and Carmelita were still inside. He peered through the window once more, but the place was now deserted. He made his way back to his doorway and, curled in his stinking blanket, settled down to wait for them to reappear. Just after dawn, as Nicky shifted uncomfortably to ease his stiffened muscles, Bernheim came out. Wrapped again in his dark cloak, he made his way down the deserted street from whence he'd first appeared. Following extremely carefully at a distance, creeping along like a hungry cat on the prowl for a rat, Nicky watched as the street opened out into a small square where a carriage had obviously been waiting all night. Both horse and driver appeared fast asleep. The driver was startled awake as Bernheim rapped his legs with a cane and, giving him a brief instruction, turned to climb inside. The carriage set off at a brisk pace, the clip-clop of the horse's hooves ringing out in the quiet early morning streets. There was no way Nicky could keep up, so, for the second time, he made his way back to his doorway to wait for Carmelita. But now he knew: whatever Bernheim was up to, he suspected Carmelita was in it too, right up to her nasty flashing eyes.

Interestingly, Carmelita stayed at the *taberna* all morning. She came out after lunch, merely to hurry back to the tenement to collect a small bag and then return to the hostelry. Nicky wondered what she was up to but decided to find out more about the third man, so made his way back to that individual's tenement lodgings. A couple of casual enquiries about the whereabouts of a scar-faced man gained him the location of his room. Once again, Nicky settled down in a cold doorway to wait patiently for his departure and grasp the opportunity to search within.

It was nightfall and the scar-faced man had left the tenement a short while before. Nicky crept silently up the narrow staircase in the seedy lodgings and found the room he sought. A few quick twists in the keyhole with the small, sharp length of metal he pulled out of an inside pocket and he was swiftly inside, the door closing behind him. Careful not to drip wax from the small stub of a candle he was carrying, he searched the untidy room from top to bottom. Finding nothing in the small chest of drawers or in or under the filthy mattress, he finally put the candle down on the small table which sat under a window, thick with grime. The top was covered with crumbs of food and a mass of papers. Carefully, he sifted through each document, ensuring he replaced it exactly where he'd found it. Most of the papers appeared to be bills of sale for goods or horses and he got the impression the man may well have been some sort of horse trader. Then he saw a couple of the receipts referring to guns and explosives and when Nicky looked at the quantities, he whistled silently to himself. Replacing those papers, he turned to two other documents which interested him much more. One was a list of names and the other a list of dates and places. He pulled a small notebook and pencil from another jacket pocket and quickly copied down the information from the two lists. He replaced the paperwork exactly as he'd found it and, with a final cursory look around the room, exited as silently as he'd entered, relocking the door behind him.

Back in his room at his own lodgings, Nicky collapsed on his bed, completely exhausted. He was cold, hungry and hadn't slept for nearly two days, but his mind was whirling with the information he'd gathered. He dragged himself downstairs to a quiet corner of the hostelry where he ordered food and drink, trying to make sense of everything he'd found, but was too tired to think straight. He retired to bed and, as the mists of slumber overtook his mind and body, his last thoughts felt like an escape from the sordid and dangerous world he now inhabited. He saw an idyllic vision of Bella, his little Sooty, shrieking and chasing after him across the fields of Firle, her plaits flying wildly, freckles live across her nose and green eyes sparkling with laughter. She caught up with him and they fell to the ground together in gales of laughter as she tickled him unmercifully to get revenge for whatever prank he'd pulled... but, as he drifted off to sleep, she changed and became faceless and the woman in his arms became *Lionesse*, still tickling him, but then tormenting and tantalising his body in another fashion until, with a groan, he slipped into blackness.

He slept like the dead, round the clock before rising late, but his head was much clearer. Once dressed and with some more food inside him, Nicky returned to his position opposite the *taberna* where he realised Carmelita was now staying. For the next few days, he watched her come and go. Interestingly, she never went near her tenement. As he sat there, he looked over the lists he'd copied from the papers he'd found in the scar-faced man's room and decided he needed to know more about him and his activities. He therefore abandoned his vigil of Carmelita's new temporary residence and started his surveillance of the scar-faced man.

For the next week, Nicky shadowed him around Madrid; to horse fairs and insalubrious *tabernas*, cafés and bars, watching and noting who he met and when. He tried to differentiate between the genuine customers from his trading and those who might be contacts for a different sort of business. When he suspected a man was in the latter group, he then followed him to find out a name and see if it matched any of those on his list. It was painstaking and frustrating work; sometimes he wanted to follow several men at the same time but obviously couldn't do so. After two weeks, he'd located two names on the list. Both appeared to be ex-soldiers and, to all intents and purposes, mercenaries for hire.

Not sure what Carmelita was now up to, he went back to her tenement and watched again. He hadn't seen her for a couple of days and

Madalena was thankfully now gone too. He casually stopped one of the other girls and asked if anyone had seen Carmelita lately. The tart shrugged and said she was obviously away with one of her customers. Nicky thought the girl looked upset and somewhat fearful. Curious, he drew some coins from his pocket and pulled her away to a nearby *taberna* on the pretext of wanting a woman for that night. He plied her with drink and after a short interlude in a room upstairs, finally discovered what had upset her. Carmelita had sent a message to say she was busy with another customer and would another of the girls like to take her place with one of her regulars? He would pay very well for accommodating his requirements and it would keep him happy. Some of the girls were well aware of Carmelita's customers and wanted nothing to do with them, but despite their warnings, others were greedy or desperate for the money. One of them had gone in the carriage sent for her, but had arrived back, whipped and bruised, black and blue, with a story that the man had tried to strangle her as he'd taken her; and that hadn't been in the normal way either. The man's depraved tastes seemed endless and unusual, to say the least.

Nicky left the girl to snore off her alcoholic over-indulgence and crept silently away, seething with anger. He knew full well that Carmelita wasn't 'away with a customer', merely residing a few streets away in rooms above another hostelry. So, despite her enjoyment of the more depraved type of sex she'd demanded from Nicky and obviously shared with Bernheim, when it came to satisfying the man's extreme sadistic requirements, she merely procured another unwitting girl for him, just like the innocent Rosita, sending her, uncaring, to her fate. That she was also up to her eyes in his other nefarious activities was now also in no doubt. Nicky wasn't sure if he could bring himself to touch her again.

Chapter Six

The worst of the winter had passed and Nicky was desperate to get word to Wellington and thence onward to Ashcroft on what he now knew was afoot. He'd finally tracked down all the names on the scar-faced man's list and had watched as the whole group had finally met up in a back street *taberna* a week before. Unknown to them, because Carmelita wasn't there, Nicky had sat nearby and appeared virtually asleep over an almost empty flagon of wine on his table, snoring periodically as he eavesdropped in to their quiet conversation. He hadn't been able to hear everything, but enough to make sense of what was being planned. The British forces had received their winter shipment of gold from Rothschild, via Portugal, but part of it was being transferred over to the Spanish rebels and guerrillas piecemeal, as they harried the French over the winter while Wellington re-grouped and waited for reinforcements from England.

Nicky assumed the dates on the list matched locations for intended deliveries. How they'd been acquired he had no idea, but that wasn't his immediate problem. Someone else could investigate informants in either Wellington's camp or on the Spanish side.

In the meantime, Bonaparte had suffered a terrible defeat in Russia and was now in full retreat from Moscow, across the frozen wastes of eastern Europe. The French were worried, on both fronts and, amidst this confusion, Bernheim thought it was the perfect time to strike. He wanted the gold shipments on their way to the Spanish rebels and a large one would be coming in spring, in time to bolster up Spanish support for a new push forward from Wellington and the allied army. If Bernheim got the gold, he was intending to use it to undermine the Spanish rebel activity and encourage them to support the French instead; to change sides and fight against the British. As Ashcroft and Nicky also suspected, a large amount of the bullion would disappear into Bernheim's personal hands and who knew what further mischief he would cause after that. Nicky also wondered how many more women he would kill, but that was his personal vendetta and even more reason now to find and get rid of the man.

Frustratingly, Nicky had no way of making contact with anyone. He'd gone to locations where he knew agents could rendezvous with contacts, or leave messages for onward transmission, but no one ever came to check for anything. He didn't know if they'd been betrayed, or killed, or both, and he had no idea if Bernheim knew the British were on his trail. He was thankful he'd kept himself well under cover, even around Wellington. He was a loner and worked best that way. It was the safest fashion in which to operate in places like this when knowing who to trust was impossible. Subconsciously, he'd been following the Dowager's last words to him, not to trust anyone and to watch his back. And that was also Ashcroft's orders and the warning from Wellington. His final idea and his only option now, was to try and find any gypsies who came from Reynard's tribe, or who knew of the Roma leader personally, to send him a coded message for onward transmission to Francis in London, thence to Ashcroft, while also getting word over to the British. Nicky's problem was his isolation. By himself, he had no means of stopping Bernheim, the scar-faced man, or his group of accomplices from stealing one or more of the gold shipments. He needed reinforcements of his own… but there was no one.

He went back to haunting the peripheries of the horse fairs, making careful enquiries for news of Reynard until finally he came across a group of men who knew of the wily old Romani. They said they thought some gypsies from his tribe would be coming to a fair the following week with some new yearlings to sell on. Nicky thanked them casually, saying he'd heard they often had some good horseflesh for sale, before he calmly strolled away.

Back at his lodgings, Nicky finally pulled out the papers from the raised soles and heels of his boots and set about drafting out a couple of short notes and translating them into Ashcroft's complex code. One was for Wellington and one for Ashcroft, care of Francis. In case the messages fell into the wrong hands or the codes had been broken by the French in the months he'd been in Spain, he was extremely circumspect with what he had to say, ensuring nothing would lead back to him and break his cover. But if either or both recipients received his information, he trusted they would find a way to send assistance. Whether it would arrive in time to be useful was in the lap of the gods. Then he pondered on how he could send the messages to Reynard without that in itself causing suspicion. He now believed the scar-faced man was a Romani of some sort, given his horse-trading activities and swarthy appearance. He trusted absolutely no one.

The following week he caught up with the gypsies from Reynard's tribe and having thoroughly satisfied himself they knew Reynard personally, proceeded to haggle with them and bought a horse he didn't need. He spun them a story about being a long-time acquaintance of Reynard from his boyhood and told them a tale about a saddle he owned that the old man had long coveted. He then produced an ornately decorated saddle and asked them to take it back to Reynard as a gift from him, in lieu of a favour he owed the man over a woman. When they laughed at this and asked him who they should say had sent the gift, he simply told them to say it came from the man with a stallion called The Shadow. With their promises to pass over the saddle and his message as soon as they returned to their camp, Nicky smiled and sauntered off with his newly purchased horse. He hoped they would pass on the saddle and Reynard would be astute enough to investigate and find the messages hidden inside and pass them on as best he could. He was sure the name The Shadow would ensure his avid curiosity and attention, if nothing else and he laughed to himself. He would tell Francis of his little subterfuge when he got back to England, if he ever made it there again. The man would undoubtedly be amused, but Nicky still shivered slightly at what lay ahead.

Chapter Seven

J ust over a fortnight later, Francis was impatiently pacing up and down in Ashcroft's office. "For heaven's sake, Man, hurry up, what does it say?" he bit out.

"And why do you think I should tell YOU, Your Grace? This is highly confidential information," responded Ashcroft, irritatingly calm as he sat and personally translated the creased and tattered sheet of paper that the Duke had brought to his office some half an hour previously, barging his way in, scattering all those who got in his way.

"Because if it wasn't for me and my network, you wouldn't have it in the first place," Francis rasped cuttingly. "My contacts have risked their lives, not to mention the considerable amount of money it has cost me, to get this information to you across Spain and France in such a short time. The very least you can do is tell me if Nicky is all right, never mind say 'thank you'!"

"Calm down, Granville, calm down; take a seat, for pity's sake. I'm nearly finished, but I can't concentrate on decrypting this with you prowling around my office like a caged tiger," Ashcroft grated at the irate Duke and went back to his scribbling for a further few minutes as he finished deciphering the complex code. Finally, with an irritated huff when he got to the last few words he looked across at the worried man opposite him. "That young man is the absolute limit," he fumed. "Notwithstanding the priceless information he has at last managed to find out, he's put a personal message on the bottom. Oh really, whatever next," he tutted.

Francis smiled questioningly. "Typical Nicky. What does he say?"

"Send love to my family. Tell them I miss them terribly, each and every one of them, including Bubbles. Bubbles?" he raised an eyebrow at the last word he'd deciphered, wondering if he'd got it right and if so, who or what Bubbles was.

Francis laughed out loud. "Thank you, Ashcroft. That means the world to me and it will do, too, for all the rest of my family; oh and Bubbles is our rather large, rather hairy dog, what else?! Now, what of the rest of the message?"

Ashcroft sighed, muttering about irrelevant dogs before he handed over the transcribed note, seemingly vague to a casual reader and with no names mentioned. However, to Ashcroft and Francis, reading between the lines, the meaning was plain. He'd found Bernheim, his expected plan was about to be carried out and Nicky was cut off and needed reinforcements to deal with it.

"What the hell does he think you can do here from London?" exclaimed Francis, waving the note at Ashcroft. "He must be desperate if he thinks you can sort out something from so far away."

"Hmmm," pondered Ashcroft as he sat back in his chair thoughtfully. "Oh, for the last time, SIT DOWN, before you wear a hole in my rug! It's obvious; he's out of contact with Wellington. We've suspected our other agents in the area, including in Madrid, have been killed. We think that's where de Bresancourt is located and, having had no word from him either, I was, quite frankly, beginning to fear the worst."

Francis had also been worriedly contemplating the very same thing over the past few weeks, pacing the house in the early hours while the rest of the family slept, frustrated and deeply anxious at his inability to find out what had happened to Nicky. When he'd received the message from Reynard's exhausted courier early that morning, he'd been enormously relieved and had hurried straight round to Whitehall to find Ashcroft. He hadn't mentioned the message that came from

Reynard with their own coded note, which had reassured him the message had come personally from Nicky - from the description he'd received from the men who'd sold him the horse and from whom he'd got the saddle. He'd also told Francis cryptically he would endeavour to pass on the second note Nicky had enclosed for his 'Uncle' as best he could.

"There was a personal message for me that came with my courier," Francis said quietly as he finally settled in a chair on the other side of Ashcroft's desk. "It appears there were two messages from Nicky passed to my man, a half Spanish, half French gypsy I've known for years. One was for me, the other for Wellington, I think, although he didn't mention any names for obvious reasons. He said he would endeavour to pass that on as best he could."

"Really?" Ashcroft sat forward, his grey eyes lighting up. "Good, good. Do you think they'll be able to get it through? How reliable are these contacts of yours?"

"I have no idea," mused Francis thoughtfully. "My man is completely reliable. Personally, I'd trust him with my life, but he is a gypsy at the end of the day and they're not accepted in all quarters, as you know. Also, getting across Spain from where he currently is, which I think is somewhere near Barcelona, won't be easy, given the French are between him and the British forces."

As Ashcroft watched him patiently, Francis sat for a while and pondered as he gazed through the window. "If I was him, I'd probably send the message by a southerly circuitous route. It might take longer, but there's far less risk of it falling into French hands that way." He sighed, "All I can say is, if it's possible to get it through, my man will find a way. Hopefully, Wellington can then send men to help. But I don't know how long such a journey will take; there are so many imponderables, not including the French."

"Hmmm," Ashcroft looked consideringly at the Duke's thoughtful face. "Capital, we'll hope for the best then," he murmured. Then, seeming almost to talk to himself, he muttered, "Interesting lot of friends you've got, Granville, for a Duke that is." He paused for a while before continuing, "You know, I don't believe that tarradiddle of nonsense you tried to fob me off with before, when I asked you about

Bernheim's father. I still don't. But I did hear gypsies were involved with that smuggler fellow, The Shadow, in that old story about the goings-on in Rouen. Interesting coincidence that, wouldn't you say?" he mused, looking speculatively at the other man.

Francis's face was impassive. "Quite possibly, Ashcroft, quite possibly, but I really wouldn't know. It was a long time ago, as you say."

"Of course, Your Grace, of course; a long time ago."

The two men looked at each other and the moment passed. "Well," said Ashcroft, "I must get on and send a fast courier down to the allied HQ myself in case your man doesn't get through with de Bresancourt's note, then we'll have to leave it to Wellington to do what he can. There's reinforcements landing in Portugal as we speak and he'll be at the French again in no time, mark my words. They may have driven him back temporarily - made a big mistake in not carrying through their advantage of course - but we must be thankful for that; and now Bonaparte is having problems in eastern Europe and pulling reinforcements over there when they should be in Spain, Wellington will finish the job, you'll see. Let's just hope that protégé of yours down in Madrid can stop Bernheim from causing any mischief that will subvert the English effort."

"MY protégé?" Francis raised an eyebrow. "Since when is Nicky MY protégé? I'm a Duke of the Realm, pillar of the Establishment, a seat in the House of Lords, I have extensive business interests and estates to oversee and run, not to mention family commitments. I've nothing to do with all this undercover derring-do. Surely Nicky is rather more yours, eh, Ashcroft?"

"Not at all, Your Grace, not at all; absolutely YOUR protégé, I do assure you. Obviously learned his skills from a master, wouldn't you say?" he replied enigmatically as he stood up, bowed and walked over to the door to show his guest out.

Chapter Eight

Midway between Tarragona and Barcelona, hidden away in a valley in a backwater near the coast, there was a small, temporary gypsy encampment. A few days after their successful and safe trip, a group of young men had finally made their way back there, well pleased with the sales they'd made at the horse fair in Madrid. They'd travelled slowly, careful to avoid any bands of marauding French soldiers and, equally perilous for gypsies, groups of Spanish guerrillas who would happily relieve them of their money and their lives, given half a chance.

It was evening before their tribe leader, Reynard, a stocky, grey haired and wily old Romani, had limped over to them to catch up with their news. They sat around the campfire and related details of the various sales they'd made and as they finally broke up to go to bed, one of the young men called out, "Hey, Reynard, nearly forgot, some fair-haired man at the fair gave me a message for you. Sent you a gift too, I've got it in my wagon. Remind me tomorrow and I'll get it for you," and with that, he promptly sauntered off, more intent on finding his girlfriend than worrying about the beautifully crafted saddle he'd brought back from the fair. Truth to tell, he'd been sorely tempted to sell it – after all, Reynard would probably never know – but there'd been a hard look in the eyes of the man who'd given it to him and at the last moment, he'd decided to do as he'd been asked and take it back to Reynard. It would be just his luck to bump into that stranger again at another horse fair and then he wouldn't care to face the consequences. There'd been something about him, that tall, handsome man with the unusual tawny hair and golden eyes. He wouldn't want to get on the wrong side of him.

It was only much later when Reynard was back in his spacious caravan, his gift from Francis and still luxuriously comfortable even after twenty years of roaming around southern Europe, that he thought about the throwaway comment from the young man. His damaged thigh, shattered by a pistol ball some twenty years previously, played up in the winter when the weather was damp and he often woke in the night to get a glass of brandy to help dull the pain and discomfort. He was a wealthy man if anyone but knew it, again courtesy of his long business relationship with Francis Granville whom he'd originally known simply as Alex, the smuggler known as The Shadow. However, even though he'd considered buying himself a villa or small farm to retire to, somewhere warm and dry most of the year round, the wanderlust was still in his veins and he continued to drift around southern Europe, minding his own business and keeping well away from the fighting, as well as gypsy-hating bigots, as much as possible.

As he sipped his brandy in the early hours, staring out of the window at the moonlit sky and contemplating the never-ending war and his future, his mind turned again to a villa and some land, somewhere to settle down and farm, maybe with his nephews so they could breed horses and he'd keep a vineyard to make wine. Perhaps in the south of France near to the Pyrenees, or in north-west Spain, on the other side of them, so he could still have a foot in both countries if the fancy took him to wander in the summer months. Until then, life was good. Not for the first time Reynard wondered if he should find himself a second, proper wife. After all the years of being a widower, he could get himself some legitimate sons, his first wife, the love of his life, having tragically died young in childbirth, along with their baby. If he did decide to put down roots somewhere, he'd like to leave the property to his own sons and his mind turned to his old friend, Francis, and the four strapping boys Cat had given him. One, Rennie, had been named for him, to his never-ending pride and delight. He reflected also how Nicky had grown into a big, tall, handsome man of whom Eddie was so proud; amazing, when he'd been such a frightened but cherubic little flower when they'd first found him.

As Reynard mused, thinking about his friends and the young men in his little tribe, that comment from one of them came back to Reynard and his curiosity stirred. He didn't know any fair men, certainly none well enough to get gifts from them, nor a message. The more he thought about it, the stranger it seemed. Then he remembered Francis... and Nicky. As realisation dawned who the fair-haired man probably was, he roared with anger and hurried out of his caravan, making his way over to bang on the door of the vehicle belonging to the young gypsy horse-breeder. The sleepy youth opened his door to Reynard's ceaseless knocking and bemusedly handed over the saddle to the irate older man, responding to his incisive questions about the fair man's appearance as best he could. When he repeated the man's message about a horse named The Shadow, Reynard swore loudly and cuffed him roundly about the ears for not handing over the message and the saddle as soon as he arrived back. The bemused youth apologised and said he hadn't realised it was all so urgent, but he was talking to thin air as Reynard hurriedly limped back to his caravan, saddle over his shoulder.

Oil lamp lit, Reynard stared at the saddle on the table in his caravan. It was beautiful. But why would Nicky send him a saddle? Was there some hidden message in the mention of The Shadow? Reynard hadn't seen nor heard from Nicky for a couple of years, if not more, in fact he couldn't remember it had been so long. Although he knew he was with the British forces there in the Peninsula, he wondered what he was doing at a horse fair in Madrid when Wellington had been holed up all winter near the Portuguese border. When he'd last seen him, Nicky had told him he had started doing some liaison work for Wellington between his army and the guerrillas – mainly because he was so fluent in Spanish – and it involved working undercover; but somehow his intuition told Reynard this was a completely different matter entirely. Again, he looked at the saddle and thought about The Shadow, his friend Francis Granville. Their last adventures, so many years before, had been very different from the lucrative smuggling enterprise in which they were both originally involved. It had included rescuing the de Mornay family, the parents and sisters of Cat and Eddie, also little Nicky as he was then, from that villain Bernheim's clutches in Rouen; and then, not quite a year later, to help rescue his old friend and Francis's uncle, Gerard Fourneval and his family. Then there was The Shadow, the Duke himself, when the Firebrand, his personal nickname for Cat, had finally killed Edgar Bernheim and his venal and vicious lieutenant, Pierre Dupont. That was when he'd sustained his wound and still gave thanks to God he'd come out of that affair with his life – it had been touch and go for all of them.

Reynard shook his head. Bernheim was long dead and The Shadow was now a distant memory; the puzzled gypsy couldn't make it out. He poked and stared at the saddle and thought; whatever it was, there had to be more here than just an ornate piece of leather. Finally, he picked up a sharp knife and started to cut away the decorative stitching, pulling back the leather to expose the flocking inside. Lo and behold, there they were, two small, sealed messages, buried deep in the horsehair and wool stuffing, wrapped inside a short note for him.

Hola Reynard! Long time, no see, My Old Friend, and I hope you are keeping well.

I am so sorry I cannot reach you at the moment to see and ask you Personally, not to mention share a bottle of nice wine or two, but I need a Great Favour – because The Shadow told me to get in touch if I ever needed Help and now I do. These two Notes need to find their way URGENTLY to their Recipients, if you can possibly arrange it. I wouldn't ask if it wasn't of the UTMOST IMPORTANCE. Also, much as I regret to inform you, The Shadow's former Nemesis has come back to haunt us all in the shape of his Son. Not that I expect you will, but if you hear anything of him, anything at all, please send Urgent Word to our former Smuggler. And be warned yourself for if you do pick up anything, you need to know he is a Bad Man, just like his Father, so keep as far away from him as possible.

Hopefully we can meet again soon in Happier Circumstances and indulge in plenty of the aforesaid wine.

Take care and thank you.

As always I am in Your Debt for your assistance in Times of Trouble.

N

Reynard picked up the two small, sealed notes. One was simply addressed to 'Francis', the other to 'Uncle Arthur'. Uncle Arthur? Who was Uncle Arthur? And then he put two and two together and Reynard hoped he was right in assuming the Uncle Arthur referred to was Arthur Wellesley, Marquess of Wellington. Sending the missive to the Duke of Firle in England presented no problem; Reynard's messengers were used to carrying information back and forth to London, they just skirted the Pyrenees and made their way into France and thence directly north, straight to the Channel. Fast horses and keeping to the back roads were the order of the day, along with plenty of money to grease palms if the Military or other nosy officials got in the way. Getting information over to Wellington on the other side of Spain, with both the French forces and Spanish guerrilla rebels in between, was, however, a different and considerably more dangerous matter.

Reynard smiled to himself. Life had been extremely quiet for years and he'd always relished a bit of action. Regrettably, he was now too old and too disabled to make a dangerous trip like that himself in a hurry, but his nephews could do it. Wily and resourceful, they would get through he was sure. He lit a cigar, went back to his brandy and sat until dawn broke over the horizon, planning out a route for them to take. As for him, he was going to Madrid. He suddenly felt invigorated, his aches and pains temporarily forgotten. Life had never been boring when Francis or his mad family were involved and he chuckled in anticipation.

Some two weeks later, late one evening at his camp near the Portuguese border, Wellington was disturbed by an almighty commotion outside his quarters. As he made to rise from his desk to see what was going on, a young officer burst through his tent flap and saluted smartly. "Begging your pardon, Sir, very sorry to disturb, but there's two gypsy sorts outside who've just ridden into the camp in rather a hurry. We would've thrown them out, Sir, but they speak broken English and say they have an urgent message for you from the, ah, Duke of Firle, I think they said; their accents are rather thick, Sir." Wellington looked up, slightly startled, especially at the mention of a familiar name. "Making the devil of a dust up, Sir, but they insist it's a matter of life and death. They won't speak to anyone but yourself, personally. What would you like me to do, Sir? Does the name mean anything to you? They're most insistent and it is a trifle odd to find gypsies who speak English…"

"Of course it does, Lieutenant," bit out Wellington, "but I'm not sure what he's doing sending me messages via gypsies." He looked thoughtful for a moment, "The gentleman concerned has connections all over the Peninsula and France, so who knows? Better bring them in, Hodges."

Wellington sighed. He was tired and it had been another long day. Dealing with two gypsies was the last thing he needed, but he was also curious. Surely they wouldn't have dared come to his encampment if it wasn't really important and, more interesting, how would they know of the Duke of Firle's name, not to mention speaking English? That name was the aspect which intrigued him the most.

His thoughts were interrupted as the officer held open the flap and some burly soldiers hustled two swarthy young gypsies into his presence. Realising they were finally in front of Wellington himself, both bowed low to him and looked venomously at their captors.

Wellington dismissed the soldiers but told the officer to wait. He was not so foolish as to think the two might not be potential assassins and trusted they'd been searched for weapons. "So, Gentlemen," he calmly addressed the two wary young men, his mien forbidding, "I understand you have a message for me from the Duke of Firle? And just how, may I ask, did you come by this message?"

In very broken English, interspersed with bits of French and Spanish, the taller of the two replied. "Eeet ees not, how you say, *precisement*, from *El Duque*, *Milor*, but from zee relative of heem. We are to saying, if we saying zee name of *El Duque*, you would be seeing us."

"Really," said Wellington coldly, as he grappled with understanding what the man was trying to say. "And?" He was at his most imperious.

The gypsy turned to look at Hodges, then leaned towards Wellington, who didn't turn a hair despite the potential danger and whispered, "Zee message we are carry, eet ees from zee blond man; a, how you say, *sobrino* of *El Duque*. You know of who we are saying?"

Wellington's eyes widened. He turned to the officer watching the two gypsies suspiciously and with a sharp nod of his head, dismissed him. "You may go, Hodges. Wait outside."

Wellington returned to sit at his desk. "Where is the message?" The gypsy pulled off his boot and tipped out the small, sealed and crumpled paper he'd kept inside it before handing it over. Wellington read his Christian name on the front in distaste, then broke the seal to look inside. He raised an eyebrow as he recognised what he thought was one of Ashcroft's complex codes and promptly got up and barked outside the tent. "Get Scovell over here, quick as you like."

He turned and looked again at the two young gypsies. "How long have you had this message and where have you brought it from?"

"Our uncle, he has eet since two weeks and one for *Londres* to *El Duque*. Eet sent to heem, in zee saddle, to our camp near Barcelona. Our cousins have eet at zee horse fair in Madrid by zee blond man. Uncle ees saying you are knowing who he ees. We are riding very hard, very careful, round ze bad *soldados* to carry zees paper to you very quick." He looked proud of what they'd achieved as he stood in front of the Commander of the Allied Forces.

"Good God!" muttered Wellington as he absorbed what they'd done. Scovell hurried in through the tent flap at that moment and without a word, Wellington handed the note to him. "How quickly can you decipher that? It's one of Ashcroft's, if I'm not mistaken."

Scovell looked closely at the paper for a few seconds then nodded at Wellington. "It won't take long, Your Lordship, I just need the cipher, it's in my tent. It looks relatively brief. Ten minutes, fifteen at the most?" Wellington nodded and Scovell hurried out.

For the next ten minutes, with a bit of difficulty, in part speaking broken French as well as English and Spanish, Wellington talked to the two gypsies; he asked about their uncle and his connection with the Duke, about which they revealed very little, then what they knew about the blond man at the fair. They told Wellington all they understood was their cousins had been approached by a tall, well-built young man with fair hair who had bought a yearling from them at a horse fair in Madrid just over a couple of weeks ago and while doing so, had asked them to take an ornate saddle back to their uncle as a gift for him. That was all they knew other than their uncle had told them to get this message to the HQ of the British Forces as quickly as possible without taking too many risks in case it fell into French or Spanish hands. Wellington listened to all this impassively and then asked what they'd seen in the way of French military activity on their way across country. On this they were as helpful as they could be and were just about finished reporting on who and what they'd seen, when Scovell hurried back in and handed over a folded sheet of paper to Wellington. He read the short note and folded the paper back in half.

Raising his head to consider the two young men, he leaned back in his chair. "You have done me a great service bringing this message across the country at such risk to yourselves. On behalf of His Majesty's Government in London and my army here in the Peninsula, I extend you my sincerest thanks. Please also extend my gratitude to your uncle." Wellington opened a drawer in his desk and pulled out a large bag of coins which he rose to hand to the elder youth, bending his head to him in acknowledgement of the service he'd rendered.

The young man looked at the bag and peered inside at the gold within. "*Gracias, merci*, zank you, *Milor*. We not looking for zee reward," he smiled at Wellington's impassive face, "but eet ees, how you telling, *apprécié*. We do zees because our uncle is big old friend wiz *El Duque*, for long times. Zat ees every-ting. Eef *El Duque* say to help, we are to help, every times."

Wellington looked at the two young men, then over at Scovell, who was also slightly stunned at these words, then back at the gypsies.

"Really?" he commented. "Well, I can't say I'm not surprised, but that man never ceases to amaze me by what he does and who he knows. Nevertheless, you both have my sincere gratitude." He paused and then continued, rising from his desk again, "Now, I have work to do. I'm sure you must be in need of refreshment and a safe place to sleep, for tonight at least. I have no doubt you'll take great care on the way back to your camp but the French are everywhere, even if they are supposed to be pulling out of Andalucía." With that, he then bowed to the two young men and personally showed them out of his tent, instructing Hodges with a telling look to ensure they both had a good meal and wine and a tent to sleep in for the night. He told him they were NOT to be harassed on any account, making Hodges' eyes widen at the implied rebuke, but saluted smartly and led the two gypsies away in a much more polite fashion than they'd arrived.

When he was left alone with Scovell, Wellington looked at the other man. "One of Ashcroft's codes?" Scovell nodded. "The one allocated to de Bresancourt?" Scovell nodded again. "You're sure it's genuine?"

"Absolutely, M'Lord," Scovell replied. "Ashcroft allocates a different code to each of his agents. That way, if anything falls into the wrong hands, the damage is limited. Also, now the French have twigged about the way Ashcroft operates, they're not so bothered about breaking his codes, unless it's for a particularly important agent they may have uncovered, as they believe it's not worth their time and effort." He looked at Wellington, "This is the first message we've received from de Bresancourt in all the time he's been in the field since you saw him at Burgos, unless he's sent something to London. I'm sure we would have heard about that by now, so there's little chance the French could have discovered anything from him and cracked his code. Besides, this is a clever note. We know what he's referring to but most wouldn't. The question is, of course, how the devil do we get a reply back to him?"

"I know," muttered Wellington. "It's the very devil. Ashcroft says all his agents in that part of Spain and around Madrid have either disappeared or been killed, presumably one and the same thing, so we've no way of getting in touch with de Bresancourt. I'd actually given him up for dead weeks ago when all the others disappeared.

Even now I don't know who to trust round there and he's obviously keeping his head down as well. But, if he's found out what Bernheim is up to and needs help to stop him, we've got to find a way to assist. I'm not having our Spanish allies subverted by that French bastard; not now, not when we're so near to achieving our objective, even if we have had to pull back for the winter and get reinforcements in."

The two men sat in silence for a while, considering the problem. Then Scovell lifted his head. "It's obvious," he sighed. "Why don't we ask the gypsies?"

"Whaat?" Wellington exclaimed, looking askance at the other man. "'Pon my soul, have you run mad, Scovell? You can't trust them from here to here." He moved his forefinger a few inches from one side of his desktop to the other.

Scovell looked at Wellington. "Well, normally I'd agree with you, M'Lord, but considering what that young pair have just done for us, maybe their little tribe are a bit different. They seem to have some connection with the Duke of Firle, strange as that may seem. Quite frankly, I don't see what other option we've got. There's no point sending men to help de Bresancourt if we don't know where to send them. As it is, we may well be too late to help anyway. I suggest we call those gypsy lads back, send a message to their uncle, whoever he is, and then see what he can do. He obviously knows de Bresancourt personally, so at least they'll recognise each other and he's obviously someone de Bresancourt genuinely trusts. We've got absolutely nothing to lose and I suggest we get a group of reliable men together and send them on their way towards Madrid, then let this gypsy fellow act as a liaison between them and de Bresancourt. What do you think of that idea, M'Lord?"

Wellington steepled his hands together, rocked back in his chair and thought hard. He picked up Nicky's note, read it through again before putting it back down on his desk and reached a decision. "We'll do it. As you say, Scovell, we've got nothing to lose and there's no other way I can see through this. We've got to protect that gold from Bernheim. You get a small group of men together. They don't need to know any details at present, the fewer people who do, the better, quite frankly. Choose who you like, but some of the men from the ranks are conniving scum, natural survivors, so they should do well for this little adventure. Offer them a bonus. I'll get those two gypsy lads back here and give them a message for their uncle. Then, well, it's in God's hands... and those of de Bresancourt." He looked thoughtful for a moment as he gazed at his officer, "Y'know, Scovell, I always thought that young man had hidden depths, despite his appalling lack of respect for his superiors." He followed Scovell out of his tent to summon the gypsies back again, muttering to himself, "Uncle Arthur, indeed!" But there was the merest hint of an amused smile about his austere lips.

Chapter Nine

Nicky was growing increasingly anxious and frustrated. He now knew the name of the scar-faced man was Carlos and also knew from his search that the first date on Carlos's list was a few days' hence. As yet, however, no-one had contacted him, so he had no idea if his messages had arrived safely at their intended recipients. Although he'd thought about trying to hire some men to help him, he didn't trust anyone enough to do so. He'd been watching both Carmelita and Carlos and the latter had met all his accomplices once more, apparently to go over final details of their first heist. Nicky wasn't sure what Carmelita's role in all this was, other than possibly to act as a liaison between Bernheim and Carlos. So far as Nicky knew, she hadn't seen Bernheim since their meeting with Carlos in the *taberna* a few weeks back. She was either keeping in touch another way, Bernheim had come to the city again to see her somewhere else, or he'd missed her leaving the city to go and meet the man at his home or elsewhere.

He toyed with getting in touch with her again but decided it was too risky and he doubted she would give him any further information. The only odd thing was that she'd apparently moved out of the tenement building permanently and had taken up residence in another similar one on the other side of the city. Nicky surmised the working girls in the first tenement had finally realised that helping Carmelita and looking after her customers was too hazardous, even for the money they could earn, so she'd obviously moved to pastures new and more fodder for Bernheim when he required it. Not long after, another body turned up on the river bank. It didn't take long for Nicky to discover she came from near the new tenement where Carmelita was now living and the frequency of the deaths disturbed him. Was the perpetrator, presumably Bernheim, using them as an outlet for his excitement over the coming gold robberies, or was he merely bored while he bided his time waiting to strike? There was no answer and Nicky grew more apprehensive and sickened than ever.

Nicky had taken to keeping a horse, ready saddled, at the back of a *taberna* near to Carmelita's tenement on the off chance Bernheim's carriage would turn up for her one day. Finally, his preparations and patience paid off and, late one morning, he watched with grim satisfaction as Carmelita left the building, strode up the dank alleyway into the main street and, as he followed her, watched her climb into an undistinguished carriage which was waiting there. He raced back to the rundown stables, grabbed his horse and galloped back to where the coach had been, heading southwards in the hope of catching it up and finding out, at long last, where Bernheim had his lair.

Luck was with him when he spotted the carriage on the main road leading south out of the city. He followed, keeping a safe distance, well back from both the road and any curious eyes. The carriage finally veered off on to an unmarked side road before continuing down a series of increasingly smaller tracks into the deserted countryside, until it was crawling along at a snail's pace. Nicky left his horse hitched to a tree, well hidden in a shady spot, before following the carriage on foot. As he stood in some scratchy undergrowth, he watched as it finally pulled into a clearing in front of a pair of big, barred, metal gates, set into a high stone wall. A large villa, with pink stucco walls covered with bougainvillea and other creepers, could be seen down the driveway. The windows were all covered either by shutters or by slightly rusty, ornate filigree grilles and some of the rooms on the upper storey led out onto small, narrow ornate metal balconettes. It was a beautiful old building, typically Spanish, graceful and full of charm. To Nicky, it looked like the country retreat of some wealthy old aristocratic family or even possibly their main family home. Whether Bernheim owned or rented it, he had no idea, but it seemed unnecessarily large and ostentatious for a single man who undoubtedly would want to live anonymously and quietly, given his occupation. Nicky found it rather odd.

The carriage didn't wait for the gates to be opened by a servant, as would normally have been expected given how grandiose the building appeared; instead, Carmelita got out by herself and rang the old gate bell as the vehicle pulled away to disappear round the side walls, presumably towards a set of rundown outbuildings situated well back behind the main residence. After a few minutes, an elderly, black-garbed woman appeared to unlock and open one of the creaking gates and Carmelita walked down the drive and followed the servant through the open, front double doors of the house where Nicky caught a brief glimpse of Bernheim as he came forward to greet his guest. Nicky's face was a mask of loathing and anticipated revenge as he realised he'd finally run his and Ashcroft's quarry to earth.

He spent the next hour carefully exploring the perimeter of the property and its surroundings, doing a couple of quick sketches in his little notebook as a reminder. Apart from the main entrance, there was a second set of high metal gates round the back where the carriage had obviously gone in. Apart from that, the place was like a fortress. Shards of broken glass had been set in the plaster along the top of the high external walls, as Nicky found to his painful cost as he'd tried to scale them to peer over - obviously to deter any unwelcome visitors like himself - and the space between the walls and the villa building was open and clear, covered with gravel which would be noisy to walk over. Finally, a pair of vicious-looking dogs had come out through the front door before it shut after Carmelita and were now sitting in the shade of the portico, occasionally getting up to wander and sniff around or drink from a bowl of water obviously left for them in the shade under one of the villa windows.

Realising he could do no more that day, Nicky bound up his bleeding hands as best he could and returned to his horse, thoughtfully making his way back to Madrid and wondering what he should do next. The first date on the list was three days away and there was just one of him.

His horse stood on a hill, hidden behind some trees, while Nicky crawled forward on his stomach where he had a good view of the road below. He was quite a way south of Madrid, well away from the French forces. He had followed some map co-ordinates he'd copied from the documents in Carlos's lodgings and without any knowledge of how the gold was to be transported, or by whom, he could only wait, watch and hope he was in the right place. An hour later, obviously in receipt of the bullion from their English allies further back near the Portuguese border, a large contingent of well-armed Spanish guerrillas on horseback appeared, surrounding a heavily laden set of covered wagons pulled by straining carthorses. Nicky was tempted to try to warn them of the impending attack but even as he considered it, a number of loud explosions rent the air. He watched grimly as a screaming melee of horses and men disappeared into clouds of acrid smoke when the hidden charges went off along a section of the road below him. As the clouds cleared, he recognised Carlos and his accomplices as they suddenly appeared from their hiding places to dispatch anyone and anything left alive from the blasts, man and beast alike. Finally, they stood laughing amongst themselves as they peered into the contents of the overturned wagons, seemingly oblivious to the horrific carnage of the large number of horses and men they'd killed on the quiet country road.

Two of the wagons had contained munitions and general supplies for the troops guarding the convoy and these were generally ignored apart from refreshing the bandits' supply of arms and food. The wagon containing the gold had survived the blast relatively well, sheltered as it had been by the bodies of men, horses and wagons to its front and rear, but a few necessary, hasty repairs were made before it was hitched up to a waiting team of fresh mules and carelessly pulled clear of the shattered bodies scattered around. Then, as if they'd done nothing more than go out on a picnic, the band of robbers set off along the road, smiling and joking, heading back in the direction of Madrid, shortly disappearing off the main road into the deserted countryside. Nicky followed them all the way as they made slow progress with their heavy load over the next couple of days and as he had suspected, they turned off to head towards Bernheim's villa.

The second heist followed the same pattern, except there were even more men on guard, but they too met the same grisly death. Again, the spoils eventually disappeared inside the gates of Bernheim's villa. The third one went the same way. Always a deserted stretch of road, well away from any civilisation. The bloody massacres sickened Nicky.

Four days later, Nicky sat disconsolately in a run-down *taberna* near his lodgings, nursing a brandy and considering his options, a half-smoked cheroot burning away between his fingers. There were now just a few days before the fourth, the last and largest delivery was due. Would the Authorities, or whoever was in charge of logistics, consider changing the planned route? Who had leaked the route in the first place? Was the informant on the English side or the Spanish? What was Bernheim planning to do after that?

Even though he knew the location of the stolen gold, what could he do about it? He took another gulp of brandy and rubbed a tired hand across his eyes before running fingers through his unkempt hair. His swarthy tan had faded over the winter, but he was now so grubby and dirty you could barely tell; he would be shunted into the gutter as a vagrant if he tried walking down Bond Street and he laughed ironically to himself. As he mulled over his seemingly unsolvable problems, a thick voice bent to whisper in his ear.

"I have to say, even your mangy, hungry lions would take one look at you at the moment and go hunt for a meal elsewhere... and as for the ladies..." a few coarse and salacious comments then filled his ears.

"Reynard! You old fox..." Nicky turned and rose to pull the old gypsy into a warm hug and kissed him affectionately on both cheeks. "What the HELL are you doing here? How on earth did you find me?" he whispered.

Reynard pulled up a chair and called over to one of the tavern wenches to bring him a flagon of wine and two glasses. The pair sat with their heads huddled together, whispering quietly. "I reckoned if I went into enough *tabernas* I'd find you sooner or later. Also, I have a message for you from your Uncle Arthur."

Nicky's eyes narrowed for a moment and then lit up as he realised what Reynard had said. "My messages? They got through?" he exclaimed.

"Of course they did," Reynard grinned. "I may be old and grey and a bit crippled, but I still have my uses," and his eyes twinkled.

"By all that's holy, that's wonderful!" Nicky laughed for the first time in weeks. "I'd just about given up hope." He paused then asked sombrely, "How much do you know about what's going on, Reynard?"

"Not a lot, I have to say," replied the old gypsy. "Your message in the saddle told me more than the information sent back to me to pass on to you, from, er... your 'Uncle Arthur'," he grinned for a moment before his whole face changed to one of anger. "But then I nearly had a fit when I saw reference to that name again. Bernheim!" He spat uncouthly on the floor. "Are you actually telling me that bastard had a son?"

Nicky looked at Reynard with ice in his eyes. "Unfortunately, yes. If anything, I believe him to be far, far worse than his father."

"Whaat?!" Reynard now looked horrified. "No, that can't be possible, Nicky. Your parents, the de Mornays, Gerard and his family, Francis, my old friend Marco, God rest his soul, then me," he rubbed his crippled thigh, "and that's only some of his victims," he murmured. His mind reeled back to the men he'd lost from his and other tribes on the dreadful day Francis had been captured and he himself had been wounded. Then there were all the other poor individuals who'd been incarcerated and either starved or tortured in the terrible fortress for no reason other than their wealth, which the avaricious elder Bernheim had coveted, or because they wouldn't comply with his local protection racket.

Nicky nodded. "I know, Reynard, but this man, he's strange." He grimaced, "Evil and quite perverted. He's a complete animal in my book and that's an insult to most furred and feathered creatures. Apart

from several British agents and no doubt plenty of others working for
the Allied cause against Bonaparte and the French, I have reason to
believe he's personally killed some half a dozen young girls, prostitutes, in the last year alone. He strangles them, after he's either beaten
or whipped them, while he fucks 'em – and that's not always straightforward either..." he explained softly, grimacing and shuddering
slightly.

"*Christos!*" muttered Reynard, crossing himself. "A nice piece of
work for sure."

"Anyway, enough of him for the moment. What's my 'Uncle' got to
say?"

"Ah yes, your 'Uncle Arthur'" smirked Reynard. "Well, the
message came back from my nephews. I sent them to see him with
your little note, good lads they are. He sent a message back with them
for me: 'Tell my nephew I'm going to send some friends over for him
to play with as soon as possible. I'm sure he'll show them where the
playground is'. That's it," grinned Reynard. "So, Nicky, are you going
to tell me about what games you intend to play in the playground with
your friends? Something tells me it's got nothing to do with skipping
ropes or skittles!"

"Bloody hell!" exclaimed Nicky softly. "I didn't know my uncle had
such a sense of humour. Wonders will never cease!" But he was hugely
relieved to know reinforcements were on their way. "Any idea how
long these friends are going to take?"

Reynard shook his head. "My nephews took some carrier pigeons
with them, in case there was need to get a message back to me urgently." He looked meaningfully at Nicky, "Well, you never know what
might have happened to one or both of them on that errand. Anyway,
a bird arrived a couple of days ago, advance information as it were, so
I've had a couple of trusted men out with me, scouring the city for you
ever since. Therefore, here I am!" he chuckled. "Good job there aren't
that many short, fat, ugly, fair-haired men around," he teased and
good naturedly tousled Nicky's long, unkempt locks. "It's dangerous
out there between your uncle's position and Madrid if they come
directly, so I think it could well be a week or so before your friends

arrive if they head south first to be on the safe side. Is that going to be a problem?"

"Hmmm, quite possibly," muttered Nicky. "Here, have another drink and a cheroot while I fill you in..." and for the next half an hour, as the older man puffed away and sipped his wine, Nicky quietly told Reynard everything he'd been up to for the past eight months or so since last leaving England.

"So, there we are; until you arrived, I had no idea how to stop them, or how to get the gold back before Bernheim moves it elsewhere. Actually, even with you here and knowing more men are coming to help, I'm still not sure what we can do."

Reynard looked at Nicky thoughtfully. "I wish Eddie was here; your Papa always seems to have a way to see through most problems and find a solution. Business now mainly, or back in those old troubled days, but we're on our own this time, M'Lad." He shook his head and sighed, "Anyway, what makes you think Bernheim will move the gold before we can liberate it back to where it belongs?"

"I don't know really," muttered Nicky, "just a gut feel." He shook his head, "If I'd stolen all that gold, I wouldn't want to leave it lying around here where the situation is so unstable, even if I was holed up in the middle of nowhere at the back of beyond. I'd want to shift it out of the country as quickly as possible, certainly much further away from Madrid. The English are in the west right now, but it's not them who concern me, it's the Spanish. They'll be livid they've lost the three consignments and their rebels and guerrillas have been causing untold problems to the French over the winter. You don't want to know what happens to any French bastard who falls into their hands," he shuddered and took a gulp of wine, thinking back to some of the horrific scenes he'd witnessed in his time liaising with the Spanish guerrillas. "For all I know, the Spanish could be making ready to try and take back Madrid tomorrow. It's not garrisoned properly, y'know, nor can I guess whether any of them knows about what's happened to those deliveries or the men who were massacred. It's difficult to gauge what mood they're in." He shrugged his shoulders as he shook his head, "Just call it intuition."

"Mmmmm, I tend to agree with you," said Reynard thoughtfully.

"Nothing's wrong with intuition. Your crazy aunt and your dear step-mother, of course, they had it in spades... females," he chuckled, rolling his eyes. "That's why they came haring over to France to help Francis when he got captured by Bernheim's father." For a moment he was lost in twenty-year-old memories. "What a woman she was, still is, my firebrand. Aaah, such passion and beauty, so wild," he sighed. Nicky grinned as he realised the old gypsy had been half in love with Cat and wondered if Francis knew. Reynard shook himself and contin-ued, "So, tell me about his villa again; it may be hidden away, but it doesn't sound as if he has many guards there?"

"No, it appears not, nor even many servants. Strange about the guards when you consider what's going on there and I don't know why he wants such a large property, but I suppose its location suits him. I dare say Bernheim feels the less people who know about him and his business, the better. That's why he keeps out of Madrid and uses the woman as his go-between, as well as for other things," he shuddered slightly yet again at the thought of Carmelita.

"Nasty piece of work she sounds too," muttered Reynard. "How well have you got to know her?"

Nicky looked at Reynard with a querying eyebrow, not wanting to admit too much. "Come now, Nicky, this is me you're talking to," Reynard smirked. "I'm damn sure you've tried your charms on her to find out what she's up to. You and Francis are so much alike when it comes to the ladies. If there wasn't such an age gap and a problem with your hair and eye colour, I'd say you came out the same nest." He chortled to himself at his joke. "Remind me to tell you some stories of what I caught him up to when we used to meet up in the Normandy ports before shipping goods over to the south coast of England," he smirked, "talk about a veritable harem, women used to fall over them-selves or fight each other, to get into his bedroom. His reputation was no fairy tale, believe me. I just got his leftovers, but there were plenty of them to entertain me and they weren't half bad... and the gossip I spread about him in certain quarters, just to wind him up and make the women even more desperate and a nuisance, you wouldn't believe how creative I got..." and he winked, guffawing quietly at Nicky's expression. "But all that's for later, over some nice brandy. Let's get back to this woman. I'd stake my life you've been fishing for information in those dirty waters," and he gave Nicky a knowing look.

"Unfortunately, yes," Nicky sighed, "I've still got the scratches." He absently rubbed his chest, "Christ, Reynard," he bit out softly, "it was like fucking a female scorpion. When I found out how she'd deliberately procured those young girls and sent them off to Bernheim to abuse and strangle, it made me want to retch. I still feel tainted even now," another mild shudder.

Reynard laughed. "Ah, the things you have to do for the greater good. You Poor, Hard-done-by, Boy."

Nicky glared at him. "It's not funny, You Old Sod. You've no idea what she's like: rapacious, insatiable, perverted," but Reynard continued to chuckle at Nicky's discomfort.

Finally, he held up his hands. "All right, all right, I believe you," then became more serious. "Well, Young Man, what are we going to do then? It looks like it's just you and me. I can get one or two of my men over to help but they're just young lads, like my nephews. Unfortunately, the majority of the tribe have just moved over the border into southern France for an Easter gathering, so I only have a few youths around, but they're into breeding and trading horses, not fighting." Nicky nodded vaguely as he remembered the group of young men he'd met at the horse fair in Madrid. They wouldn't stand a chance against Carlos and his cutthroats.

Both men sat for a while and pondered as they drank their wine and smoked. Nicky was so pleased to have someone to talk to after all these months of solitude; Reynard was a wily old fox, living up to his name, so he was sure they'd come up with some sort of plan. He prayed the men from Wellington would arrive soon.

Chapter Ten

It was nearly dusk as the two shadowy figures crept through the prickly undergrowth and made their way around the perimeter of the villa. They peered through the gates, back and front, inspecting all the villa windows and doors through a small but powerful telescope; that was an item Nicky had pinched from a shelf in Francis's study, telling him he would have better use for it and Francis didn't need it to peer through his windows, searching for naval vessels likely to be sailing past the mansion, nor Revenue men on the prowl, looking for smugglers or pirates in Berkeley Square, even if an elderly one did secretly live there!

They looked at the outbuildings and watched the guard dogs as they prowled about. The two men had been there most of the day, observing and noting the comings and goings of the few servants between the house and the outbuildings. There had been no visitors. As night fell, they crept away.

Back in Madrid, Nicky and Reynard reviewed what they'd seen at the villa. "It's not going to be easy getting in there," mused Reynard thoughtfully, "because we still don't know how many servants he's got, nor where the wagons are stored. I can't believe he's unloaded all that gold and taken it into the house, bloody stuff is too heavy, so I reckon it's still in one of those outbuildings we saw at the back. Unbelievable!" he shook his head in amazement. "I think you're right – he'll want to move it all, take it somewhere safe as soon as possible, immediately after the last shipment. Hmmm, now where would I take all that if I were him?" He pondered, drinking his wine in a dark corner of the quiet hostelry where the pair had now taken up temporary residence.

The two had decided not to bother to go and watch the final hold up. It was due to happen far to the southwest and they knew there was little they would be able to do to stop it since they had no idea where the consignment was coming from nor who was in charge of overseeing it. Wellington's reinforcements had still not made their appearance so they were now waiting for the gold to appear back at Bernheim's villa in the next few days. Then they would act.

Nicky had decided to tackle Bernheim himself. He would get over the wall, negate the threat of the dogs with poisoned meat and deal the servants in the outbuildings. He would then find a way into the house and tackle whoever he encountered there. The wrought iron, filigree bars on the downstairs windows appeared secure from what they could see, so he'd decided to climb up to one of the balconettes and try and get in through a set of doors which had no bars over them. Reynard would wait outside and keep watch. If Nicky was able to unlock the gates he would let him in, otherwise he was on his own as the old man couldn't get over the high, glass topped walls with his damaged leg. IF, definitely a big IF, he succeeded, and IF the reinforcements still hadn't appeared, Reynard's young accomplices would be called in and they would take the gold to hide among their gypsy wagons until it could be returned to the British forces, or the Spanish authorities.

As plans went, it wasn't much of one, but they were now both agreed there was nothing else to be done. They'd also discussed Carmelita and Carlos. Nicky reckoned Carlos would be paid off and then pay off his people. If Wellington's men turned up, they could pick them up as Nicky had the location of all of them for the time being. Carmelita was another problem, but they were hoping she would remain in Madrid, as she had been for all this time, apart from the odd trip out to the villa for an overnight stay. Nicky was still niggled by what her real role was amidst all the plotting and hold-ups, or perhaps there simply wasn't one. Again, his instinct told him there was more to her than was apparent, but he had no way of knowing and there was little he could do about it at the moment. He would deal with her, however, that he had sworn to himself. Rosita and the other dead girls deserved justice.

Ashcroft would have been amazed at the cold and vindictive turn of his thoughts. Not only that, the facetious and irreverent joker he wasn't entirely sure of had disappeared; in his place, and as he had hoped for, this new operative of the Department of Information was fulfilling all expectations with extreme and deadly intent.

Chapter Eleven

The final bullion consignment had arrived and was now sitting alongside the other canvas-covered wagons in a large barn among the villa outbuildings. Nicky and Reynard were well hidden, away from the villa perimeter, having maintained a vigil there for the previous couple of days. They had watched the last wagons enter through the front gates and disappear round the back of the property, driven by a couple of the men Nicky vaguely recognised from the day he'd watched the first consignment being hijacked, Carlos too. He and Reynard waited patiently for the men to reappear. They had a clear view from their hiding place, through the large, ornate, locked metal gates, towards the front door. Suddenly, the sound of muffled shots echoed over to them through the undergrowth and they watched as Carlos appeared, tucking a brace of pistols into the back of the wide leather belt around his waist. Of the wagon drivers there was no sign. Carlos went up to the front door and without him having to knock, it opened silently and he disappeared inside.

An hour or so later, he suddenly reappeared from around the back of the villa, in the direction of the barn and stables. He was leading a horse and a couple of pack mules and looked exceeding pleased with himself. It didn't take Nicky and Reynard much to conclude why. The mules were obviously laden with something very heavy as they plodded along slowly. Carmelita followed behind and before Carlos mounted his horse, she gave him a brief kiss on the cheek and they heard her bid him farewell and to have a safe journey, a sly smirk creeping round her lips. She went over to unlock and open one of the gates and watched as he went slowly through. He turned briefly to smile down and salute her goodbye as she went to shut them behind him. Except she didn't and instead, stared at his retreating back as his horse and mules slowly plodded forward up the bumpy track away from the villa. Nicky and Reynard gaped in silent shock as she pulled a duelling pistol from under her skirts, took a careful, steady aim and shot him. The deadly ball hit him in the back of the head and, without a murmur, but with a gaping hole in his skull, he simply tumbled from his startled horse and fell to the ground, stone dead.

With a satisfied smile on her face, Carmelita sauntered up the track. She carelessly kicked the body over to the side of the lane into the bushes, took hold of the horse's reins and those of the mules. Then, without so much as a look at the dead man, she walked back to the villa, turning to lock the gates behind her and took the horse and mules in the direction of the stables from whence they'd emerged not long before.

"Christ almighty," muttered Nicky, appalled, but not hugely surprised, "talk about the kiss of death…".

"That is one cold, nasty bitch," replied Reynard, "and extremely dangerous, if she can shoot like that. I don't know many men whose aim is that good, never mind on a moving target, even if it was slow. Are you sure you still want to go inside? Perhaps we should wait until she leaves? It's one thing dealing with Bernheim and some elderly servants, but her as well?" He looked extremely dubious. "What will you do if you discover she can wield a sword or dagger as well as she can shoot? She could be more lethal than my Firebrand, which is saying something," he muttered with a grim expression.

"I very much doubt that, but who knows? Anything is possible with a witch like her." The pair sat in silence for a while. "Perhaps she means more to Bernheim than I thought," mused Nicky. "Perhaps she's planning to leave with him?"

"That's not good news," murmured Reynard. "So, what now, M'Lad?"

Nicky looked at him, an unhappy expression on his face. No matter how deadly determined and vengeful he was, he was also no fool. The prospect of dealing with an unknown number of household servants, Bernheim and now Carmelita as well, was not a prospect any sane man would relish, especially after what they'd just witnessed. Carmelita was no helpless woman, she was deadly. A slightly hysterical thought occurred to him as he decided she was far worse than a mere witch and he pondered if she was a female scorpion or a Black Widow spider. He decided she was a mix of the two in human form, created by the Devil himself, and he shivered.

As they crouched in the late afternoon shadows, the front door opened silently again and the two guard dogs trotted out. It was deathly quiet, but as they watched and listened, they realised there was more activity coming from the back of the house. Very carefully, they made their way round through the undergrowth until they had a view across and in through the rear gates. Although they couldn't see well, it appeared a number of travel trunks were being carried out through the back door, presumably ready to be loaded into a carriage.

Nicky turned to Reynard. "Well, that decides it. They're obviously getting ready to leave."

It was Reynard's turn to look worried as he swore copiously under his breath. Silently, he pulled Nicky far back into the woods and settled them both down on a creeper-covered tree trunk. He looked very seriously at the younger man, placing a fond hand on his arm. He'd known him since he was a little boy of not even five, having been present when Carlotta, his step-mother, had smuggled him out of Rouen Fortress under the skirts of her nun's disguise. Over the years since then, he'd periodically made the long journey to England during the warm summer months, staying at the Firle country estate in Sussex, laughing, drinking and reminiscing with Francis and his family, including the elderly Gerard Fourneval, who'd also come over to stay when Reynard visited. He'd watched the self-possessed, scrawny, withdrawn little boy and his slightly effeminate blond curls, with his amusing childhood obsession with lions, gradually emerge under the tutelage, care and love of Eddie and Francis and their families, to grow into a big, strong, tall and handsome man; still self-possessed, something of the loner about him sometimes, but full of charm and humour when he was with his family and friends, or when he let himself relax.

He wouldn't tell Nicky, but he'd received a long letter from Francis months before, inferring the young man was involved in dangerous military spying business and asking his old friend to keep an eye out for him, if it was at all possible. It also requested he try to stop Nicky from doing anything headstrong or foolhardy in the event he ever got in touch with the gypsy for help. In Reynard's opinion, going into that villa alone, that evening, was neither headstrong nor foolhardy. Given what he now knew about the occupants, Francis's old friend believed it would be suicidal.

"Don't do it, Nicky," he stated baldly. "It's not worth it. Let them go. It's not your fault you've been left to sort this mess by yourself. Just think about it, they can't travel fast with that heavy load to transport, so we can easily catch them up when your little unit of reinforcements arrive from Wellington." He looked deeply into Nicky's golden eyes with his dark gypsy ones but his hand now bit into Nicky's forearm where he was gripping it so tightly. "Francis will never forgive me if I let anything happen to you," he whispered, "but never mind that, I would never forgive myself."

"I can't let him get away," rasped Nicky, equally seriously. "He owes me. Think of what his father did to me, to my parents and their retainers, to all those others, to you and your men, Uncle Gerard and his family, especially poor Amandine, as well as to Francis."

"But that's just it, Nicky, it wasn't HIM," said Reynard rationally. "It was HIS FATHER. Let it go, My Boy, for the love of God. PLEASE don't do this, it's utter madness," he begged.

"NO, Reynard. I HAVE to do this," Nicky grated forcefully. "If it was just Bonaparte's politics he was involved in…" he shrugged his shoulders in a very Gallic way, "but he's killed too many people, not just those girls. Who knows what else he'll do if I let him get away?

He's a menace to society and he's his father's son and I'm damn sure he knew what his father was up to in Normandy. He's not a young man, I reckon he's around forty or so, therefore he must have been somewhere between his late teens and early twenties when his father died. Either way he HAD to know what an evil bastard the man was and he's inherited the same traits, we have the evidence. I can't forget that and remember the old saying... the apple doesn't fall far from the tree." He finally whispered, "I need my revenge. For Francis, my parents... for ME!" The obsession for vengeance was alive on his face and in his voice. It had driven him for years, part of the motivation to join the British army and fight his own compatriots; those same compatriots who had overrun the France he'd been born into and destroyed it, as far as he was concerned. They had prevented him from claiming back his rightful inheritance and birthright, the Valenciennes Chateau and Estate, for centuries the home of the de Bresancourts, Dukes and Lions of Valenciennes. Until that came to pass, he was simply a Duke of nothing.

Reynard realised there was no dissuading him, his hurt and obsession for revenge went too deep, so he took a deep breath and tried to give the younger man some sage advice. "Very well," he said, "but look here, Nicky, listen to this old man for once and I'm not joking now, I'm being deadly serious, just as you are. I know you're very much like Francis in a way," he sighed. "Despite all his years as The Shadow, the men he fought," he shook his head, "he was never really the ruthless killer everyone assumed him to be. All those stories that circulated about him, I made up and put half of them around myself, a word here and there down at the docks and they soon spread and got embroidered. Like I told you before, the gossip I spread about him and his legions of women and a harem. In fact, I doubt he killed many men at all in cold blood, not that he wasn't capable of it. He was a fearsome swordsman, lethal with a knife and a dead shot, so if someone crossed or swindled him, or informed against him, they paid the price." He paused momentarily before continuing reflectively, "But that was justified, in my opinion. However, I suspect he did kill when he went off pirating for a while, as he was a different man then. I still don't know what drove him to that, maybe it was his father's death and his unexpected inheritance of the title so early, not that I knew who he really was at the time other than Gerard's nephew, just that something in England had affected him negatively. I know he had terrible fights with his grandmother at that point, he did tell me that, said she was trying to run his life and no one was going to tell him what to do..." he shrugged and Nicky's eyes widened a fraction at how much the gypsy knew.

No one really knew everything about Francis's life as The Shadow. The small group of adults in the family had all vaguely heard reference to him as a pirate in the years before any of them had even heard of him, let alone met him, but no one knew anything about that part of his life, it was a closed book so far as Francis was concerned. Nicky was fascinated, but kept his expression impassive, as if he knew all about it. Reynard obviously assumed he did and he wondered if he'd tell him more. "Benjy agrees with me, but fortunately Francis settled down to simple smuggling again after that odd time, but he is, was, never cold-hearted and unemotional enough to kill men for no good reason, for the sake of it. Wound or incapacitate them, yes. Kill them, no. Of course, he had to maintain discipline among his crews, but he wasn't cruel or without mercy like some captains. You're exactly the same as him, you have the same personal ethos and moral compass, if you can call it that. You're basically a good and just man," he grasped Nicky by the shoulder and shook him, as if trying to imbue the importance of what he was saying deep into his brain, "but this is a different situation. There's only one of you and we have less than no idea who else is inside there with Bernheim and that bitch. So, whoever you see, no matter who they are, you've got to kill them first." Reynard's look was direct and forceful. "Do you understand me, Nicky? You've GOT to kill them. It doesn't matter if they're very young, or a girl, or look like some harmless old retainer, any one of those can shoot you as easily as I can – remember they're working for Bernheim. You can't trust ANYONE. You HAVE to watch your back because I can't be there to do it for you," he swore in frustration and shook Nicky again. "Are you understanding me?" he ranted softly and vehemently.

Nicky smiled grimly back at the gypsy and lifted a grimy hand to the older man's face. "You know, Reynard, you sounded just like the

Dowager then. They were the last words she said to me before I left England: 'Take care and watch your back," he whispered in imitation of her and shook his head at the memory. "God, I loved that old woman," he sighed reflectively for a short moment, knowing in his gut she was now dead. "But you're wrong about one thing," and his golden eyes flashed with burning fire. "I'm not as soft-hearted as you and some others think. I'm not Francis with his relentless humour and jokes, no matter how serious or ruthless he is underneath, or what he might have been. I CAN and I WILL kill ANYONE who gets in my way. I want Frederick Bernheim," he whispered coldly and venomously. Reynard shivered as he looked at him, recognising completely ruthless determination when he saw it. For a moment he thought of the stories he'd heard about the old Duke, Nicky's father, what a cold-hearted man he'd been and he realised some of that blood-line may well be in his son somewhere; lying dormant, but still there.

"Very well," Reynard said, slowly and reluctantly. "Just see if you can get one of those gates open without causing any disturbance and I'll come in and do what I can, but promise me for all our sakes, be brave, but don't take any unnecessary risks. Just kill all the bastards as you find them, no one will know or care," he said, equally cold-blood-edly, "they all must know about the gold, and where it came from. There's a lot of it and it didn't appear from thin air so they're all complicit one way or another."

Nicky nodded and smiled fondly at the grizzled gypsy. "I promise; and thank you, Reynard. I know you mean well, but you must remember too, *je suis Le Lion de Valenciennes* and lions are very brave and extremely dangerous when angry," he pantomimed his hands into claws and growled, "Grrrrrrrr... rawrrrrrr," albeit with a big feral grin, "and they kill their prey mercilessly."

Reynard smiled back and prayed to God it was true; what a deep and complex man Nicky had turned into, rather like Francis in his own way, and he crossed himself.

Chapter Twelve

They crept back to where they'd tied up their horses and Nicky retrieved some items he would need: thick gloves to deal with the glass on the top of the wall, some rope, his sword, a small knife and another pistol which he tucked into the back of his belt. Then they made their way back to the perimeter wall and the spot they'd chosen near the rear of the house where it was least overlooked, to wait there until dark.

As they sat quietly, Nicky thought about what he'd said to Reynard. Of course, Reynard was right, he WAS like Francis and took no pleasure in killing anyone or anything unless he absolutely had to. But, unlike Francis, or maybe not, he mused to himself, as he'd listened to Reynard's reference to Francis's pirating days, something he wanted to know more about, he knew deep down there was a cold hardness within him that, when released, could and would turn him into a ruthless killer, just like the lion he'd joked about. For a very brief moment, a picture of his unemotional father watching his pregnant mother being beaten and raped and him being sodomised in Rouen Fortress surfaced in his mind. That man had had an unbelievably rigid, ice-cold streak inside him and it was there in himself too. He just knew it. He thought about apples and trees and merely trusted he wasn't too near the tree.

Unconsciously, his hand went to his neck, but the necklace, his father's, grandfather's and great-grandfather's necklace, of course, wasn't there. Yet again, as he sat in the falling dusk, his mind went back to London and *La Lionesse* and suddenly the coincidence of her name struck him forcefully, as it hadn't really done before. He didn't often dwell on Valenciennes, the family nickname and his father, it was too painful. But the coincidence was ironic. He smiled, they WERE indeed a pair, just as she'd said: devious, determined and passionate. He WOULD survive that night, he swore to himself, because he had another score to settle in London. For a few minutes he lay back against the stump of a tree, eyes closed and body hardening as he let his mind wander to the lecherous fantasy of how he'd take his revenge against *La Lionesse*. As he dozed and dreamed, the chilly, virtually moonless early March night closed around him.

Chapter Thirteen

Bella was in her personal little sitting room in Hertford Street. It overlooked the pavement and passers-by, rather than the pretty garden. She'd taken over the cosy room, the Dowager's erstwhile favourite haunt for herself, leaving the main study for Nicky, knowing that had been the room the old lady had used for formal meetings with her men of business. Not that she could envisage him spending much time there, his dislike of paperwork and business matters well known by his relations, but she smiled to herself as she knew he'd now have to apply himself to manage the vast inheritance he'd received. The redecorations were now finished and although the house was much the same – the paintings, ornaments and most of the beautiful furniture – it was now fresher, brighter and lighter. New drapes hung at the windows; new deep carpets and rugs covered the polished floors and new, more up to date lamps illuminated the rooms.

The key to a little attic room sat in front of her and the Dowager's secret hung heavy on her mind. She wanted to tell her Uncle Francis but was still waiting for the right moment. Bella had discovered the small upstairs room when she'd done an inventory of the house and originally assumed it was just a storeroom or old servants' quarters. She'd kept the key the Dowager had removed from around her neck and secreted it in a little drawer in the top of the jewel chest of the Dowager's that now sat in her dressing room. She'd tried it in the lock of every room in the house until at last it had worked in that small attic door.

When she'd entered the room, she'd been astonished. Speechless. Beautifully carpeted and furnished, not that there was much furniture, there were heavy velvet drapes across the small window and a small fireplace to ward off the chill. The attic chamber contained nothing except a big, deep, comfortable armchair and footstool, a rug hanging over the chairback, and there was a small table by its side on which stood a beautiful silver candelabra, a decanter and glass on a silver salver. However, the complete focus of the room was a large portrait with a curtain drawn across it which hung on the wall opposite the chair, illuminated by several strategically placed, large candelabra and lamps. Bella had drawn the curtain back and at first sight, the full-length, almost life-size portrait, was like looking at one of her Uncle Francis; except this man was wearing a kilt and full tartan, complete with plaid, brooch and flash, one hand on the hilt of a sword hanging from an ornate scabbard. He looked dashing and darkly handsome with striking cornflower blue eyes. There was a small plaque affixed to the bottom of the ornate gilt frame with a name and a date.

Lord Alexander Alasdair Kinross of Invermory
1732

Stunned at her discovery, Bella had literally tottered across the small room to sit on the chair, to gaze in awe at the painting. This then, this striking man, was the love of the Dowager's life. Uncle Francis's real grandfather. It had obviously been painted just before he left Scotland, or so Bella assumed. She wondered how on earth the Dowager had managed to get hold of it and her mind boggled. Had she gone to Invermory herself and seen it? How on earth had she persuaded his family to part with it? She'd got the impression the Kinross family weren't at all wealthy, living at the back of beyond in the Highlands, hence the reason for the man's departure to seek his fortune elsewhere; so would they have bothered, or could they afford to have such a large and striking portrait painted of a younger son? Maybe they wanted something to remember him by? Bella had absolutely no idea what life in the Highlands was like, especially back then between the two Jacobite uprisings which had proved so disastrous for Scotland. She wondered if it was a very good copy, or the original, or was the face that of the man, but copied on to an imagined body? If she had gone to Invermory herself, how had her Great Aunt Elizabeth, then the Duchess of Firle, explained her connection and curiosity to the man's family? When had she gone? Before or after the 1745 uprising led by Bonnie Prince Charlie, with the upheaval that had caused? That she had acquired the portrait, or even had some sort of a copy done, or likeness concocted from a miniature of the man's face, perhaps, didn't surprise Bella in the least, but the whole story was so sad. She imagined the Dowager sitting there in that very chair, rug over her knees, sipping a drink and staring at the portrait, full of love, regret, bitterness, anger and frustration at herself and her wrong decisions. A bitterness that had eaten away at her like a canker her entire life. She assumed the curtain was drawn across the big picture when a maid or footman came in to clean the fireplace, dust and see to the lamps. She imagined the Dowager personally supervising to ensure no one peeked at her treasured possession because of course Uncle Francis, the Duke, would have been a frequent visitor to the house and it wouldn't take much for the servants to wonder at the likeness and tattle to their colleagues about it.

Bella had often returned to the room over the following few months. She discovered the whisky in the decanter and now understood the Dowager's strange inclination to drink the stuff which had always puzzled her close family. She wondered if it had come from Invermory itself as hadn't the old lady said there was a small distillery on the estate? She decided it probably did. Bella would sit in the comfy chair and look at the portrait and think of everything the Dowager had told her, including her final letter. Then she would think of Nicky and pray he was safe and would soon come home.

Now in her little sitting room, she resolved she would go and find her uncle the following day and bring him back to Hertford Street, show him the portrait and tell him the story. In the meantime, she was overcome with a feeling of restlessness and, as ever, her mind went to Spain and she wondered what Nicky was doing. Uncle Francis had come to tell her privately a few weeks before that he'd had word from Reynard that Nicky was all right. Nothing more; but the fact he was still safe was a relief, also that he'd been in touch with the old gypsy. She suspected her uncle did in fact know more but she hadn't been able to prise anything further from him other than he truly had no idea when Nicky would return to England. Her restless feelings turned to anxiety and she rose to pace to and fro in front of the fire. Truth to tell, she felt like a veritable whale and wished the child would hurry up and come before she exploded, as she was sure she couldn't get any larger. Her back ached and her mind was full of intangible worries, not least because her mother had died giving birth to her little brother and that always fuelled her concerns. She wished Nicky was with her and she couldn't get these strange feelings that he was in danger out of her mind. She sighed and put it down to her pregnant state, but she didn't sleep well that night, tossing and turning, her head full of fears and strange dreams and she rose early the following day looking pale and drawn, with bags under her eyes.

As she'd promised herself, she summoned her carriage and went round to Berkeley Square as soon as she was dressed. Always an early riser himself from habit, Francis was already in his study and he looked up in concern as Bella almost waddled in, her hand to her back.

"Bella! What the devil are you doing here and at this time of the morning? You should be resting; the baby, it could come at any time now," he tutted like a mother hen to a naughty chick as he looked at her and rose from his chair in alarm. "You look quite shocking, Puss; get yourself back home this minute or I'll get your aunt to harangue you and you know what that means!" he threatened with an anxious smile and a comical roll of his eyes.

"Oh, stop fussing, Uncle, I'm perfectly fine, even if I do feel like a whale with a bad back. But I simply HAD to see you, I can't bear it any longer. I HAVE to tell you…"

Francis looked at his niece in despair and helped her into a chair. "Whatever is it, Sweetheart? Is something the matter? Shall I call Cat anyway? Would you like some tea or some water? Do you need to put your feet up? Some cushions? Shall I send for the doctor or the midwife?"

"No, no, Uncle, don't fret, please. I merely HAVE to talk to you. Just you and me. It's dreadfully important and I can't do it here. We HAVE to do it at Hertford Street." Bella absently twirled the Dowager's ring that was still on her little finger as Francis looked at her, completely nonplussed and concerned.

"Is it about Nicky?" he queried. "Because I promise you, I've heard nothing since that last short message."

"No, Uncle, it's not about Nicky, it's about the Dowager. And you," Bella whispered, now looking fretful herself. "Please, Uncle Francis, come back with me. I simply have to tell you before the baby is born, in case..." she whispered, yet again memories of her mother's death after Charlie's birth hanging heavy on her mind. "I can't wait any more, you simply HAVE to know. TODAY!"

"Damn me, Bella," Francis looked at Bella's worried face, "whatever is it? Why can't you tell me here, now? Why do we need to go back to Hertford Street? We won't be disturbed here, you know that." He looked more than concerned now.

"Because you just have to! Please, Uncle Francis, it's so important to me, also to you. You'll... you'll understand when you see, when you hear what I have to say," she grasped his hand, "and bring your grandmother's last letter, you know, the one with her Will."

She was working herself up into a bit of a state and Francis thought it best to do as she asked, completely at a loss as to what was the matter and now more than a little curious as well as worried. But he knew Bella was usually a sensible young woman and didn't panic over minor things, so, with a deep sigh and trying not to think about all the work he had to do, he helped her to her feet and they slowly made their way out of his study. Francis left a message with the butler to tell his secretary to cancel or re-arrange his meetings for the rest of the morning and they proceeded out of the house, into Bella's carriage and drove to Hertford Street.

The previous evening, not wanting to make the servants curious, Bella had dragged a small plain chair from a downstairs corridor into the attic room so she could sit while her uncle was in the Dowager's chair. Once they arrived back at the house from Berkeley Square, leaving Francis standing in confusion in the main hallway, she went into the dining room and collected a decanter of brandy and, holding it in one hand, she then pulled her uncle in her wake with her other. The key to the room was burning a hole in her pocket.

"Bella, wherever are we going?" Francis asked worriedly as she panted and heaved herself up the stairs one at a time. "There's nothing up here but the attics and some old servants' rooms."

"You'll see," Bella muttered, until the pair of them were standing outside the locked door. "Right, just stay here a moment, Uncle. Wait for me, but, whatever you do, DON'T come in!" With that, she pulled the key out of her pocket, unlocked the door and squeezed inside before he could see what she was doing. She'd dragged the big armchair around so it was temporarily facing away from the curtained painting and she put the brandy decanter down on the occasional table next to the one that contained whisky, unsure if her uncle ever drank the stuff; however, she deemed brandy a more reliable recuperative to cope with the shock she knew was in store for him. She then went back to the door and pulled it open a crack. "Now, Uncle, I want you to shut your eyes," she instructed Francis who was looking more than a tad irritated at Bella's mysterious behaviour as he waited in the narrow attic passageway, "just for a moment. Please, Uncle Francis, I know this all seems very strange, but just humour me."

"Bellaaaa?" Francis grumbled, "What games are you playing now? I thought you said this was serious? I've left important work to come round here with you this morning and…"

"Pleeeease, Uncle," Bella squeezed his hand as she begged him, "just do as I say. Close your eyes for a moment and just come with me… it's… it's a surprise and it really will be worth the effort, believe me."

Francis concurred, still puzzled at seeing her so agitated. "Oh, very well," he muttered and when he shut his eyes with a big sigh, Bella pulled open the door properly and ushered him inside. She gently led him the few steps over to the armchair and told him to sit down.

"You can open them now," she said when he was settled and she sat down on the plain chair next to him. "Don't turn around, whatever you do," she exclaimed as he started to look around the luxuriously furnished room in amazement, taking in the lush drapes and thick carpeting.

"Whatever is this room, Bella? I had absolutely no idea it was here."

"It was a special room of your grandmother's," said Bella quietly. "Now, sit back, as I'm going to tell you a long story. It's been driving me quite mad, keeping it to myself for the past six months and I simply can't bear it for another day!"

She picked up her diary, left on the table the previous evening, a leather-bound volume that had been a twenty-first birthday present from Nicky. Her family had laughed when she'd opened it as it had 'Sooty's Secrets' emblazoned in gilt lettering on the front and a funny inscription from Nicky on the inside cover:

> To Sooty, with my Love on your Special Birthday.
>   Now you can write down and record for Posterity, all those Countless Secrets you have Harboured over the years of the Terrible Things you have Perpetrated on my Totally Innocent Person since my Youth.
>   Nicky xxx

He'd obviously bought it and written the inscription before that torrid night when she'd invaded his bed for the first time. He'd left it with his step-father as he'd been away when her birthday had actually arrived. Inside, it now contained all her outpourings of the pent-up love and longing she felt for him, as well as what she knew of the family secrets, the stories she'd heard about The Shadow and her mother's past. After that heart-wrenching afternoon when the Dowager had passed away, unable to sleep, Bella had sat at her writing desk that night and inscribed every detail she could remember of their last conversation and the story the dying woman had related to her. She'd also copied out the contents of the Dowager's last letter to another set of sheets, now kept between relevant pages. The diary was full and she'd moved on to a second volume of *Sooty's Secrets*, all locked away in what had been the Dowager's personal escritoire that was now hers. She picked it up and opened it to the marked place, an aide memoire in case she forgot any details of what she was about to impart to her beloved uncle.

She took a deep breath and started to speak. "Do you remember that last afternoon, here in Hertford Street in your grandmother's bedroom, the afternoon she passed away?" Francis nodded. "Well, I'd come to see her to tell her about the baby. She was thrilled, of course, but she could tell I was worried about something, so I eventually told her what had happened; all of it," she whispered.

Francis grinned at her. "Did you now? Well, well... and what did my dear Granny make of that? I'll warrant she was vastly amused," he chuckled.

"She was, she laughed her head off," Bella blushed. "Almost doubled up with mirth she was. She wasn't remotely shocked, which I dare say won't surprise you. I was mortified as she teased me, but it was so good to see her laugh that much." Bella smiled sadly for a moment at the memory but then carried on, "Anyway, I had always confided in her, she seemed to understand so well what made Nicky tick and she knew how much I cared for him... so... so I told her how we'd argued again when he'd been home, how he refused to see me as anyone other than a little sister, a hoyden with plaits and freckles, how he was angry at having no money, no home, oh you know, the usual story," she tutted frustratedly. "I told her how he'd threatened to go to the Americas when he came back from the Peninsula and make a new life and to seek his fortune there," she finally whispered and Francis looked at her in shock.

"NO! The Americas? Damn me, Bella, why haven't you ever told me that? Surely he wouldn't? Thank heaven he won't need to now..." Francis realised belatedly and sighed with relief.

"No, well, I suppose not," Bella sighed and shook her head, "but at the time he was still penniless. Well not quite, as only you know, *Le Lion* and *La Lionesse d'Or* and all that." She smiled conspiratorially at her uncle, continuing, "Anyway, I told the Dowager all this – also how frightened I was that he'd go away and I'd never see him again and how much I loved him." Bella lowered her eyes as she said it, continuing, "and… and that was when she told me this story, told me never to give up on him." She then related the entire tale to Francis, just as the Dowager had told her. As she talked, she watched his body stiffen and his face gradually went ashen until he was white as a sheet.

Bella gazed at Francis in concern as he tried to take in what she'd revealed. When she'd finished, leaving him in absolute shock for a few moments, she rose to draw back the curtain from where it covered the painting and returned to him. She gently took hold of his cold hands and whispered, "Stand up and turn around," and, as he did so, almost subconsciously she grasped his shoulders and turned him to face the portrait. "Behold your REAL grandfather, Uncle Francis. That is Lord Alexander Alasdair Kinross, the late Earl of Invermory, the love of your grandmother's life and the pair of you look so alike, it's almost uncanny… the dark hair, the striking blue eyes, the height and build… no wonder your grandmother was so besotted with you…"

Francis stood there, stunned into complete silence as two tears rolled down his face and Bella shoved and pulled the big armchair around and pushed him back down into it. She noticed his hands were now shaking and, expecting such a reaction, she hastily poured him out a large glass of brandy and put it into one numb hand, encouraging him to drink.

Francis stared at the painting and Bella remained perched quietly next to him on the arm of the chair, holding his other hand. They sat like that for quite a while until eventually he whispered shakily, "Dear God, why didn't she ever tell me?"

"She was frightened you'd run away. She thought you might get some idiotic notion in your head and be too moral and ethical to keep a title that wasn't rightfully yours. Personally, when I thought after about how much she loathed your cousin Algernon, the grandson of her late husband's younger brother, so a rightful, legitimate heir being just about in the direct line, I think that had a lot to do with it as well.

She merely told me she thought you might go back to being a smuggler, or emigrate off to the Americas yourself." Bella gripped his hand tightly, "I'm not sure what all her reasons were and, of course, we'll never know now. All she said to me was she hadn't sacrificed everything to have you abandon it all, so she never told you. But she wanted me to tell you, made me promise I would and also I'm to tell Elizabeth everything when she grows up. I think she thought Lizzie has your and HIS looks and character." She pulled Francis's white face round to hers and held it between two soft hands, "Now you might understand why she wrote what she did in that last letter. Read it again with new eyes. You'll understand some of the references to ancestors and other things, as I did at the time."

"My God..." was all Francis said again, totally stupefied and lost for words as he slumped back in the chair, tipping the entire glass of brandy down his throat.

"Uncle? You're not... you're not going to do anything stupid now, are you? I'd never have told you otherwise. No one else in the world knows about this except me, and now you. I've kept this room locked and no one has come in here since your grandmother's death, other than me, not even a servant; even though Carstairs undoubtedly thinks it very odd since I've dusted and cleaned the room myself as I've come to sit in here on odd occasions, just to think about... well... things." She looked pleadingly at him, "Oh Uncle, your grandmother loved you more than anything and everything. She obviously sacrificed so much and she was so proud of you, of the family now... all of us," she faltered, not knowing what else to say to the obviously shocked and speechless man.

Francis sat there in silence, still trying to absorb it all, then merely shook his head, obviously bewildered and confused.

"I'll leave you for a while, hmmm?" Bella bent down to put the key in his hand and kiss his cheek lovingly. "I'll be downstairs in my sitting room when you're ready to talk. Just lock the door behind you... and I'll send a message back to Firle House to say you've been delayed and aren't sure when you'll be back. Oh, a final thought, Uncle..." Bella added as she stood up with a heaving breath and went to leave, her hand on the door knob, "I don't know how she came by the portrait, whether she had it done from a miniature of him she acquired at some point, maybe he gave her one as a keepsake before he left, or she had one done of him for herself for the same reason. Perhaps the painting actually came from Invermory or even, somehow, from where he settled in the southern American states. Maybe he had it done for himself when he inherited the title, to remind him of his Scottish roots. Who knows? However, I've considered all the alternatives and, given what Auntie told me about the state of the castle in Scotland he left behind to come to London, also that the family were somewhat impoverished, it did strike me it was a very extravagant painting to have done of a mere second son as he was when he left. Also, acquiring it from over in the Americas is an even bigger ask. I mean, how could she possibly explain who she was and why she wanted it, never mind know it existed in the first place? That's why I think she might well have had the portrait concocted for herself, but where she got the miniature to copy the face from, I doubt we'll ever know. Being the romantic soul I am, I'd like to think it was done just before he left and maybe he took one of her with him. However, whatever happened, the likeness to you is so uncanny there can be no doubting that truly is what your grandfather looked like, as I'm sure this portrait was done long before you were born, otherwise the title would refer to him as Earl of Invermory, not simply Lord Alexander... "

With that last little nugget for her uncle to mull over, Bella rubbed her aching back again and quietly left the room, pulling the door closed behind her.

Lunchtime came and went before Francis finally reappeared. He entered Bella's sitting room silently, his grandmother's letter grasped in his hand. He put the key down on her escritoire, the Dowager's escritoire, in the window embrasure where it had always stood, a window that looked out on to the corner of Hertford Street where she had often sat for hours, mind miles away, presumably lost in the past and full of bittersweet memories of stolen kisses, passion and so much more.

"Are you all right, Uncle?" Bella asked worriedly, putting the key safely away in a drawer as she rose from her chair, looking at his pale, drawn face. "Come and sit by the fire." She ushered him to a seat on a little sofa in front of the blazing fire and sat next to him, taking one of his hands in hers. "I knew it would be a shock, but I simply had to tell you. I'd left it far too long." She squeezed the hand she held, "Uncle, what are you going to do?"

Francis raised his head and looked down into Bella's anxious face. "Nothing," he finally whispered. "Absolutely nothing," and Bella let out a deep gasp of relief and smiled at him.

"Thank goodness for that."

"I still can't believe it," he muttered, "and thank you for telling me, Bella. You were right, I needed to know the truth." Francis stared into the flames of the fire, "So much, so many odd little things over the years make sense now, like the whisky, but my God... how could she have done that?"

Bella chuckled. "Knowing her, are you surprised? She was such a remarkable woman, but it must have been the most terrible decision for her." Bella lolled back on the cushions thoughtfully, her hands on her swollen belly. "I wonder what would have happened if she HAD upped and gone off after him, or even ran away and sailed off with him?" She reflected, "I dare say you would have been the Earl of Invermory now, wearing a tartan kilt and a furry sporran, possibly in the southern states of America," she giggled. "Not the Duke of Firle, nor would you have ever been The Shadow, or met Aunt Cat... and I wouldn't be here either... and Nicky would be dead," she whispered in momentary dawning horror. "How strange is fate?" she said quietly as she shook her head in wonder.

"I hadn't quite got that far yet," Francis admitted. "I'm still coming to terms with being part-Scottish."

"Are you going to tell anyone? Aunt Cat?" she looked at him questioningly.

"I really don't know, but yes," he finally said decisively, "I think I'll have to tell Cat. Like you, it would weigh too heavily on my mind, but that's all. She knows a lot of my secrets anyway," he grinned as he tapped his nose and Bella giggled again, wondering what else they all didn't know about his past as a smuggler. "You will tell Lizzie, won't you? When she's older? I promised your grandmother, gave her my word."

She finally pulled off the ring from her finger and held it out to him. "She told me to take this off her after she died. She said it had never left her finger since he gave it to her, other than to be resized presumably. I think it's got the Invermory crest on it, though it's very old and worn. Here," she put it into his palm and folded his fingers around it. "Perhaps you'd like to keep it safe and give it to Lizzie? It's your secret too, now."

Francis opened his hand and inspected the ring. "You know," he mused, staring at it, "I always wondered about this ring," he said thoughtfully. "I always thought it deuced odd that she wore it with all the other jewels she covered herself in when she went out and about." Then he took Bella's hand and placed the little ring back on her finger. "I think you should keep it, Sweetheart, if you want to, that is? You've got all the rest of the damned jewellery anyway, but I think this has rather a lot of sentimental value to you now?" he queried softly. "Anyway, you can give it to that little baggage of mine when she's old enough to understand. Is that all right with you?"

Bella nodded and looked at her uncle, smiling and feeling very emotional. "Thank you. I'd like that. I think about her a lot, y'know," she sighed. "Especially now I'm living here. Even though I've redecorated the place, I still feel her presence, isn't that strange? Especially in this room, or that attic one, or am I just being fanciful because I'm *enceinte*? I do hope Nicky doesn't throw it all away because of his stupid pride."

"I know, Sweetheart, I know, but he can hardly give it back," Francis laughed sadly. "Which the old meddler knew perfectly well, so let's hope he's had some sense knocked into him down in the Peninsula. When he finds out he's a father, well, that should focus his mind on being practical if nothing else does," and Francis finally grinned at his niece.

"Oh Lord, Uncle Francis, I'm dreading telling him," and she looked at him pleadingly. "Can't you let him know him first, pleeease? Then he can get over his shock and anger before I see him."

"Oh no, I told you before, I most definitely won't, *Madame*

Lionesse." Francis smirked wickedly at her. "You got yourself into this delightful mess, so you can deal with the consequences," and he patted her on her very large, rounded belly as they laughed at each other.

They sat in companionable silence for a while, staring at the flames of the fire, before Bella sat up as a thought struck her. "What are we going to do with the painting? Do you want it at Firle House, or maybe down at Firle Manor? He is your grandfather after all – and he's a deal more dashing in all that tartan than all those boring ancestors in the portrait gallery."

"Hell, no, that wouldn't do." Francis looked shocked. "Even I'd have difficulty explaining the resemblance, it's like looking at myself in the mirror. If anyone saw some of the paintings of me and him along-side the portraits of my father and supposed grandfather, it would certainly raise too many eyebrows." He looked at Bella, "I'm afraid we'll have to leave it here for now, if you don't mind? I must bring Cat round to see it as soon as I've told her." He pondered for a minute or so, "Maybe one day I'll trace my other family, my true relations, in the Americas, or see who's left up in Scotland and enquire if any of them want it, especially if it's the original, though actually, I think you're probably right about it being a concoction to appease my grandmoth-er's regrets, memories and longing; or possibly Lizzie will want it because, as you've said, it seems she does have the family look too, though I daresay she'll have to keep it shut away somewhere private as well." He shook his head, "I simply can't believe how much I resemble him. As you first said to me, it's really very eerie, isn't it?"

"Mmmmm, absolutely," smiled Bella. "Family likeness is such a strange thing; I mean, look how much I resemble Mama, except for my green eyes which come from Papa, and Auntie has them as well, but neither of them resemble Grandmama particularly, and Papa says he doesn't look much like Grandpapa, who I don't remember very well at all. Auntie says she takes after HER maternal grandmother, that's where her character, hair and green eyes come from she thinks. Papa has no idea where his brains come from although Grandpapa was quite a studious man too, but not in Papa's league.

Nicky has the Valenciennes family tawny colouring and eyes and his birthmark, yet your father looks completely different to your real grandfather, his real father, according to the portrait at Firle House; they're not remotely similar in any way whatsoever and he doesn't even resemble your grandmother either. So how did that happen? Even Papa can't explain why these things occur, which is saying something!" she giggled. "I can't wait to find out if my little lion cub has green eyes or golden ones, tawny or black hair, or doesn't look like any of us at all! Mind you, even if your face is like your real grandfather's, I'd have to inspect your knees and hairy legs too before I agreed you're his total double, to see if they match the portrait," she joked. "I wonder what you'd look like in a kilt and tam o'shanter, isn't that what they call those funny hats they wear up there, north of the border?" She burst out into gales of laughter as Francis pulled a disgusted face but he was soon rolling around in mirth along with her when she suggested Benjy, her uncle's fastidious valet, would have a fainting fit if he was asked to dress his master in a short skirt.

As the pair continued to chuckle, discussing the merits of Francis's knees with Francis putting on a terrible Scottish accent as he spoke, then wondering what the Ton would make of it if he turned up in a kilt at Almack's, Bella suddenly gasped and bent over in pain, half rising from her chair.

Francis took one look at her face and the hands that grasped her belly, then the tell-tale puddle at her feet. His eyes widened in knowing surprise. "The baby? Have you had a spasm? I take it your waters have just broken?" he asked succinctly, not entirely unfamiliar with the process of childbirth, even for a man. Bella nodded, gasping again, more loudly this time and Francis shot out of his chair as she sank back on the sofa.

"Right," he said brusquely, "never mind about my kilt, hairy knees and what I should keep in my diamond-encrusted sporran," he grinned, "no arguing or pussyfooting about now Lionesse. You, Madam, are coming back with me to Firle House and Cat can look after you and supervise the midwife and doctor... as childbirth is most definitely not on my knowledge list. I know my place, being just a mere man, which is to patrol round my study with periodic recourse to the brandy bottle every time I hear a scream. When your dear Papa arrives – I'll send a messenger straight away down to Arlington – he can patrol with me, or help me wet the baby's head more like, given how long it will take for him to get here, which is a much better idea!" Then, without so much as asking her permission, Francis gently pulled Bella to her feet, swung her up into his strong arms and strode out towards the front door, calling for her carriage or a hackney immediately, whichever was the quickest to hand, to take them straight back to Berkeley Square. He announced he was about to become a Great Uncle and watched in amusement as Carstairs ran about in a panic, shouting at the footmen to send for the doctor and clucking over Bella, still clasped in Francis' arms, offering her water, smelling salts and all manner of completely useless things.

Chapter Fourteen

Nicky and Reynard approached the rear metal gates, making just enough of a rustle to interest the quietly snarling but curious dogs, but not enough to make them bark out loud. They merely whined softly and wolfed down the poisoned chicken Reynard tossed through the bars. Within several minutes, both were lying sprawled out dead on the gravel.

Hurrying along to the place on the perimeter wall most obscured from the villa by the outbuildings, barn and stables, Nicky threw a length of rope up and over the top, the sharp grappling hook soon catching on the soft plaster. With a final hug for Reynard, the man's whispered, "Kill first, worry later and BE CAREFUL, for God's sake," ringing in his ears as the gypsy kissed the cross hanging round his neck and sent a look heavenward, Nicky scrambled up the rope and paused momentarily on the top of the wall, his thick gloves protecting his hands from the shards of glass that had cut them so badly the last time he'd climbed up. He pulled up the rope and securing the hook round the other way, let it down the other side and silently disappeared. He crept over to inspect the gate, but as they'd known, it was locked and bolted from the inside. Once again he pulled out the curiously shaped piece of curved metal from his pocket and within a few minutes, the lock was open. Slowly and carefully he drew back the rusty bolts and silently let Reynard in, to that man's enormous relief and another grateful nod to the heavens.

Under a virtually moonless sky, Reynard was just about able to make out the carcasses of the dead dogs and he picked them up one by one, to conceal in the undergrowth back outside. Then, pulling the gate closed, but not locked, behind them, the pair crept towards the outbuildings, tiptoeing as silently as they could over the gravelled drive and forecourt. While Reynard stood watch outside, Nicky crept around to the small shanty where they could see a dim light glowing through the windows. He carefully peered inside and saw four middle-aged, hard-looking men sitting at a table in front of a small fire. As well as a flagon of wine and some tumblers, they had a number of pistols and muskets on the table and were obviously in the process of cleaning, oiling and loading them, presumably in preparation for the journey the following day. He padded silently back to Reynard and whispered briefly, "There's four of the bastards inside, drivers or guards for the wagons presumably. No sign of a coachman for the carriage, he must be in the house." He gripped Reynard's arm, "Any bright ideas? I'm not sure I can deal with all four without making too much noise. They're mean looking buggers. I daren't use my pistols, obviously."

Without a word, Reynard pulled a long, evil-looking stiletto from his boot and waggled it under Nicky's nose. "I can do more than keep a look out, y'know," he whispered. "I may not be able to fight them fair and square, but with the element of surprise," he pulled a finger across his throat and shrugged with a nasty look in his eyes.

Nicky grinned back at him as he, too, bent to pull a long, jewelled stiletto from his own boot. "Courtesy of Cat, when I first joined the army and came down here to the Peninsula. She said I'd have more use for it than she would these days, being a dowdy, boring, middle-aged matron responsible for a horde of hooligan children, who no one, especially not some young, handsome rake, would want to carry off or interfere with, more's the pity... and I quote," he chuckled. "You should have seen Francis's face when he heard her, she's as daft as he is," and laughed at Reynard's amused expression as he nodded to the man's long, thin, razor-sharp weapon. "I see you've taken lessons from her as well!"

Reynard grinned and winked at the younger man, as he pulled a second knife from his belt, as did Nicky. "Great minds and all that," he said softly, "but I was always way ahead of her; and who do you think first taught Francis how to use and throw a knife when he was still wet behind the ears? It wasn't his grandmother or Gerard!" and they smiled at each other.

The deadly pair then quietly made their way round to the shanty door. They had no option but to burst in – there was only a single door and window to the one roomed cabin, the men sleeping on pallets on the hard dirt floor. However, the element of surprise was with them as Nicky calmly opened the door and stepped inside with an aristocratic bow and cultured greeting, "Ah, good evening, Gentlemen. I'm so sorry to bother you…"

The first two on their feet fell where they stood, as two daggers simultaneously flew across the room and thudded into their chests. The other two had no time to gather their wits from the surprise as Nicky flew at one with his stiletto raised and Reynard, with a speed that decried his age and crippled thigh, crossed the room and ruthlessly slit the throat of the second before the man had a chance to pick up a pistol from the table.

They tidied up the toppled wine and tumblers and pulled three bodies over to lay them down on the pallets, making it seem like they were asleep, retrieving their knives and wiping them clean on the dead men's shirts. The fourth they left sitting at the table, head resting forward on his arms, again looking like he was sleeping. To anyone checking from the outside, all would look quiet and normal. They then left as silently as they'd arrived.

"Well, that wasn't too difficult," joked Nicky in a hard whisper as he nodded his thanks to Reynard, impressed by the older man's ability and total ruthlessness.

"Hmmm, let's just hope there aren't more of them inside," muttered Reynard sceptically. "But given those four back in the shanty, plus the buggers they killed earlier, along with Carlos, it looks like they've redistributed the gold between just four big heavy wagons, the fewer the better and less noticeable, providing they can take the weight. Otherwise, I reckon there'd have been five or six of the sods in there, but there's still a coachman and at least one groom to help, given the number of horses or mules they'll need to pull those loads, not to mention the housekeeper and any other domestic servants; and then Bernheim and his woman." He growled in frustration. "I can't climb up there with you this time," he nodded to the villa balconette they were now assessing above them. They'd already crept around all the ground floor doors and windows which were now dark and covered by shutters or drapes. Each one had decorative filigree bars over the window sections which were impenetrable and the heavy doors were closed and locked. Despite their best efforts, the loose gravel had seemed noisy with each step they'd taken, but fortunately all had stayed silent within. They hoped if anyone heard anything, they'd simply assume it was the dogs wandering around.

"It's fine, Reynard, don't worry. You just keep an eye out down here. I'd never have dealt with that lot in there without your help," whispered Nicky, tipping his head in the direction of the shanty. "Maybe you could go and get those front gates unlocked and unbolted as well if you can, while I'm inside; there must be a key back in that shanty or the stables. You never know if we might have to leave and find our horses in a hurry and more than one way out would be a bonus," and with another tap on Reynard's shoulder he grasped the creeper growing up the side of the villa and started to climb.

The thick vine trunk petered out to thin branches halfway up, but Nicky just managed to grasp the side of a balconette railing and hoisted himself up and over. He was tall, broad-shouldered and well-muscled, but jumped down silently onto the narrow ledge inside the railing, as lithe and quiet as a big cat in his soft leather boots.

He peered into the room within. It was a bedroom and, to his relief, it looked deserted. There was no handle or lock on the outside of the tall French windows that obviously opened inward, so once again he pulled the little metal tool from his pocket. Not wanting to make unnecessary noise by shattering the glass, he simply described a large ring with the sharp end and pushed through the circle of cut glass onto the rug inside; then he put his hand through, unlocked the latch and crept in, breathing another sigh of relief there weren't bolts at the top and bottom of the windows and there'd been a small woven rug beneath them. The room appeared to be unoccupied and he moved over to the door and cracked it open a mere fraction. The hallway outside was in darkness. He briefly went back to the windows and looked down at Reynard, waiting anxiously below. He gave him a thumbs up signal before closing them, drawing some drapes across to hide the missing circle of glass, then returned back to the middle of the room. He checked his small pocket watch: it was two a.m. He glided silently along the corridor and made his way downstairs and towards the back of the villa, searching out the servants' quarters, his lethal stiletto poised in his hand once more. He found the kitchens and through the back of the scullery, he located several small rooms. Turning the handle on the first, he peered inside and saw the body of a man under a thin blanket, fast asleep on a narrow cot. By the clothes strewn on the single chair, he looked to probably be the missing coachman and Nicky noted the musket and pistol lying on the floor next to the bed. The man barely moved as Nicky pulled out his pillow and smothered him as he slept.

There was another man similarly asleep next door. His clothes and the smell of the small, stuffy room suggested a groom and momentarily Nicky wondered why he didn't sleep above the stables or nearer to the horses, but he had no time to ponder. The man was short and wiry and tried some resistance, reaching out in vain for the pistol on the floor by his cot as he came instantly awake, obviously a light sleeper after sensing movement – but he had no chance to make any sound before Nicky cut his throat with a quick slash of Cat's deadly stiletto, as if it were sliding through butter. He left the man face down on the bed, looking for all the world as though fast asleep, the blood from his cut throat seeping into the thin bedding beneath him.

Nicky progressed down the narrow hallway. The next room contained a man who appeared to be simply a general servant, but again he, too, kept a pistol on the floor next to his narrow bed. He didn't even struggle as he met the same fate as the coachman.

The man in the fourth room was large and fat; his clothes and the room smell suggested he was the cook. As Nicky leaned over him, his eyes opened and he pulled a wicked-looking kitchen knife out from under his pillow and slashed it down across Nicky's abdomen with a quiet cry as he tried to lift his cumbersome body off the mattress. One deep slice of Nicky's stiletto across his throat cut off his shout and he slumped back on the bed, blood bubbling from the deep and long cut, his eyes bulging. Nicky pulled the covers over the man, staggered back against the wall and ran his hand over his stomach. His clothes were slashed, but the knife seemed to have only mildly cut his skin, his leather jacket having taken a lot of the damage. Thankful for the lack of any serious blood loss, Nicky wiped his belly with his ripped shirt, paused for a moment to gather his wits and then made his way down the corridor to the last door. The housekeeper, for that was who Nicky presumed she was, was sitting upright in bed, her head drooping on her chest, a book discarded on her lap and a lone candle spluttering on the nightstand. She was of indeterminate age but her hair was gathered in a long grey plait which lay over one nightdress-covered shoulder. As he approached the bed, her head lifted and her eyes suddenly opened, flashing evilly at her intruder. She brought a hand out from under the covers with unexpected speed and Nicky looked down the barrel of a small pistol. Why she didn't cry out, Nicky never knew, as slowly and wordlessly, the woman pulled back the hammer and indicated for Nicky to raise his hands. She never saw the knife coming and before she had a chance to speak she fell back against the pillows, a stunned expression on her face as the blade buried itself deep in her chest, her hand and the gun falling lifelessly onto the soft covers. So much for harmless, old retainers, he thought. They'd all kept weapons by or in their beds. Reynard had been right.

Once more, Nicky retrieved his knife and wiped it on the old woman's nightdress, then soundlessly made his way back out into the kitchen, breathing deeply, closing his mind to the fact he'd just killed five people in cold blood, not to mention the group out in the shanty. He couldn't decide if either Ashcroft or Francis would have been proud or pleased, but he'd simply done what was necessary in order to accomplish his mission. Reynard, he told himself, would be delighted and so would the Dowager! He went over to the back door of the scullery and unbolted it, wincing at the scraping noise it made, before peering out into the night. He could see no sign of Reynard, so he merely left the door ajar and turned to make his way back into the main part of the house. His real quarry now within reach.

Slowly and carefully because of the darkness, he made his slow and careful way through each of the deserted downstairs rooms until he entered what was obviously Bernheim's study. The drapes were drawn and a single candle had burned low on the mantel but the room was empty and the desk was unoccupied and tidy. He was about to turn and make his way upstairs when he changed his mind and decided to have a quick look through the papers on the desk; picking up the candle from the mantel he went over and started to sift through them. As he bent over the documents, he heard the click from behind him and straightened slowly, his hand moving towards the stiletto he'd tucked temporarily into his belt. "Don't even think about it. Keep your hands up and out where I can see them or you'll be dead before you hit the floor." The soft voice hissed, Nicky turned slowly, raised his golden eyes and looked straight into the cold, black ones of Carmelita as she put a small lamp down on a nearby side table.

Chapter Fifteen

"Well, well, just look who we have here," the raised pistol belied the mild tone. "If it isn't my erstwhile lover. I wondered where you'd disappeared to, couldn't stand the pace, eh?" she laughed mirthlessly. "Mind you, I always suspected your heart wasn't in it, I could see it in your eyes." She shook her head, "You didn't really enjoy the ultimate painful pleasure, not your particular vice, was it? Shame really, you're quite the man otherwise," and her eyes roved up and down his body hungrily, lasciviously. "So, if you didn't want my particular style of fucking, it begs the question, what did you want, hmmm?" She cocked her head to one side as she asked the question, more to herself than him.

Playing for time while he reviewed his options, Nicky curled his mouth into a salacious smile as he let his hand rove over the front of his tight breeches, "What makes you so sure I didn't want you, Carmelita? You're certainly quite a woman yourself, more than most men would appreciate or could satisfy, but I certainly did, on both counts I rather think..."

He stared over at her as she continued to look steadily at him. She was wearing tight men's breeches in black, with black topboots and a thin, crimson red silk shirt which clung to her loose, voluptuous breasts and outlined every curve. A wide, black leather belt completed the ensemble. It was men's apparel but she looked far from manly, positively eye-catching Nicky had to admit. Most men would undoubtedly salivate over her appearance, but he found it slightly distasteful in some strange way, probably because he knew what she was like underneath. He speculated if she'd been sleeping alone, or with Bernheim. Either way, he wondered where the man was. Meanwhile, he looked deep into Carmelita's black eyes and caressed himself again, watching as her nipples hardened through the thin material and she licked her lips.

"You're very tempting, Nico, if that's your real name?" she hissed quietly. "Perhaps I ought to get Frederick to let ME whip someone for a change. The thought of stringing you up naked and taking a crop or flogger to that delicious, big, muscled body of yours is more than appealing. I wonder how much you could take before you begged me to either stop... or pleasure you?"

Not by so much as a blink did Nicky change the smile on his face. "Now there's a question for you to ponder over. You actually don't know if I would enjoy it or not, do you Carmelita? Are you a betting woman, I wonder... what odds would you lay that you could arouse me to desperation, rather than shrivel me to uselessness?" he whispered seductively. "You never went that far with me but although it's not my 'particular vice', as you put it, it wouldn't be the first time my naked body has been used and abused by someone else for their pleasure." Long buried memories of Pierre Dupont snaked across his mind. "But of course, they weren't a beautiful, tempting, exciting woman like you." His leonine eyes bored into hers, his quiet voice creeping over her like thick treacle before slowly, Nicky ran his hand up over his abdomen and chest, pulling open his shirt to let his fingers tease and pinch his nipples, tipping his head back and part closing his eyes as if enjoying his own self-torment, his feverish mind hoping in the dimly lit room she'd ignore the shredded and bloodstained lower part of his shirt where the cook's knife had slashed him.

She obviously wasn't interested in his apparel, only in what was inside. Nicky looked at her through narrowed slits; she was riveted, fascinated, tempted... and distracted from continuing to ask him his real purpose there. Slowly, so as not to alarm her, he took a couple of short steps forward in her direction. He never dropped his seductive golden gaze from hers and held his hands out in front of him, palms upwards, wrists close to each other. "Why don't you tie me up in your bed, see how much I'd enjoy that little vice, how aroused I'd be... then what would you like to do to me?" he whispered tantalisingly. As he spoke, another, disconnected part of his brain thought about *Lionesse* and his last night with her. That woman he'd trusted implicitly, knowing she only wanted to give him endless, sweetly erotic and tormenting pleasure, her 'torture' beguiling and completely harmless. But here, he was now walking a tightrope between life and a very unpleasant and painful fate, by a woman who would take enormous pleasure from actually torturing him to death, he suspected. The bizarre parallel between the two didn't escape him. He'd charmed and seduced women for fun and pleasure for most of his adult life; now, his very existence depended on his ability to charm and distract the loathsome specimen in front of him.

"So, Carmelita, *Querida*," he continued, taking another step, his arms still innocently held out in front of him, "wouldn't you like to have me at your mercy? To beat me, then you could fuck me at the same time. Think about it, you'd be so wet, I'd be so aroused, so big and rock hard... you liked that, didn't you? And you know how much pleasure you got with me, how loud you screamed when I fucked you really roughly, every which way... you could do the same to me..." he took another step, his erotic words hypnotising her.

But not quite all Carmelita's mind was so easily distracted. "Who are you?" she whispered slowly. "What are you really doing here?"

"I'm Nico," he drawled slowly in the quiet room, "and I've come to get you." With that, Nicky launched himself forward, knocking the pistol from her grasp with his outstretched hands and dragged her to him. She fought him, biting, scratching and kicking in an effort to escape his hard, enveloping arms as he in turn tried to grasp her hands and subdue her. As they wrestled and fought, she bent slightly but he caught her hand as she went to pull a long knife out of her boot. "Aaah, no you don't, You Evil Bitch. A far more capable woman than you, a good woman, someone you could never aspire to be in a million years, taught me about useful things some rather eccentric ladies might keep in their boots," and he pulled her arm hard up behind her back, making her finally cry out in pain. "In fact," he continued conversationally, "she killed Bernheim's father. Strange coincidence that, wouldn't you say?"

"WHAAAAAT?!" she screeched in shock. "Who ARE you?" she half hissed again and with a big effort, she stamped down on his foot and turned in his arms, one hand going up to scratch at his eyes while the other went to pull his own stiletto out of his belt. Nicky pulled on her hair, dragging her head back as he felt her nails scratch his cheek and then his hands were around her neck, squeezing hard as he felt her pull out his knife and try and stab him with it. Tighter he squeezed, looking down into her eyes with identical blazing hatred as hers, watching the cold, venomous, murderous malice spark out of them. "¿ Quién... ERES... tú? Who... ARE... you?" she choked again as she tried to claw him and stab him, finally abandoning her efforts as she endeavoured to pull his hands from her neck.

"Me? I'm here to get revenge for Rosita and all the others you sent to their deaths. Also, to get payback for Bernheim, but that's a personal matter." He wanted her to know before he killed her that the young girls would have their retribution.

"¿Cómo... te... llamas? What's... your ... name?" she finally whispered, now hardly able to breathe as his hands tightened and her lips turned blue.

"De Bresancourt," he bit back. "Nicholas de Bresancourt... à votre service." He spoke in French as opposed to the Spanish he'd always used with her, as he felt her clawing hands getting weaker and weaker.

"¿Er... eres... fran..cés? You... you're... Fren..?" were her final confused words as her body went limp. Even in death she was still curious about him.

Just at that moment, Nicky felt another presence in the room behind him and as he spun round, Carmelita strangled and limp in his arms, he looked across into the cold, obsidian eyes of Frederick Bernheim, holding a pistol out in front of him.

"I don't believe we've been introduced. DON'T MOVE!" His sibilant voice sent shivers up Nicky's spine as he spoke in French. "Je *m'appel Frederique Bernheim. Me llamo Frederico Bernheim,"* he repeated in Spanish. "It seems you have a personal matter to take up with me?" he continued in Spanish.

Nicky realised he'd overheard his exchange with Carmelita. Bernheim continued conversationally, now in French, "De Bresancourt? de Bresancourt? Now where have I heard that name before?" he paused theatrically, "Ah yes, my father. You wouldn't have anything to do with the de Bresancourt family from Valenciennes, by any chance?" he purred menacingly.

His instinct had been right all along. Nicky had intuitively known the son knew all about the father's activities.

Like father, like son. The two men looked at each other impassively, sudden venomous hatred blazing like a burning fuse wire between them as they recognized the other knew about Edgar Bernheim, who and what he'd been, each wanting revenge for actions connected with him that they believed had so negatively impacted on their personal lives. However, whereas Frederick Bernheim obviously used his work for Bonaparte as a convenience, Nicky believed passionately in his work for Wellington and now Ashcroft, wanting to see Europe rid of the menace who had torn it apart for nearly two decades, responsible for the death and injury of millions of soldiers and civilians across the Continent.

"And so, you know The Shadow I take it? And the de Mornays perhaps?" Nicky's stomach roiled, but he strove to keep his face impassive. "And by the way, who is this paragon who killed my father? I had no idea it was a woman."

Nicky's mind raced, aghast at what had been overheard and as he was about to drop Carmelita's body and reach for his own pistol or his knife, she stirred in his arms. He'd thought her gone, but he'd been distracted by Bernheim's entrance and she was still alive. Just.

"Fred'rico," she whispered weakly, *"Ayúdame!* Help me…"

"Now why should I do that, My Dear? I rather think our guest here has saved me a job." Bernheim's callous voice mused.

"B… bu… Fred'rico, you nee' me. I… was goin' wi' you," she whispered, hardly audible. "We're a… pair. So… suited."

"Possibly," Bernheim shrugged, "but really? What would I want with an extremely common and dirty prostitute, My Dear? You've merely served your purpose while I was here in Spain. Like all our other associates. What makes you think you're any different? Really now, getting ideas above your station? That will never do." He raised his head and looked at Nicky directly, "Your use was short-lived, but equally beneficial. With the gold I've now acquired, I can finally find out about you, your connections and finally, who killed my father; even who The Shadow is or was. Gold opens doors and loosens even the stickiest of tongues." With that, he raised his pistol, took aim and pulled the trigger.

Chapter Sixteen

C armelita died with eyes wide and mouth gaping, a look of total disbelief on her face and, as he held her in his arms, Nicky felt the pistol ball, shot from such close range, pass straight through her slender body and directly into his. He dropped her and automatically reached for his own pistol, bringing it up to take a shot, but the ball had gone deep into his body and he was too dazed; his aim was off and the ball whizzed past Bernheim's head. "Too late..." Bernheim hissed malevolently, turning to laugh cruelly as Nicky slowly, numbly and wordlessly sank to his knees, the Frenchman waiting for him to die as blood spurted out from a large hole in the side of his abdomen, turning his white shirt red and trickling down into his breeches. As he crumpled and heard Bernheim's crowing laugh, "Two for the price of one..." Nicky also heard a voice from a distance.

"Not quite, You Bastard! I'M not too late. In fact I'm just in time, thanks be to God." Another shot rang out and Bernheim gasped as the ball threw him back against his desk, blood flowering across his upper chest, near his shoulder.

In horror at what he'd just witnessed, Reynard hurried across to Nicky as he collapsed to the floor, unseeing and uncaring that Bernheim had managed to stagger to his feet and disappear out of the door behind him. By the time he'd looked around, the man was long gone.

Reynard's white face bent over Nicky's unconscious body as he put his hand up to see if he could find a pulse in the young man's neck. Finally, with relief, he found one... faint but still beating... and for the third time that night he raised his face heavenward and muttered words of thanks. He went and lit another, larger lamp and brought it back to look for the wound... and then he saw. The ball had gone into Nicky's side and was obviously lodged there, somewhere deep behind his ribs. Blood was slowly pumping out and a brief further check for injuries revealed a long slash across Nicky's abdomen that was also oozing. Reynard hurried back to the kitchens where he'd come in through the open door and picked up some towels from the pile of clean linens he spotted on a table, waiting to be either packed for the coach trip on the morrow or taken upstairs for storage. Rushing back to Nicky, he pushed a thick towel inside his blood-soaked shirt to stem the flow and with another on top, finally pulled his belt up higher to hold them in place. Unable to do more, Reynard sat back and thought rapidly about how he could get his wounded man back to Madrid, determined to do so, then find a doctor to try and save Nicky. It was down to him and he would move heaven and earth to save this man's life, if it were humanly possible.

Moments later, Reynard hurried to the stables, limping as fast as he could, to bring out four horses which he hitched to the waiting travelling carriage. It was standing on the gravel, half packed and ready for Bernheim's departure.

Nicky was a dead weight. He was big and heavy, his body hard and well-muscled from the active life he'd always led. Reynard was old, crippled and not the fit man he once was. He was quite tubby round the middle through his fondness for good food and plenty of wine; a grizzled individual, he was now the wrong side of sixty-five, with a splintered thigh bone. However, he'd been a brawny, well-built and quite athletic man in his youth, as befitted the leader of his small tribe which he'd taken on in his early twenties when his father had been killed, so some of his former strength remained. What he was lacking in fitness, however, dogged determination and bloody-mindedness was still there in abundance, along with his cool head. Somehow, therefore, he managed to half-drag, half-carry the unconscious Nicky out to the coach and topple him inside, wedged on the floor between cushions and rugs. At least he wouldn't fall off the seat, Reynard thought with grim humour. He crossed himself and prayed to God Nicky would survive as he hobbled to open the front gates and lead the coach through. He hurried back and closed the doors to the house, shut the gates after him, retrieved their own horses which he tied to the back of the coach and finally, shaking with exhaustion and no little pain in his leg, struggled up on to the driver's seat to make his way back to Madrid and seek help as fast as he could.

In the light of dawn, the remote villa stood silent and empty behind its high walls and metal gates. No one would dream there was a fortune in gold sitting in open wagons in one of its outbuildings, there for anyone to take. Reynard hadn't a care about a single gold coin, nor the concerns of the British army high command, nor some vague individual in London worried about the activities of a French agent. All he wanted was to get Nicky to a surgeon to try to prevent his death. For him, life was everything and so were old friends. Possessions, treasure or revenge counted for nothing.

Chapter Seventeen

Bernheim quickly realised de Bresancourt was not alone after all. He had no idea how many other associates might also be inside or outside the villa. The non-appearance of any of his household servants, or the men in the outbuildings, suggested they'd been captured or killed. Therefore, ever the survivor and concerned only for himself and his self-preservation at all costs, he disappeared down to the cellars where he knew a secret tunnel would lead him out, far on the other side of the perimeter wall. His injury was painful and he was bleeding, but the ball had missed his heart and lungs by inches and gone into his shoulder; he could patch it up temporarily to stop any more blood loss and at least he could still walk, albeit slowly. He knew where to find transport in the nearby hamlet which would take him into Madrid, and reckoned he could just about make it to the village outskirts on foot. His connexions in the city would help him find a doctor and then get him back to France. He couldn't be bothered with more of Bonaparte's dirty work, the man's days were numbered he felt sure. Besides, he'd made enough money over the last few years to retire from espionage and take his time to decide what to do next.

He hurriedly picked up a voluminous cloak and a bag containing money left in the tunnel for emergencies, then made his way out as fast as his injury would permit. He'd learned long ago, both from his father and others in a similar line of work for Bonaparte, to always have an escape route from wherever he was living or working.

As he staggered along, Bernheim's brain seethed and his blood boiled to the point he felt sick at the thought of all the gold he was having to leave behind. All the months and years of planning, all gone to waste. And all because of that fair-haired man, a man with a name from the past: de Bresancourt. The name that had been in his father's personal and private notebook. However, he'd always assumed his parent had killed off the aristocratic family with the unusual tawny blond hair as they'd all disappeared, but he had a lead now to the mystery of his father's unfinished business and premature demise. He would therefore go back to France, instead of somewhere civilised and safer and away from this interminable war. If it was the last thing he did, he would investigate once again what had become of the de Bresancourts of Valenciennes, trace the de Mornays and find The Shadow... and also now the woman who had killed his father, Edgar, also presumably his faithful lieutenant, Pierre Dupont.

He'd been kept well out of his father's affairs as a growing boy, invisible and away at an exclusive school in Vienna, receiving the best education and learning how to grow up to be a gentleman of leisure, a cosmopolitan Gentleman who could speak several languages and be at ease with nobility and anyone with wealth... all this while his father did his work. Edgar Bernheim had promised his son that by the time Frederick came of age they would be able to live a life of comfort and ease with plenty of money to indulge themselves and mix with the highest echelons of society. They would live somewhere civilised and warm, like Venice or Naples, or even Vienna... when Edgar had made enough money from his activities in Normandy.

Edgar and Pierre had been an efficient and feared pair. Frederick's father had governed Normandy with a rod of iron, ostensibly keeping the region safe for its residents, especially the more noble or wealthy ones, many of whom he expected unofficially to pay for their 'security'. Dupont carried out a lot of his father's dirty work when necessary, as he ran his little 'protection' sideline. Brains and brawn, a perfect duo. Well, someone had to do the dirty work and the uncouth, vicious scum that Dupont was, had been perfect for the job. His father only involved himself when necessary, or when a more 'delicate' or 'refined' solution was needed to extricate information or money from those people who tried to avoid paying their dues.

Rumour had it both The Shadow and his supposed fortune were never found, any more than his father had found that of the ducal Valenciennes family, their famed golden hoard. Either would do for him now because the money his father had salted away had never been quite enough to retire on – not once he'd bought or 'acquired' their houses in Paris and Vienna, the villas outside Madrid and in the south of France, plus a few others in various civilised boltholes across Europe where they'd occasionally holidayed during his formative years. He'd thought there was more money hidden away somewhere, for emergencies, knowing his father's habits as well as he did, but he'd never been able to locate it and that had infuriated him. Similarly, his father's unexpected, sudden and mysterious death had been the biggest inconvenience to his future life plans. But there had still been a nice tidy sum lodged in the bank in Hanover which had been his official inheritance. With that, he had led a safe and luxurious life for several years after his father's death, while the Revolution and anarchy ran its course in Paris and across France, but then war started in Europe. He'd travelled widely, spending money and generally enjoying himself and mixing in well-to-do and aristocratic circles, indulging his sexual idiosyncrasies, until his funds had inevitably started to run low as the new century dawned. With his knowledge of several languages, travel experience and the right contacts, plus a little arm-twisting or bribery in the right places, he'd inveigled himself into the diplomatic service of Bonaparte's new Republic and from there his other talents, many learned from his father, had soon made him indispensable. He was now one of the Emperor's most efficient agents, when either espionage was required or 'a little local trouble' or diversion needed arranging. It had also given him the opportunity to follow in his father's other footsteps and feather his own nest as in his view, Bonaparte's idea of reward was laughable. So far as Frederick was concerned, *Liberté, Égalité, Fraternité* were nonsense. Men never had been free, equal or brothers, it was the way of the world and always would be. Some men were superior to others in intellect and capability and it was every man for himself, look after number one; it was his father's and now his personal credo.

There were times Frederick had wished his father had invested some of the fortune he'd 'acquired', in plantations in the Americas or Far East, which would have provided a permanent income for both of them, instead of spending his capital on the assumption he would sooner or later 'acquire' a fortune from one of his targets... but then Edgar Bernheim hadn't expected to die so abruptly and unexpectedly. It was too late for Frederick to bother about that except it still niggled sometimes and he would get to the bottom of the mystery, he promised himself. After all, he was his father's son and he'd learned his lessons well, except he was going to make a success of matters and live to enjoy the fruits of his endeavours. He was far cleverer and far more capable than most other men, probably even his father. He told himself he deserved it, his father should never have let himself be killed before his work was done and carelessly leave his son to fend for himself after he'd promised him a gilt-edged life. He was far more careful that his father and no one was going to stop him achieving his ambition. He would have his gilt-edged life, just a bit later than intended.

Chapter Eighteen

I n Madrid, a white-faced Reynard staggered into the tavern where he, Nicky and now his two nephews were staying, ready to rendezvous with the men Wellington was sending to help, while Reynard and Nicky went about their deadly business. The older nephew took one alarmed look at his uncle's face, retrieved a bottle of brandy from the bar and simply thrust it into his hand.

Reynard was almost out on his feet after driving the large coach back to Madrid over bumpy or half made tracks and roads, with horses going hell for leather as the vehicle lurched and careered along; the pain in his thigh had been excruciating but desperation to get help for the man inside was paramount. As the horses had thundered along, the irony of his situation didn't escape Reynard.

Aside from his own feelings for Nicky and his long and close friendship with Francis, he owed Eddie, Nicky's step-father, his life. Eddie, himself a scarred cripple with a crushed pelvis thanks to Pierre Dupont many years previously in his youth, had rescued Reynard when he'd been shot in the back and leg. Despite his disability, Eddie had hauled him from the ruins of Rouen Fortress where they were attempting to rescue Francis, who'd been caught by Edgar Bernheim, himself determined to acquire The Shadow's supposed fortune. At huge risk to his own life and no fighter, Eddie had literally dragged Reynard out of the building and on to a cart to be driven back to the tavern where Cat, Carlotta and Benjy had been anxiously waiting. Benjy had tended his injuries and undoubtedly saved both his leg and his life. So, there was no way Reynard was going to abandon Eddie's beloved step-son. In his view, if Eddie hadn't rescued him, Benjy would have had no one to save, so he was in his debt and he was determined to repay it.

Reynard downed half the bottle of brandy in one long gulp but refused to sit down until his nephews and a groom helped him carry Nicky up to a bedroom. While he drained the rest of the brandy bottle, now sitting next to Nicky's bed and watching over him anxiously, he sent the two youths off to find the Old Moor, an Arab Reynard had sometimes consulted when his bad leg was particularly painful. The man had all sorts of medicines and therapies neither Spanish nor French doctors had heard of, or dismissed as either dangerous, useless, or barbaric and heathen; however, they'd helped Reynard recover along with massage and gentle exercises. The Moor had considered the option of cutting Reynard's thigh open again and trying to re-set the splintered bone, but decided it wasn't worth the pain and risk after so long and said he should just stick to his treatment and be grateful he had his leg and could get around. Reynard had accepted his opinion. Some of the Spanish and also French doctors had told him they'd cut the limb off if it pained him too much, their idea of a solution. Reynard's response to them all had been unrepeatable. He therefore didn't trust any surgeons, butchers he called them. He told his nephews not to come back without the Moor, to turn the city upside down if necessary to find him or where he currently was, that money was no object if the man prevaricated or was busy elsewhere. This was urgent and a matter of life or death.

The Old Moor, Ahmed Mansoor, was a skilled and learned physician and surgeon who had studied many medical treatments and ideas from China and the Far East, dismissing nothing as irrelevant and possessing all manner of herbs and drugs he'd acquired from there. With Reynard anxiously hovering, after digging around relentlessly causing more and more blood to flow from the unconscious man, he finally pulled out the pistol ball, sewed Nicky back up, then also sewed and bandaged up the nastily oozing slash across his abdomen. That he was still alive, Ahmed attributed to Nicky's youth, fitness and strength, along with Reynard's efforts to stem the flow of blood. Fortunately, the ball had hit a rib as it entered his body which had deflected it from its original trajectory and therefore avoided hitting any major organs, particularly his liver and kidneys, stomach, pancreas and spine, although it had gone through the bottom of one of his lungs. He told Reynard Nicky had lost a dangerous amount of blood and the ball had been difficult to retrieve, plus there was a lot of other tissue damage inside. Ahmed said they should all thank Allah it had been his lucky night and privately sent a prayer to Mohammed his luck would hold.

Nicky was still unconscious and Ahmed, his pocket now full of gold from a thankful Reynard, said he would call back in a few hours to check on his patient as he could do no more for him at the present.

Leaving his nephews to watch over Nicky and call him if he woke or even twitched, Reynard went to his own room and collapsed into bed, bone weary and completely drained. Despite his deep, deep fear and anxiety and the throbbing pain in his leg for which Ahmed had given him a remedy, but which had only diminished slightly, he slept like the dead for hours.

Wellington's men finally appeared the following afternoon. They were a small, disparate group of half a dozen men and their leader, Julius, one of Scovell's trusted code breakers who spoke fluent Spanish, met Reynard in a quiet corner of the tavern where his nephews had brought him from their rendezvous point in the city centre.

Without going into details, Reynard told Julius all the consignments of gold had been stolen by the French agent, Frederick Bernheim, but through the sole efforts of Nicholas de Bresancourt, they had been traced and located and were ready to be collected and returned to either the British or the Spanish forces. Unfortunately, de Bresancourt himself had been wounded in the effort to retrieve the gold and capture Bernheim. The latter, also wounded, had unfortunately escaped. However, at least the gold was safe, he said; Wellington and Rothschild's should be pleased and suitably grateful. Some of the men responsible for the actual hijackings of the gold consignments were still at large, but Reynard had acquired their locations from de Bresancourt and would pass on the information to Julius so his men could catch up with them. He, Reynard, had arranged for the care of de Bresancourt and would pass on any message to the wounded man as he was still too ill to see anyone.

Under pressure from Julius, slightly suspicious at hearing the whole story from a gypsy, Reynard took him upstairs to Nicky's room so he could see for himself that the man was indeed badly injured but was being afforded the best of care. Ahmed was at that moment in Nicky's room, carefully tending the wound with the help of a young assistant he'd brought back with him. Although looking slightly askance at the swarthy, turbaned, bearded individual in long flowing Arab robes, Julius could see the man knew what he was about, so he retreated back out of the room, satisfied he'd been told the truth.

Reynard left Julius to see to the rounding up of whatever men they could still locate who had been involved in the gold heists and he agreed to come back in a couple of days' time to meet up with Reynard again for further news of de Bresancourt and to convey any message back to Wellington.

Reynard was torn about sending a message back to England to Francis. Ahmed had told him Nicky should live, providing no infection set in, but infection or not, the man had been seriously wounded by a particularly large pistol ball and there was no telling what other damage had been done internally; his fate was down to the will of Allah. Not having any faith in Allah or Mohammed, Reynard went to church and prayed to God, Jesus and Mary, but put off sending any message. He did, however, pen a short note for Wellington, via Julius, in which he told Nicky's 'uncle' that his 'nephew' had saved the day at great risk to himself, without any assistance and therefore, in his opinion his King and Country owed him a great debt, notwithstanding he was now lying seriously wounded although there was hope of recovery.

Wellington eventually replied to Reynard with a personal hand-written message saying that he did indeed appreciate everything his 'nephew' had done, he was sorry his friends had missed the party and his 'nephew' had been sick, but he was glad to hear his 'nephew' would be able to play again another day. Also, that he would pass on this news to everyone who would be interested.

Satisfied he had done what he could to ensure Nicky's superiors understood even a small part of what he'd achieved and done for his country, at great personal risk to himself, Reynard now concentrated on doing what he could to aid his recovery.

Ahmed's concern had come to pass and Nicky tossed and turned in the grip of a fever caused by an infection in his wound, which was not caused by the bullet wound or any of Ahmed's pristine surgical instruments, but rather the carving knife. Had they but known, it had been cutting up joints of meat and all manner of other matter in the kitchens beforehand.

For over a fortnight Nicky rambled about his dungeon in Rouen Fortress, screaming out at tormented and horrifying images in his head, appearing to try to fight off Bernheim and Dupont... then raving about lionesses, masks and necklaces... and Sooty. The first three Reynard understood. The patient's torment disturbed him greatly especially when he and either Ahmed or his assistant, or sometimes all three of them, tried to calm and pacify the thrashing around and terrible child-like sobbing. Reynard had initially wondered what Nicky the little boy had suffered and seen during his time incarcerated in the terrible place but he now had a good idea, and it both appalled and angered him mightily. And then, the delirious man seemed to move on and the rest meant nothing at all to the old gypsy, although he understood references to lions and that made him laugh... but he was curious about what had happened to Nicky's chain and little lion. He, too, knew how much it meant to him, but he simply presumed it was safe in London and that Nicky hadn't wanted to risk losing it there in the Peninsula while he was involved in the war. His ramblings about

Sooty were incoherent, but at least Reynard knew to whom he was referring. One minute he was raging at her, the next he apparently wanted to kiss her. Reynard gave up, he could make neither head nor tail of any of it. He concluded a lot of Nicky's delirium was about the women in his life who were obviously confusing him. Reynard smiled to himself. Sometimes he was glad he was old and didn't have to deal with such romantic problems any longer. So he simply kept a vigil by Nicky's bed and held his hand, hoping his familiar touch would somehow percolate the mists of the sick man's delirium and provide a reassuring presence.

He thought often about The Firebrand, his Firebrand, the woman who had married his friend, Francis. This latest adventure had brought the past all back to him and he'd recognised the stiletto and knew to whom it belonged before Nicky had mentioned it. He'd been smitten with Marie-Catherine de Mornay from the moment she'd arrived in his gypsy camp with the Spanish dancer, Carlotta; he'd watched her duel with The Shadow and fall in love with him, almost love at first sight, and he'd been infatuated ever since. None of the gypsy women who had passed through his life had come anywhere near her, not even the lovely Carlotta. He'd never forgotten her beauty, her feistiness and passion, nor the many times her husband had saved his life in the years they'd been associated, smuggled and fought together; but that was all in the past. He just wanted to save the life of the young man in his care. The thought of having to send a message about his death to Francis, or The Firebrand and Eddie, would break his heart, just as he knew it would break theirs.

Chapter Nineteen

Ahmed and his assistant worked tirelessly, day and night, to care for Nicky, having been promised a large reward by Reynard if they saved his life. Not allowing anyone else near their patient, other than Reynard who insisted on sitting in his room to keep watch, they tried endless tinctures and herbs to clear his infection and break the fever. They bathed his body to keep it cool when the fever raged at its height and his temperature soared. When he shivered with the chills, they kept the fire lit in his room and Reynard brought in more furs and blankets sent for from his caravan to pile on to the bed. They forced water down his throat to keep him hydrated and frequently massaged his chest to keep his breathing clear and stop a build-up of phlegm or mucus. At one point when that didn't work and their patient was having trouble breathing, a white-faced Reynard, beside himself with fear and anxiety, gaped as Ahmed cut the side of Nicky's chest open between a couple of ribs and sucked out the fluid that was clogging his lungs through a small silver tube.

Reynard simply watched in awe and fascination and frequently went to church to pray, unable to do anything else. Finally, some three weeks after Reynard had brought him to the tavern, almost but not quite fatally wounded, Nicky's fever finally broke and he slipped into a calm, restful sleep. Ahmed smiled at Reynard and told him the worst was now over and he expected his young patient would hopefully make a full recovery. Reynard went out to church yet again, lit more candles and offered up prayers of relieved and heartfelt thanks. He then returned to the tavern, ordered a large flagon of wine with some bread and cheese and sausage and sat down to write a long, overdue, letter to Francis. When that was done, he ordered more wine and drank himself to a stupor and his nephews had to carry him to bed.

Reynard told Francis everything that had happened since he'd got the message in the saddle, at least as much as he knew. He suspected there was more to the story about Carmelita than Nicky had told him but since she was now dead, it seemed somewhat irrelevant. Bernheim was another matter, however. Reynard passed on everything he'd learned from Nicky about the man, his associates and his plans. Also, although he had shot him, Bernheim had unfortunately escaped and despite being wounded, had seemingly disappeared into thin air, with no trace. Neither his men nor Wellington's had any idea where he might be. Reynard told Francis that Nicky had been searching for the Frenchman for months before tracking him down through Carmelita, and the man was even more elusive than The Shadow had been!

Finally, he told Francis what had happened to Nicky, but he ended the letter with the reassuring news that although he'd been desperately ill, his fever had broken and he was assuredly now on the mend, under Reynard's own personal care. He told Francis he intended to take him back to his camp near the coast outside Barcelona, away from Wellington and his army, the French, the Spanish rebels and the fighting, to allow him to recover and convalesce in the Spanish sun with a bit of help from gypsy wine, women and song; the best recuperative medicine in his opinion.

When he'd finished, Reynard sat back and looked at the many pages he'd scrawled. It was quite a story he'd written and he was exhausted, but exhilarated in a way. The past few weeks had flown by since he'd got his first message from Nicky but now, as soon as Nicky was well enough to travel, he would indeed take him back to his encampment, either to stay near Barcelona or move up to southern France if they wanted to. He himself needed to rest as well.

He rubbed his leg as it had started to ache again and he made a mental note to see Ahmed for something to treat it before they left Madrid, something that didn't make him fall asleep all the time like the other medicine he'd been taking since that first night he'd arrived with his wounded friend. He smiled to himself. He'd hardly given his own injury a thought over the past weeks, he'd been so concerned with Nicky. In fact, it certainly hadn't stopped him helping Nicky when they'd broken into Bernheim's villa. He obviously needed more active interests in his life, he decided, than sitting in his caravan, eating and drinking too much and doing the odd bit of trading now and again. Some more energetic sex for a start! He concluded he'd had his last adventure and he would now redouble his efforts to find a wife and settle down, once and for all; a feisty woman, like Francis's Firebrand, or the nearest he could get to her. Also, making wine would fill his time and keep him active. It seemed a far less hazardous occupation than getting involved with the Granville family's adventures, no matter how exhilarating that was. His efforts at Bernheim's villa had brought home to him that he was getting old and he thought he needed to devote what energies he had left to fathering sons and not haring about the countryside killing or rescuing people.

Nicky slept for another two days. When he finally opened his eyes, it was to see a worried-looking Reynard sitting by his bed, holding his hand. Memory, at first hazy, suddenly flooded back and, his voice hoarse from lack of use, his first words were, "Did y'kill 'im, Reynar'?"

Reynard smiled at the pale and gaunt young man, now propped up against the pillows. Relief written all over his face, he simply shook his head. "No, I didn't, just wounded him. Unfortunately, he got away." He sighed and squeezed Nicky's hand, "But frankly, I don't care, it was you I was concerned about and thank God you're still alive. I was dreading having to write to Francis and tell him otherwise."

Nicky smiled up at the grizzled gypsy, coughed slightly and sighed as his brain fog started to clear, "Thank you, Reynard; I owe you my life. In fact, thank you isn't enough really, but I don't know what else to say."

"You don't have to say anything, it was a pleasure," he grinned down at the younger man. "What was I going to do, leave you there to bleed to death?" he chuckled. "Besides, I haven't had so much excitement for years, not since the days of The Shadow. He had to save my hide often enough."

"What happened to the gold?" Nicky asked curiously.

"Your 'uncle's' men finally arrived and I've told them we have it safe," he smirked. "In the meantime, they've traced and rounded up all the men they can find who were involved with the ambushes of the gold consignments, according to your list of addresses. Most were still hanging about the city, waiting to be paid, luckily for us, but a couple had already buggered off. Julius, he's in charge of the British unit, is waiting on instructions from Wellington as to what to do with the gold now, whether to take it back to him or hand it over to the Spanish. But it's still in exactly the same place we left it." He looked thoughtful, "Actually, given what we witnessed at the villa, I'm amazed Bernheim left so many 'loose ends'. I can only assume he'd made plans for all the men involved to 'disappear', but those plans never got carried out because we interrupted him and his exit arrangements. Maybe that was going to be Carmelita's job since she had no qualms about disposing of Carlos, but who knows..." he shrugged.

Nicky merely nodded. He looked at the new worry lines on Reynard's face, "I feel as weak as a kitten; I've been quite ill, haven't I? How long for? I don't remember much after Bernheim shot Carmelita."

"You've been out of it for about three weeks and you're still very weak. The pistol ball went straight through that bitch and hit you in the side of your chest, but it was a big bastard. The good news is it hit a rib on its way so didn't go as deep as it could have as it got deflected. The bad news is it was deep enough and caught the bottom of one of your lungs and some big blood vessels, but, fortunately, no other critical organs. My God, Nicky, you lost so much blood, it was touch and go for a bit. Then, you got an infection in that other cut you got and a fever set in, for nearly a fortnight. Heavens, Boy, did you ramble on! But thank God, you've made it," he let out a huge sigh of relief. "Now you can rest before I take you back to my camp to recuperate. There'll be no more wall climbing for you for a while yet."

Nicky tried to disagree, saying he was fine to stay in Madrid, but Reynard held up his hand. "No, don't argue with me, it's not up for discussion. I've told Francis you're coming to stay with me in the sunshine for some recuperative gypsy food, wine, women and song, so that's exactly what you're going to do. Though in your present state even that will be beyond you for a few weeks, M'Lad!" He gave Nicky a broad wink, "I'll see what I can do to find you a pretty nurse or two to help..."

Nicky went to laugh, but as he did so he was hit by an excruciating pain in his chest and abdomen and his head fell back in agony. Reynard merely looked at his white face knowingly. "See, what did I tell you? You'll have to take it easy and let yourself heal, not just on the outside. The doctor says it will take a while for the muscle and tissue inside to heal too. That ball went deep and did a lot of damage. But a bit of warm sun, sea breezes, plenty of rest and good food will work wonders."

Nicky lay back and closed his eyes for a while, exhausted by even the short conversation he'd just had. A thought drifted across his mind, "What was I rambling about when I had the fever?" he asked curiously, opening his golden eyes to look closely at Reynard.

"I couldn't understand it at all. You were talking in English, French and Spanish, confusing doesn't cover it, especially as my English isn't wonderful at the best of times, as you know, more than rusty these days. At first it was your childhood and what happened in Rouen Fortress, I assume. Oh Nicky, I hadn't a clue," Reynard gripped his hand and grimaced in disgust as he shook his head at the memories of Nicky's telling mutterings and distress, "then, you seemed to move on and there were lions and lionesses, necklaces, masks, then Sooty. You talked a lot about her," Reynard sighed.

"Really?" Nicky looked thoughtful and then slightly amused; he refused to think about Rouen.

"You sounded very muddled and mixed up. However, women tend to do that to a man," Reynard mused and sighed. "Lions I'm used to, but lionesses? I didn't understand that at all. Are you still obsessed with the wretched things, even at your age?" he chuckled.

"Only the two-legged variety, Reynard, I can promise you. I think they're even more of a problem than anything you'll find in the jungle," and with that enigmatic comment, he closed his eyes again, lay back and went to sleep, a smile curling his lips.

But interspersed with his dreams of *Lionesse*, Nicky fretted endlessly about his last exchange with Bernheim and the knowledge the man might try and trace The Shadow; that would mean Francis, Cat, his Papa and perhaps even Sooty would all be at risk. As Reynard watched him toss and turn and mutter incoherently again, he knew there was something else on the mind of the young man and resolved to sit down with him when they got back to his camp and encourage him to talk about it.

Ahmed categorically refused to let Nicky leave until he could walk properly and his wound had healed sufficiently, so Nicky lay in bed with nothing to do but gaze out through the window at the sky, doze, dream and fret, the slightest exertion still causing him considerable pain, even using a bed pan or chamber pot, which he loathed. The various books Reynard found for him had bored him rigid and his only entertainment was playing cards or backgammon with his older companion. However, one afternoon, a few days later, Reynard wandered into his room, a big, pleased grin on his face.

"Ho, Reynard," sighed Nicky. "You're looking very satisfied with yourself. What've you been up to? More than me, that's for sure."

"Finding something to keep you amused, hopefully," laughed the gypsy and grappled inside his leather jacket to pull out a small hissing kitten which he promptly dropped down on the bed covers into Nicky's lap. "There's a small litter of them in the stables at the back of the *taberna* and I rather thought one might keep you company." He smiled happily as he watched Nicky's sad face light up with pleasure.

As ever, the spitting ball of fluff soon turned into a purring furry bundle in Nicky's patient, gentle hands and a short while after, Reynard left him to it, Nicky asleep again with the kitten dozing happily on his chest.

Chapter Twenty

Reynard's lengthy letter reached Francis a couple of weeks later and he read it with mounting concern and no little distress when he reached the end and the information about Nicky's injury. It was obvious from Reynard's carefully chosen words that the damage had been serious and he prayed Nicky would come through. He was thankful beyond belief Reynard had been around to help and he knew the old gypsy would move heaven and earth to get the young man the best medical attention, even if they were in Spain with a war raging around them. Francis understood his old friend well.

He realised he should visit Ashcroft and pass on the information he now had about the gold and Bernheim, but he also wondered if he should tell Bella about Nicky being wounded. He rather suspected, if it wasn't for the baby, she'd want to drop everything and run down to Spain and nurse him herself, so he was at least thankful that the new addition to the family would prevent her from doing that.

He smiled as he thought of little Thérèse with her fluff of blonde hair and golden eyes. Nicky would have his own little lioness now as she was the spitting image of her father, even he could see that without the constant rhapsodising he got from his wife, Eddie and Bella. So he would tell Bella, but perhaps a slightly expurgated version so she wouldn't worry too much.

He read the long letter through once more and called for his carriage, setting off for another interesting confrontation with the enigmatic Head of the Department of Information.

Chapter Twenty-One

It was another month before Ahmed reluctantly agreed to let Nicky leave Madrid. He could at least now get out of bed and walk the few steps, with the aid of a stick, to and from his room door, which he did frequently to let his kitten in and out. The pair had become inseparable and Nicky spent many hours sitting in an armchair doing nothing more challenging than pulling bits of string across the floor which were attached to screwed up pieces of paper, or bunches of chicken feathers, for the frenetic animal to chase and pounce upon... all that interspersed with feeding the greedy little puss tasty morsels of chicken or fish from the meals he had no appetite for. The activity usually wore them both out and they'd then repair back to his bed to sleep off their exertions.

Ahmed and his assistant had to half carry Nicky down the stairs and help him into a carriage for the journey to Barcelona, but despite his pain and discomfort, the pleasure of finally being out of his room put a relieved smile on his pale face. Much to his amusement and Reynard's pained expressions, coloured by frequent epithets, the kitten yowled and complained continuously in her wicker basket on the seat next to him as he and the tired gypsy set off in the early summer sunshine to return to his camp.

Reynard was also glad to see the back of Madrid. He'd returned to the villa with Julius and a couple of his trusted men. While the latter had seen to the disposal of the decomposing, reeking, maggot-infested cadavers, Reynard had taken the opportunity to go through Bernheim's study and desk on the offchance there was anything interesting to be had there about the man's father and his connection to The Shadow and his associates. But there was nothing, so Reynard happily left it all to Julius, who had also taken responsibility for seeing to the removal of the gold wagons. An extremely large, heavily-armed escort was on its way to transfer them on to their original recipients.

Before he left, Julius had visited Nicky and reported that the British were on the move again and heading north-east, up towards the border, pushing the French back and everyone was expecting a major battle to take place soon. Then he took his leave, telling Nicky that both Wellington and Rothschild's were extremely grateful for what he'd done and Wellington sent him his best wishes for a speedy recovery.

By the end of the summer, the pale and injured man who could barely walk when he'd arrived, had now made a good recovery. As Nicky became more mobile, his appetite had returned and he was once again looking fit, tanned and healthy, albeit a bit thinner, but not nearly as gaunt as he had been on his arrival. He'd spent the summer helping Reynard's nephews with their horses during the day, as well as improving his guitar playing with one of the musicians in the tribe during the long summer evenings. He'd gone down to a nearby beach and swum in the warm sea, gently exercising his body on the soft sand, but the deep wound still pained him when he stretched or got jolted, as he discovered when trying to ride a particularly bad-tempered horse. It was then he realised it would be many months yet before he was fully healed internally, just as the Moorish doctor had warned him. His tawny good looks, so different from the swarthy gypsies, had been a particular attraction for the young women in the camp and he'd spread his favours evenly around so as not to cause too much trouble amongst them, much to Reynard's quiet amusement. But he was homesick and restless. September arrived and in Reynard's caravan one evening, he told him he was returning to England.

"Now that Wellington has the French in retreat, life in Spain should be a lot more peaceful and we'll have to wait and see what happens to Bonaparte on his eastern borders," he mused over a glass of wine.

"But Bernheim is still out there, isn't he?" said Reynard with concern. Nicky had finally shared with him, when they'd first arrived back at his camp, the details of his exchange with Bernheim before he'd been shot. "So I know you're not going to rest until you've caught up with him, you'll get no real peace until you do. Will you?" his eyes narrowed as he regarded the younger man, lounging indolently in a chair opposite him.

Nicky shook his head. "No, you're right, and I've got to tell Francis. He has a right to know, Papa and Cat too. Not that I think Bernheim would dare come to London, he'd be mad to."

Reynard looked at Nicky shrewdly, "But he is mad, isn't he?" he said softly. "Not a gibbering idiot, but someone extremely clever, irrational and deranged, which is far, far more dangerous. And that's why you're fretting?"

"Yes," Nicky said with conviction. "I know he'll come after us all sooner or later, unless I find him first," and he whispered again to himself, "I just know he will... it was the way he spoke, just before he shot me... I could tell..."

"Well, time enough for that, Lad, you just get yourself properly fit again before you go haring off on another mission to find him." He suddenly grinned, "When you can wield a sword, or climb up to a balcony without wincing, then you have my permission to go and get rid of him."

Nicky laughed and bowed his head to Reynard, "Oh yes, Master, whatever you say, Master."

"In the meantime," laughed Reynard back, "you'd better go home and sort your life out. Organise your women... decide which one you want, hmmm?"

Nicky looked at Reynard with raised eyebrows, "What makes you think I want any of them?"

"Well, listening to you ramble when you're asleep, let alone when you're drunk... oh yes, I've heard you... you seem to want one or the other of them, depending on what day of the week it is," Reynard chuckled. "You just don't know whether it's a lioness or a sisters that isn't a sister," he chuckled. "Boy, are you confused. Why can't you make do with an ordinary woman like the rest of us poor souls?"

Nicky chuckled too. "Ordinary? No woman is ordinary, Reynard, surely you've worked that one out by now? In fact ordinary doesn't cover it, they're a totally different species to us men. Apart from looking different, they think and act differently, nothing is remotely logical or rational; my little puss has more sense than most." He grinned and sighed, "Oh I don't know, it'll sort itself out, one way or another."

"You just need to find one who is a mixture of the two of them, both women wrapped up in one. There you are, problem solved!" Reynard shrugged and grinned at Nicky.

"Oh Reynard, if only the solution was that simple, both of them in one woman; now wouldn't that be something?" Nicky smiled ruefully. "Come, pour me another drink, I can't possibly think about them now, it'll give me indigestion for sure, so I'll make do with my little cat in the meantime..." and laughing, he held out his glass as Reynard opened another bottle of wine.

Chapter Twenty-Two
LONDON - AUTUMN 1813

Nicky winced as he climbed down stiffly from the carriage. It had been a long drive from Portsmouth but once his ship had come into the English Channel, he'd been so desperate to get home he decided he couldn't wait for it to go along the south coast, up around Kent and then down the Thames estuary to dock at Tilbury. So he'd put up with being jolted about all the way from Portsmouth and now, finally, here he was in Berkeley Square. London was grey and rainy in the late afternoon, but it was home and he was excited to see everyone again.

He ran up the steps to the front door of Firle House and it opened before he had a chance to touch the knocker. "Good afternoon, Your Grace. May I say how good it is to have you home safe again." Browning even allowed himself to smile as he greeted Nicky. It sounded like he'd been away for a mere few weeks instead of well over a year.

Nicky patted the butler on the shoulder like an old acquaintance. "Hello, Browning; yes here I am again, not even Boney can keep me away, I'm afraid," and he grinned. "Is anyone at home?" he looked around, the house seemed very quiet.

"Well, Your Grace, His Grace is at home, he's in his study, but Her

Grace is at her godmother's. Lady Aubrey has not been too well lately. And er, your..." he was cut off as Francis bounded out of his study and powered down the hallway to pull Nicky into a bear hug. "I thought I heard a carriage and your voice! My God, it's good to have you back in one piece. How are you? Why didn't you let me know you were coming? How is the wound?"

Nicky laughed as he let himself be dragged off into Francis's study. "Good God, Francis, you're worse than Cat! Give me a minute to catch my breath before I start answering all that lot."

Once seated in front of a roaring fire, a snifter of the Duke's best brandy in his hand and one of his cheroots in the other, he smilingly updated Francis with everything that had happened while he'd been gone.

"I'll have you know I had no idea what to do when I got Reynard's letter after you'd been wounded," Francis eventually confessed to him. "If I'd told Bella and Cat it was as serious as I suspected, they'd have commandeered my yacht and been off to Spain to nurse you before I'd drawn a breath, with Eddie hot on their heels no doubt, clutching a raft of medical papers in his hand." Nicky laughed. "As it was, I told them all you'd sustained a minor flesh wound and that you were fine and just recuperating under Reynard's tender care. I'll leave it to you to tell them the truth... or not... as you see fit." He looked assessingly at Nicky's features, "It was bad, wasn't it? I can see the lines round your eyes. Are you fully fit yet, or are you still healing?"

"Yes, it was a trifle nasty, but it's getting better, I promise," Nicky smiled at Francis. "Reynard found this Moorish doctor to look after me. He had to dig around quite a bit to get the ball out apparently, so that's why it's taking time to heal, apart from the damage the ball itself caused which all needed stitching up inside me. And I lost a lot of blood so that alone left me weak. He reckoned I'll be back to my usual lovely self by next spring though."

"Mmmmm, good. I remember when I was injured in Rouen, it took me months and months to heal properly too, internally far longer than externally as far as the ball was concerned. Benjy had to go fishing to find it, rather like your doctor's problem. Then those bloody burns took forever, but they did heal, eventually." Francis smiled reassuringly before his face turned serious. "You have to tell me everything that happened. Reynard wrote it was Bernheim, what else does the man know about his father, also us?"

"Not a lot, but that's too much, Francis." So Nicky unloaded all the worry and guilt he'd been carrying for the past few months as he finished his story by describing the brief exchange he'd had with Bernheim before he was shot.

"Oh my God. Cat!" exclaimed Francis. "And he knows about Eddie too? As well as The Shadow?"

"No, all I THINK he knows is that the de Mornays were involved, but he doesn't know who. He can't know that much about The Shadow, but of course he could have picked up the gossip at the time his father was killed, so we must assume he knows something about him. Look what Ashcroft found out, even now, after all this time. But he knew about my family, it was the way he said it, I just KNOW he knew what his bastard father was up to. Now, of course, unfortunately, he knows that a woman killed his father. I'm so sorry Francis, he overheard a conversation when I mentioned something, but no names, thank God." Francis looked very alarmed.

"What worries me most is, having now confronted the man, I have this deep suspicion he won't let things be until he's found out everything about us. Especially me, as I've just stopped him getting his hands on all that gold. He won't ever forgive me for that," he muttered. "Oh hell, Francis, I'm so worried and it's all my fault." He shook his head, his face a mask of guilt. "The man is callous, barbaric and evil, more than touched in the head in the worst way, you have no idea, not to mention seriously depraved. But he's going to pursue us, find out who we are, I just know he is, all because of me." He held out his hands, "What a way to repay you all for everything you've done for me, my entire life!" He looked anguished.

"Now you look here, Nicky, stop even thinking like that. This is NOT your fault," said Francis sternly, his hand reaching out to grip Nicky's arm. "I was The Shadow long before you ever arrived in my life, before you were even born. What went on in Rouen when Cat killed Edgar Bernheim was all because of ME. Frederick Bernheim obviously knew of The Shadow and what his father was up to, directly from his father. As for the rest, you, your work for Ashcroft and Wellington, well, it's just a rather unfortunate coincidence, so we'll deal with it as and when we have to," he finished firmly. "Stop worrying, we'll deal with it all together. It might never happen."

Nicky looked relieved. "Are you sure, Francis? Christ, I'm so sorry," he tried apologising again.

"That's enough, Nicky. I don't want to hear another word on the subject." Francis was very firm. "Put it out of your mind for now. Oh, and please don't tell Ashcroft any more than you absolutely have to." He smiled wickedly, "That miner keeps digging with no sign of the treasure he's seeking. He can't find out what he wants to know about The Shadow and it's driving him witless. In addition, I'm also irritating him to madness, saying I know nothing, denying everything." Nicky chuckled at that, the thought of Ashcroft trying to get the better of Francis at his most obtuse; they were well matched.

"Now then, Young Man, you're back in civilisation, so I've actually got something FAR more important to tell you." Francis deftly moved their conversation on and while Nicky poured them both another drink while munching on some bread and cheese Browning had hastily sent in to assuage his hunger temporarily after the long drive, Francis retrieved a document from the locked top drawer of his desk. He sat down across from Nicky and handed it over.

"Sadly, Grandmother died a short while after you left," he began. "I think you suspected she wasn't going to last much longer when you last saw her?"

Nicky nodded, regret in his eyes. "I'm so sorry, Francis, so very sorry. More than I can put into words. She was the grandmother I never had and I cared for her very much; you do know that, don't you?"

"I know you did and we all miss her terribly, even now," Francis smiled sadly and took a deep breath. "After she died, we, just the close family, as in me, Cat, Eddie and Bella, went to a private reading of her Will in her lawyer's office. She left this letter for all of us." He handed it over to Nicky. "I think you'd better read it first, then we can talk afterwards. I take it you never received any correspondence from her lawyers? I did tell them you were in the Peninsula and when they asked how to contact you there, said they might try and send a letter to you via Wellington's HQ, but that I doubted it would reach you. I knew they shouldn't have bothered..."

Nicky looked nonplussed but shook his head and started to read the last letter from the Dowager while he munched on a piece of cheese. Francis leaned back in his chair, lit a cheroot and watched the younger man's face intently, waiting for the reaction he knew would come.

Nicky reached the end of the letter, his cheese abandoned, his face a mask of shock. Without a word, he went back and read it through all over again, then he let it drop to his lap and looked over at Francis. "CHRIST ALMIGHTY!" he gasped, stunned. "She's left me most of her bloody fortune!"

Francis grinned at the younger man. "Well, why not? I certainly don't need it and you know how fond of you she was, like another grandson, it's all there in the letter anyway." He paused momentarily thinking about how, now he knew his grandmother's secret, some of what she'd written made so much more sense, just as Bella had said. He watched as Nicky read the letter for the third time, more slowly, taking in the comments and advice the Dowager had tried to give him – about his life, about Bella, about love and money. He watched as the varying emotions crossed his face: sadness, surprise, shock... and anger.

He was very angry. "I can't possibly accept all this," he finally exclaimed. "What was she thinking of? It should be yours, or Elizabeth's, or the boys'. She left nothing to the boys, or your sisters and their families?"

Francis was ready for that reaction, expecting it. "The boys need and want for nothing and never will, as my direct heirs. I have more money than I know what to do with and I don't even know why I keep working other than it keeps me sane, living in this household with all of you. My sisters never visited nor even saw their grandmother from one year to the next as, like my mother, they disliked her intensely and the feeling was mutual. It was all they could do to turn up for her funeral, only because it would have been noted and commented on if they hadn't appeared, so serves them right." He grinned across at

Nicky, "As for Lizzie, even a third of the Estate, by the time it all accrues as she gets older, with what she'll inherit from me as well when I go, will make her one of the country's biggest heiresses, probably the wealthiest, heaven help her," he muttered. "So who else should the Dowager leave it all to? Algernon?" he pulled a face. "You're certainly far more deserving of it than any of us."

"But I can't accept it," Nicky banged his fist on the arm of his chair. "She was mad to do this and she's still trying to manipulate me from beyond the grave. She always tried to when she was alive. I wouldn't have it then and I won't have it now!" he exclaimed, still angry, his fist opening and closing as if he wanted to hit something more than the chair arm.

Francis merely grinned fiendishly at him, leaning back indolently. "Yes, you can accept it; and yes, she was a bit mad and a serial interferer, God bless her; and yes, she's still trying to manipulate you, just as she always tried to manipulate me. I ignored her as well, tried all my bloody life, but funnily enough, more often than not, I eventually realised, in the end, she was right – and so will you." He chuckled then, "Anyway, you can't give it back, so you're stuck with it. Rant and rave all you like Nicholas de Bresancourt, you are now a very wealthy young man."

"But all that commentary about Bella, what in hell do I do about her?"

"Aaah, now there's an interesting question," smiled Francis with a strange expression on his face. "She's done the house up beautifully, by the way," he turned the conversation in another direction. "It's still the same, still as it was when Grandmother was there, but it's fresher, lighter, less cluttered, more modern somehow, so slightly different. I know you'll love it. Carstairs is still in charge with a lot of the old servants and retainers, also some new ones. Of course, Bella moved in after Grandmother died, so why don't you go round there? All your clothes and belongings are there anyway, it's your very own home now, Nicky," he finished quietly.

"Good God!" was all Nicky could manage.

"Bella hasn't done anything about the estate down in Sussex," Francis went blithely on. "She wanted you to see it first and then decide what to do with it. How to decorate the house there and so on, as it's in dire need of refurbishing. She's merely been overseeing the estate management and there's an old caretaker in the house to keep an eye on it. Bella's a very capable woman, Nicky, in case you hadn't already realised that – and she is your wife, after all..."

"A wife I hadn't ever planned on," Nicky muttered.

"Mmmmm, yes, well, we can talk about that another time," murmured Francis. "Therefore, go and talk to her, but whatever you do, DON'T. LOSE. YOUR. TEMPER," he said slowly as he looked at Nicky sternly again, obviously knowing what he was going to find in Hertford Street apart from his new home. "She's worried herself incessantly while you've been away, as have we all, but she loves you, Nicky. Truly and deeply. Grandmother knew it and so do all the rest of us, just remember that." Francis rose from his chair, "Now run along, stop fretting about Bernheim as he is NOT important right now. Please just accept all this from your Granny Granville. She's done us all a favour outwitting you and your pride; she loved you, just like we all do and always have, so be happy with it, Nicky, it's what she wanted." He put his arm around Nicky's shoulder as he too rose, "She just wanted you to be happy, with a loving family around you," Francis continued enigmatically, "and believe me, she understood what that meant more than any of us realised." He walked Nicky over to his study door as he chattered on, "I'm afraid Cat is out, your Papa is down at Arlington although due back imminently for some business meetings in a couple of days. I have an appointment at the Foreign Office in an hour sharp, so you might as well go straight round to Hertford Street now and dine there." He shooed a bemused Nicky out into the hall, calling Browning to get his carriage ready promptly to take the Duke to Hertford Street.

Francis was about to return to his study when he spied a wicker basket on the floor of the hallway, next to Nicky's few bags. The basket was moving and a yowling sound was coming out of it along with a rather noxious smell. "What the devil is that?" he enquired, peering down.

"Aaah," said Nicky, smiling at last. "That is *La Duquesa*, though I suppose I'll have to call her The Duchess now we're back in London," he mused. "She came back with me from Spain and she's been driving me mad the whole journey. Reynard found her in the stables of the hostelry where we were staying and thought she'd keep me amused while I was stuck in bed, but she never left. I realised how much I missed my little Lion after he went to cat heaven and obviously, being away so much, I couldn't replace him. This noisy bit of fluff was a crazy, spitting kitten when she arrived, forever into mischief, a complete nuisance," he picked up the basket and Francis looked inside. The hissing, manic kitten had grown somewhat and was now a beautiful, young, long haired, black cat. Big green eyes looked back at the Duke and Francis burst out laughing as Nicky grinned at him. "I was going to call her Sooty as that seemed quite apt at the time, but when I thought about it a bit more and she grew into the lovely creature she is now, Duchess seemed a bit more appropriate. Of course, she's still a complete pain: demanding, irrational and doing exactly what she likes regardless of me. So, what do you think?"

Francis doubled up with mirth, his mind going back to the beautiful bitch he'd acquired to mate with Cat's first dog, Fluffy; she'd been Bubbles' great grandmother. He'd called her Duchess for much the same amusing reasons as Nicky had named his new cat.

"I think you'd better get round to Hertford Street with your baggage as quickly as you can. I've no idea what Bella is going to make of her namesake, but she's got plenty of news updates for you, I can tell you," and, still chortling with mirth, he made his way back to his study. Nicky went out to the coach, now waiting to take him, his bags and the irate and hungry cat, over to his new home.

Francis went back to his study, poured himself another drink and lit another cheroot. He wasn't going anywhere that evening, in fact he was expecting Cat home for dinner any time soon. Eddie, too, was only round at Brooks's, not on his way to London from his Sussex home and would, no doubt, be back shortly to join them. As he stood in front of the fire, warming his back and sipping his brandy, he reflected he'd handled the matter of Nicky's inheritance rather well, not to mention the fact everyone obviously knew he and Bella were married since she was living at his house in Hertford Street. That little gem had obviously not occurred to the man, he was so bewildered about his inheritance, so it hadn't yet struck him. Francis had been expecting an explosion of resentful wrath when Nicky realised he'd been outmanoeuvred by the old lady, but apart from his first angry reaction, he seemed to have accepted it reasonably well. Francis wondered if his recent time in the Peninsula had affected the young man in more ways than just his injury. Well, they would just have to wait and see, but he rather liked to think he was getting to be just as manipulative as his late grandmother.

Wishing he was a fly on the wall in the old lady's house when Nicky discovered Bella's duplicity, and that he was now a father as well, Francis grinned to himself at the thought of the fireworks that were about to explode in Hertford Street that evening, imagining what the very upright Carstairs would make of the undoubted fracas. He strolled out into the hall when he heard his wife's voice, returning from her visit to her godmother, to tell her their favourite soldier had come home at last, safe and sound.

Chapter Twenty-Three

Carstairs, the Dowager's formidably superior and elderly butler, unbent enough to smile as he bowed obsequiously to Nicky as he walked into the hall of the house he now owned. It was a strange feeling. Nicky hadn't yet been able to come to terms with the shock of it all, just about realising during the short carriage ride that everyone obviously now knew Bella was his wife and he was puzzled about that, in fact, extremely cross. He had half a mind to go back and remonstrate with Francis about it, but realised there was little he could do. Like his inheritance, he was dealing with a *fait accompli* and he cursed his lengthy absence down in Spain.

As the coach drew up outside the familiar house, he realised he was actually looking forward to seeing Sooty and simply relaxing over dinner with some good English food, having a long hot bath, before contemplating what to do that evening. Perhaps he would go round to *Le Lion d'Or*, as *Lionesse* and his necklace were very much at the front of his mind. Just because his marriage had been announced for a reason he didn't understand, didn't mean to say he was committed to it; it was merely a problem he had to deal with somehow.

Despite all the time he'd had to think about her, he still hadn't been able to reach any conclusions about his relationship with Sooty. In the meantime, handing over a yowling and very smelly wicker basket to the affronted Carstairs, who immediately and disdainfully passed it on to a waiting footman, Nicky, feeling in a playful mood, put a restraining hand to the butler's shoulder and finger to his lips to fore-stall an official announcement of his presence, then walked silently into the Dowager's, now Bella's, little sitting room. Once again he crept up behind her to put his hands over her eyes, "BOO....!"

As he bent low over her seated form at the little escritoire in the window embrasure, a vision so reminiscent of the Dowager, a familiar scent teased his senses. Slightly confused, he was just thinking it came from the wrong woman, when Bella knocked over her inkwell and sent her papers flying in ecstatic surprise as she turned to shoot out of her chair and throw herself into his arms.

"Oh my God, NICKYYYY!" she shrieked. "Oh Nicky, you're back, oh thank heaven you're all right." Bella threw her arms around his neck and hugged him tight before kissing his face all over and then his lips, a spark fizzing between them as her mouth met his. But as he pulled back, bemused at her enthusiastic greeting and slightly stunned at his reaction to her light kiss, Bella looked up into his face. Her searching gaze took in the new lines around his eyes and mouth and despite the deep tan he now sported, she instinctively knew his injury had been far worse than her uncle had said.

"Hello, Sooty," Nicky said softly. "I take it you missed me then?" He smiled a crooked smile as he stood back to look at her, taking in her tall, graceful form, slightly more rounded than he remembered, her breasts now more voluptuous, he decided absently with a glint of appreciation, the cascade of black curls piled high on her head and falling artfully down her back, her tawny green eyes sparkling with emotion. But it was the smile that lit up her face as she looked at him with such adoration and relief that slightly took his breath away. It looked so familiar, but in another setting, as it tickled the edges of his memory. The wide infectious grin was the same, but had she always had such luscious lips, so invitingly kissable? However, the idle teasing memory evaporated as Bella once again threw her arms around him for another tight hug. "Oh Nicky, I've missed you, we've all missed you, so much. We worried about you so. It's wonderful to have you back home safe."

Bella had let her hands drop from around his neck to round his waist for her hug and as she tightened her arms about him, he winced slightly as she pressed into his still slightly tender scar. She pulled back, concern on her face. "I knew Uncle Francis was being a bit too vague when he told us you'd been wounded. What happened, Nicky?" she asked softly, worry obvious in her tone.

"Oh, it's only a slight pistol wound," Nicky said dismissively.

Bella pressed around the tender spot again with her fingers and watched as his eyes narrowed in reaction. "Hmmm, yes, obviously a SLIGHT wound, and I'm the Prime Minister," she tutted. "What really happened, Nicky? I'm not a fool, Uncle Francis told us months ago and it's obviously not fully healed, even now."

Nicky gave in. It had always been difficult keeping things from her. "I took rather a large ball that went through someone else first, at close quarters, so I suppose I should consider myself lucky." He shrugged lightly, "I lost a lot of blood because it took a while to get medical attention and the surgeon had to dig around quite a bit to fish it out as it went quite deep, then an infection set in. It's just taking a while to heal inside, is all. I'll be right as rain soon, but all the rest of me is in full working order," and he waggled his fingers at her, laughing.

"Except your brain, as ever," she laughed back at him. "Don't stand so close to people being shot at next time, if you please," she ordered bossily.

If only she knew all the story, he thought. "Yes, Madam, I'll try to remember that." He bowed slightly.

Bella pulled him over to a small sofa in front of the warm fire that was burning in the grate. "Come, sit down, I want to hear all about where you've been and what you've been up to. You realise it's been over a year since we've seen you?" She pointed a stern forefinger at him, "And please don't try and tell me you've been reading and writing dispatches all this time."

"Of course not," he grinned. "I've been playing the guitar, drinking copious quantities of Spanish wine, riding a bit, sitting on the beach in the sunshine and going for a paddle now and again." All of which was completely true, but of course Bella merely laughed at him again.

"Of course you have, and I've been knitting."

Nicky burst out laughing again, knowing that knitting and sewing were her pet hates, having spent his youth watching and listening to her swearing and muttering under her breath as her mother had tried fruitlessly to engage her in some feminine occupations, only to find her up and disappeared into the library to bury herself in some academic tome the minute her back was turned, either that or to escape outside to race about in a very unladylike fashion or to torment Nicky and make a general nuisance of herself in whatever he was doing.

As they laughed together and Bella was bracing herself to bring up the subject of the Dowager's inheritance, unwilling to break the obviously good humour Nicky seemed to be in, Carstairs knocked and entered the cosy little room, coughing as he did so. He was followed by the footman carrying the yowling basket. "Beg pardon, Your Grace, but what would you have me do with this, er, creature? I, ah, think it could do with going outside, or perhaps a saucer of milk? Would you like me to..."

Nicky jumped up, wincing at the sudden movement which didn't escape Bella's eagle eyes, then strode over to relieve the harassed footman of his burden and turned back to Bella, smiling as he sat down again and opened the door of the basket. The cat shot out at a rate of knots and ran headlong over to the window, trying to get its bearings as it stared around yet another strange room, its fur standing on end as it took in strange people and surroundings. It looked outside longingly and yowled loudly. Nicky sighed as he rose again and went to open the French windows. The cat stared outside, looking at the strange water pouring from the sky and ventured onto the small patio slowly, nervously and curiously. Having sorted out their problem, the butler and footman quietly withdrew.

"I don't think she's seen rain before. It was quite dry on the journey up through the Bay and into the Channel and it didn't noticeably rain in her little life before that." Nicky watched in amusement as the cat tried to shake off the light rain that was now watering the gardens at the back of the house before disappearing under a profusion of late flowering shrubs. A few minutes later, she shot back in, shivered in a very feline way, going straight over to the fire where she sat down in the middle of the warm hearth rug and proceeded to give herself a thorough wash while nervously inspecting her new surroundings.

Bella's eyes twinkled in amusement. "And who is this, pray? A souvenir from your travels?" Nicky shut the door and returned to sit down.

"Aaah, yes, allow me to introduce you. Sooty, meet *La Duquesa*, or Duchess, as I suppose we'll have to call her now." He grinned at Bella before leaning down to address the cat. "Won't we, Beautiful, you're so alike," he crooned to his pet, stroking her furry tummy as she stretched out in pleasure, flexing her claws and warming herself in front of the glowing coals.

Bella giggled. "I beg your pardon?"

"Well, you are. Long black hair, green eyes, very intelligent, complete nuisance and does exactly what she wants, ignores everything I say to her, and, most importantly, thinks I'm her servant."

"Ooooh, You Wretch, how could you?" She reached over to poke him in the chest, reaching to tickle him in payback for the humorous comparison. Careful to avoid his wound, she leaned forward. "Meeeeeow, compare me to a Spanish alley cat would you?" and she let forth a stream of very unladylike Spanish she'd picked up long ago as a child with big ears, listening when her mother often thought she was alone.

"Oh, noooooo! Sootyyyyyy! What shocking language... oh noooooo," Nicky laughed trying to push her away. "Just be glad I didn't call her Sooty. I nearly did... oooooooh, aaaaaah, noooooo..." and he laughed as she redoubled her tickling efforts at the affront, laughing with him. As they wrestled together on the sofa, just like they had as children, a chain that had been hanging around Bella's neck, the charm on the end hidden deep in her cleavage, fell out.

As his eyes fell on the necklace, Nicky suddenly stilled, his face changed and he reared up over her, all playfulness gone. He lifted the familiar charm in his hand, "WHERE THE HELL DID YOU GET THIS?" he yelled coldly, looking directly into Bella's now fearful features.

All prepared speeches of explanation that she'd practised for months and months in readiness for this very moment evaporated in an instant, as she sat and gazed up at him, biting her lip, guilt written all over her face.

They sat and stared at each other and Nicky shook Bella's shoulders in frustration. "I asked you a question," his voice was now ice, "WHERE DID YOU GET THAT NECKLACE?"

Bella jumped up off the sofa and stood with her back to the fire, trying to formulate the words, not quite knowing where to start. "I... I..."

Nicky was staring at her, his eyes fixated on her mouth. Slowly, he too rose to his feet to stand in front of her, his expression a look of dawning horror as he stared at her, his eyes going from her mouth, down over her body and back up to her mouth. Slowly, he put his hand up to her hair and, one by one, he pulled the pins and clips from the elaborate coiffure, letting them drop carelessly to the carpet until the long, lustrous waves were coiling down her back. Then, finally, he put a hand up to her cheek, feeling the peachy soft skin as he leaned toward her, inhaling her scent; he'd never forgotten it.

She didn't need to tell him now, she could see he'd finally recognised her, so she pulled her shoulders back and looked at him directly, into his angry, bewildered and shocked eyes. "I took it off you while you were asleep, the first night you stayed with me. There's nothing wrong with the catch. I knew if you thought you'd left it behind, you'd come back for it." As he continued to stare at her in silence, she put her hands up and undid the clasp before holding his precious chain and charm out to him. Bella continued to speak calmly, though her heart was pounding in her chest. "I knew what it meant to you, how precious it was, so I kept it in my safe in the sitting room, that's why you couldn't find it." The words now tumbled out of her, "I'm so sorry, Nicky. I was going to return it the day you left, that night, I was going to own up, to tell you, take off my mask, you know I was... but you left too soon," she ended brokenly, tears coming into her eyes. "I was going to tell you in your room, when you were packing, when you kissed me, but then Benjy came in and I... I didn't get the chance... and then... you left," she finally whispered and stood there, tears rolling down her face, her shaking hand still holding out the necklace.

White hot anger roiled through Nicky. Anger, shock and utter disbelief. He could hardly take it all in. No wonder she'd seemed vaguely familiar; no wonder she seemed to understand him; no wonder she'd beaten him at cards and chess; but it was all too much. She'd been like his sister and his brain couldn't deal with it so his temper took over. He lifted his hand and he slapped her. "You unmitigated, lying, deceitful, thieving TROLLOP," he spat out, sparks flying from his eyes, he was so angry he could hardly string the words together.

Bella recoiled at the venom in his voice as her hand went to her now reddened cheek, but somehow the slap had pulled her senses together and the tears stopped as her own temper now rose. "And you are an adulterous, unfeeling bastard! Coming to the gaming house and whoring the night away before you'd even come home to see your family, let alone your wife. There we all were, worried sick about you, thinking you could be dead or injured, never having heard one single word from you!" She bit out a furious breath, "And you returned every night, to *La Lionesse*, of your own accord, so don't you dare accuse me!" She slapped him back, hard.

They glared at each other, both now boiling over with anger. "WIFE? WIFE! I never wanted a wife, I don't need a wife, least of all YOU, You Bitch! I did you a favour and look how you've paid me back. And what the HELL are you doing running gaming houses anyway? How many other men have you enticed up to your cosy sitting room for a private game of cards, eh? To enjoy your perverted little games?"

"HOW DARE YOU!" she screamed at him, slapping him for a second time. "I TOLD YOU, if you care to remember, it's all yours, YOURS! Both clubs. I only did it to make you some money, to help you get over this obsession you have with being penniless and landless and all the rest; as if any of us care!" She tossed her head, "I borrowed the money and used it as an investment. It just went into a couple of gaming houses instead of shares or bonds."

"Hah, well I don't need it now, do I?" He waved his hand in the air, indicating the room around him. "Not now the old lady has left me all this!" He shook his head. "Christ, I still can't believe it," then he turned back to Bella, his temper still at full pelt, "so you might as well keep it all, then you can continue to enjoy yourself with any punter that takes your fancy. You can rest assured it most definitely won't be me! How many have you had then, Your Grace?" he spat the title out sarcastically. "Or should I start calling you *Lionesse*?" He grasped one of her wrists as her hand came up to connect with his face for a third time.

"YOU PIG! You know there's been no one else. You even commented on it the first time you made love to me that first night, or don't you remember? I presume, on the other hand, you've had countless women since."

For a brief moment Nicky's mind went back to the first time he'd made love to her, remembering the physical, almost virginal tightness and her gasped apprehension when he'd entered her. He knew deep down she was telling the truth, but he was beyond rationality now so bit out words to hurt her. "Dozens, scores, I've lost count, all much more talented and interesting in that department than you, My Dear, but you served your purpose while I was here on leave."

"Oh reeeally. Well you certainly seemed keen enough to see me at the time, to enjoy my little games," she bit back. "In fact, you could hardly keep away, keep your hands off me, quite the lover I thought." Her voice dripped sarcasm, "But what would I know? Maybe now I should try someone else, then I'll have something to compare you to, maybe dozens, just like you. I'm sure I'll find them more interesting, accommodating, educational; in fact, imagine what else I could experience with them."

Nicky's seething anger knew no bounds, he was incandescent. "I'm amazed you haven't already been doing that since I left, hot little bitch that you are. You surely don't expect me to believe you've slept alone for the past year or so?"

"Slept alone? SLEPT ALONE?" she screeched at him. "Hah! No, I've not been alone. Don't you want to see who's been keeping me company, Husband Dear?" The icy sarcasm dripped contemptuously and with that, she whirled and ran from the room.

He flew after her as she ran down the hall and up the stairs, pushing the astonished, shocked butler out of the way in his angry haste. "Come back here, You Trollop! Don't you run away from me," he yelled, oblivious to the gasps from gaping footmen and maids who'd joined the now speechless butler in the hallway. "I haven't finished with you yet!"

As Bella turned down the first floor corridor, Nicky was hard on her heels and he erupted with a crash into the small room she burst into, causing the contented baby, who was playing happily in her cot with some stuffed animals, to cry out in dismay. As Nicky grabbed Bella roughly by an arm, she turned and shrieked at him, "LET GO OF ME, YOU BASTARD... AND LOOK!"

At Bella's scream, Nicky shook his head and took stock of where he was and instantly his eyes went to the cot and the now crying baby, lying forlornly and holding out her arms to be picked up. As he stood rooted to the spot in shock, Bella rasped out at him furiously, "Meet your daughter, Nicky. Thérèse Charlotte de Bresancourt. She's named for your mother, mine too. The family call her Terrie. THAT is who has been keeping me company and occasionally sleeping with me while you've been whoring your way around Spain for the past year!" With that, she turned and ran from the room, sobbing her heart out as though it was breaking in two.

Unable to take in this further shock, Nicky stood completely dumb-struck, staring at the little girl holding out her arms to him. Without thought, he bent over the cot, lifted her out and sat in an armchair over by the window. As the child cuddled into his comforting arms, her tears stopped and she stared curiously into his face as he looked down at her. Golden eyes so like his own stared back into his and her honey blonde-coloured mop of fine hair, with curls here and there, had a rather bedraggled pink ribbon tangled in it. He was completely stunned and simply sat there, staring at her as she cooed and blew bubbles at him. She was so obviously his daughter that he knew what he would find as he half turned her in his arms and curiously pulled up her dress and under-wrappings to look down at the little lion birth-mark that sat, pink and fascinating, just under the curve of her bottom.

The little girl snuggled down into his arms and finding fascination in one of his shiny jacket buttons, twiddled and pulled it with fat little fingers until with a big yawn, her wide, black lashed golden eyes closed, and with a little sigh she fell fast asleep. Mindlessly, Nicky looked around the now peaceful little room, taking in the amusing drawings of a host of jungle animals that wended their way around the walls, led, of course, by a large, fluffy maned, golden lion.

As the baby slept, he sat there for a long time, his brain trying to make sense of the series of shocks he'd received in the past few hours since he'd stepped down from the coach at Firle House. His life had literally been turned upside down. He'd come home believing he was his usual landless and penniless self, to discover he was now an extremely wealthy man, beyond even his wildest dreams. He now had a daughter, so the reason for the marriage announcement was self-explanatory and, she was a miniature female version of himself. His wife, his unwanted wife, the woman he'd regarded as more like a sister, had deceived, lied and seduced him and coalesced with the woman of his dreams into... into what? He simply couldn't deal with it all and as he sat, tears of bewilderment, anger, sorrow and just pure emotion rolled down his face, until, exhausted by everything, Nicky's body and mind gave up and he fell asleep.

A few hours later, the nursery maid crept into the room. Along with the entire household, she'd heard the monumental argument between the newly returned Duke and his wife, so it was with no little trepidation that she went to retrieve her charge to feed, bathe and put her to sleep, having been informed the Duchess was indisposed. She was obviously new to the household, no nursery having been required in the Dowager's time, so she smiled as she looked at the tall, well-built man asleep in the chair, his baby daughter snuggled happily in his arms. The man was exceptionally handsome, his colouring an exact replica of the little girl, right down to his thick black eyelashes. As she bent to lift the child from him, he sleepily bent his head to kiss the baby before settling back into slumber again. The maid sighed romantically and felt sure no woman alive could continue to be angry with a man like that now he was at home with her once more.

It was well past midnight when Nicky woke, rubbing a crick in his neck from sleeping in the chair for so long. He rose quietly and spent many moments looking down at his sleeping daughter, amazement at her existence still overwhelming him. He bent down to kiss her and smooth her tousled blonde curls, then crept silently out the nursery, closing the door behind him.

He prowled through the now silent house, memories of the Dowager and his childhood visits vivid in his mind. He wandered through the many rooms, looking around him as the bright moonlight shafted in through the windows. They were as he remembered them, just more up to date, creams and pastel-coloured soft furnishings and rugs everywhere, making the rooms seem lighter, airier and brighter. A lot of the former clutter of ornaments was also now missing, just a few simple, elegant pieces adorned the tables and sideboards, everything matching and fitting in so much better. He was instantly reminded of the same taste in the apartment at *Le Lion d'Or*, but hastily shut his mind to those thoughts.

Down in the kitchen, he found the cat stretched out in front of the warm range, a half-eaten plate of chicken and a saucer of milk beside her and he grinned as she meowed at him and got up to wind herself around his legs, recognising a familiar figure in her strange new surroundings, not to mention damp, chilly weather. He picked her up, nuzzled his face in her soft fur and scritched her ears, just as she liked, and she started to purr as he continued to stroke and talk to her. But she soon had enough adoration and, contrary as ever, jumped back down to her place by the range to eat more of her chicken. Nicky chuckled, relieved she seemed settled. He foraged around in the pantry, finally finding himself some bread, cheese and ale, his growling stomach reminding him he'd hardly eaten for most of the previous day either. He sat at the long trestle table in the kitchen, munching slowly, trying to decide what to do.

Feeling a bit better with food inside him, he sauntered back upstairs and into the room that was obviously meant to be his study. He leaned against the large desk that sat in the window embrasure, looking out onto the dark garden. There was a large portrait of the Dowager hanging over the fireplace, painted by the renowned Mr Gainsborough in the previous century. He turned to look at it, whispering to the painting as if the formidable-looking woman in it was actually in the room. "So, Granny Granville, you finally got your way, didn't you?" he shook his head, "I might have known you would. None of us, except Papa and his chessmen, could ever get the better of you, not even Francis," and he sighed. "But now you've got YOUR way, what the hell am I going to do?" he asked the painting as he tapped his chest. "Me, your Nicky. I'm trapped here, so no going off to the Americas for me now, hmmm?" His thoughts went to the little golden-eyed cherub asleep upstairs and he smiled momentarily. "Well, I've got the family you wanted me to have, so I hope you're satisfied. But as for Bella," his face turned into a mask of bitterness, "she's not the paragon you obviously thought her and I'm damned if I'll ever forgive her for what she's done; how could she be so deceitful? How could I have been such a fool? Ah, damn, damn, I don't know what the hell I'm going to do with her!" he swore again under his breath and ran a hand angrily through his hair. "Well, she might have caught me once, but she can rot in hell before she lays a finger on me again. There's plenty more beautiful women out there and I'm going to get a life for myself; she can go back to her precious gaming houses and see if I care!" With that, he rose, turned and stalked from the room, while the portrait stared enigmatically down at him.

He made his way back upstairs, his emotions still seething, striding to where the master suite was located. Not sure what or who he would find there, unsure whether Bella had taken it over for her own use, he opened the door to the adjoining room next door but was confronted with the sight of his wife, fast asleep on the bed, still fully clothed. She was curled up in a ball and a sodden handkerchief was grasped in her fingers. As he crept across the moonlit room and looked down at her, he could see the tearstains on her cheeks. Her long, dark hair was fanned out across the pillows and her skirts had rucked up her legs, exposing those long limbs he remembered so well. He stared and stared, finally having a face to put to the body he'd dreamed of and lusted after for so long. But it wasn't the face he'd created in his mind, nor ever expected to see. His thoughts went back to those four torrid nights over a year before, to the passion that had exploded between them. In spite of himself and his anger, he felt his body harden in response and desire run rampant through his veins, which infuriated him more than anything. He didn't want to want her now, but he knew the angry words he'd uttered earlier were a lie. The pleasure he'd experienced with her had been sublime and he'd not found that with any other woman, nor the obvious connection they seemed to have... had always had.

As Nicky stood and stared and remembered, Bella moved and rolled over. She whispered his name in her sleep and reached out for a pillow to pull into her arms and cuddle, another lone tear running down her cheek. He looked down and saw her other hand was still clutching his chain. Very carefully, just as she'd done to him, he leaned down and slowly pulled it away from her, a sense of poetic justice running through him. As he leaned down, her familiar scent wafted up to him and the temptation to bend lower and kiss her was almost irresistible, to taste if her skin was still like strawberries and cream. But then, thoughts of her deceit and lies chased around his mind again and he stood back up angrily, determined not to give in to her or any woman who tried to manipulate him. He fixed the chain back around his neck and without a backward glance, stormed from the room, through the communicating door to the master suite, closing it firmly behind him. He noted there was no lock and determined to remedy that omission first thing in the morning.

Despite his long sleep in the nursery, Nicky felt washed out and exhausted. He ripped off his travel-stained clothes, throwing them haphazardly on the floor, realising he'd now need a valet and wondering absently if there was one already waiting in the wings, pending his return to London; knowing the efficiency of Carstairs and his wife, he wouldn't be surprised, even if the pair had not known when he would be back. He bet himself Carstairs was already making the necessary arrangements. Now naked, he threw himself down on the large, comfortable master bed, in his adopted grandmother's old bedroom, revelling in the feel of the turned down, crisp fresh sheets and soft pillows and closed his eyes. It wasn't the way he'd intended to spend his first night back in London. He'd expected to be in *Lionesse*'s bed at *Le Lion d'Or*, at last discovering what she looked like under her mask, making passionate love to her, all night, finally able to watch her respond to him and climax in his arms.

But that woman was currently lying next door, in a house that unexpectedly was now his, but he already knew her, and he didn't want her. He'd made up his mind. How could he want a woman he didn't trust? He groaned as his body told him something else, but his angry mind insisted and resolutely turned instead to thoughts of his future. He realised he now had a vast fortune to manage, as well as properties and estates and all sorts of business interests. Long ago wispy memories of Valenciennes drifted across his mind and on those far away thoughts of northern France and his childhood home, he gradually drifted off to sleep.

Chapter Twenty-Four

LONDON · WINTER 1813/14

The day after Nicky's arrival back in London set the pattern of the next few weeks and months. He spent hours ensconced with Francis and his step-father, who had surprisingly appeared at Firle House the day after Nick had arrived back in London, going over details of the vast Estate he had inherited from the Dowager. Her lawyers had been keeping a watchful eye on matters in his absence until the paperwork had been formalised and ownership officially transferred, so all three men were stunned as they discovered the extent of the personal empire the old lady had quietly built for herself once her grandson had taken the reins of the Firle family trading empire and estates.

Francis said the old battle-axe obviously couldn't keep away from business once she'd become hooked on it and obviously did it for the pure challenge, or to alleviate boredom, as she had no need of any more money, or jewellery! Given that women officially had few rights, including having their own bank account, it was quite a mind-boggling achievement. However, Elizabeth Granville had found a way around any barrier in her path. She had interests across the globe, in every new and up-and-coming enterprise hungry for investment, as well as in established industries, stocks and bonds. She also seemed to have local trading connections in territories and countries they had to look for on the globe in Francis's study, they were so remote or unheard of, as well as owning plantations and estates across the East and West Indies, Africa and South and North America. The more they delved, the more dumbfounded the men were. Between them, Francis and Eddie helped Nicky learn and understand how to oversee the running of an array of business interests that appeared, fortunately, to be very competently managed by a team of excellent men; and the more Nicky learned, the more fascinated he became. He still didn't have the patience to read every report, contract and scrap of paper that Francis always did, likewise his step-father who'd learned from Francis about the devil in the detail, but the scale and scope of the fortune that was now his to oversee was amazing. There were mines, factories and mills; new-fangled gadgets... lighting, something called electricity, engines and mechanical contraptions of all kinds, properties and agricultural land, shipping fleets... wherever the growing British Empire was spreading, Elizabeth Granville had seemingly got her foot in the door there first to take maximum advantage; if the British Empire wasn't there, she'd do business with whoever's Empire it was!

Francis was intrigued and almost jealous. He rapidly came to a financial arrangement with Nicky to buy out and take over some of the businesses and holdings which would complement many of the investments the Firle Empire owned already. That still left more than enough for Nicky to manage. Eddie was simply bemused by it all and the large figures involved in the transfer of the holdings between the two men as he sat and tried to advise both sides as what he also considered to be a fair price.

Nicky took endless files of documents and papers back with him to Hertford Street and soon a secretary, then under-secretaries and managers, visited daily and were busy with him in his study for hours. These were more capable men who had worked with the Dowager from offices round the corner in Mayfair and acted as a front for the person who was the real owner and driver of the business empire; when she'd gone into her last decline, still overseeing her interests literally until her final few weeks, these employees had expected Francis to be their new employer. Now, however, to their surprise, some had a different Duke to deal with.

When Nicky wasn't deeply involved in business matters or in meetings with his secretaries and managers, little Terrie could be found sitting on a rug on the floor beside him, playing happily with her toys, or on his lap, where he sang and talked to her incessantly... in English, French or Spanish... depending on how the mood took him. Then, in the evenings, he would disappear, coming home in the early hours, always looking in on the nursery to kiss his daughter goodnight, no matter how drunk he was.

He hardly spoke to Bella. They passed like ships in the night. Occasionally, they met over breakfast and on the rare occasions he was at home for dinner, the conversation was stilted and inane. She often stood in the hall, staring unseen through the half-open door of his study, watching him laugh and play with Terrie, rolling around on the floor, playing the fool, making the little girl crow with delight as he tickled her or tossed her up in the air. If she didn't love the pair of them so much, Bella would have been jealous of her baby, but as it was, she was simply happy Nicky took such delight in the little girl, though knowing him as she did, she would have been amazed if he hadn't.

Where he went at night, she had no idea. To Brooks's maybe, out gambling, drinking and whoring she presumed. She'd smelled scent on his clothes when she went into his room sometimes when he was out. The heart-wrenching pain was almost unbearable.

Once Nicky and her father turned their attention to the little estate at Litlington, down near the Sussex coast, they would disappear for days at a time, returning only at weekends and that she was sure was only because Nicky wanted to see Terrie.

In the meantime, Bella had her own affairs to attend to. Just because her husband ignored her and discussed nothing about the empire he'd inherited, or his new country estate, as if she understood nothing except domestic household matters, didn't mean Bella wasn't an extremely capable businesswoman. She was already deeply involved in managing the affairs of little Elizabeth Granville, a matter she happily tried to share with her uncle, but Francis was content to let her do things her own way, more than aware of what an astute brain she had and he simply watched, amused, from the sidelines. After her first meeting with some of the Dowager's secretaries, business managers and bankers, where they had treated her like an ignorant child and virtually ignored every comment and question she raised, she followed the piece of advice the old lady had passed on in her letter. For her future dealings she dressed to the nines, covered herself in jewels and stalked into her meetings, icy froideur on her face, giving every man who tried to gainsay her a cutting set down. She had very little further trouble from any of them after that, even when she was heavily pregnant.

With Nicky away or out so much, she had returned to appearing from time to time at her little gaming establishments which were still a runaway success. Through the efforts of her uncle and aunt who followed their strategy and quietly let it be known she had married Nicky before he went off to Spain, so the appearance of her baby could be explained, she was now accepted into Society as a wealthy young matron. She still went to balls and soirees with friends, or sometimes with her aunt, but took no pleasure in dancing or flirting with men who weren't Nicky; all the handsome young bucks in turn had given up trying to engage with the beautiful young Duchess who obviously had so little interest in them. Of her husband there was never a sign and she merely told anyone who asked that he was abroad, looking into his various overseas interests having been away in the army for so long; also, having been injured, she said he was no longer currently required for active service. The latter as she had no idea what her husband's status in the military was now.

It was mid-December and *La Lionesse* was making one of her rare appearances at *Le Lion d'Or*. As the evening wore on, Bella was just contemplating returning back to Hertford Street when Nicky came in. He was with a large group of old army friends and more than a little drunk. The crowd spent an hour at the various tables before a small group of them, including Nicky, sat down to play cards. She watched him from a distance, flirting with the waitresses, laughing and joking with his friends, looking as if he hadn't a care in the world. He looked so handsome and devilish in his evening clothes, the stark formality of his dark suit seeming to enhance his golden features. Deep jealousy and wrath seethed through her together with an overwhelming wave of desire. She was so desolate in her loneliness, spending days and weeks by herself, never knowing if he was going to be at home or away, unless his new valet or the butler told her. She knew she shouldn't want him as he surely didn't want her, but she simply couldn't help herself. It had somehow been different when he was in Spain, she had his return to look forward to, to sustain her. But now he was at home and she saw so little of him, he might just as well still be in the Peninsula.

She prowled up to the table where he was sitting with his companions and took a seat, all his friends delighted that the Patroness of the establishment had chosen to join their little party and they smiled in pleasure as she called over one of the footmen to bring champagne on the house. Nicky merely sat and stared at her through narrowed eyes.

Visiting there was the last thing he'd wanted to do, but he hadn't been able to object to his friends for any good reason and he'd just hoped Bella wouldn't be present. He was both angry and defiant that she was. He sat back and watched her flirt mildly with his friends and seethed inside as she threw her head back and laughed at some joke they'd made. Yet again, he asked himself how he'd never recognised her, so obvious as it was now. His own stupidity made him even angrier with himself. Then she turned to him, raising her glass in a toast. "You're very quiet, You Handsome Man," she purred, running a finger down his cheek, "and so very tanned. Have you been abroad recently?" His friends roared with mirth at her flirting while he went rigid at the feel of her glove-free hand on his face.

"I was in the Peninsula, serving with Wellington until a few months ago, when I was wounded. I'm on extended sick leave at the moment," was his bald reply.

"Reeeally?" she purred again. "You don't look very sick to me!"

and she made a play of inspecting him up and down his body, much to his friends' amusement. "So, tell me, how do the lovely, dark and hot Spanish ladies compare to us here in grey and chilly London?" she teased, again running her fingers around his chin.

"Extremely well, I'm afraid to say," he responded, his eyes now narrowed on her. "They're fiery and passionate and you always know exactly who you're dealing with."

Bella laughed with the other young officers. "Oh dear, I don't think your charming friend here likes us English ladies, or *Lionesses*, but never mind," and she picked up the pack of cards from the centre of the table and started to deal them around. "I'm sure all you Gentlemen would like to play a game with me?" As she got to Nicky, she cocked her head to one side and smiled, "What about you? Are you going to play with me tonight?"

Glaring at her now, Nicky bit out softly, "I don't think so. I only play with people I trust. What's more, I've learned to only play games with people when I can see their faces." His friends gasped at such an insulting comment from their usually urbane and charming fellow officer, puzzled at his attitude to the woman.

"Oh, what a shame, what a coward you are. You're obviously no brave lion," she purred back, the other men now curious at the interesting exchange passing between the pair of them.

"On the contrary," he replied slowly, a lecherous smile now curving his mouth, his own hand roving down her soft neck, feeling the frisson as he touched her and she shivered. "I love playing games, all SORTS of games, especially with the ladies. I just like to know who they are first."

"I'm *Lionesse*, everyone knows that, so why won't you play with me? Something tells me you'd really enjoy it," and they sat and stared at each other, now completely oblivious to the others around the table who were fascinated with the very personal banter that was obviously going on, the spark between them obvious.

"I don't think so, thank you," he whispered at her as he rose from the table and bowed. "I had a very UNPLEASANT experience the last time I played with someone wearing a mask and I would rather not repeat it."

Bella rose to her feet and went to stand in front of him, temporarily barring his escape from the table. She once again ran her hand down his face and into his hair as it curled around the nape of his neck. "That's such a terrible pity," she said softly and then leaned up so only he could hear as she whispered in his ear, "and you're such a terrible liar. I know it was an extremely PLEASANT experience the last time you played with someone in a mask; in fact, I got the impression you'd almost died of the pleasure," and she leaned back again to say softly, "you really should try it again, I'm sure you'd enjoy it; I know I would," she finally whispered to him before leaning up and placing a quick tantalising kiss on his lips, running her tongue lightly across them and taking a gentle nibble before standing back and then nonchalantly taking her seat once more as the other men goggled at what they'd just witnessed.

Nicky's whole body had stiffened at her suggestive comments and he could feel himself harden with almost uncontrollable desire as he remembered exactly what she'd done to him on that last night he'd spent with her. His body wanted him to drag her out of the card room, upstairs to her apartment bedroom, where he needed to fuck the life out of her, all night, until the morning, so riven with lust was he. But once again, his mind balked while his hand went up to feel his necklace through the soft material of his cravat and shirt.

"Yes, being the bitch in heat you obviously are, you probably would, but of course I wouldn't, that's the point," he breathed back at her. "Not with someone I don't trust, certainly not a deceitful, lying lioness." As his friends gaped at his insulting comments, he merely turned, smiled apologetically at them and walked away, back to join the rest of his group of friends playing at another table.

If she hadn't been wearing a mask, Bella didn't know how she would have coped with Nicky's insulting remarks, nor how she stopped herself from running out the room, up to her bedroom, to give in to the tears she could feel creeping out her eyes; but as it was, in front of his friends and the rest of the curious clientele, she merely tossed her head, tutted, smiled beguilingly at them and continued to play. "Now then, Gentlemen, we'll leave your crabby friend to his ill humour and continue, shall we?"

As soon as she was able, she did excuse herself and retreated up to her little bolthole where she gave in to her distress and cried brokenly for the rest of the night. Nicky, meanwhile, returned to Hertford Street where he stormed into his study, slammed the door and promptly drank himself into a stupor, finally collapsing on top of his desk where his shocked secretary found him the following morning.

Chapter Twenty-Five

I t was Christmas and as ever, there was an enormous gathering down at Firle Manor. The rambling old house was bursting at the seams as the family gathered to celebrate. Cat and Eddie's two younger sisters and their families had come as usual; their elderly widowed mother and Cat's widowed godmother, long bosom friends, sat and moaned to each other endlessly about their various ailments; the four boisterous Granville sons were with their usual parcel of noisy friends and their various young cousins ran amok around the house and gardens, despite the best efforts of their parents, Governesses and nannies to keep them well behaved. Eddie had arrived with Charlie, Bella's little brother, along with the Widow of Hertford Street, to whom he had indeed been introduced by his sister shortly after the Dowager's funeral.

A quiet, attractive and apparently conservative woman in her early forties, the blonde Lady Elise Montgomery was gentle, reserved but very kind and, as the Dowager had soon discovered, nobody's fool under her serene and pale exterior. She was thoughtful and considerate of the scarred, crippled and widowed man who so obviously still missed his late wife, whose striking olive looks and very dark hair were the complete opposite of her own fair skinned beauty. However, the pair had struck up a friendship and spent many hours playing chess, backgammon, piquet, faro and other card games, or were deep in discussion or friendly argument on all manner of esoteric, political or academic matters. With her dry wit, Eddie found Elise extremely entertaining and intelligent company, not nearly as conservative as he'd originally thought. She had yet to beat him at chess, but each time they played was getting closer and closer as she was quite a formidable player, not to mention giving him more than a run for his money at the card table. For the first time in years, Eddie had found himself less sad and looked forward to seeing the lovely Elise more and more frequently, which meant he spent more and more time back in London, which he was doing anyway in order to enjoy the delights of his new little granddaughter who conveniently lived just a few houses up the street from Elise. He had now finally taken the plunge and asked her to spend Christmas with his family down in Sussex and, to his pleasure, having nowhere else to go and no family of her own, she had readily agreed.

Nicky had planned to stay at Litlington and drive back and forth to Firle each day, now that the house had been refurbished and redecorated, but a heavy snowfall on the journey down to Sussex made that prospect impossible and it was all their coach could do to get to Firle Manor without getting stuck in drifts on the narrow country lanes over the rolling Downs. So it was that guest rooms, even in the big, rambling old house, were in short supply and on their arrival the elderly housekeeper, Mrs Collins, greeted them with a harassed smile and apologetically asked if the Duke and Duchess would mind sharing a room. As the question was somewhat rhetorical and not expecting any demur, she promptly turned and led them off upstairs, instructing a hovering nursery maid to take a grizzling Lady Thérèse up to the nursery floor. Left alone in their comfortable room, before the door had barely shut behind the well-meaning housekeeper, Nicky turned on Bella and bit out, "Don't even think I'm going to share a bed with you, You Bitch."

"Well, that's a relief," Bella responded tartly. "Sleep on the floor or in the stables for all I care, it's no doubt all you're fit for. I'm sure the mares there, as opposed to your usual haunts in London, would be pleased of your company!" The pair of them glared at each other before Nicky swore roundly at her and stormed out, going downstairs in search of masculine company and a bottle, to try and calm his already seething temper which had been slowly gathering steam in the close confinement of the coach all the way from London.

They avoided each other all evening, not too difficult in a house heaving with people. Bella went to bed leaving Nicky engrossed in a raucous game of cards with the younger Granville boys. She stoked up the fire in their room against the bitter cold outside and stood for a while, staring out at the snow-covered landscape behind the heavily curtained, frosted windows. Then, smothered from head to foot in a voluminous nightgown and some woolly socks to keep out the cold, she crept into bed, leaving a single candle burning on the mantelpiece. She eventually fell into a nervous and restless slumber.

Well into the early hours, Nicky staggered upstairs and into their room. It was bitterly cold, despite the fire burning in the grate. He looked with distaste at the rug in front of the hearth and then the warm cosy bed across the other side of the room. Bella was buried deep under the covers, right up to one edge and with a shiver he sat down in an armchair and pulled off his boots. Leaving on his shirt, pantaloons and stockings, he blew out the candle and in the glow of the firelight, made his way over to the bed and carefully climbed in the other side, keeping as far away from the sleeping occupant already there. He pulled the covers up over himself and settled down to try and sleep.

The two of them lay there like a pair of statues. Bella was furious to be woken up, thinking he made as much noise as a herd of elephants and she could smell the heavy fumes of brandy on him. Irritated, she thumped her pillow and muttered to herself as she tried to get comfortable again, keeping as near to the edge of the bed as possible. Nicky lay on his side, trying to keep his own body from reacting to the warm, luscious figure it knew was lying so close and resolutely focused his mind on going to sleep.

Bella woke up just before dawn, feeling the chill air on her nose above the covers. The fire had almost gone out as Nicky hadn't topped it up when he'd come to bed, and as she felt restless and uncomfortable, she crept out of bed and quietly added some more coals to the embers herself while they still glowed. She peered behind the thick drapes and ran her fingers down the frost covered glass; she shivered then crept back to bed, snuggling under the heavy covers, trying to get warm again. She lay there, listening to Nicky's quiet breathing. Despite her anger she admitted to herself she was so bereft and full of yearning for him, it was like a deep, permanent ache in her heart that she couldn't seem to overcome. She was desperate to feel his arms around her, to comfort her and to love her, just like he did with Terrie. She wouldn't mind if he would just laugh, or even smile at her as he used to, anything was better than this remote, bitter individual he had become whenever they were alone together.

She was so cold and lonely and as a sorrowful tear rolled down her cheek, her legs crept over towards the warm side of the bed and gently twined round his. When his legs gently rubbed hers, she shifted slightly nearer to his body and the warmth emanating from it. Gradually, she crept closer and closer until she was next to him and could gently let her arm drape around his waist. She lay quietly for a while, soothed by his presence and nearness and started to drift off to sleep again when he sighed in his sleep, shifted and rolled over, pulling her unresisting body into his arms and cuddling her protectively against his comforting, warm torso. Sighing at the simple pleasure she now felt, hugged close to him, Bella closed her eyes and dropped at long last into a deep, contented sleep.

Nicky woke slowly to find Bella snuggled in his arms, fast asleep, her soft bottom pressed against his groin and her long nightdress riding up around her thighs as her legs and sock-covered feet entwined with his. His body immediately reacted to her arousing presence and he groaned as she moved slightly in her sleep, the movement tantalising against his now growing erection. Of its own volition his hand stole down and gently stroked the bare skin of her legs, tempted almost beyond belief to pull the nightdress further up and explore the soft body beneath.

He groaned again as he came fully awake and realised he'd been asleep with her so close and his frustration turned to anger at himself that he seemed unable to keep her at arm's length even in his sleep. He pulled away from her and climbed out of bed, shivering slightly despite the fire that was now burning brightly and drew back the curtains to look at the icy landscape outside the windows. Wanting to escape her tempting presence, he pulled on his boots and jacket and grumpily made his way downstairs, fuming that he'd had to get up so early because he couldn't face staying in bed with her there as well.

He was surprised to find Francis in the dining room, Bubbles at his feet and looking hopeful as Francis finished off an early breakfast, the latter raising his own eyebrows at the sight of Nicky up so early and looking somewhat dishevelled. "Well, I'm sure I don't know what you're doing here, but this is the only time of day I can get any peace to do some work. The whole place seems to have turned into an asylum for the deranged, as usual, given the noise and chaos that appears to have taken over the entire household; there's not a quiet or silent corner to be had anywhere, unless I want to sit in the garden and turn into an icicle or snowman," and he grinned as Nicky chuckled at the familiar grouse. "I can't believe you've suddenly turned into a workaholic too, surely?"

"Not yet," laughed Nicky. "I just had a bit too much to drink with your dear sons last night, woke up early with a headache and couldn't get back to sleep."

Francis didn't believe him for a moment but said nothing. He and Cat had noticed how strained Nicky and Bella had been in each other's company over the past few months, but deciding to let them sort out their own problems, had agreed to leave them to it and not interfere. Wiping his mouth with his napkin and finishing off his coffee, he rose to take his leave, merely suggesting they might like to go out for a bracing gallop later in the morning unless Nicky wanted to be drawn into building a snowman or have snowballs stuffed down his shirt by someone's crazed offspring. Nicky hastily took him up on his offer – anything to get him out of the house and away from Bella – and agreed to meet him at the stables later.

However, on their return, Nicky did get drawn into building one of a troop of snowmen who were now lined up like soldiers on the lawns. Bella looked down enviously and sadly from their bedroom window as she watched him rolling around in the soft snow, wrestling and laughing uproariously with the hordes of youngsters attacking each other with snowballs and falling around in delight. Even the stable hands and grooms who'd been diverted to shovel snow off the paths around the house, were fooling around, laughing at the antics of the guests and occasionally throwing snowballs at each other.

It was Christmas Eve and later that evening, those that could, either trekked or rode on horseback down to the village church for Midnight Mass. Nicky managed to avoid being anywhere near Bella for the round of '*Merry Christmas*' wishes and kisses that were exchanged by everyone after the service and walked back up to the house with all four Granville boys, trying and failing miserably to keep them in order when he discovered they'd all brought flasks of brandy with them and had been surreptitiously drinking all throughout the service.

As everyone tramped into the festooned hall, stamping their feet and shaking off the snow, happily downing tankards of hot, strong wassail or mulled wine, there was much giggling as couples paused to kiss under the huge bough of mistletoe that now dangled from a low-hanging beam. Cat watched with a smirk and no little pleasure as her brother gently pulled a blushing and slightly bemused Elise into his arms. She then smiled wickedly to herself as she watched the delightful widow melt into Eddie's embrace, pink with embarrassment, as she lost herself in a rather unexpected cuddle, albeit with very circumspect but tender kisses on both cheeks the end of her nose and a final, last-minute delicious peck on the lips. They pulled apart slowly, obviously surprised at what had just passed between them, amid some good-natured teasing by his other sisters and their husbands. Cat regarded them happily as the pair wandered off, arm in arm, into the sitting room, eyes only for each other, their relationship now definitely moving on to another level. She thought how pleased the Dowager would have been to see that. She doubted her brother would ever totally get over the loss of his beloved Carlotta, but if he could find happiness with another woman who would understand and also give him companionship, affection, even love again, she was delighted for them both.

Nicky got dragged under the mistletoe by several of Bella's now slightly tipsy young female cousins amid much giggling, as she watched from a corner with no little jealousy, but wearing an apparently smiling and happy face, as he kissed them all soundly, albeit circumspectly, leaving them all blushing profusely and sighing romantically.

Mischievous as ever, despite her promise to Francis, Cat wasn't going to completely stand by and watch Nicky and Bella ignore each other, so with some innocently whispered prompting into the receptive ear of a romantic young niece, Nicky was pushed and shoved to collect Bella from her corner and give her a Christmas kiss under the mistletoe. When all he did was kiss her on the cheek, there was much catcalling in the hall and Bella stood rooted to the spot as he looked down into her impassive face, watching as hate and desire glittered in his eyes as he then pulled her into his arms and his mouth descended over hers. What obviously started as something forced and unfeeling, suddenly changed as their lips met and fireworks crackled between them. Bella gasped as Nicky was suddenly kissing her hungrily and carnally, feeling him harden against her as his tongue drove into her mouth and her mind reeled as she gave in to her own yearning desire and kissed him back, her arms snaking around his neck to let her hands rove through his thick, soft hair. It was all rather inappropriate given the round-eyed, innocent audience, except for Cat who merely smirked to herself, pleased with her interfering.

However, as suddenly as he'd started to kiss her, Nicky pulled away quickly, breaking the passionate contact, his golden eyes alive with anger and lust as he continued to stare at her for a few moments. Bella wasn't sure if he was angry at her or himself, but then the moment was lost as he turned and picked up another tankard of the hot, spiced wine from a passing footman and made his way into the large sitting room, now filled with friends and relations all milling around, full of Christmas cheer and making merry. As everyone else slowly followed him, chattering and laughing, Bella loitered in the hall and quietly made her escape back up to their room where she undressed and crawled into bed, tears yet again overwhelming her confused feelings.

Once more Nicky came to bed late, drunk and reeking of mulled wine and brandy and, once again, crept under the covers to stay on his side of the bed. Bella had worn herself out from weeping and was fast asleep. This time they kept to their own sides of the bed all night and the following day they were still acting like strangers with each other.

Christmas Day passed in a blur of noisy, riotous family fun. Everyone exchanged presents and Nicky's face was impassive as he opened his large parcel from Bella to discover the biggest box of chocolate bonbons he or anyone there had ever seen – layer upon layer upon layer of the delicious treats in all sorts of flavours, the top of the chocolate mountain and by far the biggest layer being his favourites with the soft, creamy, brandy-flavoured centre. *"A treat for the jailer's pet - not that you've been good enough to deserve them"* read the tart message which he hastily stuffed in his jacket pocket as he popped one of the delicious treats in his mouth, looking enigmatically at Bella as he did so and merely blowing her a thank-you kiss across the room with his fingers.

Bella opened her gift to discover a mask, a lioness mask. Everyone laughed, thinking it merely a beautiful accessory for a masked ball or party, but only Bella and her aunt and uncle realised the significance, being the only ones who knew about her little gambling business sideline, as well as what had happened between her and Nicky. This mask was quite stunning; large, gold, with golden decorations, whiskers and an evil look on its wild, fierce and feral face. *"Never trust a lioness, they're much too dangerous"* read his message. Bella lifted it from where it sat on a layer of black satin and tied it round her face, smiling at everyone and making them all laugh as she growled at them. Then, before he realised her intention, she went over to Nicky and bent to kiss him, just a quick peck on the mouth before leaning and whispering in his ear, "This one is obviously not nearly so ticklish. How convenient; perhaps the next person I entertain will thank me to wear it." As he looked at her venomously, she merely tweaked him on the nose and went back to sit down, carefully removing the mask and placing it back in its boxM, never taking her eyes off him.

After all the present exchanges and an enormous dinner of many courses, the older members of the family retreated to a quiet drawing room to doze in front of the fire or play cards in peace. The younger members, feeling the need to expend some energy, proceeded to tear around the house in games of hide and seek, murder, and all sorts of silly parlour games. Their screams and shrieks were enhanced and their behaviour deteriorated generally, as one of the Granville sons, notably Alex, Earl of Jevington, the eldest of Cat and Francis's two sets of twins and heir to the Dukedom, as well as supreme hooligan and endless practical joker, had seen fit to empty several bottles of his father's best port and brandy into the previously innocuous bowls of fruit punch, laid out for their refreshment.

Bella had been up to the nursery to oversee the nursery maid with Terrie and to put her down to sleep. She returned to the ballroom to find a chaotic and somewhat inappropriate game of blind man's bluff in progress and someone playing the piano so some couples could try and waltz round the room at the same time. Helping herself to a glass of punch, and nearly choking as she downed it, goggling and grinning at its obviously strong alcoholic content, which she hoped her uncle didn't come in and discover, she continued to stand and indulge herself in several glasses of the toxic brew, chatting happily to her various cousins and their friends and getting somewhat inebriated. She watched laughingly as her now slightly drunken young relations chased each other around the large room where one or two had already passed out or fallen asleep on some of the armchairs and sofas around the walls. She giggled as Nicky got himself caught by a young blonde cousin who Bella knew was barely sixteen and who proceeded to run her hands over him in an extremely forward fashion, but he laughingly extricated himself from her with good grace. In the main, it was all relatively harmless fun, though no doubt her de Mornay grandmother would be horrified if she'd seen them all and she giggled again. She was still laughing and not paying much attention when she realised Nicky had taken the blonde's place and was now being teased by a number of young girls in the centre of the room, a large kerchief tied over his eyes. Before she realised what he was at, her tall, handsome cousin, Alex, sidled over and grabbed her, grinning lecherously from ear to ear before promptly dragging her across the room and pushing her straight into Nicky's outstretched arms.

Nicky knew who he held in his arms the minute he pulled her tightly to him, he'd recognise that intoxicating scent anywhere. He ran his sightless hands up over her face, time suddenly standing still for the pair of them and the suggestive jeers and ribald jokes faded into the background as with a despairing groan he pulled her face to his and kissed her passionately. It was as if the past eighteen months had evaporated as his mouth roved over her face and neck, tasting the creaminess of her skin and then his lips returned again to hers as he pulled her body hard against his and uncontrolled, hungry passion overwhelmed them both.

"What the DEVIL is going on in here?" Francis's loud, commanding voice seared across the music and general mêlée and broke the spell that had Nicky and Bella in its grip. Ignoring the pair of them in the middle of the room as they jumped apart and Nicky tore the handkerchief from his face, Francis eyed his eldest son with a suspicious glare and took in the general chaos, as everyone held their breath and prayed he didn't decide to inspect the punch. However, it appeared he merely assumed everyone was just getting a tad over-excited and after bidding them to keep the noise down, he gave his oldest offspring another baleful glance which earned him a cheeky wink in return. That made him glare even more fiercely which was, of course, completely ignored; he then told everyone to behave themselves and beat a hasty retreat, a large grin crossing his face as soon as he shut the door behind him. Francis knew perfectly well the punch had been fortified, he could smell it the minute he walked into the room and he knew exactly who was responsible. But he sighed good naturedly, having reassured himself there was no harm being done, deciding to leave them to it and let them enjoy their Christmas fun. He'd have words with the young Earl of Jevington in the morning about his missing port and brandy, not that it would do any good. His son was just as mischievous and uncontrollable as he'd been at the same age and he grinned at long forgotten memories that momentarily wafted into his mind. As for Nicky and Bella, another smirk crossed his face; it appeared they were getting into the Christmas spirit after all, so with a happy sigh he returned back to the quiet confines of the drawing room and his game of cards with his brother-in-law, smiling resignedly, knowing the outcome before he even bothered to sit down again.

Overwhelmed by the passionate interlude that her uncle had inadvertently just interrupted, Bella tottered back over to the buffet table and helped herself to another large glass of punch. Knocking it back, she poured herself another, then a third and went to lean against the wall, trying to gather her scattered wits. Nicky had disappeared and for the next hour or so, Bella downed several more glasses and grew more and more tipsy. As time progressed, the effects of the punch caught up with most of the party and they either collapsed on the chairs or disappeared up to bed. Bella decided she had better do the same while she could still walk.

She weaved her way down the upstairs hallway, now dangling her new mask in her fingers, singing quietly to herself. She opened the bedroom door and twirled inside, only to be brought up short by the sight of her husband, drink in hand, standing in just his open shirt and tight pantaloons, looking down through the darkened window at the snowy gardens and line of snowmen still on parade.

"Ah, you've finally decided to come to bed, I see," he muttered, obviously slightly the worse for wear himself. He'd been drinking steadily since he'd left the room, hard on the heels of Francis.

"I'm amazed you even noticed I was gone," Bella trilled, twirling her mask on its strings as she continued to dance around the room. "Shall I put my mask on for you? You like ladies in masks, don't you?" she slurred her words slightly, her eyes roving lasciviously up and down his body as he turned from the window to look at her.

"You're drunk," he rasped nastily.

"So what?" she replied airily, tying the mask over her face. "You're not exactly sober yourself!" Bella prowled up to him to poke him in the chest, before taking a few steps back to catch her knees and sit on the edge of the bed unsteadily.

"I need to drink to get over the distasteful prospect of spending another night with you," he glared at her.

"Really?" she queried. "It didn't seem like that when you kissed me downstairs." She continued to stare at him, her head moving up and down as she inspected his body. "Nor does it look that way to me now, from where I'm sitting," she whispered, looking at the outline of his partial erection through the form-fitting tailoring. She licked her lips and leaned back on her elbows. "Would you like to strip for me again like you did before?" she purred. "That was a very interesting performance, y'know. I quite enjoyed it..."

Nicky tossed back his brandy and stalked across the room to tip the remains of the bottle standing on the mantelpiece into the glass, before finishing that as well. He turned to her, "I only do that for women I WANT to spend the night with. Definitely NOT unwanted wives and definitely NOT deceitful trollops," he enunciated his words carefully.

Bella's temper ignited and her eyes glittered. "You wanted me before, you couldn't keep your bloody hands off me," she reared up off the bed and stormed across the room, hissing, "How dare you call me a trollop!" She slapped him hard across the face. "I am a Duchess and extremely respectable!"

He slapped her back. "Really, where? Dressed up at your gambling houses in one of your teasing outfits for men to salivate over? I'm a Duke and a soldier, wounded while fighting for King and Country, that's respectable! And a rich Duke now, God help me, so if I say you're a lying trollop, that's exactly what you are. In fact, you should be stripping off for me. Isn't that what trollops do? Strip and spread their legs for rich men?" With that, Nicky grasped the front of her silk dress and pulled hard, ripping it open to her waist, her breasts overflowing out of her torn underslip, his eyes gleaming with lust as he looked at her.

"You Evil Bastard!" Bella seethed at him, trying to cover her modesty. "I wouldn't strip for you if you were the last man on earth, so if you think you're sleeping in here tonight you've got another think coming!" She went to hit him again, "GET OUT! I can't stand to have you anywhere near me."

"Whatever makes you think I'm going to SLEEP here?" he bit out at her, grabbing her wrist in a vice-like hold before she could touch him. "I'm willing to bet you're hot and wet for me already, You Bitch. You always were before." Nicky's golden eyes blazed down at her, his temper and lust escalating in tandem.

"NO!" Bella screeched back at him, trying to pull her hand free.

"Oh yes, My Dear Wife," he whispered venomously as he grabbed her other wrist, the frustration stoked by their kisses the night before and that evening, together with the past two nights he'd spent lying next to her, now boiling over.

They stood panting, glaring at each other, she still in the lioness mask, her breasts falling out of her torn gown and he, overwhelmed with a seething desire for her that was now running out of control.

"Oh, fuck this," he swore and with one swoop, picked her up in his arms, stormed across the bedroom and threw her down on the bed, tumbling on top of her.

As Bella tried to push him off, Nicky grasped both her wrists again in one of his, pushing them up over her head. He raised himself up and looked down at her, his little lion on its chain dangling around his neck; slowly, he undid the strings of her mask, tossing it on the floor as it came away in his hands and continued to stare down at her, his golden eyes boring into her green ones.

"I promised myself that one day I would watch your face as you climax, *Lionesse*," he whispered, "and that's exactly what I'm going to do tonight, whether you like it or not."

He bent his head and kissed her but although the desire was there, there was something missing. No underlying emotion, passion or tenderness, or playfulness. He seemed hard, cold and emotionally distant and Bella cried out, "No, Nicky, please... I beg you."

"Merry Christmas, Arabella de Bresancourt," and he ripped open the rest of her dress. "You wanted to be my wife, the Duchess of Valenciennes, so deal with the reality. I know you want this," and he bent to kiss her again, hard and hungry.

"No, Nicky, please no," Bella sobbed. She pulled fruitlessly again against his iron hands. "I don't care about being a Duchess, or whether you're rich or poor. I never have, you know that. I just want the Nicky I grew up with, the one who I met at *Le Lion d'Or*," she finally whispered.

"I am the Nicholas you know, anyone else is a figment of your imagination."

"No, you're not the man I knew, the man I want," she whispered brokenly. "Please don't do this."

"Why not? Don't pretend you don't want it." He ran his hand caressingly down her almost naked body exposed under the ripped dress, feeling her shudder and squirm as he did so, his eyes narrowed and glittering. "You want it as much as I do, *Lionesse*," he whispered.

"I'm not *Lionesse*," Bella cried frantically, sobbing. "She's a figment of your imagination, a joke. I'm Bella, your Sooty."

"You're not Sooty," he said coldly. "She's long gone. She was a lovely, mischievous but innocent little girl with her hair in two long plaits with ribbons on the ends that were always undone from their bows, freckles all over her nose, mucky hands from climbing trees, scraped knees from where she was always falling over, muddy shoes and more often than not, you had a tear in your dress and the pinafore was always grubby. That was Sooty. You're *Lionesse*, a hard, manipulative woman who runs gambling houses and who lies and steals to get what she wants. Unfortunately, you're also my wife," he added, almost snarling.

"I'm still Sooty," Bella was crying now. "Just grown up. I'm still the same person inside, the person who loves you," she whispered.

"Loves me? Hah! You don't know what love is, You Bitch. You may have been infatuated once, but now, you're just like all the rest of the women in the upper reaches of the Ton. Deceitful, devious, avaricious and sly, looking for a rich, titled husband and then doing whatever they want to entertain themselves on the quiet when they've landed one."

"No, Nicky, you're so wrong," she shook her head back and forth on the pillows, hating his cynicism, tears running down her face.

"Tears don't work on me, Sweetheart," he said coldly, "but just remember, I AM your husband, you're mine and nobody else's." He leaned down then and bit lightly on the side of her neck, taunting her by nibbling down further to the tender junction with her shoulder, making her shudder and jerk again. "This is no marriage of convenience anymore, so I'll have you whenever, wherever and however I want – and I'll kill anyone else who touches you." His voice was like ice as his free hand caressed her body again, fondling her breasts and teasing her nipples until Bella was moaning with pleasure, yet still begging him to stop. Then, as if he'd reached the end of his tether, Nicky almost tore open his own clothing and drove hard inside her, groaning as he felt himself surrounded by her hot, moist, enveloping softness.

Passion ignited like a roaring fire between them as Nicky thrust deep, making Bella cry out as the long months of loneliness and yearning dissipated in a torrent of love and lust. Her now released hands roamed over his shoulders and back, her nails raking his skin, her legs crossing behind him as she willed him further inside her. She felt a maelstrom start, she moaned and twisted under him, totally lost to the feelings he ignited within her. He filled her completely: rampant, large, hard and throbbing; his big, powerful body overwhelmed her; the scent that was uniquely him surrounded her. She didn't need him to tell her she was his, she had never been and could never be anyone else's.

Nicky closed his eyes, feeling her muscles convulse around him, as if trying to draw him more profoundly into her coils. She had haunted his dreams for months and put all other women he'd bedded in the shade, for reasons he couldn't fathom. Many were far more experienced and talented, yet he now wanted and hated this one with a venomous passion such as he'd never known. He lost control as he thrust harder and faster, wildly, then manically as if he were somehow possessed, finally feeling her muscles ripple and contract around him, then her sobbing cries. As her whole body jerked and went into spasm, her back arched off the bed and she screamed with the pleasure. He rose up for a few distracted seconds to stare down into Bella's glittering green eyes as they burst open, widened, then turned glazed and unseeing. Momentarily, they seemed to stare helplessly back into his deep golden ones and as he finally watched her climax, Nicky closed his eyes again slowly, with grim satisfaction, thrusting deeply, forcefully and possessively one more time before crying out as a release, almost painful in its impact, overtook his entire shuddering body.

They both lay on the bed, gasping and panting, each overwhelmed with the intensity of their climax, the see-sawing passions and emotions. Bella couldn't speak, she was so overcome, merely lay like a limp rag doll, listening to her pounding heart, breathing unevenly, unable to pull together a single coherent thought.

Nicky rolled off her, groaned and sprawled on his stomach, his head on his forearms, feeling like he'd been cast adrift in a storm-tossed sea. He hated how he yearned to pull her into his embrace and let sleep overtake them both after that climactic coming together; he also hated how he wanted her again, once wasn't nearly enough to assuage the rampant desire that was still thrumming around his body and mind.

The power she appeared to exert over his senses and emotions angered him beyond measure but he seemed powerless to resist. Faceless, she had haunted him in the Peninsula but now, here in England, unmasked and so familiar, it was ten times worse and as he lay exhausted and emotionally drained, he swore deeply under his breath as sleep overwhelmed him.

He woke a couple of hours later to discover Bella curled under the covers, garbed once again in her voluminous nightgown, the room lit only by the glowing coals in the fireplace. He rolled off the bed, stood and pulled off his clothes before yanking back the covers and returning to kneel next to her – memories, fantasies and images in his mind making him erect and hard. He didn't care if she was asleep or not, his body craved the feel of hers again like an addict needed a fix and he carelessly pulled at the hem of her nightgown to drag it up her body and over her protesting head.

Bella came awake at the sudden feel of cold air on her warm body and cried out as she realised Nicky was intent on pulling off her night-gown. She took one look at his grim face in the dim light and tried to retreat away from his salacious stare, but to no avail. "Please don't; Nicky, please, not again," she whispered wretchedly but it was useless; the nightdress came off and was tossed to the floor and he was on top of her in moments, his hands and mouth alive on her body. Yet again she tried to resist but there was no fighting him and he was inside her, like a man possessed, tormenting her until she was begging him for release, her body wanting one thing, her mind the opposite. This time, as she shattered around him and he climaxed deep within her, his eyes were closed, as if he couldn't bear to look at her. He never spoke, not a word the entire time, afterwards merely groaning deeply as he collapsed beside her on the bed.

Bella leaned down to pull the covers back over them, the bitter chill of the night rapidly cooling their heated, sweaty bodies. He turned away from her to return to sleep on his side of the bed as she lay there, feeling forlorn, abandoned, used and bereft. As the dawn light percolated around the curtains, Nicky woke once more and gave in to the lust that still, unbelievingly to his furious mind, raged through him knowing her enticing body was mere inches away from his. For the third time, he took her coldly yet passionately, the silence only broken by her soft cries and his final groan of release. Yet again, eyes closed, he refused to look at her, preferring to pretend the woman beneath him was still the faceless entity of his fantasy instead of the real person he hated so much.

They studiously avoided each other for the whole of the following day, Bella slightly drawn and pale-faced but Nicky as his usual charming and merry self to everyone else, with the house party now fuller than ever as visiting neighbours came and went. However, now the dam was broken, it was impossible to put back. Again that night he took her several times, silently, with a passion so intense it was as if he was possessed by some devilish entity. And so, this set the pattern for the days and weeks of the new year that followed.

Chapter Twenty-Six

SPRING/SUMMER 1814

T he more Nicky made love to her, the more he wanted her. It was like a disease eating at him, but it wasn't an act of love; it was simple fornication at its basest; carnal fucking, he told himself. He was behaving truly like an addict – he couldn't keep away and he despised himself. He'd thought if he had enough sex with her, every which way, in bed and out, using her like a common whore, he would get it out of his system, but it simply seemed to make things worse. Images of her naked haunted his thoughts day and night, her soft moans and the feel of her writhing, voluptuous body a drug he constantly craved.

He refused to stay with her, returning to his own bed when he'd had his fill, leaving her alone, sad and now increasingly angry.

One night she tried locking the door from her side, but he merely broke it down and stormed across the room to take her roughly and angrily, yet again ignoring her pleas to be left in peace. He never hurt her, no matter how angry, wild or rough he sometimes got. On the contrary, seeming to take malicious pleasure in tormenting and coldly teasing her until she cried brokenly or begged for release, or pleaded simply to be left alone. The charming, playful, humorous lover who had come to *Le Lion d'Or* and captured her soul, for he already had her heart, had disappeared. In his place was this cold, intense man who never smiled and seemed to be fighting his own demons as well as her. He became her demon lover.

She started to stay away from Hertford Street, spending her nights in her apartment at *Le Lion d'Or* in an effort to escape him. But knowing she couldn't keep away from Terrie, he merely waited for her return and would pounce on her as soon as she appeared in her bedroom to wash or change.

Winter had passed and it was early March. The spring sun was shining in through her bedroom windows and Bella felt drained and empty. She'd looked at herself in the mirror that morning and saw a drawn, unhappy woman staring back at her. She couldn't carry on like this and resolutely got up to go downstairs, determined to have it out with Nicky once and for all. She was fed up with being ignored all day and used all night, despite all her efforts to escape him. She'd realised he was fighting some demons of his own, obviously hating himself for giving in to the insatiable physical attraction that existed between them which he seemed powerless to resist, still hating her for what she'd done.

The dining room was empty so she helped herself to some hot chocolate and a soft roll which she nibbled slowly, thinking about the previous night. Nicky had been out, she knew not where, but had come through to her room on his return. He'd seemed even more obsessed and demanding than usual, taking her on and off like a man possessed for virtually the rest of the night until he'd fallen asleep, exhausted, in HER bed just before dawn, which was an extremely unusual occurrence. She'd lain awake for an age, watching him sleep, taking the opportunity to caress him, running her hands through his soft hair as, despite the torrid sex night after night, he would never let her touch or caress him if he could prevent her, nor look at her, keeping his eyes closed most of the time. She hated this strange and unnatural coupling, so different to how it had been before. It made her feel like a mere rag doll, or a helpless slave to his rampant, dominating demands. Eventually, she'd snuggled down next to him, amazed when he'd wrapped his strong arms around her and pulled her close and as soft tears had run forlornly down her cheeks, she'd finally slept, but when she'd woken, he was gone; an indentation on his pillow and the lingering scent of him mixed with his cologne, the only evidence of his presence.

Having little appetite, she abandoned any pretence at eating breakfast and rose to go and confront him in his study – but the room was empty and cold with no fire burning; of his senior secretary there was no sign. Shrugging and slightly irritated at having her intentions thwarted and assuming he was out for meetings most of the day since there was no fire, or at some other entertainment she didn't want to think about, she instead made her way up to the nursery to see Terrie. Sitting in her cot, the little girl was cooing to her stuffed animals, chattering in her own incomprehensible baby babble, now a mix of mainly English and French thanks to her father, which made it even more difficult to understand. Picking her up from the cot, Bella wandered back down the corridor and poked her head round the door to the master bedroom, but it, too, was empty. Nicky had obviously gone out early, so she made her way back downstairs to her cosy little sitting room and, having placed Terrie on the carpet where she could now crawl or toddle around, she sat at her escritoire to answer a pile of social invitations she had little enthusiasm to accept.

An hour or so later, a knock at her door presaged entry by David Sinclair, Nicky's secretary, who bowed and handed her a letter with an embarrassed cough. "I'm so sorry, Your Grace, but I think His Grace left this note for you earlier, on his desk. I inadvertently picked it up by accident with some other papers he'd left for me. I trust the delay is not important...." and with that, he bowed again and backed out.

Curious, Bella broke the seal and read the short, pithy note:

I cannot bear this Situation for a Moment Longer, living here in a house with a Woman I Despise so much. Circumstances in France are much Changed and I understand the Allies are on their way to Paris. Now I have the Wherewithal, I am therefore taking the Opportunity to go to Valenciennes, investigate the Situation there and perhaps begin to Restore my Chateau and endeavour to start to Reclaim what is Mine.

I have no idea when I will return. When the Chateau is habitable, I will *send for Thérèse, <u>MY</u> Daughter, so she may continue to live with her Father and not be brought up by an Unsuitable and Deceiving Bitch in whom I have No Trust, to whit a Gaming Saloon Hostess.*

dB

It wasn't just short, it was venomous; not even signed informally. Bella read the note with shock and reeled, hot anger flushing her cheeks. That Nicky had gone off to France, in their current state of marital warfare, she was not bothered about, in fact she was quite relieved and had expected him to do something about his old family estate now he had the monies and time to sort it out. The ongoing war with France finally appeared to be coming to an end with the collapse of Bonaparte's endeavours in Russia and eastern Europe and the retreat of the French from the Peninsula, with the English forces pushing up over the border into southern France. But the threat to take her baby from her and live in France with him was another matter. She rose to her feet to storm back and forth across the little room as rage boiled through her.

Well, he could whistle for her, she fumed. She would NEVER send Terrie anywhere without her as well. If he thought she would willingly give up her child to live in France with him permanently, the man was completely delusional. Whatever the law said about his rights, she would never accept it.

Her first instinct was to run to her uncle and ask his advice and seek his powerful protection for her and her daughter, but as she returned to sit at her desk, she realised she didn't want to air her personal problems to her family and cause divisions and arguments. She would give Nicky time and wait and see what he would do first.

Resolved, she returned to her correspondence, accepting every invitation in the pile, determined to put her misery and hateful husband out of her thoughts and go out and enjoy herself.

That afternoon, Bella took herself off shopping and ordered a new set of ball and evening gowns and for the next few weeks, went out and about, turning herself into a busy social butterfly. She flirted and danced with an endless stream of men, attracted by her stunning looks and wit. Inevitably, it was soon remarked that the former aloof Duchess was now obviously ripe for an *affaire,* in the obvious absence of her husband.

This state of affairs did not go unremarked in the Firle household and one afternoon Cat decided to call round and have a private conversation with her niece. She didn't beat about the bush.

"Whatever are you up to now, My Darling?" she asked as she eyeballed her niece. "You know you're being gossiped about and Francis is quite concerned as he says there's a book now open about you in Brooks's as to who will be the first Gentleman to have an *affaire* with you. It's a good thing your Papa is down at Arlington, but if he comes to Town any time soon, he'll be bound to see it and he'll be terribly distressed. Your uncle was bad enough, you know how protective he is of you and me."

Admittedly, Bella did look shocked at this piece of information. "Oh no! I'd no idea. But Auntie, I'd never do anything like that, you do realise?"

Cat leaned over and patted her hand. "Of course I do, My Sweet, but whatever is going on? Where IS Nicky by the way? We haven't seen him for weeks…?" she looked curiously at Bella.

"He's gone to Valenciennes," she replied with a sigh. "He went last month just before the Allies entered Paris. He wanted to reclaim and restore the chateau and endeavour get back some of the lost lands. Now Bonaparte has finally gone, I presume that will make life a bit easier." The whole of England was celebrating not only Wellington's successes in Spain but the fall and final abdication of Bonaparte.

"But why didn't you go with him, Darling? Surely he wouldn't want to go for long without seeing little Terrie? He's sooo besotted with her, especially now she's started to toddle, it's almost comical. Anyone would think no other baby had ever learned to walk before," and she laughed. "I though Francis was bad enough with Lizzie, but Nicky is much worse."

Bella was tempted to show her aunt his letter, but decided against it. "We all know the house is in ruins, so maybe I'll go over there in a while when it's a bit more habitable. It won't be a suitable place for a baby and I really don't want to stay in some nearby hostelry with her."

Cat looked keenly at her niece and knew she wasn't getting all the truth. "You're still arguing, aren't you?" she commented intuitively. "I take it he still hasn't forgiven you, hmmm?"

Bella looked at her aunt forlornly and shook her head. "If I could turn the clock back, I would. He hates me, Auntie. I don't know what to do." A lone tear ran down her cheek at the admission.

Cat pulled Bella into her comforting arms. "Oh, my poor little girl. Why ever didn't you come and tell me all this before? Come, My Love, tell Auntie Cat all about it, it'll do you good to get it off your chest and then we'll see what we can do." She sighed, "I promised your uncle I wouldn't interfere, but what he doesn't know about, he can't worry or rant about. Anyway, we ladies must stick together, eh?" She smiled at Bella, trying to cheer her up. "I know you used to unload your problems about Nicky to the Dowager, but couldn't you do that with me now? I do understand marriage difficulties, y'know. I also know what Nicky's like. Besides, your Uncle Francis and I did have our moments long ago when we first married, not that I still don't want to hit him over the head on occasion with something large and heavy when he gets some bee in his bonnet, or has one of his temper tantrums."

So, with a giggle and a bit of encouragement, Bella unburdened herself and told her aunt what had been going on and that one morning a month before, Nicky had just upped and left for France, leaving a note to say he couldn't stay there any longer, he detested her and didn't know when he would return. She left out the bit about him wanting to take Terrie from her to live in France with him.

"That idiot man obviously doesn't hate you, any fool can see that. He wouldn't spend every night in your bed if he did, that's for sure," opined Cat sagely. "Anyway, I watched him at Christmas. You thought he hated you then, but he couldn't take his eyes off you, I saw him. He eyed you like a hawk all the time. He's just had his feelings hurt, you know how proud he always was. He's taking his time getting over it, that's what I think." She looked positively at Bella, "Your uncle was just the same, when we were first married. He got some strange and wrong idea about me and it took him weeks to get over it. Evil-tempered doesn't even begin to describe him at one point, you know what he's like when he loses his rag," and she grinned. "But he came round eventually of course, they always do," and she winked naughtily at Bella. "It'll be the same with Nicky. You just have to persevere and use a little persuasion. As your dear Mama used to say to me, men can be so dense at times! And that, in my expert opinion, is an understatement!"

She patted Bella's hand. "Why not give him a few more weeks, hmmm? And then just go over there and see what he's up to? You can take Terrie, or leave her with me for a week or two; he's only along the coast from Normandy after all, not that far. I'll lend you a brandy bottle to go and knock him on the head with, if you can't find a stout branch, or just punch him on the nose if that's what it takes to make him see sense; you know, like you did when you were a little hoyden and ran around trying to get the better of him or my boys... unless of course you can find another way to persuade him...?" she smirked wickedly. "He is just a man, after all. I mean, look what happened when you took my advice last time," and she gazed knowingly over at the baby now toddling around the room, fascinated by the tassels hanging on the ends of the cords holding back the beautiful window drapes.

Bella laughed, feeling a bit better with these reassuring, amusing yet sensible words. "Oh Auntie, you are the limit, but I suppose you're right. I'll leave it for a few weeks, another couple of months at the most, then if I haven't heard anything, I think I might well pay Valenciennes a visit." She sighed, "I've always wanted to go and visit ever since I saw the Dowager's painting of it in Nicky's study."

"Good girl," smiled Cat. "In the meantime, just be mindful of the gossips. I'd hate to see your reputation sullied over nothing and, although a bit of healthy jealousy never comes amiss, after all none of us want to be taken for granted," she added, laughing, "just be careful, hmmm? The Ton thrives on tittle tattle. I'll always go with you anywhere to lend some form of respectability, just ask me any time. A clucking chaperone like Aunt Harriet, bless her heart, is something I most definitely am not!" she chuckled.

She hugged Bella lovingly. "I'll tell you what, why don't you write to him? I'm sure you can concoct something that will irritate the life out of him, then write again and wind him up even further. It won't harm him to be reminded of what he's left behind here in London, both you and Terrie..." so with that final piece of advice, Cat got up to leave. At the door, she turned and smirked wickedly, "Oh, if you need any further help on extending your French vocabulary, just let me know!"

"Auntieeeeee!" Bella giggled, feigning shock and waving as her very unladylike aunt sailed out.

Chapter Twenty-Seven

Bella wasn't surprised when her first letter didn't get a reply. So, taking her Aunt's advice she wrote again. She told Nicky about all the progress Terrie was making, hoping this would elicit a reply, if not bring him hurrying home, even for a quick visit. She'd told him in her first letter than Terrie could now walk by herself. She'd been just about toddling when Nicky had left but was now into everything; however, she was also now talking a bit too, some gibberish, but picking up new words every day that did make sense. Bella told him he was missing it all.

However, there still came no reply and she was fuming.

It was now midsummer and Nicky had been gone for four months with no word. Bella decided to give him one more month and then go and pay him a visit herself. She bunched her fingers into a fist, laughing as she remembered her aunt's advice about punching him on the nose. Angry as she was at his usual lack of communication, having absolutely no excuse now, she could think of a far more painful place to kick him, never mind hit him over the head with a stick or brandy bottle, but that thought brought back memories of one of their nights at *Le Lion d'Or* when she'd done just that, so with a sad laugh, she went off to see what mischief her little girl was now up to in the nursery.

It was three weeks later when she received a surprise visit from her father. He'd been ensconced down at Arlington all summer with the lovely Elise and despite being eaten up with curiosity at this new relationship that seemed to be developing, Bella had decided to let them have some time alone and not be a gooseberry, so hadn't seen him for quite a while. She greeted him with a big hug and kiss as he limped into the sunny drawing room and hurried upstairs to retrieve Terrie so she could be inspected and cuddled and fawned over by her doting grandfather.

As they sat over tea a short while later, amusedly watching the little girl toddle round the room, trying to catch a rather harassed black cat, Eddie turned to his daughter with a somewhat serious expression on his face. "Have you heard from Nicky lately, Poppet?" he queried.

Bella looked at him curiously. "No, Papa, actually I haven't, but he's at Valenciennes and you know what a hopeless correspondent he is," she shrugged her shoulders. "I've sent him two letters lately and not had a reply to either." She took a sip of tea, "What makes you ask, Papa?"

"Well, here's the thing," Eddie spoke quietly. "I needed to have him sign some important papers, about the Dowager's estate and moving some holdings, don't y'know. Some companies and stocks he left with me to oversee as I had an interest in that area, new mechanics and engineering and gas lighting, you know me, rather like plumbing. Nothing to interest you, Sweeting, very boring," he chuckled briefly but his face turned serious again. "Anyway, I sent them over by Special Courier and told the man on no account to come back without them signed and to be quick sticks about it."

"So?" queried Bella.

"Well, the courier fellow arrived back a couple of days ago. Said Nicky wasn't at Valenciennes, apparently hadn't been there for several weeks and no one in the chateau has any idea of where he's disappeared to. Seems he upped and left in a hurry one day... just like that," he clicked his fingers in the air. "So I was wondering if you had any idea about where he's gone?"

Bella looked concerned. "No, Papa, I don't. As I said, he's not replied to either of my letters so I was unaware he wasn't still at Valenciennes." She added, "Have you asked Uncle Francis? Has he by any chance heard from him?"

"Well, if you must know, I've just come from Firle House and Francis hasn't heard from Nicky either. Don't you think that's deuced odd, Poppet, just to up and toddle off like that without a word?"

Bella pondered as she drank her tea. "Well, Papa, knowing Nicky, nothing surprises me. Perhaps he's gone to Paris? He was going to try and reclaim some of his extended lands and properties around Valenciennes and that part of the region which used to belong to the Estate, so maybe he went there to have some meetings with the Authorities. It's probably just as simple as that. You know yourself what bureaucrats are like, things take forever as they push paper around and fuss and prevaricate. Also, France is so topsy-turvy again now Bonaparte has left, so who knows what's going on there?"

Eddie looked at his daughter in concern. "I don't think so, somehow. The courier told me Nicky had apparently gone off when he was right in the middle of a big piece of restoration that he was overseeing personally, as it was a critical part in the centre of the chateau, the main staircase or some such, so it seems a trifle strange, even for him. And, what's more, some regional government johnnies and lawyers turned up a week or so later, saying they had appointments with the Duke about his claims, so he's obviously not bogged down in the paper mire in Paris if they're coming out to him at Valenciennes. They were apparently very miffed he wasn't there to see them, as you can imagine. I don't like to bother you, Poppet, but I have to say I find it strange and I am a trifle worried now."

"Hmmm, it does sound odd, as you say," mused Bella thoughtfully, puckering her brows as she now put her cup and saucer down. "Do you know if anyone else has been to see him, any other visitors he could have gone off with? It could be something quite innocuous."

"Well, of course I don't really know, but come to think of it, my man did say something about some Englishman who'd been to call a couple of times. But that's probably one of Nicky's old rakehell or army friends calling on his way to inspect the fleshpots of Paris, now old Boney's been seen off." Eddie dismissed that comment with an airy wave of his hand.

Bella considered the teapot and another cup but was now too distracted. "Hmmm, no doubt," she tutted and she sat and thought for a while. "Look, Papa, I was actually going to go over there in the next week or two, see what he's been getting up to and take Terrie for a visit because he's been away for so long. Auntie and I were only discussing it a little while ago. I've never been to Valenciennes so I'm overdue a look around, I've heard so much about it over the years. Leave it with me and I'll go in the next few days and see what's at the bottom of it all. It's probably something quite innocuous. I wouldn't mind betting he's gone off to Paris and forgotten all about his meetings and visitors. You know how disorganised Nicky can be sometimes. It's probably some horseflesh he's after, or maybe he's located some old family friends, even a long-lost relation; it really could be anything."

"Well, I hope it's a horse or friends, though he's become much more focussed lately, at long last," Eddie mused. "I doubt it's a relation though, your Uncle Francis and I explored that avenue years ago. Every damn cousin twice removed, or even vaguely connected, all dead I'm afraid. Madame Guillotine saw to that," he muttered bitterly. "But he's really getting his head into all his business affairs now. Quite surprised me and your uncle, I have to say, but then he's got a family and responsibilities now and all this war nonsense is finished with, so he's obviously ready to settle down, finally." He leaned over and patted Bella's hand, "That's a good idea, Poppet, you go over there and see what he's up to. If you need me to come and join you, help deal with those local paper-pushers or he wants some building or plumbing advice, just send a message to the expert" he chuckled. "I'll be back down at Arlington with Elise and Charlie so it won't be a problem to hop across the Channel from there for a week or so. Might even bring them with me…"

Bella smirked at her father. "I'm glad you and Elise are getting on so well, Papa. By the way, does the Ton know you and she are there without a proper chaperone? How very inappropriate of the pair of you," she giggled.

Eddie coughed and looked a bit embarrassed. "Yes, well, ah… er… she's a widow, not a young thing like you and Charlie's there, also the butler, housekeeper and servants. We are exceeding proper, don't y'know and she's very good company. It's nice to have someone to talk to and keep me company... since your Mama..."

Bella leaned across and kissed her father gently on the cheek saying softly, "Of course, Papa, it's about time, I was only teasing. I don't think Mama would want you to be lonely for ever; you deserve to be happy again. Anyway, who gives a fig for what anyone thinks about chaperones," and she winked.

Eddie smiled sadly. "Thank you, Sweeting. No one will replace your Mama in my heart, you know that, but I'm very fond of Elise. We have so much in common and she's made me very happy over the past few months. What's more, she and Charlie get along famously; she's always wanted a child, y'see, just as long as you don't mind...?"

"Mind? Papa, I'm so pleased for you, of course I don't mind. If you're happy, then so am I. Your happiness and wellbeing is all I want." Bella sat back and smiled at her father, "Now, enough of that. Come, let's take your granddaughter out into the garden before the cat has a turn and then Terrie can go and destroy some more of the flower beds and make the gardener even more distraught than he is already!" With a light laugh, she helped him out of his chair, picked up the little girl and they wandered on to the sunny little rear terrace.

Bella was far more concerned than she had let on to her father and as soon as he left, she made her way straight round to Berkeley Square to see her uncle, marching into his study with a resolute expression on her face. Francis took one look at her and hastily dismissed his secretary, sitting back in his chair with a sigh. "I know that expression, Puss, what is it now?" he groaned, smiling.

"Where is he, Uncle? And don't tell me you don't know. Has he been sent off to do something else for Wellington? I thought he'd finished with all that now, after he'd been wounded?" Bella didn't mince her words and got straight to the point.

Francis looked at his niece through narrowed eyes and sighed. "I don't know where he is, Bella. I haven't heard from him, I give you my word. I was telling your father the truth." Francis knew Eddie was going round to see his daughter after his recent visit. "Nicky told me what I presume he told you, he was going to see about claiming back and starting the restoration at Valenciennes and get down to trying to sort out the de Bresancourt affairs over there." He looked at Bella with concern, "To be honest, I've been so busy over the past few months, now that this damn war seems to finally be over, that it hadn't occurred to me you might not have heard from him. Obviously you haven't?"

"No, Uncle, not a word – and I've written twice. Not that I expect Nicky to think about writing, you know what he's like." She took a deep breath, "And, er, matters between us have been a bit difficult lately, as you know," she finished stiffly.

"Hmmm, I did wonder, Puss, you've not been your usual sunny self for months." Francis leaned forward to pat her hand, "He'll come round, you'll see, it's just his damn pride again; just be patient, hmmm?" then he sat back again, looking thoughtful. "So, he's just disappeared into thin air, has he? That's a bit strange, even for our Nicky. I wonder...?" and he tapped his lips thoughtfully with steepled fingers as he pondered. "Leave it with me, Sweetheart, I'll make some enquiries and let you know. I promise."

"Will you, Uncle? I know you know far more than you ever tell me. We've been here before, so why can't you treat me like an adult, like a man. I have as much right to know as you," she grumbled. "I was going to go over and visit with Terrie in a couple of weeks anyway, so it would be good to know what's going on before I set off on a wild goose chase. PROMISE ME, you will tell me if he's been sent off on Army business, won't you?"

"I promise, Bella, if he's gone off on Army business I'll tell you." Francis looked at his niece with a straight face. Ashcroft's business wasn't necessarily Army business so he wouldn't break his promise. If Nicky had disappeared suddenly, he'd bet that wily gentleman would be at the bottom of it. However, Francis was worried at Nicky's sudden disappearance, although he didn't show it, and surreptitiously glanced at his fob watch, then out through the window. It was a pleasant afternoon and for once, he had nothing so important that couldn't wait a couple of hours. He thought he might take a stroll across the park to the Ministry and pay Ashcroft a little visit, to put his mind at rest.

"Don't worry, Puss," he said reassuringly to Bella. "We'll find out. It's probably something quite innocuous. He's likely to have gone off to Paris, if I know Nicky. For all we know, he might well be back at Valenciennes now, as we speak, overseeing a new roof or windows. Hah! He might even have found his infamous treasure!" On that amusing note he upped and kissed her, shooing her out of his study with a suggestion she go and have some tea with her aunt.

Chapter Twenty-Eight

Bella was an extremely intelligent young woman, academically educated and informed well beyond most of her peers, thanks to her father, whose brains she had undoubtedly inherited. She was also more than knowledgeable about both business and current affairs, even more so now she had Elizabeth Granville's inheritance to oversee, as well as her little gaming saloon enterprises. She took her responsibilities extremely seriously and she was also observant and astute, so she understood her devious and amusing uncle more and more, now she'd matured into her twenties.

She was well aware Francis Granville had made it his business over the years to have connections in various Government Departments, where he picked up a lot of information that was extremely useful to his business empire, but these contacts and information also related to the military and the endless wars that Britain was involved in, not just in Europe but over in the Americas, the Indian sub-continent and other parts of the globe where His Majesty's Empire was expanding... and that he kept most of what he knew to himself. In the main, it was of no use or interest to his family anyway... but if it was connected to Nicky, as far as Bella was concerned it was of enormous interest. She understood that sometimes State Secrets were involved in what he knew, but if Nicky was an agent of some sort – she had come to the conclusion that this was very likely the case – she wanted to know about it. She wasn't a fool and she was hugely irritated her uncle wouldn't trust her to keep a secret or thought she wasn't mature enough to deal with bad news.

She'd watched his face very carefully as they'd discussed Nicky's disappearance and she'd bet the night's takings from *Le Lion d'Or* that he was disturbed. She'd noted the slight narrowing of his eyes and pursed lips, could almost see one part of his brain calculating as he talked pacifying banalities to her with the other. Watching punters gamble in her clubs had given her plenty of expertise and experience in reading people's expressions, emotions, private thoughts and intentions; considerably more than she'd ever gained playing cards or chess with her father or extended family. When Francis had glanced at his watch and looked out of the window, Bella noticed and was positive he'd decided to go and find out for himself what was happening. Hoping against hope he'd decided to walk to his destination – hence the glance out of the window – and that it wouldn't turn out to be his club where she'd be barred from entry, she airily and noisily bade goodbye to the butler, left the house and concealed herself around the corner to wait for the Duke to leave, intent on following him.

Sure enough, some fifteen minutes later, her uncle swept through the front door and set off at a smart pace from Berkeley Square, down to Piccadilly, across the paths of Green Park to The Mall, then across St James's Park, headed in the direction of the Government buildings around Whitehall. Bella hurried after him, keeping herself at a distance. It wasn't difficult to keep the Duke in her sights, his very tall and imposing figure making him stand out amongst the general melee of people going about their business on the busy afternoon streets and strolling through the parks. As he crossed the road and headed towards Horse Guards Parade, Bella got a bit closer, needing to see which building he was aiming for. There were fewer people around here now and she herself stood out as a lone woman walking among groups of soldiers and grey, suited clerks. However, she tried to walk purposefully and when her uncle disappeared through a door in an anonymous looking Ministry building, she hurried inside after him.

Bella watched as he strode across the foyer, merely nodding at the uniformed man on duty, and thence up a wide, large staircase, portraits of long forgotten generals and politicians looking down on the scene. Aha, this was obviously somewhere connected with the military, she concluded. No surprise given the building was adjacent to Horse Guards Parade. As she made her own way across the foyer, the uniformed attendant halted her and enquired about her business there. Waving her hand vaguely in the direction of the stairs and in her best impression of her late Great Aunt Elizabeth in full flow, she looked him up and down disdainfully and haughtily uttered, "Kaindly do not look at me like that. Anyone would think you had never seen a Lady before. Ai am with the Duke of Firle, Mai Good Man. Surely you saw him enter just a moment ago? I merely dropped a glove outsaide and he is waiting for me just up there, look for yourself..." Bella turned her head in the direction of the upper floor and waved her hand airily again. "We have an urgent appointment and are late, so kaindly let me pass, or the Duke be down to give you a piece of his mind if you are not careful. He cannot abide me dillydallying," and with that, she brushed past the bemused man and set off up the stairs at a brisk pace, trying not to giggle to herself at her acting, thinking how amused the Dowager would have been to witness it.

As she got to the first floor, she looked around hurriedly, irritated her delay by the busybody downstairs had caused her to lose her quarry. But fortunately, as she peered down one long corridor, she just spotted her uncle as he turned the corner at the end of the long passageway. She followed him silently, ready at any moment to enter through one of the many doors that lined the hallway in an effort to conceal herself in case he turned back.

Francis continued to make his way down the maze of corridors until he eventually stopped in front of one of the many plain wooden doors. He didn't knock, which surprised her, just entered, leaving it ajar. Bella crept along behind him, holding her breath. As she neared the door, she was grateful for the silent corridor as she overheard the Duke's aristocratic and demanding tones enquire if 'Ashcroft' was in his office as he required an urgent word with him. Obviously, the answer had been yes, as the door was pushed to and closed firmly and her uncle stayed inside. Bella approached and looked at the simple plaque on the door: "Department of Information" was all it said and she tutted to herself. Obviously much more than that and for a few moments she stood there, trying to decide what to do. Not knowing how long her uncle would be there, she decided to beat a hasty retreat, go home and return first thing in the morning to inveigle herself in to see this mysterious Ashcroft and find out what was going on.

She wandered down more corridors and past various military offices before she finally found another exit door leading out into Whitehall itself; from there, she made her way back to Hertford Street, lost in thought.

Chapter Twenty-Nine

T he following morning Bella rose and chose her attire carefully. She wanted to look mature and intimidating enough to be taken seriously by whoever this Ashcroft was, assuming him to be some military bureaucrat or paper-pusher, yet feminine enough if she needed to exercise some womanly wiles on him to obtain the information she wanted. She'd learned the Dowager's lessons well.

With a final look in the mirror at her severe gown and restrained hairstyle she felt pleased with her appearance. Her bonnet was an artful confection, a counterpoint to the severity of her clothes. The cut of the outfit didn't stop it from fitting her figure like a suggestive glove and the restrained hairstyle beneath the hat only served to enhance the fine lines of her face with its high cheekbones. She pinched her cheeks to brighten their glow, lightly sooted her already thick black lashes and finally rubbed some soft pink salve on her lips to allow them to glimmer with moisture. With diamonds glittering in her ears, a suitably large brooch and more sparkling gems on her fingers and wrists, she deemed herself ready for battle and marched downstairs to climb into her waiting carriage. The Department of Information had no clue as to the determination of the woman on her way to visit them.

This time, the busybody on the door merely nodded at her entry, recognising her from the previous afternoon, except now much more finely dressed. She gave him a haughty stare as she swept past and made her way up the stairs before he changed his mind and tried to question her again. As Bella hurried down the corridors, she momentarily wondered if she ought to start wearing one of Great Aunt Elizabeth's lorgnettes, just for effect of course, to stare sundry upstart busybodies down as she inspected them through it; she giggled to herself once more at the vision she had. Finally, she stood again outside the familiar door. As the Duke had done, she didn't knock, merely entered purposefully and announced herself to the slightly startled clerk who was writing at the desk in front of a door towards the back of the large room. There were cupboards and paper-filled shelves around it, chairs standing near some walls and other side doors presumably leading off to further rooms. Bella had decided the entire building was a complete rabbit warren. "The Duchess of Valenciennes to see Ashcroft." Bella stared down at the man in her best supercilious impression of the Dowager. She decided a lorgnette was now a must as this individual didn't seem impressed by his visitor, nor her demeanour.

The clerk looked up at Bella impassively. "You do not appear to have an appointment, Your Grace. Perhaps someone else can help you?" his voice was as grey as he was: hair, skin, jacket and waistcoat.

"Ai do not think so, thank you. Ashcroft WILL see me. Kaindly let him know Ai am here," and she turned to take a seat in the seemingly plain room.

"But you do NOT have an appointment, Your Grace. Perhaps I can be of service? What sort of Information were you requiring? You may not have come to the right Department?"

Bella glared at him. "Ai have come to EXACTLY the raight Department, Mai Man. Now, will you announce me to Ashcroft or shall Ai go and announce maiself? Ai have not got all day to wait, y'know, whaile you dither here," and she made to stand up.

The clerk looked back at her again, his face still irritatingly impassive. "I'm very sorry, Your Grace, but that is quite impossible. Perhaps you would care to tell me your business, or perhaps leave a message and I will see it is passed on to the right quarters."

Bella knew she would get nowhere with this seemingly innocuous but determinedly and deliberately obtuse and unhelpful man, so simply stood up and before he could stop her, brushed right past him and his desk and marched through the closed door he seemed to be guarding, which presumably led to an inner office. She slammed it forcefully behind her, into the annoyed face of the clerk who had chased after her.

A tallish, slender, aesthetic-looking man, as apparently anonymous as his acolyte outside, glanced up from his desk and a pair of piercing grey eyes ran over her, assessing her in moments. "Can I help you, Madam?" he asked urbanely, a hint of steel in his slightly facetious tone. Bella instantly surmised that this man was not 'grey'.

She walked over to stand in front of his desk, putting her two hands down on its polished top as she leaned slightly towards him, trying to look intimidating. "Ashcroft, I assume?" she enquired, her tone exactly matching his, then continued as she noted the almost imperceptible widening of his eyes for a moment as she mentioned his name. "I am Arabella de Bresancourt, the Duchess of Valenciennes, and I have come to find out where my husband is. I believe you are the man to tell me... if you would be so kind," she added with another slightly facetious choice of words and voice.

"Really?" he queried in a colourless tone, staring back up at her. "And what makes you think I know where your missing husband is? This is the Department of Information, but we do not deal with Missing Persons here. Perhaps you could ask my Assistant outside and he will re-direct you." He waved a dismissive hand towards the door and returned to the papers he was reading.

Bella was growing very angry with these men and bit out, "You know where my husband is as I suspect you sent him there. Kindly stop treating me like a fool, just because I am a woman. I can assure you I am no such thing. Now, I am going to sit here until you are courteous enough to have a sensible conversation with me." She pulled forward a chair and seated herself across from Ashcroft on the other side of his desk, glaring at him expectantly before starting to peel off her gloves and remove her hat, thereby giving notice she was not moving.

Ashcroft looked across at the irate woman opposite him and steepled his fingers against his lips as he contemplated her striking looks. "How do you know I sent your husband anywhere?" he asked expressionlessly.

It had been an intuitive guess, but she had hit the bull's eye, she was sure, so Bella looked him in the eye. "My uncle, Francis Granville, the Duke of Firle, came to see you after we had a conversation yesterday about the disappearance of Nicholas de Bresancourt, my husband. Since he always knows who to go to for information, I decided to come and ask you personally."

"How did you find this Department, and me?"

"It wasn't difficult. I simply followed my uncle here and came back this morning to see you myself, in private," Bella shrugged her shoulders as if it was the most obvious thing in the world. "Whenever I ask him anything, he is so economical with the truth, I don't know why I bother anymore."

"Really? You followed him? That's very enterprising of you, if I may say so?"

"Enterprising? Hardly. Sensible more like. It doesn't really take much effort to follow anyone from Berkeley Square to Whitehall and down some corridors," Bella tutted dismissively. "He wasn't trying to be furtive, he just strolled across, so I strolled after him."

"I presume he doesn't know you did, or that you are here now?"

"I shouldn't think so," replied Bella. "But quite frankly, I don't care a jot and as a matter of fact, I'm sure he wouldn't be surprised if he did find out. He'd probably find it highly amusing."

"Yes, he does tend to see the funny side of a lot of things, doesn't he?" Ashcroft's lips curled slightly. "Interesting man, your uncle, full of secrets."

"Really?" tutted Bella again. "Well, of course, I wouldn't know anything about that, his business affairs hold no interest for me," she smiled blandly and politely. "I'm merely concerned about my husband."

Ashcroft sighed. "You really are the most IRRITATING family, but I simply can't have you bouncing into my office demanding information from me as if this is a morning gossip over tea and cake. I have serious work to do. If you want to know anything, I suggest you go back and speak to your uncle. I wish you good morning, Your Grace." He again waved his hand in the direction of the door.

"If I wanted to ask my uncle anything further, I would be sitting in Berkeley Square, not 'bouncing' in here," Bella commented forcefully and followed her intuition as she fished, "I am perfectly well aware my husband was doing work connected with you while he was in Spain and was seriously wounded in the process. If you've allocated him to another... ah... project, the least you can do is tell me, then at least I'll know what I'm dealing with. I'm an intelligent, determined and capable woman, not a tattletale. This is no more the Department of Information than I'm the Queen of Sheba, so stop treating me like some pea-brained ninny at Almack's!"

"An intelligent, determined and capable woman, eh?" said Ashcroft thoughtfully. "Perish the thought. The late Dowager was bad enough, I trust you are not like her?"

"I was extremely fond of my Great Aunt Elizabeth, I would have you know. I would like to believe the feeling was mutual. If I am anything like her, I would consider it a compliment, as I do my best to follow much of her advice. In fact, she thought enough of me to let me oversee and be the sole guardian to her great granddaughter's not inconsiderable inheritance until she comes of age. I can assure you, I am more than a match for her men of business, or most men for that matter. Fools the most of you," she tutted disdainfully.

"Well, well, how fascinating," murmured Ashcroft. The young woman was starting to interest him. "I had no idea de Bresancourt had married such a paragon. You think you have brains as well as beauty?"

"Probably far more of the former than the latter," Bella answered modestly, "for which I am exceedingly grateful, but I am not here to discuss my brain capacity nor my appearance. I simply want to know where my husband is," and she started to tap her nails on the surface of his desk in impatience.

"Do you speak French and Spanish as fluently as he does?" Ashcroft asked randomly.

"Why, yes, of course, more or less, though my Spanish has no doubt got somewhat rusty since my mother died as I have no opportunity to speak it these days. But my father and his family are all French and we often converse in that language if we are by ourselves. What has that got to do with anything?"

"Interesting," murmured Ashcroft again. "So, I wonder, just how clever are you?" he muttered to himself. "Do you play cards, or chess by any chance?" another random question.

"What an extraordinary question," responded Bella. "I can also add up columns of figures in my head, discuss Plato or Shakespeare, politics or current affairs. If you wish, I can talk to you in Greek or even Latin, if you're interested in my intelligence. But to answer the question, yes, I do actually, both, all cards and games of chance, but look here Mr Ashcroft…"

"It's Lord Ashcroft actually, but never mind, you may simply address me as Ashcroft."

"Lord Ashcroft, Sir, I apologise. However, I came here about my husband as he seems to have suddenly disappeared without trace. If you have anything to do with it, as I rather suspect you do, I beg you to tell me. I was going to travel to Valenciennes next week but if he's not there, or you know if he's disappeared to Spain again, or somewhere in France or some other country, or he's gone back to Wellington's headquarters wherever they currently are, I wish you'd tell me. At the least I should like to know if he's not going to reappear again for another year… or two," she finished sarcastically.

"My Dear Duchess, I'm afraid I couldn't possibly tell you anything. These are Government and military matters and you are a lady. We have to maintain security, surely you must appreciate that?"

"Ooooh!" Bella fumed and thumped her fist angrily on the desk in front of her. "Why do you ALL treat me as if I am the Village Idiot, just because I wear skirts? I am just as capable of keeping my mouth shut as any man, probably more than most men if you but knew it. Give me the benefit of the doubt, for pity's sake!"

Ashcroft leaned back and studied the irate and rather beautiful woman seated opposite him, tapping his fingers together in thought. Finally, he sat forward. "I have a proposition for you, Your Grace."

A proposition? Typical man. Bella looked at the impassive face in front of her suspiciously; she'd already decided womanly wiles wouldn't be worth wasting on him, he seemed too much of a cold fish, but perhaps she'd got him wrong. "What sort of proposition?" she asked dubiously.

"Play chess with me, or cards if you prefer, but the former doesn't rely on the run or luck of the cards, merely skill and intelligence. If you win, I'll answer your questions. If you lose, you will go from here and not see me or speak of this office or Department, to anyone; ever." His voice was soft but Bella didn't mistake the implicit cold threat in his tone.

Bella's eyes first widened with surprise then narrowed as she looked at Ashcroft assessingly. This wasn't at all what she'd expected when she'd barged into this unknown man's office and she wondered what he was playing at. Also, this wasn't Nicky she'd be toying with here, not that he hadn't challenged her somewhat when they'd played at *Le Lion d'Or*. This was Serious, and she had the distinct feeling the grey man in front of her would test her to the limit. But she was desperate, so she merely smiled slightly and nodded. "If that's what it takes?"

"It does."

"Very well, chess it is then." The pair stared at each other, consideringly, for a moment. Bella decided it was turning out to be an exceedingly strange morning.

"Capital," said Ashcroft urbanely. "It's about time I crossed swords with someone who can put up a fight and I'm sure you will, won't you, Your Grace?" The mere ghost of a smile hovered around his lips. Ashcroft had no idea why he thought this woman would be an adversary worthy of him, it was simply intuition, but then he always paid attention to his sixth sense and the woman fascinated him. His mundane morning had taken a rather unexpected – and interesting – turn.

Bella smiled more widely. Perhaps he wasn't such a cold fish after all. She knew if she played well, she might win his respect and some help. But she wanted to win. She had so much at stake.

Ashcroft got up and walked purposefully round his desk, over to cabinet on a far wall and pulled out a board and a box of pieces which he set up on a small table between two chairs in front of the empty fireplace. Gesturing Bella to join him, she got up and undid the tight collar of her jacket and put her gloves and hat down on her chair with her reticule. As he arranged the men on the board, she settled herself in one of the chairs and sat back ready for the game of her life. Before beginning, Ashcroft went over to the door of his office and Bella heard him quietly instruct the grey clerk outside that he did not wish to be disturbed unless something very urgent came up. He then closed the door and returned to sit down opposite her.

They battled silently for the next two hours and, apart from her father, Bella had never come up against such a worthy adversary. The Dowager had been very good but not in this man's league. Strategic and cunning, Ashcroft was a masterful player. The game was at a critical point when Bella got up and retrieved her reticule from the chair where she'd left it. She pulled out a narrow silver case and went to sit down again, extracting a long thin cheroot which Ashcroft then lit for her, his eyebrow lifting in some fascination and amusement. This woman was exceedingly unusual, he realised, noting that she obviously didn't care what his opinion was regarding the social niceties for aristocratic ladies.

As she sat, smoked and thought, the cigarillo sitting between her long, elegant fingers, Bella was totally engrossed. Across from her, Ashcroft was entranced. The woman was indeed a worthy opponent and he took a few moments off from his concentration of the game to wonder how he could put her to use for him and his operations. He also wondered at the relationship between her and her husband, which he had ascertained a while ago was not quite what de Bresancourt or Granville had inferred, certainly not with the arrival of a child. He fancied they were well matched. The apparently insouciant, irreverent charmer who concealed deep passions, ruthlessness and a strong will, who was undoubtedly far more cunning and clever than anyone suspected, even him, had gone up hugely in his estimation after he'd discovered what had transpired in Spain... and this beautiful, very determined, clever and intelligent woman. He'd bet fireworks were common between the pair of them. As Bella pondered, Ashcroft returned his thoughts to the game, time enough after to consider her potential to the Service, even if she was married with a child; there were still all sorts of possibilities here in England. There were plots and spies everywhere.

Bella finally moved her man and sat back. She'd taken a risk, but, after much consideration and deliberation, decided she had no other option. The game was headed for a stalemate and she was desperate to win. She didn't know if Ashcroft would tell her anything if they drew. She undid her jacket and took it off, revealing the thin, silk blouse underneath. Ashcroft gazed impassively across at Bella, down at the board, then back at Bella and looked thoughtful, but Bella knew he hadn't been affected by her action, not that she had actually had any ulterior motive, she was merely hot. He, too, then sat back and pondered and twirled a signet ring around and around his little finger, his only sign of mental agitation... and the game continued. For another two hours they battled. Ashcroft got up and patrolled back and forth across his office as he thought and strategised. Bella smoked continuously until she ran out of cigarillos as she fought the game of her life. Finally, her risky gamble paid off and she struck. "Check, I believe, Lord Ashcroft?" Bella whispered as she leaned forward and moved her knight.

Ashcroft considered the board and then looked at the woman who'd just beaten him. He nodded his head. "Congratulations, My Dear. You're quite a formidable player, even if you do take risks," and he smiled at her thoughtfully.

"I had a lot at stake, Lord Ashcroft. Stalemate wasn't an option."

"Mmmmm, yes. Sometimes we have to take risks or grasp opportunities when they come up, but may I ask, where on earth did you learn to play like that?"

"My father taught me. He's the only person who can beat me," Bella laughed at Ashcroft.

"Aaah, yes, the Baron de Mornay," Ashcroft nodded at her. "Your husband mentioned him to me when we first met. I meant to catch up with him, but it slipped my mind." He shook his head, obviously cross with himself. Forgetting things was not a common occurrence in Miles Ashcroft's life.

He sat back and regarded Bella, his face turning serious. "You can learn a lot about a person by the way they play, I find. Your gamble paid off, My Dear, because I pay my debts. So, what do you want to know?"

"I don't want to know your State Secrets, Lord Ashcroft," Bella said softly. "I simply want to know where my husband is. I'm not precisely sure what your connection is with the military or what the Department of Information does, but given your location here in Horse Guards and in this building, I have to assume you work hand in glove with them... and I know my husband was working on some special mission for the army in the Peninsula, so was he under orders from you in some way too? In which case, have either or both of you sent him off on another... ah... mission, for want of another description of what he does?"

"Hmmm, well, to answer your first question, I'm not exactly sure where he is, to be frank; somewhere in France probably, or at least I assume so. And as to the last question, I'm afraid the answer is yes, but not exactly another mission, more a continuation of what he was doing for both Wellington and me in the Peninsula." Ashcroft, once again steepled his fingers against his lips for a moment. "Tell me, what do you know about a man called Bernheim?"

Bella's head shot up and she went rigid. "Bernheim?" she whispered, obviously shocked. Ashcroft smiled knowingly. So, the entire Granville and de Mornay families were involved with the mysterious Shadow and his affairs all those years ago; even this young woman was aghast at the mention of the hated name. Once again, although he didn't show it by so much as a flicker of emotion, Ashcroft cursed with frustration at his ongoing battle with the Duke of Firle to get to the bottom of what had happened in France over twenty years previously. By now, he was sure the Duke and the infamous Shadow were one and the same; not that he gave a toss that the man had been involved in criminal activity. On the contrary, he found it rather amusing and it was an impressive attribute, to have lived two such different lives at the same time and no one had a clue about any of it. Except his close family and now him too. As with many secrets Ashcroft discovered about people in the course of his work, details were never put in writing, most of it was in his head and he wouldn't ever reveal them to anyone, especially the Authorities, if he thought those concerned had earned the right to keep their past quiet. The enigmatic Duke was certainly one of those and his devotion to his country over the past two decades and more had been proven many times over, including information he'd picked up through his business dealings overseas and here in England, not to mention his charity work about which he kept very quiet. The only reason Ashcroft wanted to know was pure curiosity, especially in connection with the younger Bernheim. The man had surfaced again and was causing Trouble. There was some kind of link to the members of this close-knit family who had the formidable Duke at its head. Now, he decided to go fishing in new waters.

"You know of this man?"

Bella was instantly on her guard. "Only by name. He was Governor of Normandy when my French grandparents and aunts were held for a while in the old Rouen fortress at the start of the Revolution," she answered carefully. "It was a long time ago, before I was even born, so what has he got to do with Nicky?"

"The man we are interested in is that individual's son. He's been an agent of Bonaparte for many years and has caused endless trouble for those fighting him across Europe. He turned up in the Peninsula a couple of years ago, trying to subvert the Spanish support for Wellington's forces and then attempted to steal one of Wellington's gold shipments destined for the both the army and the Spanish guerrillas and rebels. However, he wanted it for himself as he is an extremely venal individual. He almost succeeded, stealing a number of consignments worth a vast amount, but your husband thwarted him at the last minute, that's how he got wounded. Wellington, the British Government and Rothschild's, all owe him a large debt of gratitude for what he achieved, virtually unaided, except by an old gypsy fellow, a man named Reynard. Do you know him by any chance?"

"Uncle Reynard?" Bella nodded, amazed at the mention of Reynard's name in connection with the affair, but was astounded to finally learn what Nicky had been up to in Spain. "Good heavens," she muttered, "I had no idea. I suspected he was perhaps working with the guerrillas, fighting the French, a sort of liaison between Wellington and the rebels and resistance forces." She shook her head in wonder then asked, "How did he get wounded? Will you tell me, he was very vague when I asked?"

Ashcroft wondered if he should tell her, but she'd asked, so shrugged to himself. If she really wanted to know what her husband was doing, determined to poke her nose into affairs her uncle was trying to shelter her from, she would have to deal with the reality. Also, if she was to be of use to his Department in the future, she would have to cope with these things, so this would test her reaction. She wanted to be treated like a man and be told everything, therefore she would have to come to terms with it. Consequently, Ashcroft spoke mildly, as if the action was commonplace. "Your husband had been involved with a woman called Carmelita Benitez, a common prostitute who was Frederick Bernheim's mistress. Nicky used her to get information about Bernheim and to trace him and the gold. She was a very nasty piece of work, we understand, like Bernheim." He watched as Bella blanched, but she said nothing, just sat and listened to his explanation. "We found out she pimped for Bernheim, in other words, supplied young girls for his, er, rather depraved tastes. Some of them even turned up dead. Extremely unpleasant individual, as I said. This Carmelita was of the same ilk. A fine pair. Bernheim shot her in your husband's arms, the bullet went straight through her into him." Bella gasped. "Oh, it's not as straightforward or simple as that, My Dear," Ashcroft almost smirked. "I gather your husband had just strangled her, or thought he had."

"Merciful God!" Bella was stunned and horrified. She sat with her hand over her mouth, eyes like saucers.

"I'm sorry it's all so unpleasant, My Dear," Ashcroft said conversationally, "but you did ask. This is the reality of things my men have to deal with. So to answer one of your previous queries, yes, your husband does work for me now; he's been temporarily transferred, re-assigned if you like, from the military to my operation, but as you surmise, I do have very close links with both the Army and Navy.

While he was in the Peninsula, his activities served both Wellington and my Department."

Bella was still sitting wordless as she absorbed what Ashcroft was telling her and he continued, "My men have to do whatever it takes to achieve their objective. It's why I usually only have unmarried men in the field." He sighed, "Apart from the high casualty rate, we can't have wives finding out about such things. I do have women agents as well, naturally," and he stared at her directly. "They become friends and mistresses of men we are suspicious of. They are NOT prostitutes or courtesans in the usual sense, although one or two have been, but they will also do ANYTHING, absolutely anything, to get the information we need." He looked at Bella's dazed expression, "So, My Dear, now you know. THAT is why your uncle wouldn't tell you what was going on. He was only trying to protect you."

"Uncle Francis knows all this?" Bella whispered, still overwhelmed.

"Not all the details, actually, but quite a lot of them. It was through his auspices we managed to make contact with Nicky when he got cut off from both Wellington's and my lines of communication. That's how we got to know about the gypsy, Reynard."

Bella sat for a long while in complete silence, trying to take in everything Ashcroft had told her, as that inscrutable man watched her closely. So much was now clear. Not only why they never got any letters from Nicky, but why he never talked about what he'd been doing. He'd always been something of a loner, she knew that, that deep part of him, hidden away behind the superficial charm. That part of him no one had ever been able to reach – not her, nor her mother, father, uncle, not even her Great Aunt Elizabeth. In a way, it made him perfect material to work for this strange man she'd just met, and she finally also understood why her uncle had been so reticent.

"But why did you take Nicky on when you knew he was married?" she asked curiously. "And, now we have a child, why have you sent him off again?"

"I was initially told it was only a marriage of convenience and you were going to have it annulled. He assured me you were like a sister to him, but you now have a child, so obviously matters have changed." Ashcroft smiled curiously back at her. He couldn't imagine how de

Bresancourt could view this beautiful woman as a sister, but obviously he'd overcome that little problem. He let out a small sigh, "Unfortunately, although he, too, was injured at the same time as your husband, shot by the gypsy as I understand, Bernheim escaped capture, recovered and has resurfaced to make further mischief. Your husband is the only man who knows what he looks like and," Ashcroft paused, "Nicky seems to have a personal vendetta against the man, because of what happened between his family and the man's father. He was responsible for his parents' demise, I gather. He is determined to get rid of him and stop his latest schemes. He appears, ah, how can I put it... somewhat obsessed with him?"

"But that's ridiculous, how can he hold the man responsible for what his father did?" Bella was confused.

"I'm not sure either, to be frank," replied Ashcroft musingly, "but he says the man is as bad as, if not worse than his father; considers him frighteningly insane and evil, I mean seriously and dangerously irrational about some matters, not a jabbering lunatic in an asylum. You see, Nicky is concerned for the safety of his, your family. Bernheim apparently wants retribution against those who were involved with The Shadow," Ashcroft returned to his fishing.

"Oh my God!" Bella gasped softly as her hand went to her mouth again in horror.

"You know about The Shadow then, what happened to him?" Ashcroft asked mildly.

"Oh, it was all a long time ago, before I was born," she responded airily as she pulled herself together rapidly. "My father and aunt are French, as I told you. My late mother, who was Spanish, was living in France as well at the time, that's where she met my father. I think they mentioned him once or twice years back, tattle and reminiscences from the old days before the Revolution got out of hand and the King and Queen lost their heads; but that's quite extraordinary, surely this Bernheim fellow must be mad to even think about such a thing. The Shadow is long gone."

"Well, one would think so, wouldn't one?" replied Ashcroft knowingly.

Bella's mind was working frantically. A conversation with her uncle was top of her to-do list before anything else. She also knew how Nicky felt about Edgar Bernheim and the bitterness he carried with him about how the man had destroyed his life. She shivered. This was far more complicated than she'd ever imagined. But she wasn't going to discuss any of this with Ashcroft. It was an Unspoken Rule in the family, amongst those who knew, that nothing was EVER mentioned, to ANYONE, about The Shadow or any of the events that had happened in Rouen all those years ago. Although SHE knew, her Uncle Francis's sons didn't even know, neither did her de Mornay relations either, even if her aunts and grandmother had been rescued by him. They just thought it was her uncle, in his Ducal capacity, who had helped; her late Uncle Gerard had also never mentioned anything about what had happened either to him or his family in Rouen.

"So, Lord Ashcroft, back to Nicky. Where do you think he is now? On this Bernheim's trail obviously. How long ago did you see him?"

"I take it you know of what has been happening politically in France?" Ashcroft now realised he was dealing with a woman who might be as astute as the late Dowager Duchess of Firle, or was a much younger version of her.

"Yes, of course." Bella looked annoyed Ashcroft should even consider asking such a question.

"Well, we picked up some rumours that Bernheim has been involved with a faction that wants rid of the Monarchy again and Bonaparte back from Elba. They are willing to pay vast sums of money to people who could help restore him to power once more and Bernheim loves money more than anything. That was why he went after those gold shipments in Spain, so we have reason to believe he has been working with them. We understand there have been threats against the new King and all sorts of other plots. Quite frankly, it's hard to know what to believe given the current turmoil in the country, but there's no doubt Bernheim is causing mischief. It's in the interests of the Allies to stop these threats and try and maintain some stability in France. The last thing anyone wants is to go back to war again. Personally speaking, I wish someone had had the guts to shoot Bonaparte, not merely send him into exile. That would have done everyone a favour and there'd be no figurehead for all these plots to remove the

Bourbons again and reinstate the man in power. I believe he'll be a menace to us until he is disposed of, permanently."

Bella was fascinated at this insight and nodded. "But why Nicky? Surely the French Government can put a stop to any insurgence before it gets off the ground and deal with these various factions? I can't believe most rational French people aren't as fed up with the war that has been going on around them for years, as are all the rest of us here in England and across the Continent. The impact constant war has on any country's economy is appalling, surely people realise that, never mind the thousands of people, soldiers and civilians who get killed or injured or lose their homes and incomes."

"Quite so, and one would think so, but of course everything has changed since Bonaparte went into exile," replied Ashcroft. "The Government is a mess, between you and me, national and regional," he shook his head despairingly, "not that it wasn't always, years ago during the previous Monarchy, again in my personal opinion, until Bonaparte got them by the scruff of the neck and reorganised everything. That was perhaps the only useful thing he did. Even if the ordinary people have had enough of war, the Allies can't and won't rely on the French to sort out their own dirty laundry, there's too much at stake. As I said, Nicky is the only person who knows what Frederick Bernheim looks like and the extent of the danger of the man because of what he's like, having been on his trail for months back in Spain and understanding how he operates. He really is a threat to the country's stability if he can somehow help facilitate Bonaparte's escape from Elba and return to Paris and then rally the people and the French army to his cause again. The consequences of that could be incalculable. Nicky is the only person we know who could recognise Bernheim, also that Reynard fellow; but he's an old man now, not to mention a bit of a cripple. He's holed up somewhere in Spain, we're not sure currently where, itinerant gypsy that he is. So I'm afraid I had no other choice but to approach your husband again. This threat is a very serious and dangerous one." Ashcroft's voice was momentarily apologetic but he soon moved on. "So serious, I went over to France personally to meet with him at Valenciennes. I'm afraid he didn't take much persuading, if anything he seemed overjoyed at the prospect of returning to undercover work and disappearing again." Ashcroft looked questioningly at Bella with a raised eyebrow, but she ignored him.

"I see," she merely mused. "Therefore, he could be anywhere, as you said before. So realistically, where do you think he's gone?"

"Well, to Paris for a start. We understand Bernheim owns a house there, in a quiet, upmarket, residential district, not that he appears to have lived there for any time over the past few years. But, quite frankly, he could be anywhere. I haven't heard from Nicky since I saw him a few weeks ago – actually, I was rather hoping to by now but presumably it's because he has no news."

Ashcroft leaned forward and looked at Bella very seriously. "What are you going to do with this information? Are you still intent on going to Valenciennes? Because I can tell you he won't be there." The beneficial prospect of two agents on Bernheim's trail was not lost on the crafty Ashcroft.

"I'm not sure, Lord Ashcroft. I hadn't expected things to be so, er, complicated. But I need to consider. I have a young daughter, you may remember. I have responsibilities, I can't just go running off willy-nilly and abandon her."

"Of course not, perish the thought," replied Ashcroft sympathetically, but then dangled some bait. "You're very concerned about your husband, aren't you? Worried about Bernheim and what he might do? You care very much for Nicky, don't you?" Ashcroft probed, almost sure he knew the answer.

"Of course I do, why do you think I'm here in the first place?" Bella tutted brusquely. "But there are things I have to consider, he could be anywhere," she muttered to herself and then, "but Bernheim, The Shadow…" she whispered to herself and Ashcroft watched her as she shivered again. He really wished he knew what had gone on in Rouen. Whatever it was, the trauma had never left the family. De Bresancourt had inferred the son was worse than the father, not that Ashcroft could understand quite why he believed that when he'd barely met the man, but if so, no wonder they were all so agitated.

"I'm going to think about it," Bella finally said slowly, "but I promise if I go to France I will send word to you, if you give me your proper direction and tell me how?" she looked at him with raised eyebrows.

Ashcroft smiled to himself, his Cheshire Cat smile that never reached his eyes. He'd lay odds she'd be on a packet over to France within the week, if not sooner. Then he'd have two people on the case, which was better than one, even if they were slightly at odds with each other. He wasn't a fool, they'd obviously had a Marital Disagreement which was why he'd found de Bresancourt all alone at his former French home. Angry, close-mouthed, short tempered and looking for a distraction from his domestic problems, not at all like the man he was getting to know. He'd even been doing heavy manual labour alongside his estate workers when Ashcroft had come upon him. He thought that a sure sign of frustration at the way he'd been driving himself even harder than his men, breaking up heavy stone blocks around the ruined chateau with a sledgehammer, like a common navvy. But their marital difficulties were not his concern. Bernheim was, which was all he was interested in. If he could harness their personal and private concerns to settle a British Government and Allied problem, that was perfect for him.

So he smiled at Bella. "Just address any communication to me here at the Department of Information. If it's that important or confidential, your husband will know how to send it in code. Otherwise, just be very discreet in your language; I'm sure I'll get the gist of what you're trying to say... if you get my drift? There are eyes everywhere, Your Grace."

Bella was slightly taken aback that Ashcroft had assumed she would go to France and find Nicky. But he was obviously no fool. The fact she'd gone to all these lengths to track him down obviously revealed how desperate she was, how deep her worries were about her husband.

"Very well, Lord Ashcroft. Thank you for confiding in me. I do appreciate it and understand the whole picture now." She added for good measure, "I just wish someone had done so, long ago. It wouldn't have stopped the worry and heartache, but at least I would have understood everything so much better."

"Not at all, My Dear. It has been a very illuminating day. I enjoyed our game immensely and you must give me an opportunity to take my revenge when you get back. Oh, by the way, don't concern yourself too much with what I told you about your husband's activities in Spain. Needs must, King and Country and all that, y'know," he tipped his head towards a portrait of the King which hung on his office wall, over the fireplace mantel. "It wouldn't have meant anything to him, it was purely business, I do assure you. Remember, he'd already tried to kill the woman, so don't let it bother you."

"Don't worry, Lord Ashcroft, I won't," said Bella calmly. "I'm perfectly well aware of what my husband is capable of. Remember, I've known him literally all my life. He held me in his arms the day I was born, when he was just five years old. I'm told he tried to tie a ribbon round my neck shortly after, like he did to his cat and pet rabbit, except he inadvertently almost throttled me. I grew up with him so I probably know him better than anyone."

Ashcroft's lips actually twitched at that piece of amusing intelligence, "Well, as long as you understand, that's reassuring," he muttered as he rose to see her out, politely helping her with her jacket and watching as she put on her hat and gloves, returning once again to the severe-looking woman who had marched brazenly into his office, not the seductive, beautiful creature with whom he'd played chess. Oh, yes, she was absolutely perfect material for one of his operatives, albeit in a part-time or superficial capacity.

He kissed her hand as she left and watched her breeze past his assistant before disappearing through the main door of the office of the Department of Information. As he sat down to recollect what he'd been doing before she'd erupted into his life several hours before, his assistant entered. "THAT, is a very beautiful, enterprising and determined woman, My Lord," he commented. "You've been sequestered with her for nearly six hours. That is quite something, if I may say so, for someone you didn't know or weren't expecting."

"Absolutely," replied Ashcroft thoughtfully. "Enterprising and determined describes her well. Intelligent, forceful, strong-willed, also willing to take risks... just like her husband, albeit in a completely different way." He smiled knowingly, "She plays chess extraordinarily well, better than most men in fact, but not quite as extraordinarily well as me, Chalmers, though it was a close call." He looked up at his assistant with a gleam in his sharp grey eyes, "But she'll never know that..."

A cunning look stole across his austere features. "She'll be off to France in a matter of days. She's tri-lingual like him, very useful. She'll track de Bresancourt down, you mark my words, and then we'll find out what's going on. Now we'll have two of them to tempt that bastard Bernheim out of hiding. He won't be able to resist the potential of taking his revenge on both de Bresancourt and a de Mornay family member if he discovers who she is. Then hopefully, they'll deal with him and our worrying French Problem will be solved once and for all. In fact, it's all quite perfect. I couldn't have planned it better myself," and with that, he settled back in his chair and returned to reading his papers. As his assistant was about to shut the office door, Ashcroft looked up suddenly, "Oh, Chalmers, some coffee and water please and a bite to eat, but before I forget, have a little dig into the background of Baron de Mornay, will you? That was his daughter I've just been entertaining. He sounds like a person we should know, remind me to facilitate a meeting. I have a feeling he's cleverer than the whole damn lot of them and I think it's about time I caught up with another member of that rather unusual and eccentric family."

Chapter Thirty

Bella went straight round to Berkeley Square, intent on finding her uncle and discussing the whole Bernheim issue. However, when she arrived, she was frustrated to discover he was out, but her aunt was in her sitting room so she hurried in there as she needed to speak to her as well.

"Bella, Sweetie, come and have some tea," her aunt rose and kissed her on both cheeks. "What brings you here today? How's my favourite great niece?" and she laughed. "Still rampaging round your garden and giving the cat a fit of the vapours?"

"I've just had the most extraordinary morning, Auntie," Bella blurted out, ignoring her aunt's domestic enquiries. "I was looking for Uncle Francis, but come to think of it, you'll do just as well. I need to ask you a favour too." She settled herself next to her aunt and gulped down some tea, then attacked the plate of delicate sandwiches, suddenly realising she'd had nothing to eat all day, apart from a glass of water during her epic chess game with Ashcroft.

She sat back after appeasing her hunger and looked at her aunt, "Tell me, Auntie, truthfully, how much does Uncle Francis tell you about Nicky and about his business generally?"

Cat looked at her niece, somewhat surprised. "That's an odd question, Darling," she reflected, "but to be frank, he doesn't tell me much. Not that I actually want to know about his business or estate affairs, far too boring. I leave all that to your Papa, they're thick as thieves with it all," she sighed. "The only thing he did mention a few months back, last year when Nicky got home, was how he'd come to an arrangement with him to buy out a lot of the enterprises that were part of the inheritance from his grandmother. They apparently fitted in well with whatever business it is he's so busy organising all the time. I know he was quite excited about some factories with new manufacturing equipment, also new inventions which sounded extremely complicated, as well as tedious trading contracts in places I've never heard of... and your Papa told me he paid Nicky very well for them, so he's got even more money to fret over," she chuckled. "Anyway, that aside, I do get frustrated and worry about Nicky when he's away, just as you do. I know Francis knows far more than he tells us. He thinks he won't worry us if he keeps any bad news to himself, but it's just the opposite of course. It's the not knowing that gets to me. If something bad has happened, I'd far rather know and deal with it than sit here in ignorance and still worry anyway." She looked at Bella curiously, "Why, Darling, have you found out something? Do you know what's happened to Nicky? He's been gone quite a while now. Your Papa told me he's getting quite worried," she put her tea cup down with a frustrated thump. "Men! I wish they'd realise we're just as capable of dealing with bad news as they are, probably better most of the time." She took another look at her niece's expression and realised she was full of news and her face looked concerned. "Bella, Darling, what is it? You've heard something haven't you? Oh, for God's sake tell me. What's happened?"

So Bella told Cat the whole story. How she'd followed her uncle and discovered the mysterious Ashcroft, then her visit there this morning. She then asked her to tell her the entire tale about Bernheim and what had happened in Rouen, in detail, all those years previously, before she'd been born.

The two women sat and talked for nearly two hours and by the time they'd finished, Cat got up and raided the brandy, her face taut with the terrible memories. "You know, Bella Darling, practically every time you come round here, seeking advice, I end up looking at the bottom of the brandy decanter. But this time, it's beyond quite extraordinary. I'm going to give your uncle more than a piece of my mind now I know all about this Ashcroft fellow and his suspicions about Bernheim. Good God! Can you imagine what would happen if anyone found out your uncle used to be a smuggler? It was quite an operation he ran all along the French and English coasts, not just the odd keg of brandy now and then. The scandal! He could be arrested, even after all this time. It's a Capital Offence, for heaven's sake. And now Nicky is chasing after that bastard's son, who's a threat to all of us, you think?" she tossed back a glassful, "I knew absolutely nothing about it. Piece of my mind? I think I'll kill him this time!" She looked daggers at Bella as she referred to her husband.

Bella couldn't help but laugh. "Well, wait until I leave before you do it, if you don't mind," knowing well how hot tempered both her aunt and uncle were, their arguments the stuff of legend in the family.

"But the thing is, Auntie, I can't possibly sit here a moment longer. I have to go after him." Bella got up and started to pace up and down the room. "Oh, not that I can do anything about his mission, it's just, Nicky and I, well, things aren't right between us, not since he's been back from Spain. All that *Lionesse* business and Terrie, you know, you've seen... and I told you a bit about what had been going on a little while ago..." Bella then turned and looked at Cat with a haunted expression in her eyes. "But you see, what I didn't tell you was when he left, when he went to Valenciennes, he left me a vitriolic message to say he was going to move there, permanently, without me, including that he wanted Terrie to go and live with him. He wants to take her away from me," and she burst into tears, finally getting the terrible worry she'd been carrying for months off her chest.

Cat sprang to her feet and immediately went and put her arms around her niece. "Oh no, Bella, Darling, NO! He wouldn't do that, he couldn't. I'm sure he didn't mean it." She was horrified. "Men say such dreadful things at times, he just wanted to hurt you, that's all." Cat put her hand under Bella's chin and tilted her face up so she could look directly at her. "He obviously had a terrible time down there in Spain, which we now know all about, but then to come home and find out about you, about Terrie, about the Dowager and the money...it was probably all too much for him to deal with and he's just run away to come to terms with it all." She sighed, "His life has been turned completely upside down and it would be too much for most people, I have to say, so he does have my sympathy; but Darling," she hugged Bella tightly as she sobbed, "I'm sure he'd never do anything to hurt you, not my Nicky; he's just hitting out at you where he knows he can torment you the most. He doesn't mean it, I'm sure." Cat tried to sound as reassuring as she could. "He'll come round, he will, he must. I'll throttle him myself otherwise, after I've murdered Francis!" Bella laughed at her aunt's belligerent tone, despite her tears.

They sat down again. "So you understand, I've got to go and find him, have all this out with him once and for all." Bella wore a very determined look on her face now. "I'm damned if I'm going to let him go, I love him too much and I know he wants me, even if he won't admit it to himself." She turned to her aunt, "You understand, don't you, Auntie? So will you look after Terrie for me while I'm away? I'm going to Paris. Ashcroft thinks that's probably where Nicky has gone. Bernheim has a house there, apparently."

"Good God, Bella, are you sure? It could be dangerous. Can't it wait 'til Nicky finds Bernheim and deals with him once and for all? Then you can talk properly together and sort out all your problems."

"No, Auntie, it's gone beyond that, really it has. I have to go and find him. I have this terrible premonition it's not all as simple as Ashcroft is making out. I also have a niggling suspicion he let me beat him this morning. I can't be sure, but that man is the very devil and I have this horrible feeling I'm being manipulated." She shook her head in frustration, "Oh, I can't put my finger on it, just call it intuition. But Nicky is in danger. This Frederick Bernheim is worse than his father, Ashcroft is certain of it. Crazed, irrational and extremely dangerous, to the Allies and us, he said. Nicky agreed with him, apparently, or it's the other way round. Either way, I'm going. I've decided. I can't sit here and worry a minute longer."

Marie-Catherine Granville sat and looked at her niece. Her mind travelled back over twenty years to when she'd gone chasing after her husband for much the same reasons: an argument and her premonition of danger that simply wouldn't go away because she was worried about him and couldn't face sitting there in London doing nothing and waiting. So, she patted Bella's hand. "I understand completely, My Darling, I really do. More than anyone. But you have to take someone with you, you can't go chasing off by yourself."

"Who will go with me? No one I know would be right. Anyway, I can't be doing with some maid who'll keel over with shock when some French man goes 'boo!' at her."

Cat laughed. "I know what you mean." Then she said reflectively, "When I went chasing after Uncle Francis, I had your mother and Benjy with me. At the time, your dear mama was carrying you as well. We were a motley group to be sure. Of course, your Papa had insisted on going with Uncle Francis, so he wasn't by himself either. Therefore, you absolutely MUST have some sort of companion. Now just let me think... hmmm, Benjy... Benjy..."

She sat pondering for a while, gazing through the window deep in thought, sipping from her glass of brandy, before she smiled beatifically. "I know just the person, not at all who you would expect. But he'll do perfectly. You never know, he could be quite useful, which is why he's so ideal. Bella, do you know who Jack Vallance is?"

Bella looked at her aunt curiously. "Young Jack? The groom from the stables at Firle?" she raised her eyebrow.

"That's him," and Cat told Bella how she'd come across the youth a few years before in the notorious Seven Dials area in London. "So you see, he's turned out to be a very bright boy, extremely intelligent in fact. Mrs Collins told me he's in and out of the library borrowing books every five minutes. Seems to be like a veritable sponge; he reads anything and everything apparently, now he knows how to. But what is most useful, of course, is his background. Although he denied it, I know he was thieving. He had to be to keep his family and the other young children from starvation in that dreadful garret I found them in. I reckon he has talents that may prove quite useful, just like Benjy had all those years ago after his stint in the Navy, then smuggling with your Uncle Francis. In Jack's case there's nothing like a reformed criminal to be just the job. He's seen everything in the Seven Dials, so I daresay NOTHING will faze him."

"Good Lord, I didn't know that! He's a personable and cheeky lad from what I recall, but he's only a boy surely? How old is he? It's been a while since I've actually seen him."

"I'm not sure, but neither is he to tell the truth. Do you know, when I found him, he didn't even know what a birthday was? Well, not as we know it." Bella gasped. "I know, terribly sad, but not unusual in those places where getting food is the only thing that's important, as well as keeping some sort of roof over one's head. But he's filled out quite a bit now from the scraggy, filthy, starved boy I found. He thought he was about twelve or thirteen then, so that would make him about fourteen or fifteen now. But he looks around sixteen to me, if not a bit more given his size, so he may well be as old as that. Anyway, I think he'd be ideal. He can look after you, sort out transport, find lodgings, run errands, keep an eye out and, not least, he's big enough to throw a punch if necessary. I think he can speak a bit of French too, only a bit mind. Old Mr Crichton, the boys' tutor, is retired now and lives in a cottage down in Firle village. I think he's given Jack a few lessons, at least enough to say hello and thank you and a bit more. I originally got him to teach Jack to read and write and improve his accent, but he threw in a bit of French and Latin, arithmetic, history and geography while he was about it as he told me how bright the lad was and was very taken with him. He's been going to the local village school as well, so you won't be travelling with a complete idiot – he does know where France is – which is more than some London villains do," she laughed.

Bella looked doubtful. "Are you sure, Auntie?" The family all knew of her aunt's predilection for picking up waifs and strays, both human and animal. "I really think I'd be better off alone in spite of what you said. I can look after myself and once I find Nicky, he'll look after me."

"IF you find him, Darling," Cat waggled her finger at Bella. "Remember you said Ashcroft only THOUGHT he'd gone to Paris. He could be anywhere," she shrugged, "and although I'm not as cranky as your uncle about going out and about unescorted," and the pair grinned at each other at the Duke's obsession with all his family's safety, especially the women, to whit her and Bella, "I really don't want you running around all over France without someone with you. He can at least send us a message if... if you need help, or something," Cat tailed off, not wanting to say any more on that front.

"Very well," Bella sighed. "I suppose it's sensible. But it'll be like trailing around with an older Charlie in tow, except Charlie is like Papa and always has his nose stuck in a book. I hope Jack is a bit more worldly-wise than my little brother."

"Oh, I think you'll find him quite an entertaining companion, My Love, absolutely NOTHING like Charlie," and she winked. "I'll send a message straight down to Firle to tell him to get ready and you can pick him up *en route* to the coast." Cat smiled, knowing the youth would look after Bella at all costs as well as keep her amused. He was forever thanking Cat for what she'd done for him and his little family of orphans, asking how he could repay her. And he'd grown into a charming and amusing lad, neither boy nor man at present, just a tall gangly teenager. But he was clever, resourceful and streetwise, so Cat thought he'd be an ideal, if slightly unconventional servant for her niece to accompany her and to keep an eye out for her. Maids were two a penny, but a resourceful, streetwise and trustworthy young man, who was also probably an ex-thief to boot and who also probably knew how to use his fists and a knife, was another matter, even if he was officially a groom.

They talked on for a while, discussing arrangements for her trip, including sending Terrie round to Firle House, before Bella finally rose and took her leave. As she headed towards the door, she turned once more to her aunt and ran back to hug her again, "Thank you for listening to me, Auntie. You're so wise, so different to Great Aunt Elizabeth in so many ways. I can talk to you about absolutely anything. You always support me whatever I want to do, never criticising. I love you so much, like a second mother and very best friend all rolled up in one. I don't know what I'd do without you now..."

Cat sniffed, hugely moved by her niece's thanks. "Oh, Bella, Darling, if my little Lizzie grows up to be half the woman you are, I'll be pleased as punch!" She gave her a big kiss and tight hug. "You just remember, take NO NONSENSE from that husband of yours, or from anyone else. You're a Duchess and an intelligent woman. Men will underestimate you all the time, fools that they are, brains in their breeches more often than not, but just come back safe with my Nicky." The Dowager's words from another lifetime ago suddenly came to mind and she felt herself well up with emotional tears.

"I'll try, Auntie," Bella whispered softly and then a final thought, "and you will tell Uncle Francis all about Ashcroft, won't you?"

"Oh, you can rely on me to do that, My Love, the minute he walks through the front door," and Bella left the room laughing at the belligerent look on her Aunt's face.

She was just going out said front door as her uncle arrived home. "Hello Puss, been visiting your Aunt?" he bent and kissed her. "Off anywhere nice?" he queried amicably as he handed his hat and cane to the waiting footman.

Bella turned round and Francis suddenly found himself in a big hug. "Yes Uncle, I've just had a long conversation with Auntie, she'll tell you all about it as soon as you go in." She grinned wickedly, "But I'm off, going away for a short trip, so I just want to say goodbye and give you a kiss," and she leaned up, hugged him once more and planted a smacking kiss on each cheek. With that, she turned and hurried out of the door, just as her aunt's angry screech floated down the hall.

"Francis Alexander Granville? Is that you I can hear? You excuse for a man, imbecile, idiot, bumpkin... I want a word with you, RIGHT.THIS.MINUTE. Come and see what I've got for you..." and with a giggle at her uncle's horrified face, Bella fled, half reminding herself to buy some more items of French porcelain to send home, sure the current crop in the small sitting room were about to end up in pieces, via her uncle's head.

Chapter Thirty-One

J ack did indeed prove a lively companion. He'd never been on a ship before and Bella watched in amusement as he enthusiastically absorbed every new experience; even the rolling of the packet in the Channel swell, which sent quite a few green-looking passengers below decks, didn't deter him as he stood at the rail, the sea breeze ruffling his thick brown hair. He was so excited to be going to France and badgered her the entire time on the road to Dover about what it was like.

As she, too, stood at the ferry rail next to him, Bella was lost in memories. She hadn't been to France since the brief peace of 1802, after her mother died, when she'd been just eleven and Nicky was sixteen. Her aunt and uncle and the Dowager had taken her and Nicky and her grieving father over to Normandy on the Duke's yacht in an effort to cheer her father up; but it had been a subdued trip and despite everyone's best efforts, he had stayed silent and withdrawn most of the time while she had chased Nicky along the sandy beaches at Deauville or he'd gone off fishing with her uncle while she, her aunt and the Dowager had strolled happily around the shops of the little coastal villages, leaving her father in the hotel staring out at the distant view, totally lost in his sad, painful reminiscences. She laughed to herself as she remembered Nicky creeping up on her one day and dropping a little wriggling crab down the back of her dress, making her shriek in alarm. The startled guests at the hotel where they were staying had looked on in tutting disapproval as she'd let loose a stream of very unladylike invective at him in French, screeching, hopping and prancing around the reception area, lifting her skirts way too high, in an effort to dislodge the creature. The Dowager had caught them, told her in no uncertain terms to mind her language and sit down, since she was supposed to be a Genteel Young Lady, not a fishwife, nor an opera dancer. She had then given Nicky a severe telling off for Inappropriate Behaviour by a Gentleman to a Lady, which he'd totally ignored, but she'd also seen the old lady's suppressed grin and sudden coughing fit. She knew she'd had the devil of a job keeping a straight face and her mirth at bay at the whole event. Bella sighed as she reflected how long ago it all seemed.

Now she was alone and making a trip with far more serious intentions. She was excited, but apprehensive too, and decided she was glad her aunt had made her bring Jack along.

Before she'd left, she'd gathered her diaries, *Sooty's Secrets*, to fill in extra pages with all the gaps in the story of The Shadow. It was now recorded for posterity as she knew she would tell Elizabeth one day, to help her understand part of the Dowager's story and why she feared her grandson would run off and abandon the title if he had known the truth.

"Penny for your thoughts, Your Grace?" the pleasant tones of the young man were a far cry from the gutter language he'd spoken a few years previously, as he looked round at the young woman stood next to him, obviously lost in thought, her gaze far away.

"Oh, just memories, Jack. It's been quite a while since I've been to France myself."

"Really, Your Grace, how long ago was that?"

"Not since 1802, when there was a brief peace in the wretched war with Boney," she reflected and then laughed lightly at him, "You've really got to stop 'Your Grace'ing' me every time you open your mouth. It's making me feel like my aunt or the Duke's old grandmother. Besides which," she paused, "I'm not sure what everyone in

France makes of aristocrats these days, even if they have stopped chopping all their heads off. Boney created a whole new lot of them from some of his Marshals, ministers and extended family, so perhaps we'd better think of another way for you to address me, just in case."

"Yes, Your Grace, ooops, pardon Your..." He laughed cheekily back at her, his sherry-coloured eyes with their long thick lashes, sparkling at her in amusement as he pantomimed a slicing action across his throat.

"Oh, You Wretch, come along, do be sensible for five minutes," it was like talking to a naughty little brother. Bella thought for a few moments, "I know, you must refer to me as Madame de Bresancourt, for that is in truth who I am. Also, you must try and speak to me in French when we are around people. I think the less we draw attention to ourselves, the better. I have a feeling the French people dislike us English as much as we dislike them. The War went on for such a long time, feelings run very deep on both sides of the Channel."

"*Mais oui, Madame, bien sûr...* But yes, Madam, of course," Jack managed, though with a somewhat execrable accent, then made a sweeping, grinning bow at her.

"Hopeless, you're absolutely hopeless, I just give up," Bella laughed as she looped her arm through his. "Come along, You, no doubt you're hungry again; I'd forgotten how much boys eat. Let's go and find something edible on this crate before you faint at my feet. And then, Young Man, I think you and I might have a game of cards to pass the time," and with that, the Duchess and her unusual escort made their way below.

As the little ferry boat rolled across the swell to Calais, Bella and Jack passed the time playing cards. Master of every trick in the book when it came to cheating or sleight of hand, the youth decided this was not the occasion to practise his talents in that direction and for probably the first time in his life, he tried to play a straight game. "No, no, Jack, you have to memorise the cards that have gone. Try to remember them in your head, then you can better decide the odds on what are still left to come and gamble accordingly." Bella sighed as she tried to show the youth how to assess the odds. Finally, after a while, to her pleasure, he soon got the hang of it and his face became a mask of concentration as he furiously muttered and counted to himself.

"Oh Lord, you're supposed to do all that in your head and keep smiling and pretend to admire the décolletage of the lady opposite you, or the fall of a Gentleman's cravat or his waistcoat design," she chuckled, "but practice makes perfect, so I'm sure you'll have plenty of time on our little trip to get the hang of it." She eventually got up to look through the grimy porthole to the outside, but could see no sign of land. Sighing, she returned to her seat and sat back wondering what to do next. Suddenly, a gleam came into her eyes. "Do you know how to play chess, Jack?" she asked.

"Chess?" he looked puzzled, "Is that another card game?"

"No, My Lad," Bella replied. "It's an exercise of the brain. It's all about strategy, attack and defence." She looked at him, "I think you'd be rather good at it."

Jack eyed her worriedly. "Exercise my brain? How does that work?" He scratched his head.

Bella grinned at him. "Well, just like your body gets fat and lazy if all you do is sit around every day and eat pies, puddings and pasties, if you don't use your brain to think, dream, plot and learn, it'll go to seed too." She made a silly face at him as she got up and went to rummage in a large portmanteau. She pulled out a little travelling chess set she often used to play on with her father when they made the tedious coach journey from London to Firle or Arlington. "Now then, My Lad, watch and learn; you are about to be taught by a master, well almost," and for the rest of the journey, the pair sat engrossed as Jack tried to get to grips with Pawns, Rooks, Knights, Kings and Queens.

Chapter Thirty-Two

J ack was quite glad when the little packet finally pulled into the harbour. His head hurt from all the memorising and thinking he'd been doing for hours on end, but he had to admit, chess had him fascinated, especially the strategy and planning. His new mistress had been kind and patient with him. Yet again, he thanked his lucky stars he'd tried to thieve the reticule off the Duchess of Firle that day in Bond Street three years before. The note the Duchess had sent him, to him personally much to his amazement, for he never got letters from anyone, let alone on thick paper with a ducal crest at the top, had told him to look after her headstrong niece as he'd cared for his own little family; never to let her out of his sight and to protect her with his life if need be... and not to be afraid to use the talents he'd acquired in his life before they'd met! If he did his job, he would be well rewarded, she had promised. That the Duchess thought him capable of such responsibility filled him with such pride, he swore to himself he would follow her orders to the letter, or die trying, irrespective of the reward.

As Bella waited patiently on the dock with her baggage, Jack disappeared off to rent them a carriage, determined to try out his broken

French that he'd been practising all the way since they'd set off from Firle. Soon, a smart carriage pulled by reasonable horses appeared and the smiling young servant helped his mistress inside, pleased as punch with himself to have managed everything to her satisfaction. Trusted with a bag of gold pieces to rent the vehicle, he was more than a match at haggling with the liverymen, even if he couldn't understand much of what they said. Gesticulating, pointing, counting on fingers and much swearing had ensued – understood in any language – but he got the price he felt was fair, with horses he'd personally inspected.

The carriage set off and Jack initially had made to get up alongside the driver, as befitting his servile status, but Bella had insisted he do no such thing and to sit instead, with her, to keep her company; so he soon forgot about his unusual circumstances and sat inside, distracted by the passing foreign countryside and the different style of buildings.

Bella had a yearning to visit the de Mornay family home, repossessed by her father many years before after a lot of belligerent negotiation. It was currently looked after by elderly caretakers, trusted retainers of the family from before the Revolution. Eddie had located the old, impoverished couple in a nearby village and brought them back to take care of the house until the War ended and circumstances allowed visits and residence there by the family again; once it could be restored from its current state of disrepair. It was in completely the opposite direction to Valenciennes from Calais, but Bella didn't care. She decided after so long, another couple of days before she reached her intended destination wouldn't matter.

She strolled around the empty, dilapidated house and gardens, thinking how fate had conspired to have her aunt and father in London when Edgar Bernheim's men had stormed in one day and carried off her grandparents and aunts to the Fortress in Rouen. Everything was recorded in her diary for posterity. Jack merely wandered about, looking at the old country manor with interest, thinking about how the family had managed not to get their heads chopped off.

They also stopped for a night in nearby Rouen and Bella sauntered through the streets near a small market, close to where the old Fortress building had once stood. It was a ruin still, what was left of it charred and blackened, a monument to despair and terror by those with long memories. She found and purchased an old print of the building from a stall in the market, as it had been in its intimidating heyday, but as she stood and stared at the broken, dark stone walls, looking from the picture to present reality, a shiver ran up her spine as she remembered the story her aunt had recently re-told her about the terrible events in there, so long ago. Now she was an adult and deeply involved with the latest incarnation of the Bernheim family, she had heard the tale in much more frightening detail, including how her aunt had rescued Nicky, a terrified but brave little boy, from Bernheim's second-in-command, a hideous man called Dupont. Then, how her mother had refused to leave him behind, so smuggled him out to safety with her, concealed under her long, heavy skirts as she'd been disguised as a nun. Following on a year later, her Uncle Francis had been nearly tortured to death in the place and she shuddered with horror as she thought about the nightmarish burn and lash scars she'd seen on his back when they'd been sailing some summers on his yacht, him temporarily shirtless whilst helping man the sails up on deck. Unbeknownst to Ashcroft, the memories of those scars were one of the reasons she readily believed Nicky's assessment of the danger and barbarity of the man whose activities were now his mission to stop.

"Are you all right, Madam?" asked Jack at her side, as he watched her stare at the ruins then down at the print she'd bought, lost in deep reflection. "That must have been a right dreadful place in its day," he muttered. "A sight worse than the Fleet or Newgate. Glad someone blew it up. I'd bet some terrible things went on in there."

"You have absolutely no idea, Jack, really," Bella whispered as she finally turned to hurry away. "Come, I've seen enough ruins here for a lifetime. Let's go and find Valenciennes."

And so they'd finally arrived at the old de Bresancourt chateau, family home of the Dukes of Valenciennes for centuries. They drove in through a pair of huge, ornate, open gates with two enormous, black rampant lions sitting atop pillars on either side and a small gatehouse which, by the look of the new roof, had also been restored but seemed currently unoccupied as no one came out to enquire about their business. The stone lions looked freshly painted, but Bella wondered if the gates were new or simply the old ones which had been restored. Either way, it was a very grandiose entrance as they proceeded up the long drive, far more imposing than the entrance to the estate of her old de Mornay home and she couldn't help but be curious as to what the chateau would be like.

Despite Nicky's disappearance, she discovered the place was a hive of activity with men scrambling over the beautiful old chateau like ants, new windows and roof now being put in place and a huge pile of rubble sitting to one side, waiting to be cleared, the remains of the partly torn down building. The hatred of the local people and tenants of their former master, the long dead Duke, had been so immense, they wanted nothing left to remind them of his uncaring cruelty and the harshness of their poverty-struck existence while he sat in luxurious, extravagant splendour and spent most of his time at Versailles while the remote Duchess was always covered in satin, lace and jewels. They'd known nothing or seen hardly anything of his ignored little son and heir, consigned to the care of servants, nannies, a Governess and tutor.

Bella found and introduced herself to a new housekeeper and a new estate manager but, as with all the others, they could offer no explanation as to why their master had suddenly upped and disappeared so suddenly. The estate manager shrugged his shoulders phlegmatically. He well remembered the vagaries of the aristocracy, even if the new young Duke had shown no airs and graces as he'd happily worked shirtless alongside the carpenters and stonemasons he'd employed to bring his family home back to its former glory. Much to their astonishment, he'd laughed and joked dirtily with them on occasion, speaking much the same as they did, certainly not in the cut-glass accent they'd expected.

The chateau itself was beautiful and, despite her aunt's reassurances, Bella was filled with anxiety that Nicky wanted to live there without her, keeping little Terrie to himself to bring up in France. As she stood at the windows in what would soon be the grand salon again, looking out over wonderful views of distant lakes and woodland, she took a deep breath of determination, promising herself that would come to pass over her dead body. She would put things right between them, she had to believe in that, as she was sure, somewhere deep down, Nicky did care for her. He may not love her as she loved him, but he wanted her and she was sure he had some feelings for her. He used to... and she was determined to try and make him care again. All she had to do now, was find him...

Chapter Thirty-Three

Bella and Jack left Normandy behind them and set off for Paris.
While they'd played the early rounds of their game of
chess, sizing their opponent up as they'd made their first
moves, Bella and Ashcroft had chatted idly about what Nicky had
been doing in Spain over the many months he'd been out of touch.
Bella was curious to know how he'd finally located people he was
searching for, after Ashcroft had told her, in vague terms and without
mentioning names, that it was an essential part of his work.

Ashcroft had considered her thoughtfully and then proceeded to
tell her how he understood Nicky had either worked in a number of
livery stables or horse markets, looking for people who may have
known or come across his quarry, which of course she now knew was
Frederick Bernheim. When that had brought no results, he had begun
to tour the bars and taverns as an itinerant singer, searching out and
befriending all the local prostitutes to see if any of them had been
picked up by his target. Ashcroft explained he thought that was how
Nicky had found a lead through a particular tart, which as a strategy
had obviously worked. He also explained, reassuringly, that it was
common practice for his agents to follow such tactics when trying to
locate a single man alone in a strange city. Depending on the wealth

and status of the man, the standard of prostitute and location would be taken into account – from high class courtesan at social events attended by the *demi-monde,* to street whore in lowly taverns. Bella had merely raised an eyebrow at this explanation but made no comment.

At the time, the vision of Nicky entertaining a bar full of people had made Bella burst out laughing. She knew he could play the guitar a bit, had indeed learned some Spanish folk songs from her mother, just as she had, but an entertainer? The thought was absurd, although she conceded to herself he could sing in tune, even when he was drunk, but she could hardly hear him when they sang hymns in church, let alone loud enough to keep a room full of noisy, inebriated customers happy. His friendship with the prostitutes was another matter and she'd closed her mind to what exactly Ashcroft had been inferring by his term 'befriend'. Obviously, he'd had an affair with this Carmelita, Bernheim's mistress, but all those prostitutes? It wasn't something she wanted to contemplate.

Now, however, she was on her way to Paris and she had to start somewhere in her search for her husband. Ashcroft had given her Bernheim's address, located by chance in his desk at the villa in Madrid on a bill of sale, scrunched up and lost at the back of a drawer. However, he'd also told her the house had been watched by his agents for months with no sign of any occupant, other than an elderly house-keeper and a strange caretaker who came and went from time to time, with no apparent schedule.

Bella had wondered since she'd left England how to explain to Jack what she was doing in France. All he knew at the moment was she was travelling to meet up with her husband who had been there for the past few months, overseeing the repossession and restoration of his family house, now that Bonaparte had abdicated, the Monarchy restored and life was starting to return to some semblance of normality. It was difficult for Jack to understand that the two countries had been at war since before he was even born.

But it was obvious Nicky wasn't at Valenciennes and Bella could give the youth no straight answer when he'd innocently enquired where they were to meet up with the Duke in Paris. As the carriage rattled along the pot-holed roads, headed south to Paris, Bella wrestled with her problem, searching the young man's face for an answer as to whether she could trust him with the reality of what she was doing. Presumably her aunt wouldn't have suggested he accompany her if she didn't think he was suitable, but Bella had only known him barely a fortnight and the lad was only fourteen or perhaps sixteen at most. Bella looked at Jack, lounging on the seat across from her, staring out of the carriage windows. She tried to work out his age by comparing him to Nicky when he was a teenager, or her Granville cousins and their friends. Like Nicky, the Granville boys had all been strapping youths at sixteen, but their friends were a varied mixture... and to her, Jack seemed like Nicky and her cousins. He certainly looked and acted more mature than fourteen, even fifteen. She concluded he was older than he thought, agreed with her aunt and settled on sixteen.

After much deliberation and wrestling with her dilemma, finally she gave in. She decided to go with her instinct and tell him the truth so, after they'd stopped for some lunch and to stretch their legs at a roadside inn, when they got back in and set off again she told Jack about the real purpose of her trip. She explained her husband had worked on special missions for Wellington in Spain and was now on the trail of a Frenchman who had been causing problems in the Peninsula, but was now on the loose again in France. Since he was the only one who could recognise this man, her husband had been tasked with tracking him down and capturing or killing him. Bella said she was worried about him since they'd had no word for months, so she had decided to come to France to try and find him.

It all sounded so simple.

Jack, however, sat open-mouthed and goggle-eyed as he listened to her explanation and her insistence that he not breathe a word of what she'd told him to anyone, EVER. He was still gawping as the carriage rolled into the outskirts of Paris and through the old, outer city walls before pulling up at a fashionable and comfortable hotel near the city centre. Since the recent return of Louis XVIII and the restoration of the Bourbons to the throne, Paris was now full of Allied military, diplomats and general visitors, so their arrival was completely unremarked. Bella registered at the hotel as Madame de Bresancourt with her nephew, Jacques. She had originally assumed the lad would sleep in the servant's quarters or the stables during their travels, as he had been at the various inns they'd stayed in since their arrival in France, but over the past fortnight she'd become quite fond of him and she thought it would be amusing to put him up in his own room as if he were indeed a young Gentleman, not a servant, to watch his reaction. She'd bought him some new clothes in Rouen and had his hair trimmed properly and fashionably and he now looked quite presentable, with a bit of a swagger when he thought she wasn't looking. As they were hustled upstairs by an obsequious footman and shown to their rooms, Bella could hardly wait for the comedy she knew was about to unfold.

They were first shown to her suite where her trunks were unloaded and she asked for a suitable lady's maid to be provided for her use during her stay. Then, turning to the waiting Jack who was staring around him in awe at the palatial rooms, Bella shooed him out. "Come along, Jacques, we're going to your quarters now," and marching in front of him behind the footman, they were soon shown into a much smaller, but still luxurious room, furnished sumptuously with a large four-poster bed and views out over the river Seine. Bella gave the footman a handsome tip and waved him out of the room before turning to Jack. "Well, what do you think, do you like it?" She went over to the window, "Ooooh, look, you can see the river from here and there's Notre Dame Cathedral."

Jack looked puzzled. "It's very nice, Madam, though not as lovely as yours. Is this room for His Grace then, when you find him?" he asked curiously, frightened to touch anything in the beautifully decorated room. He'd been into Firle Manor many times, having the express permission of the Duchess to use the library as often as he liked when she and the Duke were absent, then also with her permission when they were in residence, so long as he kept his visits to the early mornings before anyone was up and about. But the library was the only room he was allowed in, although he had sneaked a peek in some of the others when no one was watching him, seating himself at the head of the vast dining table as if he were the Duke himself, or lolling on one of the deep, comfortable sofas in one of the many sitting rooms.

Bella turned to the young man, waiting politely by the door, his hands behind his back as he stared around him with wonder, obviously waiting for her to dismiss him down to the stables or wherever servants were housed in that establishment.

She grinned at him. "No, *Monsieur* Vallance, this is YOUR room. I thought you might like to sleep in a four-poster bed for a change, instead of the loft over the stables or a servant's attic room. Do you think you might manage to put up with that while we're here?"

Jack was speechless and once again gawped at Bella, so much so as to forget his newly acquired, cut glass and slightly aristocratic tones which he'd learned at his elocution lessons and had copied from the family whenever in their presence. "Wot? Nah, yer jestin' me, Mum. I can't doss dahn in 'ere, that's fer peeps like yous; gentry an' all that."

Bella laughed and went over to ruffle his hair, grasping his hand to lead him over to the huge, soft bed where the covers had already been drawn back ready for its next occupant, the freshly laundered sheets smelling of lavender. As he looked at her, still stunned, she gently pushed him backwards and he toppled onto the deep, comfortable mattress, a look of both amazement and complete bliss stealing over his surprised face.

"So, is the bed to *Monsieur's* satisfaction? Does *Monsieur* think he'll be able to sleep well there tonight?"

"This is all fer me? Truly, Mum? Yer ain't jestin' me, like?" the youth was stunned.

Bella looked at the lad, so overcome with surprise and utter pleasure, still slightly disbelieving he would be sleeping in this room by himself. She was enormously pleased and amused with her gesture, as she knew she would be. She took such things as a proper comfortable bed and clean, scented linens for granted. To him, it was something he'd never experienced or even knew about. He was such a kind, considerate boy, constantly running after her to make sure she was comfortable or didn't want for anything, always trying to be protective as she wandered around the shops and sights by herself. She remembered what her aunt had told her about where she'd found him and how he'd been struggling to look after the little gaggle of young children, not all of them even related to him, but all orphans like himself.

He was a bright, intelligent lad too. To give him a taste of comfort and luxury was so easy for her and would give him such pleasure.

"It's all yours, Jacques. Just don't steal any of the ornaments!" She grinned at him.

He sat up, affronted. "Your Grace," his elocuted tones now returning as he recovered from the shock at his new temporary abode. "I haven't stolen anything since the Duchess took me to Firle," then he suddenly reddened. "Well, only some cakes or biscuits from Mrs Farthing sometimes when she's not looking." Bella's face creased with mirth, suddenly reminded of Nicky often doing exactly the same thing from the gifted fat cook at Firle Manor, bringing his stolen hoard up to where she was always waiting, like his little shadow, to share his ill-gotten gains. Her wild Granville cousins, too, had been just as bad, often feeling the end of Mrs Farthing's rolling pin on their backsides when they'd been caught. The woman was a true battle-axe and had no care whether her thief was the Duke's son, a maid or a stableboy, they got their ears bent and boxed if they were caught with sticky fingers in her domain.

"I know plenty of other young rogues who've done exactly the same thing," she winked, "so I wouldn't worry too much about that and anyway, they really are delicious pastries aren't they? I never got caught either," she added, giggling like a naughty little girl for a moment.

She left Jack lolling around in unreconstructed bliss on his bed, bidding him to come and find her in a couple of hours for dinner, before returning to her room to oversee her unpacking and instruct the young girl who would act as her maid. She ordered a bath, also one for Jack with plenty of soap and scented masculine cologne while she was about it. Another first for the young man she presumed, though he would have to experience that new little treat all by himself and she laughed.

Since Jack had no evening clothes, they couldn't eat in the exclusive hotel's dining room so they ventured out and found a small, typically Parisian, upmarket café restaurant where the food was delicious and Jack ate his way through the menu, finally finishing with a rich chocolate confection that sent his face into further paroxysms of bliss.

"I swear, I don't know where you put it all," laughed Bella. "You really must have hollow legs."

Jack grinned back at her, carefully wiping his mouth on his napkin. He'd watched carefully as Bella had picked up each different piece of cutlery before following suit, terrified and bewildered when they'd first sat down and perplexed at the array of silverware laid out on the table. "I spent so many years not having enough to eat, sometimes for days at a time, that I think I'm making up for it now. I can't bear to leave anything untouched, it's such a waste."

Bella smiled fondly at him, gazing at his clean, glossy hair and scrubbed skin with just a hint of beard now showing, the mild cologne she'd ordered for his bath water still lingering on his skin. No one would ever suspect he'd been an emaciated, bedraggled and dirty thief who couldn't string two intelligent words together just a few years back. He'd had such a hard life, but she put the sad thoughts to one side and, as they sipped their fragrant coffee, she put her mind to the task in hand and what they would do the following morning.

She explained that when Nicky was in Spain, he'd spent time working in the various livery stables and horse markets, looking for people who might know of Frederick Bernheim, or someone like him if he was using a false name, the man he was chasing. Then, he'd apparently started singing in taverns and bars. Bella laughed at Jack as she told him, explaining she thought this was somewhat far-fetched, but that they would have to go round as many as they could anyway, in an effort to try and track him down. So she suggested Jack made his way round the various livery stables across the city while she tried to find out where the most popular taverns, bars and cafés were situated and they would visit as many of them as they could each evening after dinner.

Jack said he'd been expressly ordered by the Duchess not to leave her alone, he was her protector and bodyguard, so he couldn't go off and poke around livery yards and stables all day. But Bella was adamant, pointing out it would be difficult for her to achieve her task accompanied, but she promised she would stay in or near the hotel or take a carriage to the more exclusive shopping streets to make enquiries there while exploring the new Parisian fashions. Not happy at being overruled, Jack became quite belligerent, but Bella firmly took him to task and said if he disobeyed her, she would merely send him back to Firle.

Dismayed at the prospect of being sent home in disgrace, he reluctantly gave in and, friends again, they made their way back to the hotel where they sat for another hour, playing cards and taking the opportunity to practice French vocabulary which would assist Jack on his visits to the liveries.

Chapter Thirty-Four

So the days progressed and after two weeks, they'd achieved nothing. They could find absolutely no trace of Nicky. It was like looking for a phantom.

In frustration, Bella decided she may as well go and visit Bernheim's house, since she had nothing to lose. After a creative discussion with Jack the night before, she dressed herself in her plainest dark dress and went out early to purchase a drab, dark bonnet and encompassing shawl. Then, with Jack in tow carrying an acquired charitable collection box, the origins of which she didn't want to know, she approached the quiet, leafy square of the address Ashcroft had given her.

The houses there were large and well kept, each set back from the street and surrounded by high railings and gates. They weren't the mansions of well-to-do aristocratic families who still had their heads intact because they'd got out of France before the bloodbath, or the *nouveau riche* who'd benefited from Bonaparte's time running France… but neither were they the homes of ordinary working people. Wealthy middle class, Bella told herself, business owners perhaps, or lowly nobles, if there were any of those left in Paris. Definitely a suitably discreet address for people who might have money but didn't want to display their wealth. Bernheim's residence looked identical to the others except the blinds were shut or curtains drawn at all the windows and although the gardens were tidy and well kept, they somehow looked a little abandoned and untended, with few flowers planted to relieve the sparseness of the plain, empty soil.

The street was quiet as Bella made her way to the gate. It was locked, so she pulled the chain to ring a noisy bell. She waited several minutes with no response and was just about to turn away and leave when a tall, hulking brute, a veritable giant of a man with a dark, swarthy appearance, wearing just a leather waistcoat and some heavy cord trousers, all muscles and shaven head, a solitary gold earring in one ear, lumbered down the drive and peered at her questioningly through the railings. He said nothing, merely cocking his head on one side. "*Bonjour, Monsieur,*" she said brightly. "I'm collecting for the Wounded Veterans Charity," she tilted her head meaningfully at the box Jack silently held up, "and I wondered if your master or mistress would like to give a donation?" She looked sad and mournful, "So many men have come home, maimed, with terrible injuries and lost limbs, like my own husband and some of his colleagues, so I'm sure your employers would like to assist?" She raised her big green eyes at the swarthy man, trying to look pathetic and pleading.

His face impassive, he merely shook his head and went to turn away. "Oh, please, *Monsieur,* could I not come in and plead my case? I'm sure your employer must have some sympathy? There are so many, such dreadful injuries: frostbite and starvation from Russia, mortar wounds from the Peninsula..." Bella tried to think of something sad in an effort to produce a couple of tears in her eyes and a vision of Nicky and Terrie playing in the gardens at Valenciennes while she was sat at home in Hertford Street, sad, lonely and abandoned, sprang into her mind. Tears plopped on to her cheeks in moments.

The swarthy man looked at the attractive, tearful woman but still shook his head. "Oh please, is there no one at home who could spare even a few coins?" Bella looked up, "It's such a beautiful house, surely a little money would be nothing to your master, is he not at home?"

Again, the man shook his head and as Bella poked her hand through the railings to try and grasp one of his, he leaned forward and opened his mouth; there was no tongue, and Bella reared back in shock. The man pantomimed at her that he obviously couldn't speak and his eyes flashed with suspicion as he looked from her to Jack, who was standing quietly, merely holding out his box, occasionally rattling its few contents and also trying to look serious and pathetic. He gestured to them to go away and stood back, crossing his bare, muscled arms, obviously waiting for them to leave. Realising she was getting nowhere, Bella turned to go, only to hear Jack whisper in her ear that the mute was watching them carefully so they had better visit some of the other houses or he would be suspicious.

For the next half an hour, Bella and Jack went through the same ritual at all the other upmarket residences in the street while the big, swarthy man watched them through the railings of Bernheim's mansion. They were quite successful, obviously the other house-owners far more sympathetic to their cause than Bernheim's caretaker. Finally, they slowly made their way from the last house and turned the corner, out of the leafy square and only as they did so, did the mute guard finally turn and make his way back inside the shuttered mansion.

As Bella leaned up against the railings of another large house and let out a long breath, Jack shook his head. "Phew, he was a nasty piece of work and no mistake. Did you see his eyes?" he shivered.

"I wasn't looking at his eyes," whispered Bella. "I've never seen a man with no tongue before," she grimaced. "I wonder if he was born like that or had it cut out?" Her grimace turned to a shudder at the thought.

"Trust this Bernheim fellow to have a man who can't speak and tell anyone anything. Very convenient," muttered Jack. He'd seen too many maimed, scarred and limbless beggars in and around the Seven Dials to be personally affected by a man with a mere missing tongue.

"Well, that's that, I suppose," sighed Bella, "not that I really expected him to come to the door and welcome us in with open arms," she muttered in frustration. "So we're back at square one. Back to the stables, bars and taverns tonight then, I'm afraid."

Jack rattled his now almost full collection box. "What are we going to do with the money, Madam?" he asked.

"What do you suggest, Jack?" Bella asked curiously. For her part she wanted to give it to exactly who they had collected it for, but she was interested to see what her young, hopefully reformed, thief would say.

"Well, I think we should find the real Veterans' Charity and give it to them. Surely they must have one? All those wounded soldiers," he shook his head and sighed sadly, "even if they are Frenchies, they're still men, a lot no doubt with families to support or too wounded to find any useful employment. There were enough ex-soldiers begging in London but it seems to be the same in Rouen, here in Paris, and some of the other towns we stopped at. Can we do that, Madam?"

Bella smiled at Jack, delighted at his response. She rather thought she'd have been very surprised if he'd said anything else, she was getting to know him quite well now. "Of course we can. I'll make enquiries when we get back to the hotel. Tell them we found the box while we were out visiting a museum or something, ask where we can take it." She smiled at him, "Young Man, in the meantime you are back on your rounds of livery stables, I'm afraid."

Jack pulled a face. "Do you really think I'm going to find anything there? I mean, I can understand when the Duke was in Madrid, but apart from the fact that anyone up to no good wouldn't use their own name, why would Bernheim want to hire a carriage or horses in the city where he already has a home? It doesn't make much sense to me. He can just hail a hack surely? He's obviously not short of a few *francs*, given that nice mansion he owns, to hire one all day if need be, so why bother to rent a carriage or hire horses?"

Bella looked at him and considered his opinion. "You know, you're quite right, Jack. I presumed since he didn't seem to live here permanently, he might just hire a carriage and horses when he needed one, instead of keeping his own stables, but unless he was going on a journey, why bother?" Bella sighed. "I suppose I was just following what my husband did when he was under cover before." She paused to reflect on their other options then suggested, "But working the cafés, coffee shops, bars and taverns is another matter, don't you agree?

Everyone goes out to eat and drink occasionally, even if they live in the city. If Bernheim has been at home recently, he surely must have gone out, perhaps picked up a woman, being a single man. He did that in Madrid and I was told he killed some of them," she said starkly. "He's a nasty piece of work, Jack, that's why I'm so frightened for my husband."

"Bleedin' 'ell, 'e killed some of 'is tarts?!" It popped out before he could stop it. "Oh, begging your pardon, Madam, I didn't mean to swear in front of you."

Bella smiled at him. "That's quite all right, Jack, my language isn't quite the thing at times, I can assure you."

"But you're a Lady, a Duchess, Ladies don't swear like that."

Bella laughed at him, "You've obviously not been around my aunt when she's in full flow, nor me for that matter," she tweaked his nose, just as she'd often done to Nicky. "We're far from perfect, You Idiot, Ladies or not. We lose our tempers or get frustrated or shocked just like anyone else," and she smiled reflectively. "But thank you for apologising. You really are quite a young Gentleman you know, you should be very proud of what you've achieved over the past two or three years, it can't have been easy." However, before he could answer, she pulled his arm through hers and set off down the street. "Come along, *Monsieur*, I'm sure you must be starving, so let's go and find some lunch. I swear all that begging has made even me feel hungry and it must be at least two hours since you last ate." She grinned at him, increasingly glad she had his amusing and cheerful presence with her to take her mind off her concerns over Nicky.

Another couple of weeks went by. They had abandoned visiting the livery stables and other places to hire or buy carriages and horseflesh. Instead, they passed the time visiting the museums and taking in the sights of Paris. They finally agreed it was pointless searching for someone when they didn't know what he looked like and would no doubt be using a false name. Also, Bella told herself, finding Bernheim wasn't why she'd come chasing over to France; her priority was to find her missing husband and resolve her own personal problems.

Bella hadn't been to Paris before so she enjoyed being a tourist as much as Jack. She pointed out the fearful *Conciergerie* where the tragic

Queen Marie Antoinette had spent the last months of her life; the large square where the guillotine had once stood and at the majestic Notre Dame Cathedral where they climbed the tower to look down over the river and spectacular views of Paris spread out below. Every evening, they visited a variety of inns and taverns, seeking out someone, anyone, who may have heard or seen an itinerant, golden-haired singer or guitar player, but their search proved fruitless.

Chapter Thirty-Five

They had been away for weeks and Bella was now despondent and in despair. She missed Terrie and was even more worried about Nicky. Messages sent back to Valenciennes and Hertford Street confirmed he hadn't reappeared in either location. One evening, she told Jack she had a bad headache and was going to bed early. She couldn't face traipsing round more smoke-filled, frequently raucous taverns, full of all manner of people, mainly men. She hadn't been sleeping well, worry often making her patrol back and forth across her room in the early hours, nightmares about finding Nicky shot or butchered in a gutter soon bringing her awake, damp with sweat, if she had even managed to get to sleep beforehand.

Looking at the pale, drawn features of the young woman to whom he'd become devoted, Jack gallantly bent to kiss her hand, making her smile forlornly and bade her a good night. She told him to go to bed himself and not get into mischief, that she would see him in the morning when they needed to work out what to do next; just like in a game of chess, she said.

As he set off down the hallway, Jack had absolutely no intention of going to bed. By himself for the first time, he had his own ideas of where to go and look for the missing duke, not necessarily in an inn or tavern. Having changed his apparel to his own original, simple, home-spun clothes he normally wore for work, he set out from the hotel and headed for the slums and the teeming stews of Paris, home from home for a youth like himself, intent on making his own investigation and asking some questions in his hesitant but rapidly improving French. Coached and corrected by Bella, he'd been speaking it day and night since they'd arrived in France and as well as his fluency, his accent was also now much better. Bella had commented he seemed to have a real ear for languages and was inordinately pleased at his progress.

However, he, too, had no success that night and staggered back around dawn to fall into his wonderful bed, still overcome with bliss every time he put his head on the soft feather pillows and pulled the crisp fresh sheets up around his naked body, the glorious feel of them against his now always clean skin something he thought he would never get over.

The next day, Bella was still out of sorts, running a slight tempera-ture and then she started sneezing. She took to her bed with Jack hovering in concern over her, not knowing what to do other than hand her a fresh handkerchief every time she sneezed and asking constantly if he could get her some tea, or hot chocolate, or water, or visit an apothecary for some medicine. Finally, simply wanting peace and quiet to allow her to sleep, she muttered, "Oh for heaven's sake, Jack, I've only got a bit of a cold, an unusual occurrence for me though, I have to say. Go on, be off with you. You've got plenty of pocket money, go and spend it, amuse yourself for the day. Eat sweetmeats or all the pastries in Paris, whatever you want, just let me be to sleep a bit, pleeease. I'm sure I'll feel a lot better then."

So, reluctantly, Jack departed alone and spent the morning roaming up and down the main shopping streets, gazing in wonder and fasci-nation at the beautiful clothes and accessories there, so much the same, but somehow so different to Bond Street in London. He resolutely ignored the temptation of the reticules of the wealthy ladies he watched strolling up and down as they stared in the shop windows; he'd put that life behind him and didn't need to steal any more. After indeed stuffing himself with all manner of pastries and treats for lunch, he made his way back to another part of the dark, dank, dangerous and filthy alleys of central Paris to continue his enquiries for a tall, good-looking, blond singer who had been working the bars and 'making friends' with the local ladies of the night.

Bella was still unwell the following day, though somewhat improved, so Jack disappeared off again and repeated the previous day's activity, making his way through more crowded and noisome tenements and dingy taverns full of thieves, vagrants, beggars, drunks and prostitutes as night fell. As he wandered down a maze of squalid passageways and narrow lanes, populated by the destitute and starving, the desperate and the villainous, he found himself at a small crossroads with a busy tavern on one corner, full of people loitering around, drinking and trying to listen to someone who was singing inside, accompanied by a Spanish guitar. As he heard the strummed notes, Jack edged his way through the crowd and peered round a smelly, overpainted and raddled prostitute, who on close inspection was obviously nearer fifty than thirty, with rotting teeth and hennaed hair. She was sighing as she listened to the romantic song the entertainer was singing.

Jack took one look at the man perched on a high stool and his face beamed with satisfaction. He'd run his quarry to earth.

He recognised the Duke from his visit to Firle the previous Christmas when everywhere had been covered by the heavy snowfall. He remembered watching him as he'd helped the other grooms, stable hands and gardeners clear the paths around the house. The Duke had built a short and fat snowman for the little girls to dress up, playfought and laughingly rolled around in drifts with the younger boys and he'd then had a seriously rollicking snowball fight with the older Granville sets of twins and their friends. He'd seemed such a charming and kind man, with no airs and graces despite his title. Jack had trouble reconciling the merry joker from Christmas with the undercover agent of his wife's description.

But here he was, the very aristocratic and wealthy Duke of Valenciennes, singing in a murky tavern in the centre of the infamous Paris slums on the *Île de la Cité*. Pulling himself together and full of excitement at his discovery, Jack ran as fast as he could back to the nearest main thoroughfare and hailed a hack to take him back to the hotel.

Totally forgetting his manners when he arrived, he simply ran up the stairs, down the corridor and erupted into his mistress's room, waking her up in complete fright as he burst out, "I've fahnd 'im, I've only bleedin' fahnd 'im! Come quick, I've fahnd 'im!" He was hopping up and down in glee.

Bella shot out of bed, her voluminous nightgown and warm shawl flying around her, her long plait swinging wildly. She grabbed Jack by the shoulders, "Where? Jack, where? Oh, You Darling, Clever Boy!" She hugged him tight and gave him a smacking kiss on the cheek. "Where is he?"

Startled by the informal and unexpected show of affection, Jack smiled back at Bella, thrilled to pieces he'd done something to please her and got his brain and accent on track again. "He's singing in a tavern, Madam, in the slums down on the *Île de la Cité*, not far from Notre Dame, there's quite a crowd there listening to him."

Bella gazed back at him, "Good God! So it's true then?" Jack nodded. "Wait here, let me get dressed and we'll go back straight away." She ran into the small adjoining dressing room, threw on some clothes haphazardly, not bothering to undo her plait, just winding it up on the back of her head – and in minutes, she and Jack were running back down the corridors, across the hotel foyer and out onto the now deserted streets, startled late night hotel staff scattering in their wake.

It was around three in the morning when they finally arrived at the tavern and Nicky had obviously finished singing for the night. Bella spotted him leaning against the bar, a beautiful Spanish guitar on the floor next to him, drinking a tankard of ale, chatting with a group of scantily clad young prostitutes. He looked very different with his longer, un-styled hair, unshaven cheeks and cheap, scruffy clothes, but he was still the man she loved. She watched for a while, standing in the shadows, as the girls laughed and flirted with him. He plied them with glasses of cheap wine, speaking to each in turn, his whole demeanour that of a handsome charmer looking to choose some bedroom company for the night.

Hot, tearing jealousy shot through Bella as she stood there spying on him from her hidden corner. She gazed in silent pain as one young girl seemed to catch his interest and he engaged her in deep conversation before throwing a lazy arm around her shoulder and disappearing up a rickety side staircase at the back of the tavern, her in tow, to one of the rooms available to rent upstairs for the night.

Jack, too, was watching and saw the sadness and pain creep across his mistress's face as she saw her husband go off with the prostitute. Not knowing quite what to say to dissipate her evident distress, he merely grasped her hand and whispered, "I'm sure it's nothing, Madam; she must have some information or know something he wants to find out. He wouldn't go with someone like that otherwise. Why should he? Not when he has someone as lovely as you for a wife."

Bella looked at the youth tearfully. "I know, Jack, but it still hurts. You wouldn't understand, you're too young," she whispered back forlornly.

Jack wasn't that young or ignorant that he didn't know what the Duke was doing upstairs. If anything he was jealous of him as that young girl was pert and reasonably pretty and he'd already discovered the joys of sex with some of the saucy young scullery maids at Firle or the kitchen maids down at the tavern in the village. They'd regularly visit him late at night in one of the hay lofts over the stables at Firle. But he kept a straight face as he knew pain and distress when he saw it and, throwing caution to the wind at his completely inappropriate behaviour, put his own arms around Bella, hugging her to him, seeking to comfort her in the only way he knew how, just as he had with the little children under his care in the old draughty garret. He was tall for his sixteen years, his rangy, gangly limbs starting to show the promise of the man he would become. Although he wasn't much taller than Bella, his comforting hug and understanding words were a salve to her sorrowful heart.

"Come on, Madam, let's go back to the hotel," Jack murmured quietly. "He's apparently booked to sing here for another few nights, that popular he is. Look, see that poster over there," he pointed to a tatty sheet of paper pinned up near the door that had a likeness of Nicky on it with details of when he was due to perform scrawled underneath. "We can come back tomorrow and you can talk to him then, hmmm?" So he led his tearful mistress away from the tavern and back to their hotel.

Bella was very subdued the following day. She dressed carefully, wanting to look her best but in simple clothes that wouldn't stand out where they were going, before setting out the following evening. She told Jack he need not accompany her as she was going to talk to her husband, now that she'd finally located him. But Jack would hear none of it, saying it was his duty to look after her and there was NO WAY he would let her go wandering by herself, down those fetid, dangerous alleyways at night, or even during the day, full of thieves and cutthroats as they were. He told her she'd be dead and her body floating in the Seine before she even got to the tavern! He produced a small, nasty looking knife from the inside of one of his boots, saying he'd cut the throat of anyone who tried to do her harm. Bella surveyed him and smiled. He looked like a boisterous puppy, full of aggression and hot air, but truth be told she would be glad of his protection; she'd been so overwhelmed with finally discovering Nicky the night before, she hadn't really absorbed just where Jack had found him and had been aghast as they'd hurried along the narrow passageways to and from the tavern. She knew her Uncle Francis would have a complete raving tantrum if he had even an inkling of what she was up to! Perhaps she could send Jack on his way, back to the hotel, once she'd found Nicky and could go somewhere private and safer with him, to try and put things right between them, not to mention find out what he was up to.

Arriving early, the pair of them found a table in a dark corner, able to see but not be seen in the dark, smoke-filled hostelry. Jack brought back a flagon of wine and two glasses and they sat and drank in silence for a while, each lost in their own thoughts.

"He must do this to get information," Jack finally spoke, voicing the thoughts he knew were running around his mistress's head. "It's a good idea, the street girls always know what's going on. They talk to each other, compare clients and pimps, warn each other if one of them should be avoided or someone has nasty tastes, or won't pay; well, usually, that is." He spoke with an experience well beyond his years and another world to Bella. "Some keep themselves to themselves, especially if they get their claws into a regular or gent with a bit of money, but mostly the grapevine is a reliable source of gossip." He tailed off and took a long gulp of wine. This was not the usual conversation one would have with one's mistress. It was all very bizarre.

Bella nodded slowly. "Yes, I can appreciate that. I suppose they need to stick together sometimes." She watched as a small group came into the bar and sauntered round the tables, laughing coarsely, pulling down their bodices quite brazenly, or lifting their skirts, to show off their attributes, offering their services to any likely-looking man on the premises. One or two even eyed up Jack, staring curiously at Bella as she sat there looking slightly shocked.

Jack chuckled when he saw her expression. "They obviously think I'm with you... you know," he winked at her and smirked. Bella looked even more shocked. "Anything goes round here, Madam, same as London. No one would think it strange, age is irrelevant, believe me."

"But you're so young. That's appalling!" she whispered, her eyes widening.

"Not that young, Madam," he winked, "and anyway, you're a very beautiful and desirable woman, especially tonight, if you don't mind me saying, pardon for being so forward!" He grinned wickedly at her.

"Jack Vallance, behave yourself!" Bella had to laugh despite herself, the lad was incorrigible. But the little exchange had broken the pall of sadness that had seemed to hang over her and the pair of them sat back to wait for Nicky to appear, periodically exchanging whispered comments on the tavern's customers and the 'ladies' who were preying on them.

By midnight, the dingy tavern was heaving with people, some even standing around outside, waiting for the evening performance to begin. There was a sudden hush and Bella sat gripped as she watched her husband make his way slowly through the crush of tables and customers to perch on a stool on a makeshift dais at one end of the room, in front of the hostelry's dirty bay window.

He smiled captivatingly at his audience and began to play his guitar, the soft notes of the tuneful Spanish folk songs so familiar to Bella, they made her heart lurch with old memories of her mother. He was very good, his guitar playing enormously improved from his boyhood. Bella was amazed; she wasn't to know that he'd spent his time the previous summer in Reynard's camp being tutored by a couple of masters of flamenco guitar there, practising his musical skills as well as working with the horses. It was the ideal occupation for someone who needed to sit and rest a lot, and recuperate from his serious injuries.

After a while he started to sing. Bella's mouth nearly dropped open as his melodic voice stretched to the back of the crowded room and out the door, a quiet hush falling over the formerly rowdy occupants. He sang in Spanish, then switched to French romantic ballads which had the women in the room rapt as he crooned the words, making them feel he was singing just for them. He sang for quite a while, chatting to the audience between songs, asking them for requests and drinking occasionally from a glass of wine sitting on the windowsill behind him. Bella was completely entranced and absolutely stunned. As she'd told both Ashcroft and Jack, she'd had no idea Nicky could sing like that, let alone keep an audience entertained. They were in the palm of his hand, completely engrossed in his performance, clapping wildly as he finished each song and calling for more.

Eventually, he stepped down from the stool and started to stroll around the room, strumming his guitar and singing at one or two of the tables, making a bee-line for the females in the party, if there were any, smiling and flirting with them as he sang. He was quite unbelievable and, as he got nearer to the bar, thankfully not in the direction of the far corner where Bella and Nicky were cowering, ready to flee, he finished singing and turned to bid the audience buy more drinks while he took a break, promising to return again in a while. He then sauntered off, loud applause ringing in his wake.

"My God," breathed Bella as the room calmed down and customers flocked to the bar or called over the now busy serving wenches. "I genuinely didn't realise he could play the guitar that well, nor sing like that. That was unbelievable!"

Jack smiled at her astonished face. "He certainly knows how to hold an audience, he's quite some performer, and his voice is more than good. If he wasn't a duke and didn't need the money, he could make a nice living on the stage in London, that's for sure. What's more, the ladies of the Ton would love him; what a turn that would be at some of your fancy *soirées*. Imagine, he could be The Singing Soldier..." and the pair of them laughed at the ridiculousness of that and drank some more wine as they waited for The Disguised Duke to re-appear.

About half an hour later, he took his seat again, but this time with another man, also holding a guitar. Once more, he started out with a few instrumental tunes, traditional French ones, concentrating and paying attention as he played his Spanish guitar even more competently. After much calling out and clapping, he put down his guitar and went to stand near the edge of the dais. The second man, who'd been standing quietly, starting to strum the notes of a well-known opera aria. The audience started cheering and shouting, *"Chantez! Chantez! Nico, chantez Orphée et Eurydice....* Sing, Nico, sing Orpheus and Eurydice; Nico, sing Orpheus..." with much stomping of feet. Bella looked puzzled at Jack as the customers called out their encouragement, obviously waiting for what was presumably the highlight of his performance. But they were calling for opera – from Nicky? Surely not? Suddenly, he held up his hands to pacify them and spoke quietly, the clamour of the audience dying down as he addressed them. "This is dedicated to someone I've loved and lost too..." his face was sad and then, as the introductory notes of the haunting melody wafted around the bar, just on a simple guitar, no violins in this slum tavern, he began to sing. *"J'ai perdu mon Eurydice...* I've lost my Eurydice..."

A shiver ran down Bella's spine, hairs stood up on the back of her neck and her mouth finally did gape in disbelief. Jack's warm, supportive hand stole over hers as he, too, was riveted. You could hear a pin drop in the formerly raucous room. This was classic opera and Nicky had a beautiful light tenor voice. But he didn't sing the aria of lost love, of the death of a beloved wife, as if he were on a grand theatre stage. He sang it more quietly, intimately, just to the accompaniment of the guitar. As he sang, he seemed lost in the theme of the moving aria, his eyes closed, a break in his voice. He fell to his knees as he empathised with the hero's torment and his wish to die because he'd lost his wife. Overcome with what she was watching, Bella felt tears roll down her face. Who was this man pouring out his sorrow in a song as if it was really his own? She'd never seen anything like it and she felt Jack push a crumpled handkerchief into her numb fingers.

The room was stunned into momentary silence as the music finished and the aria ended, Nicky bowing his head as the hero was lost to grief. Then the audience erupted and applause rang to the rafters. Even the uncouth riffraff, the majority of the clientele, had appreciated what they'd witnessed and heard. While everyone around them stood to applaud and call for an encore, Bella merely sat, rooted to her chair and Jack watched her with concern. He hadn't understood the lyrics, just the introductory first line, but he'd got the gist of what was going on and the effect on his mistress. Nicky stood up, smiling, and was mobbed by the clientele, women grasping his hand, kissing him and throwing their handkerchiefs at him, then a shower of coins. Suddenly, it was all too much for Bella; she lurched to her feet and fled from the bar, shoving and pushing her way past the still cheering customers until she reached the street where she leaned back against a wall, breathing hard, tears running down her face.

"Madam, Madam? Oh no..." Jack ran after her and once more pulled her into a hug. "What is it? Tell me...?"

"I can't stay here, I can't see him tonight, it's too much," she whispered as she wept. "I'll come back tomorrow. Take me back to the hotel, please Jack?"

As they sat in the hack carrying them back to the hotel, Jack looked angry. "He's hurt you, hasn't he? What are you really doing here, Madam?"

Bella looked at the worried youth across from her and blew her nose as she stuttered, "Yes, Jack, he's hurt me. But you see, it's all my fault. I... I... did something terribly, terribly wrong and I hurt HIM, so he can't, won't, forgive me. That's why I'm here, that's why I needed to find him, to try and put things right, so he'll come home again. His undercover work aside, I'm frightened he'll stay here in France, at Valenciennes, that he'll abandon me."

Jack swore. "No, he couldn't do that, not to YOU!" He looked at her, besotted admiration obvious on his face.

"Oh, he might well, Jack, you don't know him like I do. And you see, I really couldn't bear it. I love him so very much and I'm so frightened he'll do something rash while going after this man, Bernheim, but if something happened to him, I'd never forgive myself because it's all my fault. I drove him away, I'm sure of it..." She broke down in pitiful sobs.

Jack swore again. "No, I can't believe it's all your fault, you're not like that, the man must be a fool to want to leave you."

"Oh, Jack, it's not that simple. I wish it were," Bella blew her nose and pulled herself together as the carriage pulled up in front of the hotel entrance and they got down and went inside. At her door, Bella sighed ruefully. "Just wait 'til you fall in love, Jack; it can be the very devil."

"Hah, I know what you mean. I'm never going to fall in love, people always get hurt when they do," he muttered.

"Not all the time, Jack. Some live happily ever after." Bella laughed sadly, "Like my aunt and uncle, the Duke and Duchess, also my Uncle Richard, the Earl of Keswick, the Duke's oldest friend. Still, I'm going back to see him tomorrow and I'll have it out with him before he disappears again, I promise." She ruffled his head, in the now familiar gesture, "Goodnight, Jack. Thank you."

"Goodnight, Your Grace," he bowed low and reverently as he kissed her hand. "Sleep well and try not to fret too much. I'm sure he'll come round..." and he watched as she went into her room, closing the door quietly behind her before making his way down to his own room, at a loss to understand how anyone could abandon such a kindhearted and beautiful young woman who obviously loved them very much.

They returned the following night, but despite the clamour of the audience, strangely, Nicky didn't sing the aria again. Bella had spent the day thinking about him and she couldn't get his performance out of her mind. How had she not known he could sing like that? And the way he'd performed it? Had he been thinking of her, or another woman? Or was it all theatrics? He was obviously a consummate performer as he entertained his audiences extremely well whether singing, playing or just bantering with them. And all those women throwing themselves at him after he'd finished singing the previous night? Had he taken another upstairs to his bed? She couldn't get images of him in bed with the laughing prostitute of the night before out of her mind, picturing him kissing and making love to the young girl as he had with her. The more she thought, the more confused and angry she became, so she was wound up like a spring by the time they'd got to the tavern once more. She sat there drinking all through the evening, her eyes glittering as she watched the performance, Jack surveying her in growing alarm. That morning, in exchange for a few coins, he'd quietly asked one of the helpful clerks on the hotel's reception desk who amazingly spoke a bit of English, to give him the gist of the words of the aria from the night before, but it had left him just as puzzled. He'd come to the conclusion the Duke and Duchess were obviously in a seriously confused relationship.

As on their first evening, after he'd finished his performance, Nicky went over to the bar and spent the next half hour surrounded by the local street girls, laughing and joking with them, all the tarts obviously vying for his particular attention. Bella watched jealously, her rage growing, her frantic imagination running riot. She watched as he bent to whisper in the ears of a couple of them and then, blowing kisses at them all, he bowed his head and strolled away from the bar, making his way upstairs, alone.

Bella made up her mind; standing up and grasping their latest bottle of wine and a couple of glasses, she turned to follow him. "Go back to the hotel, Jack," she ordered. "I don't need you now. I've got unfinished business to deal with." She raised her eyes to the staircase. "I'll see you there tomorrow."

"But, Madam, what if… what if he doesn't want to see you?" Jack murmured. "I'd better wait for you down here."

"Oh, he'll see me." There was a determined glint in her eyes, "I'll be just fine. Go on, you don't need to wait. Go back."

Jack could see there was no arguing with her, so he merely nodded and then watched as she strode over to the stairs and made her way up, disappearing from his sight. He went over to the bar and bought a tankard of ale and sat back down in their corner. Never mind putting things right with the Duke, he sensed she was now spoiling for a fight with the man. She'd been in a funny mood all day, not really paying attention when they'd played a game of chess that afternoon and obviously distracted over dinner, merely toying with her food and hardly eating anything. So there was no way he was going to leave her in the tavern alone. Heaven knew what was going to happen and he settled down to wait. He was only sixteen, according to his mistress, but he had plenty of coins still in his pocket and one of the young girls at the bar was giving him the eye. The Duchess would be occupied for hours yet, maybe all night. He grinned at the young girl, curled a surprisingly long, elegant finger and beckoned her over.

Chapter Thirty-Six

Bella walked down the narrow, dim corridor upstairs, unsure which room to enter but, as she hovered, a giggling pair of girls, the ones she'd seen Nicky whispering with downstairs, appeared from the other end of the hallway, having come up a different back staircase in the ramshackle building. She watched as they tottered towards her, slightly drunk, looking at the numbered doors until they paused outside one, primping their hair, rucking up their skirts and pulling down their already obscenely low-cut gowns to expose all they had to offer. Without thinking, Bella marched up to the pair of them and shoved them out of the way. Letting loose with a stream of gutter French even her aunt would be shocked to hear, she told them to get lost in no uncertain terms.

"Sez 'oo?" muttered one, looking belligerent. "We saws 'im first, 'e's ours."

"'E's promised me five francs if'n I 'elp 'im," giggled the other. "As if 'e's gotta problem," she made an obscene gesture with her fisted hand as she rolled her eyes. "I saws wot 'e's got in them tight britches o' 'is, but 'e's got two o' us ter 'elp 'im wiv 'is problem ternight," she muttered coarsely.

Bella held up a ringed hand, the gold band all the adornment there. "Sez 'is wife," she bit out, "so fuck off!" Along with a rude finger gesture, it was language they understood, but which rarely crossed Bella's lips unless she was hugely angry, albeit not with that coarse accent; however, she was now in a towering rage, to put it mildly.

Looking sullen and cross, but realising their prospective night's plans and money had now dissipated into thin air, the pair retreated back along the hallway and disappeared down the stairs, swearing and muttering to each other. Still grasping her bottle of wine and glasses in one hand, Bella knocked on the door, still not one hundred per cent sure she had the right room.

"*Entrez*," came a familiar voice from within and Bella turned the handle, a satisfied smile on her angry face.

He was standing with his back to the door, leaning to peer out through the small window, still wearing the creased shirt, loose cravat, form-fitting pantaloons and boots he'd worn for his performance. His guitar was leaning against the far wall but other than that the room was empty of any belongings.

"Well, well, Your Grace, it seems there's no END to the talents you possess. I thought your little striptease was quite a performance, but last night definitely topped that." Her voice dripped icy sarcasm, "And who was your little song dedicated to? Very touching that, I almost cried."

Nicky spun round, his face registering complete shock. "What in HELL are you doi..." he never got the words out as Bella marched over and slapped his face, hard and viciously.

All her pent-up rage and hurt poured out, fuelled by the copious amounts of wine she'd drunk on a virtually empty stomach. "How DARE you run off without a word. How DARE you threaten to take my daughter away from me. If Bernheim doesn't kill you first, I'll do it myself before I let you take her off to France without me!" she yelled at him. "And as for all your women, you're welcome to them, but you have the unmitigated gall to tell me you don't trust me? You complete and utter piece of horse shit. You're worse than the dirtiest sewer rat. What sort of a proper father, never mind a duke, a wealthy aristocrat, spends every night with common, dirty whores? There were two on the menu tonight I gather; I've just seen them off. If they're not riddled with the pox, I'd be surprised, and that's another thing. How…",

She went to hit him again but he grabbed her hand and looked at her in fury, cutting off her towering rant. "Drunk again, I see, Your Grace. It's getting to be a habit," he bit out angrily. "What the HELL are you doing here and what the devil do you know about Bernheim?"

"I came to find you, God knows why now, but I had an extremely illuminating conversation with your friend Lord Ashcroft several weeks ago." More sarcasm dripped from her. "My, my, Your Grace, you have been a busy bee. Rescuing gold shipments, consorting with Spanish prostitutes, even strangling one. How bad tempered of you, didn't she come up to scratch then?" She leered at him maliciously, "At least I never seemed to have that problem, you used me enough a few months' back, but at least my neck is still in one piece."

Ice cold anger raged through Nicky at her words. "You HAVE been poking your nose into my affairs, haven't you?" his voice dripped sarcasm too. "Ashcroft must be losing his touch to fall for your wiles. I would have thought he at least would be immune to your beautiful, treacherous face."

"Apparently not," she bit back, "any more than you can resist every cheap whore on the Left Bank."

"At least they're honest with their feelings, they don't pretend to be somebody they're not," he spat back at her.

"Are they so wonderful then, your pretty little tarts?" she seethed. "I watched you with them, they certainly seem to make you smile and laugh," then Bella added slyly, "did Carmelita make you smile too?" She watched his eyes blaze at the mention of the Spanish prostitute's name. "When was the last time you smiled at me, were even civil to me?" she raged bitterly. "You won't even let me touch you, never mind kiss you."

"Why should I smile and laugh with you? You do nothing to please me, absolutely nothing. I can't stand the thought of you touching me now, certainly not kissing me. I DESPISE you!" he finally raged at her.

Her temper completely boiled over at his rejection. "Hah! You didn't seem to hate me enough to keep out of my bed after Christmas, You Lying Bastard..." and, beside herself with hurt and anger, Bella brought up her other hand which was still holding the heavy bottle of wine and glasses and cracked it over the side of Nicky's head.

"You Evil Bi..." he cried as she hit him and he dropped like a stone, as did the glasses, toppling back across the low wooden bed, the only furniture in the room, apart from a simple chair.

Bella fell across him, completely enraged, meaning to hit him again, so angry she could hardly speak, but she paused when she realised he was out cold. She'd actually forgotten she was still holding the wine bottle, its cheap, thick glass still intact. She'd brought it up with her, fully intending to try and sit down and reason with Nicky over a civilised drink, but the sight of the two prostitutes in the hall had swept all her good intentions out of the window. 'Hit him over the head...' for a moment her aunt's words came back to her and an amused smile crossed her lips. She obviously had more of her aunt's de Mornay characteristics in her than she realised and was becoming just like her... and she remembered she'd still not bought any more French porcelain to send back to Firle House as she recalled the imminent battle she'd left behind when she'd last exited the mansion in Berkeley Square.

As he lay across the bed, shirt falling open over his muscular chest, the usual tight pantaloons fitting his long hard body like a glove, Bella stared down at Nicky and a huge wave of drunken lust surged over her as she still seethed with hurt over his callous remarks. All these other women could have him, love him, take their pleasure from him, but not HER, his wife, the mother of his daughter. He said she did nothing to please him and she grinned maliciously. She'd show him. She'd pleased him enough once, it was about time she did it again.

Reaching down, she roughly pulled off his undone cravat still hanging around his neck and rolling him over, face down, she tied his limp wrists tightly behind him, then rolled him back again and sat back to wait for him to regain consciousness.

While she waited, she poured herself a glass of wine and pulled out one of her long cigarillos from the case in the small reticule which had been dangling from her wrist, lighting it from the low fire that was sputtering in the small grate. Then she scrambled onto the bed again, perching at the bottom, sitting cross legged, waiting, drinking slowly and blowing smoke rings towards the ceiling.

He came to a short while later, with a feeling groan, but when his hand wouldn't move to put to his throbbing head, Nicky opened his eyes and they instantly locked with Bella's, glinting malevolently across from him as he shunted himself back up the bed to rest against the rough-hewn headboard. Angry hate burned in his eyes.

"Well, here we are again it seems, *Milor*, except this time I don't appear to have my mask with me," she spoke conversationally as she finished off her wine and tossed the last of her cigarillo over to the fireplace.

"What do you want, Arabella?" Nicky could hardly think for the rage boiling inside him. He never called her by her full name.

"Why you, of course, Your Grace," she purred, malice still in her voice. "It's what I've always wanted, you know that. You can keep your wonderful fortune and title and go to hell your own way, but now I've had a taste of you and that glorious body of yours, enjoyed your undoubted expertise, just like all your other conquests, I simply can't resist having a bit more," and she started to undo the buttons of her jacket.

As he watched, Bella silently got off the bed and began to peel off her clothes, layer by layer, in a teasingly slow fashion, deliberately taunting him, until she was left in just her thin, virtually transparent, short silk chemise and silk stockings held up by lacy black garters just over her knees. Her eyes glinted as she watched him pull uselessly at the tight bindings round his wrists, unable to do anything but watch as she stripped off her clothes. She climbed back on to the bed and strad-dled his lap, settling back down to look deeply into his burning, golden eyes. Beneath her thighs she could feel his erection swell in his tight clothing and she smiled to herself in satisfaction, like a feral cat.

"So, Your Grace, I don't please you anymore?" she purred. "Is that the way of things?" She tore open his shirt and leaned down to run her tongue over first one, then the other of his flat hard nipples, feeling his reaction as she did so. Nicky bit his lips to stop the sigh of pleasure rising to them. Scooting back slightly, she let her hand rove over the front of his pantaloons, feeling the immediate reaction and growing hardness there. "You OBVIOUSLY don't like me touching you, hating me as you do. I don't please you anymore either, such a shame," and Bella ripped open the fastenings and took him in her fist, bending her head to lick the top of his instantly rock-like erection, making him throb, a pearl of moisture leaching from the top. He couldn't stop the moan from his lips.

As she pleasured him, Nicky threw his head back and closed his eyes, giving in to the intense feelings coursing through his veins, his mind and body again at war over his reaction to the woman above him.

"Oh no you don't!" Bella lifted her head and hands away from him and roughly pulled his face forward, her fingers now running through his soft, thick, tawny hair. "Open your eyes, Nicky," she ordered, her lips inches from his. "You wanted to watch this once, so now's your chance. Watch and know who it is who really loves you," and she bent her head, kissing him hungrily, the copious amounts of alcohol she'd drunk making her lose her usual inhibitions.

Bound as he was, his wrists sore from pulling against the tight length of his cravat she'd wound and knotted around them, Nicky could do nothing but lie back and succumb to her carnal attack. No matter how much he denied it to himself, he still craved her like an addict long without his fix. He moaned as she kissed him and then her mouth moved slowly down over his torso, licking, kissing and nibbling, until it returned once more to his throbbing hardness. She took him in her mouth again, lasciviously, sucking hard then stopping periodically to tease and torment him slowly by hand, until he was squirming and jerking, begging her for release, hating himself as he did so, watching her ministrations with eyes that glittered ferociously as they burned at her.

"Do your other women make you plead with them like this, Nicky?" Bella looked up at him and whispered, her green eyes locked with his golden ones. "Do they please you as much as I do? Admit it,

Nicky, even if I may not be as experienced as them, you can't resist me, can you?" She set to, trying to remember other tricks her aunt had suggested to her.

His body on fire, his heart pounding, Nicky stared at Bella, almost overwhelmed by the level of passion and rage teeming through him. "I LOATHE YOU," he grated slowly and moments later let out a loud, hoarse cry as he exploded deep in the back of her throat, his body shuddering and pulsing with reaction to the intensity of his epic release.

As he lay there, helpless under her, trying to gather his wits, Bella snaked up his body and kissed him deeply on the lips, her tongue curling around his, dancing around in his mouth. "Taste me, Nicky," she purred. "Can you taste yourself and me together? Don't try and tell me you can't stand for me to touch you now."

Slowly Bella raised herself off him and went to light herself another cigarillo and pour out a further glass of wine, then with both in hand, she sat back on the end of the bed, cross legged once more, watching him through narrowed eyes. "Can I interest you in a drink? Would you like a drag on this?" She raised her glass in his direction and blew a smoke ring towards him. He shook his head and she could see the temper in his face as he glared at her, red flags on his cheeks. She smiled like a satisfied black spider with her helpless prey caught in her web.

They sat watching each other for a while, then, as if he couldn't help himself, Nicky finally bit out, "Where did you learn to do that, all those clever tricks of yours? How many men have you entertained in your nice little apartment while I've been away? I sure as hell never taught you anything."

Bella laughed at him, lying across from her like a rumpled and angry captured lion and, taking another sip of wine, she mused, "Well now, there's an interesting question." She paused to draw on her cigarillo. "Why would you assume I needed to entertain men to further my education? What a narrow-minded male opinion, to be sure, as Great Aunt Elizabeth would surely have said. Some ladies, those who have more than half a brain or are not brainwashed by their fathers or husbands to think themselves worthless and generally inconsequential to the world, discuss all manner of matters over morning coffee or chocolate, or afternoon tea, I'll have you know, far more interesting and diverting than bonnets and reticules and babies... then all you need is a willing captive to practise on." His eyes widened and she grinned to herself as she recalled her conversations with her aunt before continuing, "But then, of course, there are also the weekend house parties..."

Nicky's eyes narrowed as he obviously assumed what most would about the extra-marital carrying on at country house weekends, away from the watchful, gossiping eyes of the Ton. But Bella continued, "So, one goes away to these bucolic weekend breaks in the fresh air, mixing with a houseful of the weird and wonderful of Society, with some local country bumpkins and worthies to make up the numbers... all in an effort to escape the interminable weeks and months of worry in London, when one doesn't hear a word from one's loved one, who one thinks is away fighting battles in the war against France. One lies awake in a strange bed, unable to sleep, trying not to think about them lying dead on a foreign battlefield, or wounded and bleeding in a ditch somewhere, with terrible visions of them with a lost limb or two, or slowly bleeding to death from terrible injuries because there's nobody around to help them. Or else one imagines them captured by the enemy and being gruesomely tortured or starved to death in some foreign prison camp..."

From looking at him with a hard, unforgiving expression, Bella's face changed as she blithely continued, "Giving up on sleep, one goes downstairs to inspect the library. It's quite amazing what one finds there to take away and read for the rest of the night, especially in the grand mansions of large, aristocratic estates. Everything from Horace and Ovid to Chaucer and Shakespeare, alongside weeks' old copies of the news sheets; ideal, tedious material to send the most intellectual of people to sleep eventually. But then, of course, one also finds Catullus, or strange Indian literature with interesting illustrations, obviously brought home by someone who has visited that country and translated some of the Sanskrit text into English in the margins; or even the scandalous writings of the Marquis de Sade. Really, the mind boggles at what one finds on the shelves of the most upstanding pillars of Society, sitting there, in plain view of everyone, albeit sometimes on a high, difficult-to-reach shelf. Obviously, some people never expect a mere woman to peruse their shelves, climb a ladder, let alone understand such 'interesting' literature in its original tongue. I do use the term 'interesting literature' loosely, by the way. Catullus: Carmen Sixteen, for instance. Are we by chance familiar with '*Paedicabo ego vos et irrumabo*'? The page in that dusty tome was even marked. How shocking to deface all this fascinating classic literature," she tutted.

Nicky knew Bella's grasp of Latin and Greek was of an exceptionally high standard, thanks to her father. He was amused to picture her grappling with the translation of the Latin poet whose pornographic writings about extremely dirty or erotic sex in all its forms had been required midnight reading material for all fourth form boys when he was at Eton; far more interesting than Caesar's Gallic Wars with details of sieges and other boring ancient military campaigns which they were supposed to be studying; and he'd heard of the Indian writings but never actually seen them, not knowing of any English translations. But as for the depraved French aristocrat, "You read de Sade?" he asked, astonished. "That's worse than Catullus. What the hell did you make of that?"

Bella looked at him curiously, "Oh, I see you're familiar with his writings as well. I suppose I shouldn't be surprised," she added nastily. "Well, not to my taste, I have to admit; makes our innocuous little games seem like a children's party, don't you think? I personally fail to see how being painfully tormented in certain ways, sodomised and whipped, can give anyone pleasure, protagonist or recipient, but I suppose it takes all sorts," she grimaced. "No wonder they locked him up."

Nicky's face was impassive until Bella asked maliciously, "Is that in your extensive repertoire with the ladies too, then?"

When he didn't answer Bella was somewhat shocked. "Nicky! Don't tell me you indulge in those practices, surely?"

"They're not to my taste either, I do assure you," he replied softly, "but as you say, some people enjoy them and all manner of other perversions he doesn't even cover. Take Frederick Bernheim, for instance; he is one seriously depraved and perverted bastard. He could have walked out of the pages of one of de Sade's books, even had his own chapter on further unmentionable practices, but of course dear Ashcroft won't have told you that," he added sarcastically.

"Whatever do you mean?" Bella whispered, horrified. "How do you know? That's a very personal and private thing."

"He occasionally strangles the women he fucks, it gives him an additional thrill when he climaxes, feeling them pleading, gasping and struggling for breath. I saw one of the bodies, knew the girl, she was only fifteen," he said quietly. "But if he doesn't kill them that way, he half beats or whips them to death. Dominance and pain is his game; especially the latter. He likes inflicting it, he gets aroused by doing it, just like de Sade."

"How do you know he does that, Nicky?" Bella asked again very quietly.

"I just know, all right, leave it at that. I simply want you to understand what sort of a man Bernheim is. This isn't a game I'm playing here, Arabella, whatever you may assume, and it's not about squalid carnal practices either; they just happened to be an unpleasant sideline of the man who was causing mischief to the Allied cause in the War, mainly for his own ends. Unfortunately, he's still at it."

But Bella persisted, thinking back to what she did know, what Ashcroft had said to her. "Carmelita Benitez. She was involved with this, wasn't she?"

Nicky sighed. "Yes, she was. She was a sometime prostitute and Bernheim's mistress. She was almost as perverted as he was, enjoyed the same sort of practices. Pain aroused her, receiving it, that is, as well as dispensing it. She procured the girls for him, most didn't know what they were letting themselves in for..." he paused. "I killed her. That's all you need to know."

"You were strangling her, weren't you? Then Bernheim shot her and that's how you got injured. My God, Nicky," Bella was almost speechless. "I can hardly believe it all. Why didn't you tell me?"

"You didn't need to know. I don't want to talk about it as it's my work – and it happens to be extremely important work. Enough now,

Arabella. Let me go." He pulled on his bound wrists again, looking at her angrily.

"Stop calling me Arabella. You sound like Papa when he's cross with me, or my old Governess," she complained.

"Well I'M cross with you. No, actually, cross doesn't even begin to describe what I feel." He stared at her then, "What ARE you doing here, Arabella? What do you want?"

"What do you feel for me, Nicky? Tell me the truth for once. You know what I'm doing here. I came to find you."

They stared at each other across the length of the bed. "Untie my hands, Bella," he sighed. "I haven't got time for another argument with you. I've work to do and I'm bloody tired."

"You're so busy then? At, what time is it? It must be around two or three o'clock in the morning. My, my, I had no idea being a government agent was such a hectic occupation. All that singing for instance, which reminds me," she sat up a bit straighter, "where did that all come from? And opera? I couldn't believe it."

"There are a lot of things you don't know about me."

"Obviously, just like there are lots of things you don't know about me either," she smirked at him, her anger starting to recede.

She slid off the bed and went to refill her glass with yet more wine before clambering back to kneel at his still booted feet. She took a sip, "Are you sure you don't want some?" she held out her glass and then smiled naughtily. "I haven't got any chocolate treats this time, or champagne, I'm afraid. This little establishment didn't run to such delicacies."

"Release me, Bella," Nicky said slowly. "I don't want your wine, or chocolate bonbons, or champagne. I don't want anything from you," he looked at her steadily.

"You don't want any chocolate bonbons?" she tossed back the remains of her wine, even more tipsy now, and leaned down to put the glass carelessly on the floor, looking back into his golden eyes. She started to pull off one of his boots, "Are you sure you're Nicholas de Bresancourt?" She tossed it on the floor and started on the other one, smiling as his temper started to mount again. "*Le Duc de Valenciennes*," and he tried to wriggle away from her, but of course couldn't back up any further. "Absent aristocratic French husband of Arabella de Mornay, oops, sorry, I still forget sometimes, Arabella de Bresancourt." He glared at her. "Long-lost lover of *La Lionesse*, proprietress of *Le Lion d'Or* and *La Lionesse d'Or*, renowned, high class gaming establishments in London." Then tempted beyond her control, she tickled his feet.

He howled and swore at her, vituperative French and English filling the small room as he tried and failed to kick her off him. "Oho, you are Nicholas de Bresancourt after all," she grinned saucily back at him, "but obviously having a bad day, or rather, a bad night if you don't want any chocolate trifles!" She tickled his feet again, laughing as he cursed and swore and writhed on the bed, now viciously trying to kick her away from him and get up.

"I swear, when I get my hands on you again, I'll thrash your backside so hard you won't sit down for a week, then I'll...." she crawled up his legs and started to pull down his tight pantaloons.

"You'll what, Nicky? What will you do to me?" Bella purred, leaning down to lay light butterfly kisses along his leg as she gradually removed his form-fitting clothes. "It's been a long time since you spanked me, well, apart from your little episode at *Le Lion d'Or*. I think I was only about ten or eleven the last time you put me over your knee if I remember right; a bit young, even for you no doubt," she taunted.

"Get off me, Arabella," Nicky seethed. "Let me go, you've had your fun. Go back to wherever you're staying and then go home and leave me alone."

She tossed the clothing on the floor and started to run her hands up his legs, then his thighs, until she reached his belly, then she grasped his partly torn shirt and ripped the rest of it open, pushing it back from his shoulders and down his arms, as far as it would go with his bound hands behind him.

She sat back, straddling his thighs and looked down at him, desire curling insidiously around her belly as she ran her fingers through his golden chest hair. She grasped the hem of her shift and slowly pulled it upward, inch by inch, finally kneeling up before dragging it off over her head. Then, slowly, she pulled the pins out of her hair and shook her head, letting the fully glory of her long black waves tumble over her shoulders and down her back. She was naked except for her silk stockings and black lacy garters.

Nicky's chafed wrists were rubbed raw from his efforts to escape, but despite twisting and tugging them, he still couldn't get free. He was forced to watch her pull her shift off, her full creamy breasts rising high as she lifted her arms to tug the garment over her head and then let down her hair. The familiar surge of lust poured through him at the sight of her; it happened every time he looked at her tall, slender, full breasted body. Hot anger seethed in his mind that he couldn't control this overwhelming desire he always had for her.

"Let me go! Get off me," he bit out, trying to writhe away from her caressing hands. "I don't want this again. For God's sake, you had what you wanted before."

Bella leaned down until her face was mere inches from his. "Ah, you've got it all wrong, Nicky, My Love," as she nibbled the side of his neck, "apart from the fact that you do want me." Her hand stole down to caress his now rampant erection. "This isn't about you again," and she kissed the other side of his neck. "You've had your fun and I don't care if you don't want it again. This is about ME. I want MY fun and I want you. I want to touch you, explore you, caress you, wherever I want." Her tongue ran up his neck and across the seam of his lips. "I'll never stop wanting you. I don't want anyone else. There's never been anyone else," she whispered. "As I've told you before, I'll NEVER let you go." She kissed him then, deeply and passionately. "You're mine," she breathed, "all mine, you always have been, no matter where you go or what you do. As one of those tarts tried to tell me, except she was wrong, I saw you first. Me. Remember that, Nicky, MY husband." She rose up then and impaled herself down on his throbbing length, moaning in pleasure as she did so, drowning out his muttered denials and final groan of surrender.

She made love to him just as she'd dreamed about sometimes, enjoying the freedom to caress and kiss him as she wanted, moving on him slowly, taking her time, intoxicating him with the vision of her body taking its pleasure, her face a mask of sensual abandon. Gradually, the smouldering heat between them grew hotter and she rode him harder, kissing him hungrily, her nails now digging into his shoulders as she became lost in the welter of feelings spreading through her body from deep within her belly. "I love you so much, Nicky," she cried softly against his mouth as her nails raked down his chest. "I wish to God I didn't, as you're breaking my heart," and for a long moment, their eyes met and a strong, deep, unspoken connection flowed between them.

Nicky swore and cursed as he yanked uselessly on his bound wrists, his body helplessly writhing and thrusting under hers, his desire to touch her, caress her and hold her in his arms, almost over-whelming in its intensity, the hatred and resentment confused by their passionate connection. He felt the spasms start deep inside her, strong and intense, as she rose and fell on him one final time, crying out his name, her head thrown back in abandon, her long hair swirling around her. He was lost too, carried away on a tide of hatred and yet extreme yearning and intense desire for her.

"Aaaaarrgh... Sooty..." he cried as an immense, powerful and emotional release tore through him, and Bella collapsed on top of him, their hearts pounding together, breath coming in gasps.

Bella fell into a drunken slumber on top of him, her arms around his neck and as Nicky lay there, unable, and for reasons he refused to address, unwilling to move under her weight, he tried and failed to dismiss the feelings he had for her and how much she affected him still, like no other woman. His wrists hurt like hell and his arms ached, but he didn't move. Eventually, giving up the unequal fight with his emotions, he too fell asleep, strangely comforted by the feel of her warm body draped around his.

Bella stirred in the pre-dawn light and opened her eyes to look at the man who was the centre of her life. His face looked relaxed and peaceful in sleep with a smile curving the sensuous lips she loved to kiss so much. He looked like the humorous and charming Nicky she knew and loved, not the remote, hard-faced man he had become with her since his return from Spain. She desperately wanted to feel his arms around her and so, slowly and carefully, trying not to disturb him, she slid from him and the bed and bent down to retrieve the sharp stiletto she'd seen tucked inside one of his boots. She pushed his body gently and he sighed as he rolled over enough for her to cut the tightly knotted cravat around his wrists, noting with regret how he'd rubbed his skin raw in his efforts to escape. She replaced the knife and crawled back onto the bed, half expecting him to push her away and roll over to sleep alone or even get up and leave her.

Nicky groaned softly as the circulation returned properly to his hands, arms and shoulders and his eyes opened to look at Bella. He rubbed his chafed wrists and gave her a speaking look and for a moment, they just lay there in the dimness, watching each other. Then, with a deeper groan he reached for her, pulled her into his arms and kissed her deeply, slowly and hungrily. He kissed her face, then moved slowly down to her neck, her shoulders and her breasts. He kissed and tasted her soft skin, gently, teasingly working his way down her body, allowing her in turn to kiss him back and caress him as she wished. "Aaah, Sooty," he murmured. "You still taste like strawberries and cream," and she laughed softly as he returned to kiss her lips again, intensely pleased to hear him call her by her nickname once more.

"Love me, Nicky, like you did before at Le Lion d'Or, that's all I want," Bella whispered against his lips, revelling in the simple plea-sure of being held in his arms as he gently caressed and kissed her. He said nothing but continued to make love to her, really make love to her, not the cold acts of before. This was loving and tender, kissing her all over her body, her whispered moans and mewls of pleasure and surrender making his golden eyes gleam as he watched and revelled in her, the anger and resentment temporarily suspended as they came together with a quiet but powerful and intense passion. She cried his name again as she climaxed, clutching him to her as if she never wanted to let him go. As he felt the spasms contract around him and her loving embrace, he gave himself up to the pull of another gripping and emotional release, his mind a maelstrom of confusion. As he poured himself into her, he kissed her deeply and muttered, "I hate you so much, Sooty, I hate you."

Bella just held him tighter and murmured back, "And I love you so much, Nicky, I love you enough for the both of us."

They fell asleep in each other's arms, but Nicky woke a short while after, his mind again working overtime – in turmoil with thoughts of Bella but also now jumping to pursue a snippet of information he'd picked up earlier the evening before, from one of the girls. He carefully pulled himself away from Bella's warm embrace, rose and dressed hurriedly. He disappeared from the room for a short while, hurrying silently downstairs to the deserted bar to find a scrap of paper and something with which to scribble a note. He left it near Bella's pillow, picked up his guitar and jacket and then, with a final distracted look at the woman sleeping soundly still, stole out of the room once more, closing the door quietly behind him.

Chapter Thirty-Seven

J ack had enjoyed a sublime night. A willing and uninhibited student, keen to improve his carnal knowledge, as well as being a paying customer, he'd learned and experienced more from the young Parisian prostitute in a few short hours than all the nights he'd spent frolicking around with mostly inexperienced, but giggling and enthusiastic local kitchen and tavern maids back home at Firle. He'd left the garret room soon after dawn and was now seated in a dirty doorway across from the entrance to the tavern. Unsure as to what had transpired overnight between the missing Duke and his wife, he'd decided to sit there and wait. If the Duchess came out alone, then he would be on hand to escort her back to the hotel and if they were together, he could make his own way back. If it was only the Duke, Jack had decided to follow him. Some sixth sense told him even if the Duchess did make it up with her husband, there was still the outstanding matter of his mission and if he was any sort of a man, he wouldn't want to take his wife into danger. Innately curious, Jack wanted to know, for his own reasons, where he went and what he was doing.

As he patiently waited, his mind roved back over his previous night's carnal discoveries and a glazed, happy smirk covered his face as he rubbed his crotch appreciatively. He was so absorbed in his reverie, he almost missed the Duke as he quietly exited the tavern and set off down the narrow alley with a purposeful expression on his face. Shaking off his stupor, Jack rose to his feet and crept after him, keeping his distance in the almost deserted, early morning streets.

Nicky headed straight back to his own digs, left his guitar with his other possessions, replaced his torn shirt with another scruffy one, then set off to find the tenement in the *quartier des Arcis,* among the Right Bank slums where he knew the local prostitutes shared rooms. One of the girls he'd been joking with the previous evening had revealed some very radical views, railing against the restoration of the despicable Bourbons and hinting darkly that Bonaparte would return soon to take France back to its Revolutionary glory. Slightly tipsy, she'd intimated people in the south of the country would be waiting to welcome him with open arms and bring him back to Paris. Nicky had been waiting for her and her friend to come to his room for some further 'entertainment' overnight, as he'd expressed interest in her views, intimating he wanted to hear more as he might want to help her and her fellow anti-monarchists bring Bonaparte back too. His intention had been to inquire more closely about the prostitute's radical customers or acquaintances from the south of France. He wasn't sure quite which they were, surmising the uneducated girl was merely repeating much of what she'd obviously overheard, since she didn't appear to have much of a brain herself. However, he would find out as much as possible while she was in a post-coital haze. Unfortunately, the pair had obviously been seen off by Bella, so he now had to find the girl and pick up with her again to pursue his enquiries.

Jack watched curiously as the duke disappeared into a dirty, squalid tenement and sat down in another foul smelling doorway opposite to await his reappearance. As he watched the intermittent arrival of a number of prostitutes fresh from their night's work, he wondered what on earth the Duke was up to, but merely sat back and waited, his mind returning to its former reverie.

Nicky had two choices: he could either use force to get the information he wanted from the girl, or spend a few hours with her to coerce it out of her willingly, if unknowingly. The more time he spent on the latter endeavour with these dregs of Parisian life, its teeming underbelly, the more he hated it. The women were invariably coarse, dirty and often diseased, worse than in Madrid if that were possible, and he was having more and more difficulty closing his mind to what he was doing, each time he picked one up to follow any leads he thought they may have. But distasteful as he found it, he couldn't bring himself to torture a woman for information, just because she held anti-monarchist or radical views, and this simple whore was no Carlotta. With a deep sigh, therefore, he pasted a charming smile on his face and asked around inside the damp, rat-infested building, finally running to earth the girl he wanted, watching her greedy expression as he pulled a few coins from his pocket and she hassled her roommates away to leave her and the supposedly impoverished singer alone for a few hours.

It was nearly noon when he finally emerged with a determined expression on his face. Jack followed him back to his lodgings where he collected a small portmanteau and his guitar, then hurried to a busy livery yard where he hired a travelling carriage, leapt inside and told the driver he would receive a bonus if they got to their destination in record time. Unable to follow further, Jack strolled casually into the stables and, his broken French stretched to its limit and with the assistance of a few coins, he managed to discover the small coach was set to take its passenger to the Coat Daz-yewer. He had no idea where or what that was, but he loitered unnoticed in the stable yard while the vehicle and horses were being readied, overhearing the coachman muttering to one of the hands about a place called Neece. This was also unknown to him, but at least he now knew where the Duke was going. What his mistress was going to do was another matter.

Armed with his nuggets of information, Jack returned back to the hotel to see what the situation now was between the Duke and Duchess. For all he knew, the Duke might have taken his wife into his confidence, but he doubted it somehow. That was why he'd followed the man, just in case, so at least one of them knew his destination. The Duchess was still absent, so he threw himself down on his bed, making the most of the indulgence for a minute or two, feeling sure they would soon be leaving and he'd be back in his stable loft, his palatial bedroom a mere fond, but never to be forgotten memory. He rolled over, worrying about his mistress alone in the slums, thinking he should go in search of her to escort her back, but was so worn out after his sleepless night, he inadvertently fell asleep, dreaming of practising his new-found talent for fornication on the lucky maids back at Firle.

Bella woke around noon to find the bed and room empty. As she stretched and sat up, her head throbbing from too much cheap wine the night before, her hand touched the note lying on the dishevelled bedding near her head. Picking it up, she opened the folded note in trepidation...

Go Home, Arabella, back to My Daughter whom you should be Looking After, not Traipsing around France, poking your nose into my Affairs and Work. Whatever Ashcroft may have told you, you have No Idea what is going on here and I cannot Cope with the Distraction of dealing with You and your Nonsense, and doing my Work at the same time, which is not the Frivolous Business you seem to think it is. It is both Serious and Dangerous and needs my full Concentration if we are to catch Bernheim and put an End to his Mischief, once and for all.

I am probably leaving Paris anyway, so STOP trying to follow me and Interfering. Go Home, back to London, where you belong!

Bella read through this terse, angry missive twice before screwing it into a ball and throwing it into the now cold fireplace. Then, realising the information it contained, she got up, struck a light and burned it. In high dudgeon, she got dressed, left the tavern and made her way back to the hotel, uncaring or unseeing of the furtive or avaricious looks she attracted as a lone woman, obviously not a slag or prostitute or resident of the slums she was hurrying through. It was just as well she was in a hurry and looked determined and purposeful, as it put off more than one would-be cut-purses, eyeing up her reticule. Her uncle, also her aunt, would have been aghast to see her on her own in such surroundings and the protective Jack should have known her head-strong fearlessness by now.

Safely returned to the hotel, she paced the floor in her suite, trying to decide what to do. Simply because he'd told her to go home, Bella felt extremely disinclined to do so. If Nicky had stayed to talk to her before he left, explained or gave her sensible reasons, she might well have done so. But to disappear without trace once again, leaving just a short, sarcastic message... well... she was damned if she'd be told what to do. The trouble was she had no idea where he was. Was he still there in Paris, singing in the inns and taverns? Or had he gone off some-where else, as he'd intimated? If so, where to? And matters were obvi-ously still not resolved between them, whatever had happened the night before. That note showed he still bore considerable animosity towards her. She remembered his last words to her, 'I hate you so much, Sooty,' and she paused in her pacing to stare through the window, trying to tell herself he didn't mean it. The way he'd finally made love to her contradicted his words; or was she fooling herself?

Then there was the matter of Bernheim. Bella had a bad feeling about the whole thing. She just couldn't explain it, but the matter obvi-ously had worrying connotations for her family as well as Ashcroft's concern about the activities of Bonaparte's supporters. On top of everything, she'd been away for weeks and she was missing Terrie dreadfully. All in all she was completely confused, tired and irritated and so she kept wearing a groove into the floorboards, her brain working overtime and getting nowhere.

She was still pacing restlessly around an hour later when Jack knocked on her door to see if she was back. He was hugely relieved to see she'd come to no harm in the slums without his escort and asked nervously what had transpired between her and her husband.

"Suffice it to say he's disappeared off again," Bella said shortly, "and I haven't a clue where he's gone. To be frank, I feel inclined to pack all this in and go home." She sighed, "If only I didn't have this horrible, niggling feeling I shouldn't. Oh Jack, I can't explain it, but I just don't know what to do." She plumped herself down on a sofa and looked over at the concerned youth.

His intuition had been right, thought Jack. "Well, I might just be able to shed some light on that," he added, coming to perch on the sofa next to her with a short, "may I?" before he sat down.

As she patted the space next to her, Bella looked at him curiously, "Whatever do you mean, Jack?"

"It's like this," he muttered. "I, er, didn't come straight back here last night like you told me to. I, um, had more to drink at the bar and I got talking to this, er, girl."

"Reeally?" said Bella, looking at him with a raised eyebrow.

"Well, yes, and I, er, we, er..."

"Oh Jack, you didn't? But you're only fifteen or sixteen. That's shocking," Bella didn't know whether or laugh or tell him off.

"Please don't be angry with me, Your Grace. I, er, just wanted to stay at the tavern in case you needed me."

Bella gave in and burst out laughing. "You're an absolute disgrace, Young Man, you really are. It's a good job I've grown up with a horde of reprobate male cousins, so I well appreciate what boys of your age get up to!" She held up her hands. "I don't want to know anything about it, but what has that got to do with the Duke?" she asked curiously.

"Well, you see, I left the tavern soon after dawn while everyone was still asleep, so I went to sit in the doorway opposite. I was really waiting to see if you would come out alone, or with His Grace. I wasn't sure what had happened last night between the pair of you as it was obvious to me you were very angry with him and, um, well, you'd had quite a lot of wine. But, anyway, it wasn't long after I got there that, lo and behold, out crept the Duke. There was no sign of you, so I followed him."

"Good gracious!" exclaimed Bella. "Where did he go?" Jack looked rather uncomfortable and shifted around, not quite knowing how to explain where the Duke had spent the rest of the morning. "Come on, Jack, spit it out. I know he's been spending time with some of the local prostitutes, so you might as well tell me," Bella said resignedly.

"I'm so sorry, Your Grace, but, well, he went back to his lodgings, left his guitar there and then went out again to this dirty tenement on the Right Bank, deep in the stews and alleyways, not dissimilar to where the tavern was where we were last night and disappeared inside for a couple of hours. I think a lot of prostitutes live there and I recognised a couple I'd seen in our tavern last night." Bella just sat with a tight face as he continued, "But when he came out, he had a very determined look on his face and he hurried back to his lodgings again, packed his bags and guitar and went straight round to a big livery yard, hired a carriage there and left straight away."

Jack looked at his mistress's distressed features and sighed. "I'm sure he went to that tenement in search of some information, perhaps not what you think. Mayhap that was what he was doing talking to all the girls last night? Anyway, whatever it was, he certainly left in a hurry. And, what's more, I know where he's gone..."

"Oh my Lord," Bella sighed, "I can't deal with this anymore, I really can't."

"Oh, Your Grace, I'm certain it's not what you think. How could he want any of those women after he'd spent the night with you?" Jack took Bella's hand, patting it reassuringly, "I simply can't believe it. I'm sure he just went there looking for some information. Perhaps he had to wait til someone returned home, who knows. He certainly didn't look like he'd spent a pleasurable morning when he came out. Not that anyone could spend a pleasurable morning in that place. What a filthy hole. Like a lot of the Dials or the Rookery," he tutted.

"Do you really think so, Jack?" Bella looked at him hopefully.

"I'm absolutely sure, Your Grace," Jack said forcefully. More positively than he believed, but he didn't want to upset the Duchess and he really did think the Duke was up to more than just visiting a prostitute for her favours, although he suspected that was probably part of the deal.

"So, how did you find out where's he's gone?" asked Bella.

"I followed him to the livery and hung around and listened. I couldn't understand much as they were speaking to each other so quickly, but I did manage to ask inside where the coach had gone, very casually of course, whilst I was ordering a drink, and they told me to the Coat Daz-yewer. Do you know where that is? And when I went outside to loiter while it was being readied, I heard the coachman say he was headed for somewhere called Neece. I think he was on a bonus if he got there in record time. That's what it sounded like, I'm pretty sure. *Une prime?* Is that right?"

"Well done, Jack... and reeally?" Bella was now much more enthused and interested.

"Yes, Your Grace. The Duke was obviously in a hurry, so whatever information he found out must have been important, enough for him to hire his own carriage and not wait to go on a mail coach or regular transport to wherever Neece is. How lucky was I to have actually been following him at such a critical moment? We'd have lost him for sure otherwise. It has to be Fate working in our favour, Your Grace."

Bella thought a while. Although the story about the prostitutes had upset her, now that she knew there was obviously far more to it, she felt somewhat relieved. Maybe Nicky hadn't gone after the girl for some amusement, but what had he discovered to send him chasing off to the South of France in such a hurry? She looked over at Jack and pondered. "Well, Jack," she finally mused, "the Duke is obviously on the track of something to go off in such a hurry and I want to know what it is. You're right, it is Fate and I'm not going to ignore it. So..." she looked at the young man next to her, "do you think you could go back to the tenement and find out who he saw there? Perhaps find the girl and ask her some questions yourself? You might need to... er... pay her for her services," she finished delicately. "Do you think you can make yourself understood well enough in French to do that?"

Jack grinned at her. "Oh, you mean I might have to take her to bed and fuck her to find out? Don't you think I'm a bit young for all that? You certainly did fifteen minutes ago?"

"Don't you get cheeky with me, My Lad, You Saucy Jackanapes," tutted Bella as she poked him in the chest, "and you mind your language, that's completely shocking in front of a genteel lady, especially a Duchess," she tutted again with a choked-back laugh, not in the least offended, but her lips were twitching and she gave up trying to tell him off as she grinned. "But I suppose now you're on the path of no return, you might as well make the most of it!"

Bella went over to her reticule and took out a handful of gold coins, tossing them over to him. "Here you are, I have no idea what the going rate is, but I'm sure YOU do now. This should cover any activity you need to indulge in, even if you just have to pay her for some information. I don't want to know, far too sordid for a respectable matron and highfalutin', very proper Duchess like myself..." and she pinched the top her nose with a disapproving expression, making Jack grin, "so I think I'll leave it all to you," she concluded, grinning back at him.

"Yes, Your Grace, just leave it to me. I'll find out what we need to know, see if I don't. But could I just ask you something first?"

"Yes, of course, what is it, Jack?" Bella looked curious.

"Do you think we could have some lunch before I go?" and Bella burst out laughing.

Chapter Thirty-Eight

Before leaving Paris, Bella scribbled a few hasty letters for her Aunt Cat and Uncle Francis, also one for Ashcroft, all care of the Duke of Firle in Berkeley Square. Unsure of the security of the post, she was careful with the content, but felt sure that her relations and certainly Ashcroft, would understand her news, interspersed as it was with other ramblings to disguise its real meaning.

Dear Auntie,

Jack has proved every bit the Best Combination of Servant and Companion you could wish for. Thank you so much for sending him with me. We have Toured Normandy, all the Places you told me about and we discussed before I left. Everything has so much More Meaning when you see it in Real Life for Yourself.

I could not find what I wanted in Valenciennes, which was such a Charming Place, just as I'd heard, with lots of Interesting Ruins to look over, so travelled on to Paris. Oh Auntie, you should see the Fashions here, so Different to London, so very French! I'm sure you know what I mean! There should be some Rather Large Boxes coming to Hertford Street soon. Could you please send Clara along to oversee their unpacking when they arrive, as there are some Little Trifles in there for you too. I am sure Uncle Francis will appreciate them!

Bella really had enjoyed her shopping expeditions and bought piles of new clothes and some particularly beautiful and enticing underclothes, nightwear and fripperies. She knew her aunt would love her gifts too and had giggled at the thought of her uncle when she'd written that part of her note.

Paris is teeming with All Sorts of People, so many Foreigners as well as English, and do you know, I actually found Someone I recognised just the other Day. Someone I hadn't seen for simply an Age, here in Paris of all places, but they were just leaving for the South of France so I thought I might go there myself and take Jack to see the Mediterranean. It was just a Passing Meeting, barely time for more than a Short Conversation, which was a tad frustrating. They went off before I had the chance even to have Dinner with them, so mayhap I will find them again in Nice and have a cosy Catch Up and Gossip there.

I do miss Terrie, so much, but thought I might as well go South while I am here and I know you will look after her for me. Just in case Anything Might Happen, you never know, French Highwaymen... stand and deliver, your money or your life! Ha ha and oooh la la!! Don't tell Uncle Francis I said that!

I promise I will write again when I get to Nice. Give my love to Uncle Francis, I have written him a separate Short Note as well, just so he will not feel Left Out... and of course give my love and kisses to Papa when you next see him and please tell him I miss him too.

Your Loving Niece
Bella

Having sealed that note, Bella now applied herself to something a bit more informative to her Uncle and Ashcroft.

Dear Uncle,

Well, here I am in Paris seeing the Sights and on the Lookout for Long Lost Friends and Acquaintances. Paris is a Fascinating Place, just as Papa always told me, and I feel as if I have been Everywhere here and seen Everything, from the most Tempting Shops where I wanted to buy the Entire Store, (do not worry, I restrained myself!) to the Conciergerie to Notre Dame to even the most Talented French Bar Singer in a Dirty Tavern off an alleyway on the Île de la Cité. He sang with a Spanish Guitar, tunes I remember Mama used to sing to Nicky and me when we were Young. He even sang some Opera; it was Quite Amazing and Totally Unexpected in a Disreputable Hostelry full of Prostitutes, Thieves and other Low Life. I am not sure how I found myself there, Quite By Chance, you must believe me! However, please rest assured I have my Devoted Servant and Companion from Firle with me At All Times. He carries a Deadly Weapon, just in case you were worried I was Traipsing Around by myself, Unprotected; as if I would ever do that?!

I gather this Itinerant Singer is going South to Nice, so who knows, I might see him Perform Again as I intend going down there myself now, as I have been told it is THE Place to go. I have never been and I am also told it is such a Perfect Time of Year to visit. I remember Uncle Reynard telling me all about it, how it was one of his Favourite Places to stop for a while when he was on one of his Excursions years ago, and how Lovely and Quiet it was and the views of the Bay from the Surrounding Hills are supposed to be Breathtaking.

I have not seen Anyone else I know or have heard of, Famous or Infamous, even though I had hoped to in such a Fascinating City. But you never know who I might bump into in Nice, apart from the Singer that is.

I have also written a Short Note to Aunt Cat. No doubt she will Share her News with you and I'm sure you will do The Same with yours to her, you know how she Always Appreciates that. There is a Gift for you too, as well as her, in some Boxes that are on their way to Hertford Street, though I trust you will enjoy Hers just as much! Also, something for Papa and Charlie. Perhaps you can arrange to pass them on with My Love and tell Papa I think of him every day.

Bella giggled as she thought of the numerous bottles of the best and rarest French brandy and cigars now on their way to London for the pair of them. The brandy all bought legitimately! Also, the dig about her Uncle keeping her Aunt informed about Everything!

By the way, Uncle, there is a Little Note here enclosed for Uncle Ash, such a Dear Old Man. I am sure having a Little Note from me will cheer up his Dull Life no end, so perhaps you could pass it along as well as the Gifts for Papa and Charlie, as I am such a Silly Girl, I completely forget his Precise House Number, you know what a Ninny I am at times! I only know it by the Door Colour – and everything here is such a Whirl, especially now I am off to Nice in such an Unexpected Hurry.

Your Loving Niece
   Bella

Bella smiled to herself. Really, she should be writing penny novels she thought, as she surveyed her missive. But now, the final one to 'Dear Uncle Ash'.

My Dear Uncle Ash,

   How Clever of you to suggest I should make a Little Expedition to France to see the Sights. You somehow seemed to know it would be Just The Thing to take my mind off Life's Little Problems and my current Distraction. As you rightly said, there was Nothing Much to Interest Me in Northern France, knowing what Entertains Me as you do, so I have been enjoying the Sights of Paris, exploring all the Places you suggested. However, I have not yet managed to locate that Old Acquaintance of yours you told me to look up, but I did come across that Itinerant Singer you told me about. He was quite A Find I must say, but Unfortunately, just as I had located him and watched a

Performance, he left Paris for the South of France so I never got A Chance to speak to him about what he was Doing These Days, or if he was Coming to London any time soon, so I could pass on the news to you. Such a Shame.

Anyway, Gossip tells me Anyone who is in The Know is now going down to the South of France, so that is where I am off to now, Nice to be precise. Quite a Little Community of English there I hear, as well as All Sorts of other Interesting People gathering there, so I understand. Well, the Climate is Absolutely Perfect for them, it is So Quiet and I understand the Town has now been, or about to be, ceded back to the Kingdom of Piedmont-Sardinia, so is not Officially French anymore, not that I understand Anything about all that. Politics are so way Over My Head and Tedious. The ennui is enough to send me to sleep. Especially discussions about the recent War, who did what, who went where, who fought who, especially in the Peninsula... it quite overwhelms me!

Well, that is all My News for now. I promise I will try and write again from Nice and send you any Further News of Friends and Acquaintances I bump into there. It is a Much Smaller Community, of course, so it surely will not be So Difficult to find Old Friends and Discover their Latest News.

By the way, I did enjoy our last Game of Chess, but I am Warning You, Uncle, next time I mean to Win Properly, not because You Let Me! You really are a Conniving, Manipulating Gentleman!

With Very Best Wishes
Arabella

Bella hoped her aunt would understand the gist of the information she'd written and would also know there was more to be had from her uncle, which she knew now he definitely would share with her. She grinned. She wished she'd been a fly on the wall during the 'conversation' that had no doubt ensued after she'd last left Berkeley Square. As for Ashcroft, having reviewed their game in detail in her mind, she knew she'd been had and he'd let her win, no doubt for his own devious purposes. Furious at being manipulated in such a way, Bella wanted revenge, but conceded it would have to wait. In the meantime, she just wanted him to know she knew. For now and the foreseeable future, Nicky was her utmost priority.

Chapter Thirty-Nine

They'd been in Nice for a week but had found no trace of Nicky.

Jack had checked all the local liveries and posting houses, but apart from one where an ostler could vaguely recall a hired coach from Paris that had arrived late one night and set off back to Paris early the following morning, a couple of days before their own arrival, there was nothing. The passenger had alighted and disappeared and the ostler hadn't seen enough to know anything other than it had been a man. Bella and Jack had agreed it could have been Nicky, but it could have been anyone. Coaches came and went all the time. Nice was becoming increasingly popular with the English and other nationalities who wanted to spend their winters in warmer climes and was a long way from Paris and politics. Although British visitors had dropped off during the War, the area was now becoming popular again. Bella likened it to a French version of Bath, full of wealthy old biddies discussing their ailments. Also, with the fall of Bonaparte, the town had returned to being part of the Kingdom of Piedmont and Sardinia, so no longer under the auspices of France. Very convenient for Bernheim and any potential plotters, Bella decided.

One particularly sunny afternoon, Jack had hired a gig and he and

Bella had driven off along the coast where they'd found a deserted cove and eaten a picnic on the beach. Bella watched, highly entertained, as Jack cavorted in the warm blue waters of the Mediterranean. He'd learned to swim a bit, courtesy of some of the other young male servants and grooms from Firle, in the chilly Channel waters off Brighton where it was all the rage for one's health, with the bathing machines there doing a roaring trade. However, he'd never experienced warmer seas like this and was in his element, splashing and paddling back and forth in just his breeches, like an excited child, the warm sun turning his pale rangy body a light golden colour. Bella kicked off her shoes and stockings, and, unheeding of her young companion, tucked up her skirts and paddled in the shallows. Her mind went back to long ago summer holidays when she and Nicky took picnics down to the nearby beaches at Firle and frolicked in the sea, building sandcastles when the tide was out and marvelling when the softer sea-bed was revealed beyond the stones and pebbles of the beach. She'd always spent hours decorating her castles with shells and bits and pieces she found on the foreshore. He'd always been more interested in constructing complicated forts with moats that filled when the waves crept up the beach. She sighed. Every one of her memories appeared to have some connection to Nicky. Her life was inextricably linked to his, there was no escaping it.

Jack had also visited all the local taverns but none had heard of a golden-haired singer with a guitar. He was now in the process of checking the many hostelries and lodging houses for any trace of a man of his description. As Bella sat on their shaded hotel terrace, drinking a glass of chilled white wine late one hot September afternoon, Jack came hurrying through the reception rooms and excitedly pulled up a chair at her table, talking to her in urgent, hurried undertones.

"I've found his lodgings," he whispered, "right at the back of the town, on the way out to the hills. He got there a few days before we arrived. It must have been him, in that posting house we called on, do you remember? When the old biddy, the landlady, *consee-erge* or whatever they call them here, went out shopping, I crept back into the lodgings and had a look round his room."

"Ooooh, Jack, you clever villain! How did you get in? I hope no one saw you?" Bella sat back looking excited, pleased and alarmed, all at the same time.

"Aaah, no problem for someone of my talents," grinned Jack, waggling his fingers in the air with a smirk, but his face became serious. "It was his room all right, but it looks like no one's been in it for a few days, it was just a feeling I got. His guitar is there and all his belongings. I checked his bag and there's quite a lot of money in it, Your Grace. I hope that old nosy parker keeps her fingers out until he returns. I didn't like to take it for safe keeping, Madam, or he'd know someone had been there. Did I do right?" he looked worried.

"Really?" Bella herself looked concerned. "Oh yes, best to leave everything as you found it, but missing for a few days?" She pondered. "Tell you what, Jack, why don't you go back there, have a chat with the *concierge* and check when she last saw him. If it's been a while, see if she has any idea where he went and pay up his rent for another week or two just in case. Say you're his cousin from London, or a friend or something, in case she wonders why you want to know; she'll know you're not French, so tell her you're passing through the area and will come back and find him again in a few days. Give her a few coins for her trouble, then have a dig around the local area and see if anyone else has seen him." She tossed him a bag of coins, "Also, get yourself some dinner while you're about it in case you come over all faint," she grinned at him. "I'll have a quiet dinner here and see you later, or in the morning. Then we'll decide what to do. I don't really know what I'm doing here myself and he'll be mad when he finds out I've followed him again, but I've still got this niggling feeling that I should be around..."

"Very well, Your Grace," Jack got up and kissed her hand. "Will you be all right by yourself? Promise me you won't go out alone, will you?"

"No, Jack, I'll be very well behaved and do what I'm told," Bella laughed. "Now go on, be off with you. I'll be quite safe here. Lady Wentworth, you know, the old dear who wears those dreadful green turbans, is dying to tell me about her rheumatics, so I'm sure I'll be in for a riveting evening!" Laughing, Jack bowed briefly to her and turned to make his way out of the hotel once more.

Bella called a waiter over and ordered another glass of wine and some savouries to nibble on, then sat back to watch the sun set over the Mediterranean, thinking about the information Jack had gleaned and wondering for the umpteenth time where Nicky was and what on earth she was doing there. To be honest, she seemed to be chasing after a man who probably didn't want her anymore, if he ever did in the first place. If it wasn't for some deep-seated, unexplained feeling of disquiet she simply couldn't put into words, she would simply pack and go back to London and her little daughter.

As Bella gazed unseeingly into the distance, leaning back in her chair and slowly sipping her wine, eating an olive now and again, a tall, leanly muscled man along the other end of the terrace had been observing her and her interchange with the youth who had come and gone briefly. He was quite a presentable looking gentleman, not bad looking, around 40, black-haired with high cheekbones, thin lips, aquiline nose and a clear if slightly olive complexion. He was very elegantly and expensively, if conservatively, dressed. His dark, obsidian eyes watched the Lady sitting alone, obviously lost in thought as she took in the sunset. As he surveyed her, he too sipped from an early evening aperitif, his thin lips curling into a fascinated smile.

It was unusual to see such a beautiful and elegant young woman all alone in Nice, he mused to himself. He'd been in the town since the early spring and, apart from the locals, the place seemed full of middle-aged or elderly, sedate individuals who did nothing but gossip and stroll up and down the promenade all day under their parasols, discussing their aches and pains or complaining of the heat. Why they came to the South of France in summer and then moaned that it was too hot was beyond him, but then Foreigners had their idiosyncrasies and, in his opinion, the English were more eccentric than anyone, a strange nation altogether.

But this woman had caught his attention. With her thick, luxuriant black hair piled high on her head and ringlets artfully falling down her back, her very cream-coloured skin, sensual lips and slender but voluptuous figure giving her a slightly exotic look, she vaguely reminded him of some of the beautiful Spanish women, or Carmelita; but this woman was definitely no common whore. From the way she held herself he could see she was a Lady, quite aristocratic in her demeanour. Beautifully and expensively dressed in the latest Paris fashion, he watched an elegant hand carry her glass to her lips from time to time and the arch of her long neck fascinated him as she drank. Although she was wearing a wedding ring, there was no sign of a husband, just the youth who had come to join her for a brief conversation, then left.

Frederick Bernheim owned a villa in the hills behind Nice, another inheritance from his late father, another bolthole. It was well off the beaten track, among the wild flowering shrubs, surrounded by olive and palm trees, discreetly hidden away from prying eyes and therefore ideal for him to carry out his business privately and quietly. He periodically came down into the town to dine in one of the better hotels or restaurants, or in search of entertainment. As he rose and surveyed the solitary female, he reminded himself he hadn't had a woman in his bed for weeks, months even, unless you called the handful of local prostitutes women, which he didn't; simply dirty, uncouth, venal tarts most of them, who served a useful purpose for the shortest possible time, nothing more. But this woman was special and there was something about her that fascinated him. He reflected he hadn't been with a Lady like that since he'd worked in central Europe, before he went to Spain, some three or so years back. Even then, none of them had been aristocratic, or as beautiful. Frederick Bernheim stared and felt his body harden in response. He wanted her.

As if casually strolling along the terrace, he made his way past the assorted tables full of hotel guests taking their early evening aperitif in the dappled shade under wide awnings, until he reached Bella's. Brushing past her, he gently jolted her chair, causing her drink to spill ever so slightly. Just a couple of drops, nothing to spoil her gown. It was masterful.

"Oh, My Dear *Madame*, I am so desperately sorry. How clumsy...

please... allow me..." Bernheim pulled out a large white kerchief with a flourish and dabbed her hand, bowing effusively and presenting the cloth for her to dab the virtually unnoticeable drops on the skirt of her gown.

Bella looked up briefly and took little notice of the man who had accidentally bumped her chair. She'd been so lost in thought she hadn't seen him at all. "Oh, 'tis nothing, I assure you, but how kind. I was miles away, not paying attention," she responded, looking up to hand back the borrowed kerchief. Green eyes locked with obsidian black ones and an instant feeling of dislike wriggled down her back. However, she was far too ladylike to show anything but good manners, so she merely smiled and nodded her head, expecting the man would continue on his way.

He didn't. "*Chère Madame*, Dear Lady, please allow me to get you another glass," and he summoned over a waiter with an imperious hand and ordered a bottle of champagne.

"Oh no, really, 'tis quite unnecessary. Please, *Monsieur*. I assure you," Bella demurred.

"*Madame, au contraire*, on the contrary, please allow me, I beg you," and he bowed again, punctiliously. Bella had put her glass down and was thinking of making her excuses to go in to an early dinner, but as she made to pick up her shawl and reticule the man continued to address her in a drawling voice with a slight lisp. "May I introduce myself, *Madame*? *Chevalier* Bernheim, Frederick Bernheim, *à votre service*," he bowed again.

Good job she'd put her glass down. As her reticule fell back to the table from suddenly numb fingers and Bella's body and mind went into complete shock, her heart started to thump and her blood turned to ice. Slowly, reeling, she looked up at the bowing man, trying to keep her face impassive and gather her shattered wits. "How do you do, *Chevalier*," she managed.

"May I?" Bernheim nodded towards the other chair at her table.

"Oh, of course, please do," Bella answered, her brain suddenly whirring round at a rate of knots, as she smiled at him politely, wondering if her face had gone as bloodless as she felt.

The waiter appeared at that point and served their champagne, giving Bella a few moments to collect and compose herself. She was completely stunned and overwhelmed. The nemesis of Ashcroft, Wellington, Nicky, possibly also her family now, had just come up and introduced himself to her, even using his own name, so obviously feeling completely secure in this coastal backwater. He was plainly intent on making her acquaintance, presumably totally ignorant of who she was. She now wondered if the bump had been intentional. It wouldn't be the first time some lovestruck young swain had tried to do the same thing to her at various Society balls, parties or at Almack's. What an extraordinary coincidence. What a frightening one.

But Bella was now on her mettle, her brain engaged and her senses on full alert, though none of that showed under her polite, ladylike demeanour as she raised her glass to the man now sitting opposite.

"Are you here on holiday, *Madame*?" Bernheim asked conversationally as he sipped his wine, politeness itself.

"Yes, it seemed an ideal time of year to come; past the intense heat of summer and before the autumn rains. I've always wanted to come down to the southern coast of France and it is as beautiful here as I had heard. An acquaintance enthused mightily about the views of the Bay here in Nice and I have to admit, they were quite right." The conversation was banal.

"You have a very slight accent, *Madame*," Bernheim looked at her through narrowed eyes, "are you French?"

Bella smiled at him. "Well, yes and no, the Revolution, you understand; my family fled to England and I grew up there," she explained vaguely.

"Really?" Bernheim twirled his glass in his long, elegant fingers, a signet ring with a black stone glinting on his little finger. It had been his father's, taken from the dead man's finger, the only personal item of Edgar Bernheim's that his son had kept, apart from his notebook and his property portfolio.

"Mmmmm," Bella nodded. "Fortunately, they got out before everything really deteriorated, but now Bonaparte has gone and this tedious War finally seems over, well so we assume, but of course who knows..." she waved her hand airily "...he may yet return eh?" and she looked at Bernheim, shrugging. "Therefore, I may well come back and live here again, it is so much more cultured and warmer."

"You don't like England then?" Bernheim enquired. "Do you live in London?"

"Yes, in London. It is all very well, but of course, it's not Paris," another Gallic shrug, an imitation of her aunt's. Bella wasn't sure why she wanted him to think she was more French than she was, not that she was French at all, having been born and bred in London.

"And your husband, is he not with you?" Bernheim fished.

"My husband?" Bella raised her eyebrow.

Bernheim nodded towards her ringed hand. "Oh, my husband," Bella waved that hand airily again, "well, he's away, he's always away, travelling you know. His business affairs take him abroad a lot."

"Really?" Bernheim's eyes gleamed. "So are you here, holidaying alone?"

"Not quite," Bella smiled. "I have my nephew with me. I thought he could do with a bit of polish so we've been to Paris; so fatiguing, all that sightseeing with the hoi polloi, the shopping and socialising; consequently, we're now here to recuperate for a week, or two or three, whatever takes our fancy really. I had wondered about going on to one or other of the Italian states to introduce him to some of the art, in Florence or Rome, or maybe visit Venice, such a fascinating place, but I hadn't made up my mind. I'm not sure he's old enough to appreciate it all yet; he's not terribly discerning, one artist is much like another in his eyes," another vague wave of her hand in the air.

"Is that the young man I saw you with earlier?" Bella gave him a curious stare. "Oh, I couldn't help noticing you from across the terrace, *Madame*. You are quite a beautiful woman you know. I observed you had a young man with you."

So, he'd been watching her. Again, the frisson of dislike ran down her back. But Bella merely continued, "Yes, he's only fourteen although he looks bigger, a growing spurt his mother says. Regrettably, his brain hasn't kept up, as you can imagine at that age," she sighed. Bella decided for some reason to make out Jack was just a typically idiotic youth. "He found Paris terribly exciting, unfortunately here, less so; there's not a lot to do for a boy always full of beans and needing to be distracted every minute of the day, given he's not very studious; however, he enjoys the beach and the sea," she sighed again, sounding bored, "and he's found some fishermen who are going to take him out, that should keep him amused for a few days," again she waved vaguely in the direction of the sea, seeming rather disinterested with the topic of her 'nephew'. "In fact, that's where he's gone now, off to find himself some sort of excursion for tomorrow."

"He certainly does look rather a big lad for just fourteen?" commented Bernheim.

"Oh, you know young boys, one minute they're scraggly nuisances and then suddenly they spurt gangly arms and legs all over the place and think they've grown up." Bella shrugged, "His father is very tall too, a veritable beanpole, but he's a good boy, easily amused," she said dismissively. "So, *Chevalier*, what brings YOU to Nice, or do you live here?" Bella changed the subject and sat back, sipping her champagne slowly. She wanted to keep a clear head.

"Actually, I own a villa up in the hills, directly behind the town, not too difficult to get to in daylight. I'm staying there for a few months on business, but in the main I am a Gentleman of Leisure," Bernheim informed her. "I have several homes and tend to drift between them all, depending on the season, the weather, my business affairs and what takes my fancy at any given time. I'm afraid I'm something of a restless soul."

"It actually sounds a delightful existence," responded Bella. "What sort of business are you in, if you don't mind me asking?"

"Oh, nothing to mention really, this and that, a bit of import and export here and there, investing in lucrative opportunities, anything that will generate a profit, I suppose. Just a sideline, naturally. As a Gentleman, I don't really like to get my fingers dirty and dabble in trade personally," Bernheim responded vaguely and rather disdainfully.

"Of course not, but most Gentlemen still have to manage their affairs and be sensible in business matters when necessary," Bella smiled. "There's not much point doing anything if one doesn't make a profit."

Bernheim's eyes narrowed. "That's an interesting comment from such an aristocratic Lady," he said. "What do you know about business and profit?"

"Ah now, there's the thing," Bella smiled at him seductively. "Not all Ladies are interested in reticules, shawls, shoes and bonnets...or music, painting and embroidery."

"Really?" Bernheim suddenly looked more interested than ever. "What a combination, a beautiful woman interested in business. What did you say your husband did?"

"Oh, this and that, diplomatic matters, Government matters, he knows people everywhere. He's sometimes a special envoy, or facilitates introductions between interested parties. I don't really understand, terribly boring, he's always away. But I like it that way, it leaves me free to follow my own interests. He has his affairs and I have mine," Bella responded suggestively, wondering what Bernheim would make of her comment; 'affairs' could mean a lot of things.

"Really?" Bernheim was fascinated. "And what 'interests' would they be, these 'affairs' of yours?"

Bella looked at him archly. "Now wouldn't you like to know, *Chevalier*..." and she rapped him lightly on the knee with her fan.

Bernheim jumped as if he'd been scorched and looked across at Bella, raising his glass in her direction. "*Madame*, or should it be My Lady?" he queried. "You are not only beautiful, but quite fascinating. I was wondering, would you care to have dinner with me so we can continue our interesting discussion? It is the time to dine and your fellow guests are all departing to change their dress for dinner." He looked over at several couples who were finishing their aperitifs and disappearing back into the hotel.

"Well, it is My Lady actually," Bella spoke slowly as if she was considering his request, "but I'm not bothered with titles these days, they have their uses sometimes and sometimes not, depending on where one finds oneself. For certain, the Americas now have a different viewpoint and in France, well, one minute a duke was respected, the next they had their heads chopped off. There appears to be a strange new crop of them, no lineage of course, but who knows where we are or how long that state of affairs will last?" Another Gallic shrug. "The world and the old order are changing, are they not *Chevalier*? She paused, "And yes, I think I would like to dine with you. The hotel is full of boring old biddies and my nephew's conversation does pall after a while. It is so delightful to meet a sophisticated, interesting Gentleman for a change, especially down here in this social backwater."

A slow, sensual smile crept over Bernheim's thin lips as he surveyed her and Bella's nerves jangled. "How perfectly divine, thank you, My Lady... er...?" he raised an eyebrow, obviously now waiting for Bella to introduce herself. For a moment, she was caught short, she couldn't give him her real name, or even her maiden name. Then she smiled as an idea came to her. "Well now, *Chevalier*, let's just leave it at My Lady for now. Then, if our acquaintance progresses over dinner, I may tell you my name and perhaps about my 'interests', even my 'affairs'." Bella gave him her best flirtatious look.

"Aha, a woman of mystery. How delightfully intriguing," said Bernheim seductively as he glanced at his pocket watch. He was obviously ready to dine but Bella was still wearing an afternoon dress. "Shall I meet you again in the foyer in an hour, or two? How long will you need to dress for dinner? Meanwhile, I shall arrange for a table. Would you like to eat here? Or dine somewhere else in the town? I know one or two delightful restaurants with delicious fish dishes. The chefs are very creative and the venues are perfect for those with more discerning tastes."

There was no way Bella was going anywhere with the man by herself, it would be totally inappropriate, even if it wasn't Bernheim, so she merely smiled. "Actually, I've had quite a busy day and don't want a late night, so here would be perfect, if you don't mind. The food is reasonably tolerable... and an hour will do."

Bernheim rose from the table and held out a hand to help Bella to her feet, very punctiliously, before allowing her to precede him off the terrace and back into the hotel reception rooms, acting almost as if he was following royalty. Once in the main foyer, he bowed to her again, more formal and obsequious than ever as she turned to make her way upstairs. "An hour, My Lady?" Bella nodded at him aristocratically as she sauntered upwards. As soon as she had disappeared, Bernheim went over to the reception desk and booked himself a room; he didn't want to make his way back to his villa up in the hills late at night and, who knew, perhaps he could persuade her into his bed? He doubted it for that night, unsure of where the nephew would be, but one could hope? The woman was intriguing and definitely not the usual conservative, properly behaved Lady, or he doubted she'd even consider dining alone with him, even in the hotel dining room. As he signed the hotel register, he ran his finger down the list of recent arrivals. No aristocratic name jumped out at him but a suite and an adjacent room were booked to the name of Vallance. Vallance. He pronounced it the French way and smiled to himself. He went back to the table on the terrace, poured himself another glass of champagne and sat back to wait.

Bella had watched Bernheim go over to the reception desk as she peered down through the balustrade on the first floor. Thank heaven for the stroke of luck that she had sent Jack in to register them at the hotel while she oversaw the unloading of her boxes and trunks from their carriage. She smiled at the knowledge the staff thought she was Madame Vallance. The idea had made her and Jack laugh as he'd taken the small pleasure and pride of registering at a hotel for the first time, bespeaking appropriate rooms to match the Duchess's high standards where money was no object. He'd learned by listening to her when they'd arrived in Paris. Another minor addition to his growing knowledge of appropriate social behaviour and etiquette.

As Bernheim made arrangements for a room, Bella turned slowly and walked down to her suite, deep in thought. She rang the bell for a maid and ordered a bath to be brought up as quickly as possible and then sat down to write a note to Jack. The last thing she wanted was for him to bounce in to the dining room and interrupt them, so she left a short explanatory missive on his pillow telling him on no account to do so, then scribbled another note for him to leave at reception with his room key, telling him to read the URGENT note in his room before coming to find her. Finally, as an afterthought, just to be on the safe side, she put a postscript and told him if he should bump into her that evening when she was in company with anyone, he should address her as 'Aunt'!

Then she set to, to bathe and dress for dinner, asking the maid to re-style her hair and taking a long time over her toilette and decision of what to wear and the impression she thereby wanted to give. That she was now involved in a seriously dangerous situation didn't escape her and Bella knew she would have to watch every word she spoke, consider every action. She thought about Ashcroft. The man would have a fit if he knew what she was up to, so would Uncle Francis, probably even more so. More than a fit, the pair of them. But some deep instinct, some sixth sense, told her Bernheim was at the root of Nicky's apparent disappearance and she meant to find out where he was, before she herself grappled with the problem of *Chevalier* Bernheim himself. The latter was something she wasn't quite yet ready to contemplate. At the moment, it was just her and a boy of sixteen... up against one of the most dangerous men in France, Spain and who knew where else. Bella shivered. Uncle Francis wouldn't just have a fit or lose his famous temper, he'd be frantic, completely beside himself; her solitary walk through the teeming and dangerous Parisian slums would have nothing on her current situation. The thought made her giggle hysterically and she told herself firmly to get a grip. She had to think like her Great Aunt Elizabeth and be brave and determined like her Aunt Cat. Inspirational women, the pair of them, more than equal to ANY man, Bella reminded herself.

But they were incomparable and a hard act to follow. Nevertheless, she had no choice, as she simply couldn't walk away, no matter how much sense that option made. She had to become a combination of both aunts; her husband, her family and probably her country needed her best efforts, not to mention herself and Jack. Lives were at stake; one wrong word or move could spell disaster. However, Arabella de Bresancourt, formerly Arabella de Mornay, had never shirked a challenge. And she told herself it wasn't only her aunts she had to emulate – both her mother and crippled father had risen to the occasion when faced with a crisis - and she was their daughter. Now it was her turn... after all, wasn't she now a lioness? Lions might be the head of and protectors of their pride, but lionesses were the hunters for the pride, and therefore extremely dangerous. The Duchess of Valenciennes, *La Lionesse de Valenciennes*, told herself the time had come to live up to her name.

To Be Continued...

Read on to Part 3 in the series, <u>Hunting Lion</u>.

Bella is in France, trying to find and follow Nicky in an effort to repair their broken relationship, but has unexpectedly come face to face with the dreaded Frederick Bernheim. He has no idea who she is but is fascinated by the enigmatic, exciting woman he accidentally happens upon in her hotel, and wants to pursue their acquaintance...

Bella is on her own with only a young groom from Firle to aid her and knows the safety of her family, her country, not to mention herself and young Jack is all now down to her. She must to rise to the challenge, like a determined, clever and fierce lioness. In the meantime, just where has Nicky disappeared to?

To give you a little taste of what is coming up next, keep reading…

HUNTING LION

Preview

Chapter One

As he and his alluring dinner guest sat and chatted over their meal, Frederick Bernheim was almost salivating. Although outwardly he appeared urbane, cosmopolitan, charming and appropriately restrained, as befitting the manners of a refined Gentleman, inside, his senses were on fire. The woman opposite him looked stunning, and although she appeared cool, aristocratic, ladylike and reserved in her elegant and obviously expensive, empire line cream evening gown, with the neck-hugging, single string of exquisite pearls, matching earrings and bracelets, and their understated diamond clasps, he sensed she had hidden depths; he could see fire in her green eyes and he meant to find out what those depths were.

While Bernheim waited in eager anticipation for his dinner companion on the terrace of the hotel bar, unlike others doing nothing more than sitting with their aperitifs and relaxing while watching the sun go down over the beautiful *Baie des Anges*, Bay of Angels, and contemplating the delight of the superlative view, Bernheim's mind was elsewhere. It had drifted to what was transpiring up at his villa...

He'd been more than surprised to discover none other than Nicholas de Bresancourt, the man behind his untimely departure, his empty-handed and wounded departure he'd reminded himself angrily, from Spain, had turned up there in Nice. He'd thought the man dead, back in his villa outside Madrid, along with the whore, Carmelita. However, when his faithful manservant, Mustapha, who silently kept an eye on all the comings and goings to Nice, essential activity in his line of work, had reported on the arrival of a tall, well-built, golden-haired man, late one night in a privately hired carriage from Paris, his curiosity had been aroused.

Mustapha, a Turk, former guard to the Ottoman Sultan himself and part of his personal retinue, had had his tongue ripped out for talking to one of the women of the seraglio, usually guarded by eunuchs, was glad to have escaped from Constantinople with his life. Devoted to Frederick Bernheim who had picked him up in Naples a decade previously when he was virtually destitute and seeking employment, the giant normally kept an eye on his master's house in Paris, when he wasn't accompanying and guarding him on his travels or any particular missions. He'd been with him in Madrid but had left there in advance of his master's departure with his golden hoard to return to Paris to check on the house and ensure it wasn't being watched for any reason, so Bernheim himself could return in safety; also to relay some confidential messages to other contacts in the French capital, and then await further instructions. But of course, those plans had all gone awry. When his master had taken up residence in his villa outside Nice, after a recuperative and safe sojourn in Venice from where he could watch events in France and Bonaparte's downfall, and decide what to do next, the devoted Mustapha had once again been with him... but had since been tasked once again with relaying confidential messages between there and Paris. Which, ironically, was why he happened to be at Bernheim's old home when the 'charity collectors' called and had left a few days later to return to the *Côte d'Azur*.

Mustapha had soon run the golden-haired man to earth in one of the cheap lodging houses at the back of the town and Bernheim had quietly stood in the shadows and watched for him, recognising de Bresancourt instantly when he'd arrived back there one evening. It was too much of a coincidence to find de Bresancourt there in Nice, just when he'd been plotting an escape from Elba for Bonaparte, on behalf of a group of wealthy individuals: armaments suppliers and bankers in the main, apart from a couple of wealthy radical zealots, all of whom wanted to see war in Europe resumed and the Bourbons thrown out again, either for their own commercial or political benefit.

A couple of the armaments suppliers owned or had interests in munitions factories across Europe, so the more countries who got drawn into conflict again, the richer they became. It mattered not to them which side they supplied. As for Bernheim, he had no interest whether war recommenced or not, or whether Bonaparte or the Bourbons ruled France, but the gold he was being paid to facilitate the former Emperor's return to French soil, lay the ground for another coup, and see him safely esconced in Paris once again with his old faithful soldiers guarding him, was considerable, more than considerable, and that interested him over and above anything. Bernheim had no intention of losing out a second time, especially to de Bresancourt, even if this amount of gold didn't come near to what he'd lost in Madrid. However, it was still a small fortune and that was what mattered.

Nicholas de Bresancourt. The French *Duc de Valenciennes*, yet also a man with close connections to Wellington, obviously one of his agents, and with knowledge of The Shadow... and therefore all those involved with the mysterious and inconvenient death of his father, and the consequent loss of his potential fortune which had changed the course of his life. De Bresancourt owed him in more ways than one.

De Bresancourt was therefore now enjoying his hospitality in the cellars up at his villa, and before long he would have details of what the man knew about his dealings with the pro-Bonapartist group, as well as information about The Shadow and the woman who had killed his father. Maybe even information about the treasure his father had sought from both de Bresancourt's father and The Shadow.

Bernheim smiled a self-satisfied, malicious smile as he thought about that, casually sipping his champagne, looking for all the world as if he was merely contemplating and enjoying the beautiful sunset over the tranquil, blue waters of the Bay of Angels.

So far, beating and whipping, starvation and other physical torture from Mustapha, no mean exponent of the art, had produced few, if any, results. However, now the Chinaman had arrived from Paris, with his little box of needles, Bernheim trusted he'd shortly have the information he sought. In the meantime, this little diversion here at the hotel with the enigmatic and exciting woman he'd accidentally discovered, would keep him occupied. He always needed the release of sex when one of his missions or plotted activities was coming to fruition, and the restless stimulation of anticipated success bubbled through his veins seeking an outlet. The woman had arrived like a ripe peach on his plate, at exactly the right time. And a peach she certainly was, with her long lustrous hair, her soft, creamy skin and alluring scent tantalising his vision and senses in anticipation of devouring her. Between her discovery and that of de Bresancourt, Fate was definitely conspiring in his favour.

Chapter Two

They discussed art, music, commerce and politics, and while Bernheim found her both extremely intelligent and very well informed on all topics they touched upon, while they talked over their dinner, Bella's mind was racing as to how to turn the conversation to his current activities there in Nice. Apparently idle queries concerning his views on the current regime in Paris and the state of French foreign affairs had elicited little comment from Bernheim, and although he seemed well informed about investments and foreign trading opportunities, he gave little away. Now being in charge of little Elizabeth Granville's not inconsiderable business and investment portfolio, Bella decided she knew far more than he did about the subject, but didn't push. After all, that wasn't the information she was after.

"So, *Chère Madame*, My Lady," Bernheim leaned back in his chair, sipping from his coffee, "you are most surprisingly well informed on a wide variety of subjects. It has been such a delight sharing dinner with you." He paused for a while to finish the fragrant brew and then he leaned forward and studied her face intently. "However... you have said so little about your personal 'interests' and 'affairs', or even your name. I don't suppose you would care to enlighten me?"

Bella fanned herself calmly and looked back into Bernheim's

obsidian eyes, considering her words carefully. "Well, *Chevalier*," she began, "as I said, my husband has interests overseas and spends most of his time away, so I have developed my own little business interests in London to keep me occupied."

"Really? A Lady with her own business interests. Most unusual. And what sort of little business interests are they, if I may be so bold?"

Bella continued to fan herself slowly. "I suppose one could say I am in the entertainment business," she mused.

"Entertainment?" Bernheim obviously wasn't expecting that. "You mean singing, dancing, the theatre...?"

"Oh, no, *Chevalier*," Bella leaned forward and her fan tapped Bernheim playfully on the hand. "Much too commonplace and there's little money to be made in that sort of enterprise, at least not at the level I am interested in." She looked at him consideringly, "I have expensive tastes which I like to indulge," and her fan idly touched on her necklace of large, perfectly matched pearls. The intimation was she'd bought them for herself; Bernheim wasn't to know they lived in the sixth drawer down of the late Dowager's jewellery chest. Below the diamond drawer, then one for sets of rubies, sapphires, emeralds and amethysts. The pearl drawer; and it was full of ropes of them, in all sizes and lengths with accompanying earrings, bracelets and brooches. "Actually, I am in the gambling business" Bella said softly.

"Gambling?" Bernheim's eyebrows rose. "Now that IS fascinating," he lisped.

"Mmmm, isn't it now." Bella replied slowly and archly. "I own two gaming houses as a matter of fact, and even though I say it myself, they are currently the toast of London, absolute gold mines," and she sat back and smiled at him like a cat.

"TWO gaming houses? *Chère Madame*, I am seriously impressed, and you are so very young?" He was no stranger to flattering women but in this case he thought he was right as he looked at her beautiful, flawless, peachy skin, with no blemish or wrinkle in sight; and concluded she was still in her twenties, mid-twenties he finally decided.

"Well, why have one when you can have two, or three or four?" Bella mused coquettishly as she regarded him over her fan, "and age is no barrier to being successful in business. If I was a man, you wouldn't think it so odd" she said slightly tartly.

"Perhaps, no, obviously not, My Lady..." said Bernheim expectantly as he hovered over her title once more.

"Ah, I can see you are determined to have my name," Bella smiled at him seductively, her womanly wiles working overtime. "Well, *Chevalier*, since you are SUCH a charming and gentlemanly Gentleman, SUCH an intelligent man for a change, and I have had SUCH a pleasant evening, I think I may tell you." Bernheim looked at her expectantly, completely riveted and strung out.

"You may call me *Lionesse*. That is how I am known in my saloons, *Le Lion d'Or* and *La Lionesse d'Or*." Bella paused for effect as Bernheim looked surprised at the nickname. "Of course, I always appear incognito there. I wear a lion's mask to keep myself anonymous and my life private, but down here in Nice, this little backwater," she shrugged her Gallic shrug, "I don't have to worry about irritating matters like that. Actually, if truth be known," she added conversationally as she leaned towards him, "one of the reasons I came over to Paris, and then on down here, was to see if it would be worth opening more of my saloons there, but especially here, to get in before anyone else does. The place is apparently getting more and more popular and Gentlemen are always looking for upmarket entertainment on quiet evenings, and the social scene here is very quiet and I am exceedingly upmarket..." Another seductive smile as she leaned forward, her voluptuous bosom and cleavage more exposed in the low-cut gown she'd deliberately chosen. The dress was artful, seeming plain, elegant and conservative on appearance, but when the wearer moved or bent, it became a study of enticement if one had the appropriate assets, and supporting undergarments!

"*Lionesse*?" Bernheim murmured. "That is a very interesting nickname. What made you choose that and the names of your little enterprises?"

"Wouldn't you like to know..." Bella purred quietly and flirtatiously, and tapped him with her fan again, looking deep into his eyes.

Bernheim leaned forward to whisper at her, "I would like to know very much, *Lionesse*."

"It's because I claw people who get in my way, or don't pay their debts; don't you know that lionesses are the hunters of the pride, so I hunt my prey down," she mouthed slowly and curled her long, elegant fingers with their beautifully buffed and manicured nails into claws. "Rawrrrrrrrrr," she purred as she carefully drew one clawed fingernail down the side of Bernheim's face and then sat back to survey his reaction. It had been a serially inappropriate thing to do and she wouldn't have dreamed of behaving like that in London, but then this wasn't London and the situation she was in was surreal.

Bernheim's body hardened immediately as his black eyes glowed. He knew she had depths, and what depths! *Madame*, how wonderfully... feral," he whispered, "and do you scratch and claw people often?" he enquired.

"Oh, now and then, when the fancy takes me," Bella replied airily before saying slowly and maliciously darkly in a soft voice, now full of implied viciousness, "or when I need to teach somebody a lesson. I particularly enjoy that. No one cheats, crosses or owes me and gets away with it. The downside of gambling enterprises is people losing money they don't have to lose, and one cannot buy a gown or bracelet with an I.O.U., but no one gets away with not paying what they owe *La Lionesse*, one way or another. I always take pleasure in ensuring that."

"Do you really? Now what an interesting coincidence that is," Bernheim said slowly and a salacious smile curled his thin lips. "I sometimes find I need to do that too in my line of business. But of course," and he looked at his own hands with their fastidiously manicured nails, "I don't scratch people."

"*Chevalier*, how fascinating. How do you take your revenge then?" Bella purred.

"Let's say, I have my own methods," he replied enigmatically, "but I find dispensing the punishment is so rewarding."

Bella shivered inside but kept her face smiling impassively, wondering what the hell she was getting into, something way out of her depth or comprehension, she suspected. However, she'd had enough for one night, her nerves were in shreds and she'd laid out her lures, telling herself she deserved a standing ovation for her acting.

"Each to his own then, *Chevalier*," and she sat back and sighed slightly. "Well, it has been a most delightful and illuminating evening and time has flown, but as I told you, it has been a rather busy day for me, so if you..."

Bernheim interrupted her. "*Chère Lionesse*, do you have to go? Can you not stay a while longer? It's still early." Bella merely shook her head, trying to look regretful, so Bernheim pressed on, "In which case, would you give me the pleasure of your fascinating company over dinner again tomorrow? Perhaps we can try one of the restaurants in the town, then we can continue to get to know each other better?"

Bella had been aiming for an invitation to his villa, but perhaps it was a bit premature. She therefore merely smiled. "*Chevalier*, how delightful. It is somewhat unconventional of course, and slightly inappropriate for an unaccompanied Lady, but then," she appeared to consider, "we are not in London now, nor even Paris, and I know you are a complete Gentleman, one of your many attractions, so I should be delighted to accept."

"Capital!" he smiled at her, almost oozing gratitude as he preened under her honeyed compliments, "and *Lionesse*, please, call me Frederick." Bella smiled again and rose to leave, picking up her reticule and long evening gloves. She held out her hand to him regally as he rose and bowed over it punctiliously. "Goodnight, Frederick, until tomorrow then. Shall we say six o'clock here at the Hotel? Would that be convenient?"

"Absolutely perfect, *Lionesse*," and he bent to place a kiss on the back of her outstretched hand, before turning it over to place another in her palm, his tongue describing a small circle.

Bella pulled her hand back, disgusted at such a forward action and wishing she'd kept her gloves on to dine, but then remembered herself and smiled flirtatiously and batted his hand with her fan. "Oh, tut, tut, Frederick, reeeeally!" She looked at him archly, "How VERY inappropriate of you and a bit premature for a first evening and for such a Gentleman, and a Lady such as myself. I'm tempted to change my mind about tomorrow, but you will no doubt behave more appropriately then, I'm sure, so perhaps I won't," and she gave him the hint of a knowing smile which could be taken any way, as could the word 'appropriately'. She turned to go, acknowledging his bow with an aristocratic inclination of her head. "Until tomorrow then. It has been a real pleasure to make your acquaintance and have such a delightful dinner. Thank you so much."

"*Bonsoir*. Goodnight, *Lionesse*. Tomorrow will be even more pleasant. I promise you..."

Chapter Three

Bella hurried up to her suite, her breath now coming in distressed gasps. She lurched into her room and banged the door shut behind her, leaning back against it, her eyes closed.

"My God, Your Grace, are you all right? Whatever have you been doing?" Jack sprang up from the sofa where he'd been sitting waiting for her, the notes he'd been holding falling to the floor.

Momentarily distracted, Bella stared in surprise at Jack. "How on earth did you get in here, Jack?" she asked.

Jack merely rolled his eyes at her. "Now what sort of a silly question is that to ask someone like me?" and he grinned, going over to her hurriedly to take her hand and shoo her down to the sofa, alarmed by her pale face. "Come along, what on earth have you been up to?" he bent to pick up her notes from the floor where he'd dropped them. "You look like you've seen a ghost. Can I get you a glass of water or perhaps something stronger?"

Bella didn't know where to start, but she desperately needed to talk to someone, and there was only Jack. So, taking a deep breath she took his hand in her shaking one. "Jack, I have to talk to you, seriously. There's much more to what we're doing here than I told you before, but I need your word you won't speak to anyone of this, and, it's suddenly become very dangerous. I need advice, and help, and I have no one to turn to except you." She seemed disturbed, very shaken and on the verge of tears.

Jack looked at her with a straight face. "Your Grace, I realised a while ago there was much more going on than you let on. Oh, I know you and the Duke have obviously fallen out, but what he's doing, this man he's after, there's something about him, isn't there? The Duchess, back at Firle, told me to guard you with my life and never let you out of my sight. You don't ask that of someone if you were just coming here to France to chase after an errant husband, or visit the sights, or go shopping for frilly petticoats or a new reticule. And then, of course, there's the curious question of why I'm here at all? Me, Jack Vallance, with my, let's just refer to it as a 'somewhat interesting background', not to mention slight lack of social graces, manners or knowledge, and why you have no lady's maid or proper female companion with you, or even a footman; all much more appropriate than a young groom from the stables..."

The young groom from the stables stared straight into Bella's eyes. He continued to stare at the obviously disturbed woman, the silence ticking in the large hotel suite as he then picked up Bella's numb hand and eventually spoke again, quietly and seriously. "I give you my word, Your Grace, and although I'm not a Gentleman, far from it as you know, my word still means something to me; therefore, whatever you tell me will stay between us." He spoke very solemnly for a youth from the streets. "Surely you realise you can trust me now? You've done so much for me since we've been away, shown me so much, taught me so much, treated me with respect, as if I wasn't just a poor lowly groom, a boy from nowhere except the gutters. I can't believe any titled lady, especially a duchess, would ever do that for someone like me." Jack went down on one knee in front of Bella and looked up at her, for once a serious expression on his face. "I would do anything for you, Your Grace, anything to repay you for your goodness, both you and the Duchess of Firle. I know I was just a dirty beggar, and a thief," he hung his head briefly, "but only because I had to be, and I've changed now, and I want to help you, so please trust me? Talk to me, tell me what's going on, and what's happened to you tonight, for I know something has."

Bella pulled Jack back to his feet, both moved and reassured by his simple and heartfelt words, and tugged him down on to the sofa next to her again. "Oh Jack, you're such a sweet boy, not so different from all my cousins really, despite your birth, and you've done so much for me already. But yes, you're right, there is much more to all this than just chasing after a French agent who caused Wellington a few problems in Spain." And for the next half an hour, as she gripped his hand, Bella told Jack all about what Nicky had been doing in Spain. About the gold, about Bernheim, about Carmelita and what evils he believed the pair had perpetrated on the young prostitutes, and all she'd found out from Ashcroft about what had really happened to Nicky, and what he knew about Bernheim. She also told Jack a bit about what Nicky had said the night they'd found him in Paris and the note he'd left her. Finally, with a deep breath she told him about her family's connection with Bernheim's father, just over twenty years before at the start of the French Revolution. She left out mentioning The Shadow, merely saying Bernheim Senior, a corrupt, venal and evil man, had been responsible for carting off Nicky's parents to Rouen Fortress where they'd perished as a result of being tortured to reveal details of the location of the family fortune; and the same had happened to the family of her father and the Duchess. She also explained how the Duke, the Duchess and her mother had helped the de Mornays and Nicky escape from France and that Bernheim's father had subsequently been killed by the Duchess although she didn't go into details of the circumstances of that. However, Bella explained it was because of what had happened to Nicky's family that her husband had a personal vendetta against Bernheim, saying he believed father and son were out the same nest of vipers, and in return, Bernheim knew who Nicky was and blamed his family, ie Bella's family including the Granvilles, for the death of his father. At the end of her story she sank back against the cushions with a big sigh, glad she'd finally got it all off her chest and he would now understand the reality of what was going on.

"That's an unbelievable tale, like something Mr Crichton might have told me in my lessons with him back at his cottage at Firle. But so much makes sense now, Your Grace. When you were in Rouen, your fascination with that ruined building? I wondered about that at the time." Jack was fascinated with Bella's tale. "But what happened tonight? You looked terrible when you got back up here? Your note merely said you'd come across someone, here in the hotel, connected with your husband's activities and to keep away from you, not to let on who I really was and just to call you Aunt if we accidentally happened to bump into each other."

"I was just sitting quietly, on the terrace where you left me, when this man, a complete stranger, effected an introduction. I didn't like him, something about him gave me the chills, but just as I was about to take my leave and go and have dinner, he introduced himself." She grasped Jack's hand again, "Oh Jack, you'll never guess, it was HIM! Bernheim."

"WHAAAT? NO!" Jack's mouth dropped open in shock. "Bleedin' 'ell, Mum," he gawped.

"Precisely," nodded Bella. "I didn't know what to do. And then, he asked me to dine with him. It was so inappropriate, but I had to," she whispered. "So I did. That's where I've been and, oh Jack, he's the most repulsive man. I can't explain as he looks and acts perfectly normally, quite the Gentleman in fact, but it's the feeling he gives me. Nicky, my husband, the Duke, he told me some terrible stories about what he was like. His personal perversions, so shocking I couldn't possible repeat them to you, I can barely get my head around them myself. But now I understand, when he kissed my hand it made my flesh crawl," and she shuddered at the memory and flexed the hand in question as if it was tainted. She couldn't wait to wash it.

Jack had pulled a handkerchief out of his pocket which he handed to Bella as tears ran down her face. "Oh, Jack, I flirted with him, tried to find out more about what he was doing here. He's got a villa up in the hills behind the town, but I'm so frightened. Do you think he's found Nicky? Do you think that's where he is? Why he seems to have mysteriously disappeared and just left all his belongings and money lying around?"

A storm of weeping finally overtook Bella as Jack sat and patted her hand. "Well, Your Grace," he said, "consider this. I went back to His

Grace's lodgings and had a nice little conversation with the *concierge*, got on really well despite the language problems, if I say so myself. My French is really coming on, it's amazing, talk about practice makes perfect; well, not that perfect yet, but I'm getting there!" and he grinned proudly for a moment before continuing. "Anyway, I paid her some more rent like you said, but she's seen nothing of him. All I found out is that the Duke went out one morning, charming as you please, said good morning to her and asked the way to the local market as he wanted to buy some bread and cheese, and then... poof!" Jack clicked his fingers in the air, "or *rien*, as she put it. Nothing. Gone. She hasn't seen him since. BUT," and Jack paused before delivering his big piece of news, "she described another individual who had come around asking questions, looking for a golden-haired man who had recently arrived. A huge, swarthy, dark skinned, foreign looking man with a shaven head, a single gold earring and no tongue; a man who had to write down all his questions..."

"Oh God, Jack, the servant from Bernheim's house in Paris; it has to be!" Bella blanched.

"I think so, Your Grace." Jack now looked at Bella worriedly. "I wandered around all the local shops and bars, and one or two people recognised His Grace's description. He does tend to stand out with his colouring. He bought some cheroots from a *tabac*, and some wine and fruit at the local *épicerie*, but no one has seen him for days. As we wondered and you just said, it's like he's disappeared into thin air and I'm sure he wouldn't go far and leave all that money behind... nor these," and as he spoke, Jack got up and went behind the sofa to retrieve Nicky's portmanteau from which he withdrew his stiletto and a brace of pistols.

Bella recognised the jewelled stiletto instantly. It had belonged to her aunt and she knew she'd loaned it to Nicky when he went to Spain; it was also the knife she'd used to cut his bound hands that last night in Paris. "I'm sorry, Your Grace. But when I heard about the man with no tongue, I had a bad feeling, so I crept back up to His Grace's room and brought most of his things back with me. His guitar is over there by the fireplace," he nodded towards it, "but surely he wouldn't go anywhere without these?" and he held out the stiletto and a pistol again. "He must have gone on a quick errand to buy some food and been abducted on the way, that's what I reckon." Jack didn't want to mention or even contemplate he might have been killed, not just abducted, although he thought it was a distinct possibility given Bernheim had already tried to kill the Duke in Spain. The only thing against that possibility was no body had been found, but Jack knew it could easily have been quietly disposed of in a variety of places.

Jack put the weapons back in Nicky's portmanteau and took both of Bella's cold, numb hands in his, looking at her frightened face. "You have to be strong, Your Grace, but I'm almost sure Bernheim has done something to your husband."

Bella was distraught and as she burst into another round of tears, Jack swore and pulled her into his arms and hugged her. "Look here, Your Grace, you can't go to pieces now, we have to DO something, find out exactly what's happened to him and if necessary, rescue him. We'll do whatever we have to…"

Bella blew her nose and shook herself. Jack was quite right, this was no time to have a fit of the vapours. Of course, this was all supposition. She refused to consider he might have been killed. Instead, she wondered if Nicky might have gone off somewhere else, or been captured by someone else, maybe the conspirators plotting to bring back Bonaparte from Elba? Because, deep down, she knew he wouldn't go out without his stiletto; she was amazed he'd even gone to a market without it. Her aunt had taught Nicky to fence with a rapier way back when he was a little boy, newly arrived from France, and he'd then been coached and taught to fight and shoot by her Uncle Francis, no mean swordsman, even now so she'd heard, and of course he'd been The Shadow so knew about fighting in all its forms, as a Gentleman and as a criminal, and he'd passed on to Nicky all he knew. And that included NEVER to go out unarmed. Some of her earliest memories were of watching Nicky duel or fight with one or other of her aunt and uncle, in the gardens at Firle Manor or in the long portrait gallery there, or in a spacious empty upstairs room in Firle House in London, and she remembered jumping up and down as she watched them, chewing one of the ends of her plaits, shouting out and encouraging Nicky in the most bloodthirsty fashion, which had amused her uncle and aunt no end, especially if he was engaged in fisticuffs with her uncle, a very different type of duel to crossing swords with her aunt, eccentric lady that she still was.

"You're quite right, Jack," Bella sat up and pulled her shoulders back, "this will never do. My aunt and the old Dowager would despise me for being so feeble, but we must think." She paused, "I'm having dinner again with the bastard, tomorrow evening, heaven help me. You must follow him after and find out where his villa is. I tried to encourage him to take me there tomorrow, but we are only going to have dinner in the town again." She shook her head sadly, "I'm no *femme fatale*, as in a trained agent or subversive, I'm afraid," she muttered, "but tomorrow I'll do whatever it takes to get him to take me to his home. Anything, I swear. If he's got Nicky there, you're spot on, you and I will have to rescue him. We're on our own, just the two of us, so it's as simple as that," she finished forcefully.

"Well said, Your Grace, that's the spirit." Jack tried to look positive, more than he was currently feeling. "I'll tell you what, why don't we take a picnic up into the hills tomorrow anyway, and have a look around. There can't be that many houses up there, surely, and it will help if I familiarise myself with the roadways and lanes that lead there from the town." Bella nodded. "You ride quite well, don't you, Your Grace?" Jack then asked.

"Reasonably so, I suppose," Bella responded, "though not very much these days now I spend most of my time in London, I'm too busy. But I used to ride out regularly over the Downs at Firle and Arlington a few years ago, and all through my childhood. I'm afraid I was a terrible hoyden... why?"

"Well, I thought I'd hire a couple of horses, rather than a gig or a trap. We can go much further and down some tracks we could never access in a gig, then we can be a bit more nosy. Can you manage with an ordinary saddle or do you want a lady's one? I know it's not conventional, but it..."

"Didn't I say I was a hoyden?" sighed Bella. "I'm past worrying about convention now. As long as I don't show myself up here at the hotel, no one will know or care. That's a good idea, Jack, we'll set off first thing. I'll order a picnic when we have breakfast, and you can pick it up when you come back with the horses. Now you go off to bed, it's late, and I'm tired too. Not that I think I'll sleep much after all this, but we must try."

Jack nodded and rose to go, bowing and kissing her hand tenderly. "Sleep well, Your Grace, and try not to worry, hmmm?"

"I'll do my best," Bella sighed wistfully. As Jack was about to open the door and go to his own room, Bella suddenly thought of something. "Oh, by the way, Jack, how DID you get in here? Did you get a duplicate key from the maid?"

"Who needs a duplicate key?" He winked at Bella, "There's not a door can keep Jack the Lad out, nor a lock I can't pick, and I was just learning how to crack these big, new, heavy iron cabinets, safes, with complicated locks, when the Duchess found me." Then he looked serious, "However, I give you my word, Your Grace, I was telling the truth before. I've not thieved anything other than Mrs Farthing's pastries and biscuits since I met Her Grace. You CAN trust me. I might have come from the worst stews in London, but I promise, your family secrets are safe with Jack Vallance." His bright sherry eyes looked straight at her.

"I know they are, Jack," Bella whispered. "I believe you, and thank you." Bella blew him a kiss and he winked back at her before disappearing out the door.

Chapter Four

The next day Jack appeared at the hotel with two sturdy ponies in tow and collected the waiting picnic, then met up with Bella a few streets away where, to his amusement, in a narrow alleyway, she removed her skirt to reveal herself in a pair of tight men's pantaloons tucked into sensible boots that she'd hurried out to buy before he'd arrived. They then trekked up into the rocky hills behind the little town.

As they traversed what were little more than mule tracks in many places, they viewed where *La Grande Corniche* now started as it curled its cliff-fronted way towards Monaco, Menton and Italy in the east, following the ancient Roman route known as Via Julia Augusta. Bella told Jack it was the road Bonaparte had apparently commissioned for his troops to march along to facilitate his ambitious Italian campaign in 1796 and the pair of them marvelled at the men still working on it here and there in the distance, in what was to them a wonder of road engineering given how high they were and that the road was on no more than a cliff face.

Deeper into the hills, away from the new road, here and there were little houses with small allotments or fields where farmers grew vines or local produce, and a few chickens scrabbled around the odd barn or ramshackle stable. Behind tall gates, some newly built, large villas could be seen, screened by shrubbery and palm trees. The pair followed tracks that went right to the top and sat and had their picnic, looking at the stunning views of the Bay and the beautiful Mediterranean spread out below them, the blue sea glittering in the sunlight. It was an even more breath-taking view than from the hotel terrace and finally Bella understood what her Uncle Reynard had rhapsodised about. For a moment, thoughts of the grizzled gypsy came to mind and she wished he was there with her, just as he'd apparently been with Nicky in Spain, to offer advice and lend assistance in her hour of need. But he wasn't, she was on her own and there was no one else to turn to, other than Jack.

They sat and talked over their simple meal of bread, cold meats and cheese, and fresh ripe peaches which Jack couldn't eat enough of since he'd discovered them for sale everywhere on the stalls around the town. While insects hummed and buzzed around, and now she had got to know him better and there was a real feeling of camaraderie between them, Bella finally asked Jack to tell her more about his childhood and how her aunt had found him and taken him to Firle.

Just as Cat had been, she was in turn appalled, distressed and amazed to hear details of the story of his terrible life in the gutters of the Dials, some of the worst slums of London, and home to a hard core of beggars, pimps, whores, thieves, murderers and general villains of all description.

Hesitantly, Jack had related how his mother had died and left him to fend for a little half-brother and half-sister when he was about eight or nine, he didn't know for sure; and somehow he had taken in a couple of little boys, brothers, who'd lived downstairs from the small, rat-infested tenement garret room Jack and his siblings existed in when the boys' mother, another prostitute like Jack's mother, had died. And then, one day he'd found a pair of little girls, no more than tots, begging in a doorway, emaciated and literally starving, and so he'd taken them in as well. All seven had lived in his garret room and struggled to survive and look after each other, though they all relied on Jack, the eldest. The little children had begged, and he'd found what work he could: holding horses for the gentry or cleaning out stables or privvies, anything that would earn him a coin, or otherwise he'd thieved; he'd had to in order to get money for their rent and food. It had been a hard existence, literally living from day to day, until that fateful one when he'd tried to cut the reticule of the Duchess of Firle near Bond Street, desperate for some money to get medicine for one of the children who was sick.

Something about the desperate, painfully thin and dirty boy had got to Cat, and so instead of handing him over to the Magistrates, when he'd begged and pleaded with her not to because his little family would all starve without him, she'd gone back to his garret to see if he was indeed telling the truth. She'd been overwhelmed and distraught at what she'd found; exactly what he'd told her. It took her all of five minutes to decide to haul the bedraggled, freezing and half-starved children from their garret and transport them down to Firle, where she'd found homes for the little ones among the estate tenants or neighbouring country folk, and Jack had gone to work properly, for the first time in his life, as a lowly stableboy, intent on learning how to be a proper groom. Desperate to better himself, and watched curiously by the Duchess who had taken an interest in the kind-hearted and determined boy, she had arranged for his schooling in the local village and some extra tutoring from an old retainer of the family who had taught the young Granville boys before they'd all gone off to Eton, and kept an eye on them during the school holidays. Jack had blossomed beyond all expectations in his new environment, mentally and physically, and now, here he was, trying to repay Marie-Catherine Granville for saving and literally changing his life.

Bella was stunned at his story but said little, other than she was finally glad to know about it all, simply because she didn't know what else to say, she was so overwhelmed with what he'd come from and how he'd managed to better himself, even if he was still working in the stables at Firle. She finally said she was glad her aunt had chosen him to accompany her and she didn't know how she would have managed without him. Hugely embarrassed at her praise, Jack had endeavoured to change the subject to more mundane matters and focus on the remains of their meal.

Everywhere was quiet in the hot afternoon sun and Jack pulled off his shirt and lolled back against a rock, looking at the view and dozing in the heat, another new experience he was revelling in. Bella simply sat quietly under a shady tree and considered the evening ahead, wondering if Nicky was inside one of the shuttered houses they had passed on their way, and both frightened yet determined to inveigle herself deeper into Bernheim's acquaintance and gain an invitation to his home. Some deep, inexplicable inner feeling told her Nicky wasn't dead and Bernheim knew either what had happened to him or where he was. Moreover, despite everything that had happened between them, she knew she would go to any length to find her husband and rescue him if he was in trouble, which she now believed he was. She'd told herself her imagination was running away with itself, but she simply couldn't shake off the chilly sense of foreboding that wouldn't go away.

Bernheim both fascinated and repelled her. He was obviously a well-travelled and extremely clever individual, fastidious in his manners, appearance and dress; not so much as a speck of dust or crease had marred the perfection of his beautifully tailored jacket and waistcoat and his cravat was a masterpiece even Benjy, her uncle's sometime valet, would have been envious of. He was also excessively punctilious, to the extreme. He'd mentioned over dinner his schooling in Austria and she'd put his almost militaristic mannerisms down to that. However, under all his various idiosyncrasies, she sensed a leashed power about him, a restless energy and deep passion. As an attractive woman, Bella was used to dealing with men, their effusive addresses and attempts to flirt and more, but now she was experienced in bed matters, courtesy of Nicky's practised endeavours, she could sense and see it in those black, obsidian eyes that had looked at her as if he was mentally removing her clothes and assessing what else he'd like to do with her; he'd licked those thin, cruel lips of his as he'd talked to her and Bella didn't need Nicky's warning to somehow know the man's perverted lusts just simmered beneath the surface of his outwardly urbane, polite, courteous and gentlemanly exterior. She shivered as she contemplated their forthcoming dinner and what she suspected Bernheim would want from her afterwards.

Bella had kissed a lot of men, especially over the past year, in her efforts to shake off the hold Nicky seemed to have over her. Some of the most charming and flirtatious rakes amongst the Ton had amused and tried to take her fancy, and endeavoured to please her, young and old, and her aunt would no doubt be amused and aghast at what she'd done in unseen quiet corners at balls and parties and out in gardens where no one else could see, although it had never gone further than kisses and some exploratory caresses. That was why there was a betting book about her. However, accomplished and good-looking lover that he was, Nicky was a hard act to follow, as legions of women could have told her, so most other gentlemen had left her stone cold, unimpressed, even occasionally disgusted, and none could hold a candle to the feelings she got when Nicky kissed her. Because she loved him, that was the difference, she realised, and nothing she did or tried could change that fact, no matter how many other accomplished rakes and lotharios did their best to try.

The thought of kissing Bernheim, however, made her feel slightly nauseous, but she was resolved that she would do it if that was what it took to further her investigations. That manipulative bastard, Ashcroft, would be proud of her, she decided. Her final thoughts before she, too, dozed off in the heat were of her last night with Nicky in Paris, and the way he'd made love to her before they'd fallen asleep. Even now she could remember how it felt to be held in his strong, protective arms, of the way he'd kissed and caressed her and then moved inside her. Surely he couldn't pretend he didn't have feelings for her after the way he'd made love to her? He couldn't hate her, or could he? She sighed as desire for him curled round her belly and her heart ached as she drifted off to sleep.

"Your Grace? Wake up, Madam, Your Grace...?" Hands shook her. "Your nose is going rather pink." Bella came to dazedly as Jack peered laughingly down into her face. "You're not in the shade any longer, Your Grace, and you've caught the sun." His own tanned features grinned down at her. "We need to make a move if you're to be back at the hotel in time for your dinner appointment." The residue of her pleasant dreams rapidly dissipated as Bella let Jack pull her to her feet and they returned to where their ponies were themselves dozing in a little shady stand of trees.

They slowly made their way back down the hilly tracks, still silent in the afternoon sun, only the sound of crickets intruded into the peaceful scenery. As they trekked down in companionable silence, Bella's mind again wandering to her forthcoming dinner, Jack suddenly pulled up his mount as they were going along a wooded pathway. He sat still for a minute or two, his head cocked to one side. "Did you hear that, Your Grace?" he turned to Bella whose own pony had now pulled up alongside his.

"Hmmm? What?" she mumbled, her mind far away.

"I thought I heard a cry," Jack said quietly, his head still bent to listen in the silence.

"I didn't hear anything," Bella whispered, but they sat quietly for a further few minutes, the hot air only full of the sound of crickets humming and lazy buzzing bees. Jack shrugged and let his pony move on. His ears were far more attuned and alert than his mistress's, and he could have sworn he'd heard a cry. No, it had been more like a scream... a few minutes before. It had come from a distance, drifting across the hot silent air. He shuddered, perhaps his mind was playing tricks on him, still full of the amazing and lurid story he'd heard from the Duchess the night before. He shrugged to himself and paid more attention to where his pony was now picking its way down a rocky pathway, but nevertheless, instinct told him he HAD heard a scream. An agonised, long scream. Obviously, horror was just as prevalent in this quiet, rural foreign backwater as it was in the Seven Dials in London; but where had it come from and, more to the point, who had screamed in such torment...

Get the book here and carry on reading.

If you've enjoyed the story so far, and there's a lot more drama to come, I'd love you to leave a review <u>here</u> and tell others about it and the rest of the books in The Pride of Lions series: Fighting Lion and Wounded Lion. Nicky's adventures are quite a journey ...

This is the second set in the whole **Granville Legacy** series, lots more to come, and don't forget, if you're interested in joining my little group and getting advance reader copies of the books to review as they come out, or to hear about special offers, or read my occasional blog, or get a monthly newsletter, go to my website, https://antoinettegeorge.com/ and join my lists. You'll find out about all the rest of the **Granville Legacy** series there, especially the contemporary stories which are being published next, starting with *Soldier Banker*, all about Francis Granville's direct descendant, Marcus Forsyth.

Thank you so much and... keeeeeep reading!

This is
THE GRANVILLE LEGACY

Coming soon, the full series of The Granville Legacy

18th and 19th century

The life and times of Francis Granville and his friends

Behind The Shadow

Pride of Lions

Publish And Be Damned

To Catch a Thief

21st century

The adventures of Marcus Forsyth, Francis Granville's direct descendant, and his close friends and family.

Soldier Banker

Lions and Feathers

Matilda's Diamonds

Never Left Behind

The Chameleon and The Swan

The Cat's Whiskers

Pins and Noodles

Acknowledgments

Barbara – thank you for your continued enthusiasm and support, endless useful comments on everything, and of course, the editing.

Zivan – thank you for your graphics and covers and grappling with a coat of arms!

Clare – thank you for the formatting and pulling all the content into shape.

www.ingramcontent.com/pod-product-compliance
Lightning Source LLC
Chambersburg PA
CBHW050916250626
47155CB00001B/262